COMBAT:
Parallel Lines

A Jock Miles-Moon Brothers
Korean War Story
Book 3

A Novel By
William Peter Grasso

D1215058

Novels By William Peter Grasso

Jock Miles-Moon Brothers Korean War Story

Combat Ineffective, *Book 1*
Combat Reckoning, *Book 2*
Combat: Parallel Lines, *Book 3*

Moon Brothers WW2 Adventure Series

Moon Above, Moon Below, *Book 1*
Fortress Falling, *Book 2*
Our Ally, Our Enemy, *Book 3*
This Fog of Peace, *Book 4*

Jock Miles WW2 Adventure Series

Long Walk to the Sun, *Book 1*
Operation Long Jump, *Book 2*
Operation Easy Street, *Book 3*
Operation Blind Spot, *Book 4*
Operation Fishwrapper, *Book 5*

Unpunished

East Wind Returns

Sign Up For New Release Announcements at:
wpgrasso@cox.net, with Mailing List as the Subject

Connect with the Author on Facebook
https://www.facebook.com/AuthorWilliamPeterGrasso

Follow the Author on Amazon
https://amazon.com/author/williampetergrasso

Dedication

To all those who could have gone home but chose to stay and fight.

Author's Note

Often called the "forgotten war," the Korean War of 1950 to 1953 remains overshadowed by the vastness of WW2. Yet it marked an escalation of America's military misadventures on the Asian mainland, where US domestic politics continued to distort foreign realities, provoking disaster after disaster on the battlefield. In no way, however, does the fictional story presented here mean to denigrate the hardships and sacrifices of the individual American soldiers forced to fight an enemy they did not understand and for whom they were—at least at first—woefully ill-prepared.

Dialogue often uses derogatory terms for African-Americans and people of various Asian ethnicities. The use of those terms by the author serves no other intent than to accurately represent the vocabulary of some military personnel in the early 1950s.

It would take a host of maps to fully depict the locations visited in this novel. Since this novel focuses on the exploits of fictional characters and doesn't intend to be a history textbook, I've chosen to include no maps. Those readers who wish to put the fictional action into a geographic context can visit a number of sources, any of which can provide far more useful maps than could be included in these pages. Here are a few helpful links:

https://history.army.mil/books/maps.htm
legacy.lib.utexas.edu/maps/ams/korea/

Chapter One

South Pyongan Province, North Korea

Late November 1950

The driving snow cut their visibility of the road ahead to a quarter mile or less. Perched in the commander's hatch of his Pershing tank, Master Sergeant Sean Moon, US Army, told the driver, "Slow it down, pal. Keep it to ten miles *per*, okay? Let's not get anybody strung out and lost because he couldn't see the guy in front of him."

There were a dozen M26 Pershings in column behind Sean's tank, all replacements for vehicles that had gone unserviceable during 26th Regiment's fighting withdrawal from the grasp of the CCF, the Communist Chinese Forces, who'd poured into the battle for Korea just weeks ago. It hadn't been Chinese weaponry that knocked out those tanks, for the swarming hordes of the CCF possessed little in the way of anti-tank capability. The Pershings had gone out of action due to their inherent mechanical weaknesses; transmission failures had been the biggest cause.

I don't imagine this new batch is gonna hold up much better, Sean told himself. *They're still underpowered and got the same damn transmissions. But maybe they'll last until the M46s finally start showing up, whenever the hell that'll be.*

From what I'm hearing through the grapevine, though, the M46s—Pattons, they're calling them—ain't gonna be much better.

Well, they couldn't have a better tanker's name, at least.

The Chinese had hit hard at first, knocking the GIs of 26th Regiment south across the Chongchon River toward the North Korean capital of Pyongyang. They'd expected to be driven back across the 38th Parallel, perhaps to Seoul...

Or maybe all the way to Pusan, just one step away from being pushed into the sea, like they'd nearly been last summer.

But as quickly as they'd appeared, the CCF vanished, leaving behind nothing but fields strewn with their dead...and the numbing fear that they'd suddenly appear by the tens of thousands once again, washing across the GIs' positions like an unstoppable tide. The retreating UN forces—five US Army divisions, nine South Korean Army light divisions known as ROKs, one division of US Marines, and the assorted brigades and battalions of Allied nations—had stopped to form a ragged defensive line across the width of North Korea, the center of that line rendered broken and discontinuous by mountain ranges. Twenty-Sixth Regiment was dug in thirty miles north of Pyongyang along the Taedong River.

There, they'd wait as politicians around the world engaged in cautious debate as to what their next move should be, although on one point there was no need for discussion: nobody—save the American high commander in Asia and his admirers in Congress—was willing to risk an escalation of this small cold conflict in

Korea into World War III.

But that didn't mean they'd be willing to yield a win to the communists, be they Korean, Chinese, or Russian.

Sergeant Moon didn't need much visibility to know where he was; he'd been on this highway more than a few times. The railroad tracks that paralleled the road on its east side had just crossed over to the western shoulder; that put them less than ten miles from 26th Regiment at Sunchon. "See if you can raise Regiment on the radio," he told his loader. "Ain't no mountains in the way from here. Just give me a second to make sure the antenna base is clear of snow. Don't need to be shorting out a brand new radio right outta the box."

As he leaned aft from the hatch to dry the antenna mount, the driver's voice filled the crew's headsets: "We've got company coming the other way like a bat out of hell, Sarge. Some deuces all bunched up."

Sean had a pretty good idea what he was looking at: *That's a bug-out, plain and simple. Ain't no other reason for a regular convoy to be driving like that in this weather. The only question is whether they're GIs or ROKs.*

And there's only one way to find out.

It wouldn't take much to transform his column of tanks into a roadblock. There'd be no driving around it; the snow had made the terrain on either side of the highway impassible for wheeled vehicles.

"Form a wedge on me," he radioed to the other tanks. "It looks like we gotta save some scared and confused boys from themselves."

When confronted with this wall of steel, the drivers of the *deuce-and-a-halfs*—bunched up and barreling as they were—couldn't stop fast enough. The lead truck slid into Moon's tank, bouncing off her bow and then sliding backward until quickly shuddering to a stop. Two deuces foolishly tried to leave the highway and bypass the roadblock; they stalled twenty yards off the pavement, their wheels hub-deep in the snowdrifts. Five more trucks emerged from the veil of blinding snow; with little traction to stop, they collided with each other nose-to-tail in sequence.

Men leapt from the beds of the deuces and tried to run off-road around the Pershings. Finding themselves bogged down in knee-deep snow, they didn't get far as tanks plowed effortlessly through the drifts to encircle them. Sullenly, the hundred-strong mob milled about, their hands deep in the pockets of their parkas. None of them were carrying a rifle. All of them were Koreans.

A ROK lieutenant climbed from the cab of the deuce that had bounced off Sean's tank. He approached the Pershing, waving his arms imperiously while calling out in excellent English to clear the road for his trucks.

"I don't think so, my friend," Sean replied, peering down from his seat on the turret hatch ring. "And you got a little explaining to do. For instance, how do I know you and this great unarmed rabble of yours ain't KPA infiltrators?"

"We are ROKs, not KPA," the lieutenant indignantly replied. "There is no more KPA. The North Korean Army is finished. Everyone knows that."

"I wouldn't be so sure about that," Sean said. "And those trucks you're driving...they got GI markings all over 'em. Second Infantry Division, in fact. Where'd you steal 'em from, pal?"

"They are not stolen. They were reassigned to us."

"Bullshit," Sean replied. "As bad as the Second got

beat up on the Chongchon, they ain't in a position to be giving nothing away. Admit it…you found these vehicles sitting around somewhere and figured they'd be a quick way to bug out. Pretty typical scenario…throw down your weapons and run, like you decided that you ain't part of this war no more."

"We are not bugging out," the lieutenant insisted. "We have orders to…"

Before he could finish the sentence, two more deuces emerged from the curtain of snowfall. With two dull *thuds*, they added themselves to the daisy chain of trucks nestled nose-to-tail along the roadway.

Sean's radio had no trouble establishing communications with the regimental command post. It only took a few minutes for the CP to confirm with 8th Army what he'd suspected all along: the ROKs were, in all likelihood, from several companies that had bugged out that morning from the regiment on the right flank of the 26th. A platoon of ROK MPs was looking for them at that very moment.

"I just got the word that those *orders* you're talking about are bullshit, too," Sean told the lieutenant. "You got two choices. You can get on those deuces, turn them around, and go back to your unit. We'll follow along behind you just to make sure you don't get lost or nothing. With a little luck, this *motor movement* of yours just might get written off as a big misunderstanding."

"And the other choice?"

"I hold you here until those MPs come and lock your asses up. From what I've seen of how your MPs operate, though, I'd say the first option looks much more promising."

The whole time this discussion was taking place, the

encircling tanks had been inching steadily forward, forcing the ROKs into an ever-shrinking circle. The creeping forward progress of Sean's tank forced the ROK lieutenant to keep backing up. In a few more feet, he'd have to jump sideways to avoid getting crushed between the Pershing and his deuce.

For added menace, the tanks' turrets slowly traversed through narrow arcs, as if putting groups of deserters in their sights.

"Can we shoot them, Sean?" the commander of *Number Two* tank asked over the radio.

"Only if they shoot at us. But it ain't likely they're gonna do that unless they wanna get turned inside out by a bunch of thirty cals. Just don't let no asshole climb up on your deck. He could have a grenade on him."

"You still think these clowns might be KPA?"

"Nah," Sean replied, "they're just scared shitless gooks from down south."

A Pershing made nose-to-nose contact with one of the snowbound deuces and was pushing it backward toward the road, the muzzle of its long main gun hovering over the cab as if ready to smash it. Thinking the tankers might be intent on flattening him along with his vehicle, the deuce driver panicked; in his hurry to exit the truck, he slipped on the icy running board and fell to the ground. Quickly pinned beneath the front wheel of his vehicle as it came to a stop on top of him, he disappeared into the deep snow.

"YOU ARE KILLING MY MEN," the lieutenant shrieked. "I'LL SEE TO IT YOU ARE COURT-MARTIALED FOR THIS, SERGEANT."

Casually, Sean replied, "I don't think so, pal. He ain't dead yet, probably...just pushed down into the snowbank. But if we don't get him out real soon, he's gonna suffocate."

He signaled for the Pershing driver to shove the truck back a little farther. No longer trapped beneath the wheel, the driver was pulled from his airless captivity by two ROKs. He was gasping for breath but otherwise unhurt.

Sean told the lieutenant, "See? What'd I tell you? He's gonna be okay. Just a little accident. Happens all the time. The snow saved his ass from getting crushed. Like falling into a big soft cushion."

After letting the Korean officer sulk for a moment, he added, "So what's it gonna be? You going back of your own accord? Or are you gonna let the MPs do a little dance on your head?"

The lieutenant said nothing. He just stared into the distance, as if the surrounding mountains held the answer to his plight.

"What the hell are you running from, anyway?"

"The Chinese. They're coming."

"Nobody in Eighth Army's seen a chink in over a week," Sean replied. "According to that patch you're wearing, you're from ROK Sixth Division, right?"

His gaze still miles away, the lieutenant nodded.

"You're telling me your outfit got hit?"

He shook his head.

"Then what the fuck are you running from?"

"The Chinese have no choice now. They're coming."

"Yeah, and so is Christmas. You're telling me you ain't even been up against the chinks yet, but you're running anyway?"

Another nod.

"In other words, you're just yellow."

He hadn't meant *yellow* as a racist pun, but his crew took it that way. They found it hysterically funny.

"It's not what you think, Sergeant," the lieutenant said.

"Then maybe you'd better hurry up and fill me in. I'm wasting gas here."

The lieutenant took a moment to compose himself. Then he said, "If I surrender to the MPs, they will kill me."

"Figured that already. So I guess you've gotta turn around and get your asses back to your unit, right?"

With a slow shake of his head, the Korean replied, "If I order these men to return, *they* will kill me. Perhaps not here, not now. But in time..."

The cordon of tanks had squeezed all the ROKs back onto the road. In the process, they'd pushed the two mired deuces back onto the pavement, as well.

"Tell you what I'm gonna do for you," Sean said. "I'll be the bad guy here. I'm placing your men under arrest. They're my prisoners now, got it? I can't arrest you, you being an officer and all, but the rest of 'em are fair game." He winked, hoping the lieutenant understood the favor he was doing him.

"You can do that, Sergeant?"

"You bet your sweet ass I can," he replied, tapping the six stripes on his sleeve with a gloved finger.

"But they're not even in your army."

"I beg to differ, pal. You're all part of Eighth US Army and so am I. If I catch them breaking regs...and being deserters, they sure as hell are breaking regs right now...I can take them into custody. Now go tell your men what I just did, get 'em back on the deuces and outta this damn snowstorm before the stupid bastards die of exposure. We'll escort you back to Sunchon. If they give you any shit, blame it on me. I don't figure they'll argue much with a bunch of tanks."

Then he added, "And if your C.O. gives you any crap, you can paint yourself the hero of this little fiasco for all I care, because I ain't got no dog in this fight except keeping my unit's flank covered, which is the job you and your men are supposed to be doing right now."

The lieutenant understood completely. He smiled and said, "Thank you, Sergeant. Maybe I can pay you back someday."

"Yeah, right…but I won't hold my breath."

As the lieutenant turned to begin policing up his men, Sean called after him, asking, "Hey, what's your name, anyway?"

"Moon. My name is Moon."

"You gotta be shitting me," Sean replied. But he wasn't really surprised: *With all the people named Moon in this damn country, I'm surprised it ain't happened before now.*

When his crew finally stopped laughing, his gunner said, "Gee, Sarge…the son of a bitch don't even look Irish."

*****

By 1500 hours, the ROKs had been returned to their units. As Sean had figured, there was a great deal of huffing, puffing, and draconian threats by ROK commanders about the would-be deserters' *treasonous behavior*. But there was little chance those threats would evolve into action, for one simple fact remained: the only force with an abundance of manpower was the CCF…

And the ROKs are hurting for people just as bad as we GIs are—maybe worse—so when the shit hits the fan, even a man you had to drag into that fighting hole by the scruff of his neck is worth a hundred men sitting on their asses in the stockade.

And the good ol' US Army ain't had no qualms about turning a blind eye to its troopers who decided to pull a runner, neither.

*****

Master Sergeant Melvin Patchett, *top sergeant* of 26th Infantry Regiment, broke into a rare grin when Sean Moon walked into the CP. "Well, look who's finally back," Patchett said as he stepped away from the big situation map on the wall. "I *hear tell* you got to visit with kin on the road up from Pyongyang."

Sean knew what his fellow NCO was referring to by *kin*: the ROK lieutenant who shared his surname. He'd figured his tankers wouldn't waste any time spreading word of the confrontation on the road between the two Moons. But he didn't take it as the good-natured ribbing it was meant to be.

"That ain't fucking funny, Patch. Give it a rest, all right?"

Too late, Patchett realized the nerve he'd struck. The last mention of *kin* around Sean Moon had been the *next of kin* notification he'd received a few days ago. It had informed him that his brother, USAF pilot Tommy Moon, was MIA: *missing in action* over North Korea.

Quickly trying to make amends, Patchett said, "Hey,

Bubba...you know I didn't mean nothing by—"

"Just drop it, Patch. I said give it a fucking rest, okay?"

Hands raised, Patchett backed off, telling himself, *This is gonna be one of them days, I reckon. Seems like everybody's got a case of the ass. First, the colonel gets that damn telegram. He ain't been right since...*

And now Bubba Moon's got his knickers in a twist because I made a bad joke.

Ah, come on, Melvin Patchett...who are you kidding? It wasn't just a bad joke.

You pissed on the man's head...and maybe his brother's grave, too.

The colonel—Jock Miles, commander of 26th Regiment—appeared at the door to the CP, shaking the snow from his galoshes. He looked every bit the man whose thoughts were thousands of miles away.

Patchett asked, "You get that telegram moving, sir?"

"Radiogram, *Top*. It's a radiogram...and yeah, I got it sent. Don't know if she's ever going to get it, though." He sounded like the world had collapsed on top of him.

It took Colonel Miles a few moments to acknowledge Sean was even in the CP, as if he hadn't seen him standing there. It seemed an odd behavior for a man usually as observant as a hawk. But he finally told him, "You did a great job out there on the highway with those ROK runners, Sergeant. I heard they were green troops. Is that true?"

"Yes, sir. Bright green. Like *throw your weapon away* green."

"Well, you saved us having to adjust our lines to fill in the gap they could've caused. We're stretched thin enough as it is." Sounding even further down in the dumps, he added, "And just when I was beginning to believe bug-outs were a thing of the past…"

He paused to trace with his fingertip some new line Patchett had drawn on the map's overlay. It seemed a vacant gesture, like somebody intently gazing on a work of art he didn't comprehend.

Sean and Patchett exchanged worried glances. They'd served under Jock Miles through the darkest days of this Korean War and he'd never seemed in the least bit unfocused, no matter how bad things were. But now, they both had the same alarming thought:

Did the colonel have a breakdown?

"Just leave me be for a while," Jock told them. "Let me sort this damn thing out."

*****

The *damn thing* boiled down to this: his wife Jillian, who'd relocated to California with him and their two young children when his tour as military attaché in her native Australia ended, was being threatened with deportation.

In fact, she might've already been deported. The goddamn cable from her that just showed up this morning was dated a month ago. Whose desk did it sit on all that time? The deportation hearing she talked about happened two weeks ago.

For all I know, my wife and kids have been kicked back to Australia already.

I'm not worried about them starving or having a roof over their heads. Hell, her family back in Oz has more money than God.

But not knowing where they are...when I'll get to see them again...and not being able to do a damn thing to help...

It's tearing me apart.

Who the hell did she tangle with to get kicked out of the country?

And why?

Jill's never been one to back down from a fight. She's ten times tougher than I'll ever be, for cryin' out loud.

But deportation? That smacks of some real shady politics.

I've got to get my shit together, though...right here, right now.

The lives of nearly five thousand men depend on me.

I've buried far too many of my soldiers in this war and the last.

Shame on me if any more die because I was in some kind of fog.

Whatever it is she's up against, Jill's going to have to handle it on her own...

At least for now.

Chapter Two

For Major Tommy Moon, the ejection from his crippled jet had been brutal. Falling from an altitude of over 30,000 feet, the emergency oxygen system on his parachute pack had malfunctioned and he'd blacked out. But he'd come to a minute and a half later when he hit the denser air below 10,000 feet, giving him enough time to pull the ripcord and make a semi-controlled descent onto a windswept mountainside strewn with trees. Luckily, he didn't strike any stout branches and came to an unceremonious stop with the soles of his boots swaying just inches off the ground, suspended from the parachute canopy snared like a fluttering dome in the limbs above. Aside from some bumps, bruises, and a frostnipped face, he'd survived the descent intact.

He had no idea where he was; somewhere in west central North Korea was about as close as he could nail down his location. But no matter where he'd dropped into that war-torn country, now frigid and glazed in winter, the escape azimuth to friendly lines was southeast.

The icy, mountainous terrain made progress on foot agonizingly slow. His flying clothes protected him fairly well against the bitter cold: *Hell, without this getup, you'd freeze in a heartbeat if the cockpit heat craps out. As long as these clothes don't get torn to shreds, I shouldn't have to worry much about dying of exposure. I'd better wrap this scarf around my face, though, to ward off frostbite. And there are plenty of fallen branches lying around to build fires.*

Water to drink might've been a problem if there hadn't been several inches of snow on the ground. He'd remembered eating snowballs as a kid in Brooklyn and telling himself they were ice cream. But his grumbling, empty stomach wouldn't allow him to indulge in that fantasy now. The first few days, he'd sustained himself on the chocolate bars in his survival kit. Once they were gone, though, the quest for food became every bit as harrowing—and as important—as the trek to the safety of friendly lines.

He was hungry, but not yet to the point where he'd cook rats, which seemed to be everywhere, inhabiting every abandoned shack he came across.

There were Asian soldiers everywhere, too, but avoiding them hadn't been too difficult. The rugged terrain offered plenty of hiding places for a lone man. He suspected at first they were KPA—North Korean troops—but he couldn't be sure. The only Korean soldiers he'd ever laid eyes on were the ROKs around Pusan, and they all had American-style uniforms and GI weapons. The troops he was seeing now had neither.

He'd nursed a nasty suspicion they were Chinese. They seemed to be moving in the same general direction as he was—southeast, away from the Yalu River and Manchuria—but only at night. During daylight hours, they bivouacked in the concealment of forests and villages. Tommy figured he knew why:

When the sun's up, they're hiding from our airplanes. I've heard plenty of ground attack ships overhead, too, but I guess they never see these guys. I can't blame those pilots, though. I know how hard spotting people on the ground can be...especially those who don't want to be seen.

I'd love to signal those pilots somehow—maybe with this dinky signal mirror in my kit—but that would probably only give me away and get me captured. It looks like rescue is going to be provided by my feet...or nothing.

The Asian soldiers seemed to have little concern for perimeter security. They didn't patrol; Tommy sometimes got within a hundred yards of their bivouacs. Nobody noticed him.

Sometimes being a small guy has its advantages, I guess.

It wasn't difficult to avoid civilians, either. There were so few of them, all primitive farmers who received nothing from this world but the ravages of war.

Whoever those soldiers were, their rations were the only source of food in this barren wintry landscape now that the chocolate was gone and the rats were still taboo. The trouble was he'd have to steal that food from under their noses. After shadowing a unit for a day, he had a plan:

These troops seem a pretty disciplined lot, but like all soldiers, they lose a lot of that discipline when they're unsupervised, away from their officers and sergeants. They joke around, play games...mostly grab-ass.

Right around sunset, they have a meal: a couple of them light a communal cookfire and put big rice balls in a pot of boiling water. After they eat the rice, they break camp for the march through the night.

But while that rice is cooking, they're usually horsing around...

And while they are, I can sneak up, swipe some of

that rice from the pot on the edge of a bivouac area, and beat it out of there.

By the time they realize something's missing, I'll be gone, too. I don't imagine they'll bother launching a search party at twilight for the missing handful of rice.

The plan worked better than Tommy imagined. Though sure his pounding heart could be heard a mile away, he managed to swipe an entire rice ball from the pot and slip away just as the soldiers stopped *smoking and joking* and returned to their fire.

From a wooded hiding spot on a hillside not very far away, he munched on the rice—the size of a baseball—as he watched the shadowy figures of several soldiers argue in the dim glow of the cookfire. The argument quickly devolved into a shoving match.

Those dummies must be accusing each other of glomming the rice.

This little tactical victory over hunger and the Asians was exhilarating. The rice—mushy and tasteless, probably full of dead insects—was a prize to be savored.

During the next week of his long walk to the southeast, he pulled off similar heists three times more, each theft from a different unit. Somehow, those balls of rice kept him going.

*****

For the first time in the two weeks since he'd been shot down, Major Tommy Moon heard voices that weren't speaking some Asian language. Those voices spoke the English of Britain, in accents to which he'd grown accustomed while stationed there in 1943 and '44, before Operation Overlord and the move to France of the

US 9th Tactical Air Force in which he served.

I guess I've finally made it to the UN lines...some Brit outpost, for sure. And they sound pretty jumpy, too. All the noise they're making, I guess they figure it's no secret they're here.

Now all I've got to do is approach them without getting myself shot. Looking as shabby as I do right now, they might take me for anything but an American airman.

From behind a boulder, Tommy started singing at the top of his lungs. The song—*The White Cliffs of Dover*—had been a sing-along every night in every pub he'd ever been in while in England:

There'll be bluebirds over
The white cliffs of Dover
Tomorrow, just you wait and see...

He even sang it in the warbling style of the Irish tenors his mother had loved to listen to on her old Victrola. His big brother Sean had most likely stolen that phonograph so she could have a Christmas present during a particularly lean year of the Depression.

By the time he'd finished that first verse, Tommy figured it was safe to stand up and show himself.

A gruff voice called to him, saying, "You can come out now, Yank. Just do us a bloody favor and don't sing anymore. You aren't exactly Vera Lynn, you know."

*****

A burly British sergeant major named Peel was astounded that Tommy had survived two weeks in the desolate mountain wastelands of North Korea, in the midst of numerous Red Chinese divisions, before reaching friendly lines near Unsan.

"So they're Chinese, eh?" Tommy said. "I suspected as much, but not speaking the language, I couldn't be sure."

"We think they're coming down from Manchuria in droves," Peel added. "They hit us hard...and then they vanished. Haven't seen or heard them in over a week. You really don't know about the Chinese attack, sir?"

"I've been a little out of touch, Sergeant Major. The last thing I heard was MacArthur telling the whole world the chinks wouldn't dare get involved. I guess he called that one wrong."

Peel replied, "Let's hope his latest pronouncement isn't wrong, as well, because now he's claiming the Chinese assault was merely a probe—a *demonstration*—by a force incapable of doing much more."

"I take it you don't believe that, Sergeant Major?"

"No, sir, I do not. I don't know why the Chinese broke off their attack, but if they hadn't, probably none of us would be standing here right now. So you see why we're more than a little apprehensive."

Tommy ate another spoonful of the stew the Brits had given him, cautioning himself not to overload his shrunken stomach. He washed it down with a few sips of hot coffee. Food had never tasted more delicious.

Watching him eat, Peel said, "I'm still amazed you don't have *the trots*, sir. Especially after the swill you've been eating. Even here in our unit—with regular rations—we've got about a dozen lads down with dysentery. It's the bloody water. No matter what you do, somebody takes in a bad batch."

"Yeah, I guess I am pretty lucky," Tommy replied. Eager to change the subject, he asked, "How about showing me on a map exactly where we are? Maybe then I can figure out where I was when I got shot down. It might help me look a little smarter at the debrief…"

Rather than just some dumb-ass who didn't know where he was and got jumped by a MIG he never saw coming.

The British C.O.—a colonel named Rigby—joined them. "How are you getting along, Major Moon?" he asked.

"Just fine, sir. Thanks for the hospitality."

"You're very welcome. But I'm afraid you'll have to enjoy that hospitality until morning. The liaison plane picking you up won't arrive until then. The weather, you know? In the meantime, I was hoping we could have a discussion of what you observed while among our Chinese friends around here at Unsan and farther north."

Tommy filled them in on everything he'd observed: the small arms they carried; the absence of motor vehicles, armor, and radios; the horses ridden by men who were apparently officers; the lack of heavy infantry weapons; and, of course, what they were eating.

"All they seem to have a lot of is people, sir," Tommy said. "I mean, some of those bivouacs were so crowded they looked like Times Square on New Year's Eve. A couple of five-hundred-pound bombs would've wiped them all out."

Having already fought the CCF, none of this came as a surprise to the Brits. But Colonel Rigby was encouraged by one piece of new information: the lack of security patrols around the Chinese bivouacs and assembly areas.

"I figure that's the main reason I didn't get myself caught," Tommy explained. "Nobody was looking. The only chinks you'll find outside a perimeter are there just to relieve themselves."

"Very good to know," Rigby replied. "Very good, indeed."

*****

The pilot of the liaison ship was a US Army lieutenant named Joe Novarro. Tommy asked him, "What're our chances of making a stop at Sunchon on the way to Kimpo?"

"The chances are pretty good, sir," Novarro replied. "I've got to stop for gas somewhere along the way. I was going to make it Pyongyang, but Sunchon's just as good. The latest field report says the engineers have packed down the snow on the runway nice and hard, so getting in and out should be a snap. I saw a couple of C-47s land there on my way up here this morning. If they can do it, we sure as hell can. What've you got going on there?"

"My brother's around there somewhere. He's a tanker with Twenty-Sixth Regiment."

"They're part of Twenty-Fourth Division, right?"

"Yeah, they are. You don't happen to know exactly where the Twenty-Sixth is, do you, Joe?"

"Sure do, sir. They're not too far from the airstrip. We can give them a heads-up you're coming once we're airborne. Does your brother know you got knocked down?"

Tommy replied, "I hope not. He doesn't need the extra worries."

*****

The only person waiting for the liaison ship when it

landed at Sunchon was the GI driving the fuel truck. Joe Novarro checked his watch and told Tommy, "You've got about an hour, sir. If we take longer than that to get airborne again, you'll miss the Tokyo flight at Kimpo. Those transport jockeys are on pretty tight schedules. I don't imagine they'll hang around for you."

Making that Kimpo connection meant being back in Japan for supper. But an hour wasn't much time to find Sean, who was somewhere, presumably, in the regiment's zone.

He'd started walking toward the operations tent when he heard the roar of a vehicle engine echoing across the valley cradling the airstrip. In another moment, the source of that roar barreled into view as a Pershing tank crested a rise, avoided the carefully plowed aircraft ramp so as not to chew it up, and came to a stop behind the tent. Climbing from the turret hatch was none other than his brother.

"I knew you wasn't dead, *Half*," Sean said, calling him by the nickname Tommy had been saddled with since childhood, one only family and close friends dared use. It had always seemed so natural to refer to a diminutive person with that surname as *Half Moon.*

Neither said another word as they locked each other in a brotherly bear hug, the much smaller Tommy practically lost in the embrace of his tall, burly brother.

And neither was ashamed of the tears he shed.

*****

As scheduled, the C-54 from Kimpo deposited Tommy back in Tokyo in time for supper. But he was more interested in a long, hot shower, clean clothes, and a sound sleep, one in which there was no danger of being discovered by rats or enemy soldiers. After hours of medical examination, the flight surgeon—a fellow major—pronounced him fit for duty.

"I still can't get over the fact that you don't have any intestinal problems, Tommy," the doctor said. "And I'm still amazed how you kept up your energy level eating the little you did."

"Sometimes you just get lucky, Doc."

"I think it's more than that. Face it, Tommy…you're not the biggest guy who ever strapped on a fighter plane. Your caloric demands are probably quite a bit lower than a larger person's. How'd you ever make the height requirement for flight school, anyway? I mean, you're not quite five foot four. Close, but no cigar."

"That'd be my little secret, Doc. And sure, I was hungry as hell out there in the cold. But wouldn't you say it's pretty hard for a guy who'd been eating pretty well all along to starve in just two weeks?"

"Maybe you've got a point there, Tommy."

*****

Mercifully, the debrief was not scheduled until 0800 the next morning. He wasn't prepared for the crowd that filled the conference room where the debrief was held. Aside from a twenty-strong phalanx of USAF officers led by the three-star general commanding Far East Air Force, there were six Navy and Marine Corps officers, all wearing aviator's wings.

Damn, when I got shot down behind enemy lines in France, the debrief committee was my C.O. and just a

*few other officers. Some adjutant did most of the talking,
trying to figure out whether I qualified for an escaped
POW's immediate ticket out of theater.*

This is a much bigger show...but I'm not sure why.

The minute the *three-star* opened the proceedings, it
became painfully obvious why this was a *much bigger
show*: there was a good chance that *Moon, Thomas P.,
Major, USAF*, was the first American pilot to be shot
down by a Soviet-built MIG-15 jet. The fear that the
Americans had nothing in their inventory or tactics to
equal, let alone best, the MIG hung heavily over the
room.

When the general finished his introductory remarks,
Tommy asked, "Sir, you said *there's a good chance* I
was the first. Who else is in the running?"

"An F-80 was lost over North Korea earlier the
same day, Major. We're not sure what happened to him.
He'd been separated from his flight and no one saw how
he came to grief. There's been no trace of the pilot or the
plane, either. But you're sure how you came to be shot
down, am I correct?"

"Yes, sir, I'm quite sure what happened and who
did it."

"Then you're the only one who does, Major. Tell us
every last bit of it," the general said. To the room, he
added, "Strap in, gentlemen. This is going to be a long
and bumpy flight, I'm afraid."

Chapter Three

A relative calm had settled over the line of contact in the week since the Chinese attacked, wreaked havoc, and then disappeared. While the shock of that assault had begun to wear off, the GIs were convinced beyond all doubt the combat momentum still lay with the CCF. Nobody below the rank of general believed it had just been a *probe*, a one-time event that wouldn't be repeated. As Jock Miles told his assembled regimental staff, "Holding the chinks off is all well and good, but we need a plan to take back the offensive. And at the moment, dammit, neither Division, nor Eighth Army, nor MacArthur and his boys in Tokyo have one."

The only plan Tokyo seemed intent on implementing was a daunting logistical one: provide a traditional Thanksgiving feast—hot turkey with all the trimmings—for every GI and Marine in Korea, no matter how remote his current outpost happened to be. So on November 23, 1950—Thanksgiving Day—every American mess section prepared and served the planeloads of holiday food they'd received.

"This turkey's mighty fine," Patchett said. "Keeping it hot for the men on the far outposts was a little tricky, though. By the time they got from the serving line to where they set themselves down to eat, that hot chow wanted to freeze all over again."

"How'd we solve that problem, Top?"

"Simple, sir. Everybody kept their gloves on while they heated up their mess kits over a fire. That held off the cold for a coupla extra minutes."

Then he asked Jock, "You ready for seconds, sir?"

"Not unless every man in the regiment has already had a shot at seconds, Top."

"They all have, sir," Patchett replied. "Every last swinging dick. So what's your pleasure...white meat or dark?"

"Actually, I had my heart set on another piece of that cake."

"Coming right up, sir," Patchett replied as he headed for the serving line.

In this moment of solitude, Jock thought back to a Thanksgiving during the last war. The *holiday fare* had been much more spartan in the jungles of Papua and New Guinea. Jillian, being Australian, had no concept what Thanksgiving celebrated. When he'd explained to her back then what the holiday meant, she'd listened quietly and then asked, "These *pilgrims*...they were English?"

"Yeah, they were, Jill. Some of my ancestors, in fact. The Miles line goes way back in Massachusetts."

She shook her head. "It all sounds like another of your bloody Yank fairy tales to me, Jock. The English would be more likely to kill or enslave the natives than break bread with them."

What began as a pleasant reminiscence had now turned painful: *Where are you and the kids now, Jill? How long am I going to have to wait to find out?*

Patchett returned, setting the chocolate cake on the field box they were using as a table. He said, "Here's your pleasure, sir, as requested."

"Thanks, Top. But you know what my pleasure *really* would've been?"

"A case of Scotch whiskey, maybe?"

"No, seriously...I would've loved to see all the cargo planes that delivered this food loaded to the gills with ammo and automatic weapons instead. I've got a nasty feeling we're going to need that stuff real bad before long."

*****

At a village nestled between jagged mountains in central North Korea, Gunnery Sergeant Jim Ramsay and the men of his Marine Corps tank platoon were downing their Thanksgiving dinner, too. The hot turkey with dressing, steamed vegetables, fresh-baked bread, and pumpkin pie was a delicious treat that seemed completely out of kilter with the hostile environment and the imminent jeopardy of combat.

This whole thing's been a goat rope from the git-go, Ramsay told himself. *These Army generals we're stuck under get dumber by the day. After we fucked around on board ship for a couple of weeks, sailing from Inchon to Pusan and then to Wonsan—where those generals told us we'd be making another amphibious assault—we sat offshore for a damn week, waiting for the swabbies to declare the harbor free of mines. When we finally hit the beach, we found out the ROKs were already there...and so was Bob Hope and his USO show.*

Like I said, a goat rope. Typical Army hurry up and wait bullshit...

Just like the Inchon landings back in September.

From Wonsan, we drove north, into these fucking mountains, where there's only one road—we call it the MSR, for main supply route. Main supply, my ass...it's the ONLY supply route. And now we've stretched that

ONLY supply route for over fifty miles, to this little shithole town called Hagaru-ri, which sits at the southern tip of this big lake called the Chosin Reservoir. We're just begging for that supply route to get cut off by the chinks.

To get around and past the Chosin, the road north to the Yalu and Manchuria is straight uphill, through the highest mountains in Korea. My tanks will never make it up those grades through the passes. Half of them have broken down already. Once we're in those mountains, we'll lose the other half, for sure.

It makes no sense why that Army general who's running this show—that General Almond, like the nuts— has his Tenth Corps dispositioned the way it is, extending like gnarled fingers of an arthritic hand, each moving up its own deep valley. The Marine division is on the hills to the west of the Chosin, an Army regiment is on the east side. We couldn't support each other with that fucking lake in the way if our lives depended on it ...

And they just might.

I don't know much about the big picture—I'm not sure anybody does—but with all these mountains in the way, none of the UN forces in North Korea can support each other.

If the Chinese decide to hit us here, we're on our own.

But those Army generals keep telling us that'll never happen.

I guess they figure we haven't heard that it's already happened to Eighth Army on our left flank...

On the other side of the damn mountains.

*****

Three nights after Thanksgiving, the Chinese struck the UN lines across the entire width of North Korea with a renewed vengeance. Jock Miles' 26th Regiment had just been designated as 24th Division reserve, remaining at Sunchon while Division's other two regiments deployed to forward positions along the Taedong River a few miles to the north. From Sunchon, Jock's regiment could deploy in any direction to plug breakthroughs in the defensive line, surrounding and destroying any marauding Chinese before they could do serious damage in rear areas of the division.

It would fall to Division to make the call when to commit the reserve. Jock and his staff figured that was why Brigadier General Ellis, the 24th Division assistant commander, was camped in front of the situation map in their CP. As battle reports from the other regiments flooded in, Ellis became alarmed as Sergeant Patchett drew a particularly large bulge on the map near the boundary of 24th and 25th Divisions, an indication that a Chinese breakthrough was imminent...or might have already happened. The general wanted the reserve committed immediately to reduce the bulge.

As Jock was formulating a respectful way to disagree with the general, Patchett beat him to the punch.

"If I may, sir, the bulge is just an approximation," Patchett told the general, "a *worst-case scenario*. You know as well as I do these reports in the middle of a fight—especially a night fight—are never one hundred percent on the money. Let's not light our hair on fire until we get some confirming information. Nobody's reporting a breakthrough yet, just a readjustment of boundary lines between us and Twenty-Fifth Division."

As Ellis dithered, Jock added, "We've got to be certain before we commit the reserve, General. We'll only get to do it once, and it'll be damn near impossible to stop it or change its direction after it gets going. It'll be like a boulder rolling downhill, so we'd better be right when we pull the trigger. In my opinion, we're not there yet."

Ellis replied, "Maybe you should just send a tank company or two up there to support them, Colonel?"

Even in the CP's dim lighting, Jock could see Sean Moon's face twist into a scowl. He understood why his armor sergeant hated the general's idea: *Tanks rolling around in the dark, without dedicated infantry support, are easy marks for sappers.* So he told Ellis, "When we commit, sir, we commit *everybody*—infantry and armor—together. Otherwise we're begging to get destroyed piecemeal."

"But surely, Colonel, there are times that call for exceptions to the rule…like taking an aggressive action to seize the initiative."

"Yes, General, there are exceptions, but this isn't one of them."

Patchett and Sean watched the discussion in silence, fully expecting the general to issue an order mandating his half-baked tactical idea. Both sergeants were thinking the same thing:

What is it with the generals in this man's army nowadays? They still ain't seeing the difference between aggressiveness and tactical stupidity.

Patchett had come up with a name for this tendency, which he kept to himself; he called it *MacArthur's Disease.*

But to their surprise—and relief—Ellis issued no order.

Battle reports continued to spill into the CP. The regimental intelligence officer—the S2—had been listening intently to a radio conversation. Turning to Jock, he said, "Sir, we've got a call for artillery support from a Twenty-Fifth Division unit on our right flank. Looks like all their batteries have their hands full at the moment. Our one-five-five guns can handle it."

Patchett already knew the coordinates of the fire support request; he'd been listening to every radio in the CP simultaneously, sorting out what was critical and what were just the babbling voices of men under extreme pressure, their words doing little but chronicle the terror and uncertainty swirling around them. The ability to sort out the confusion was a talent successful combat leaders developed early, one that enabled them to steer their units through the chaos with as little deadly misdirection as humanly possible.

"I recommend we put a hold on that fire mission, sir," Patchett said, stopping the artillery liaison officer as he was about to relay the request to the firing battery. "The Twenty-Fifth's already got their artillery engaging that target."

"Negative, Sergeant," Ellis said. "You don't know that. Honor that request for fire."

Patchett replied, "Sir...with all due respect...the coordinates are within thirty yards of a fire mission the Twenty-Fifth's guns already started shooting less than a minute ago. The first rounds impacted while we were standing here talking. Target description is near identical: *troops at the wire, danger close.* Just a case of different eyes on the same thing. We'd be shooting at the same damn bunch of chinks, sir…and wasting a ton of precious ammo in the process."

Looking deflated, Ellis asked Jock, "Do you go along with the sergeant's assessment, Colonel?"

"Affirmative, sir."

Ellis threw up his hands, a gesture that meant *so be it.*

The CP's switchboard operator called out, "I've got General Bishop on the line, sir."

General Bishop: 24th Division's mostly absentee commander, frail and racked with arthritis. A man famous for *leading from the rear*, he'd rarely visited frontline units during his three months as division commander. Right now, he was at 8th Army Headquarters near Pyongyang, forty miles from the front. In all fairness, his physical condition would've made constant travel to and from his units in small aircraft and jeeps a painful ordeal. But in all honesty, it should've precluded MacArthur from blessing him for command in the first place.

Jock replied, "Who does he want to speak to?"

"You, sir."

Jock held out another handset to Ellis so he could join the conversation.

But the general looked stricken and waved the handset away. "Don't mention I'm here," he said, just above a whisper.

Patchett had to turn away to hide the smirk on his face. *Sure, he don't want Bishop to know he's here, with the reserve regiment. He's probably supposed to be bird-dogging the line units.*

There don't seem to be no physical defects to our General Ellis here, but I reckon he's taken to being a rear-echelon commander just like his boss.

Jock hadn't had a chance to say anything to Bishop yet; the general on the other end of the line was doing all the talking. What he was saying was startling, especially from a commander who'd bought into the misunderstanding of every situation Tokyo had ever offered.

But surprisingly, Bishop's words made tactical sense this time.

Jock rang off the line, still seeming a bit stunned as he told his staff, "You're probably not going to believe this, but we're being ordered to *pull back.*"

Ellis asked, "Back to where, Colonel?"

"Pyongyang, sir. Eighth Army wants to trade space for time so we can set up better defensive positions. If the CCF plans to continue trying to overwhelm us with sheer manpower, Eighth Army wants to fight them on more favorable terrain."

Patchett had one more question: "We're gonna do this move in daylight, right?"

"Negative, Top. We're going now."

*****

Eighth Army, General Walton *Johnnie* Walker's command, was holding the left—or western—half of the UN line, just as it had since summer without interruption. General Almond's X Corps was scattered throughout the mountainous and desolate eastern half. But all across that line—which stretched over one hundred miles across the Korean peninsula from coast to coast—the Chinese were attacking once again with what seemed an unlimited supply of light infantry. They still possessed little artillery, no armor, and no air support, but that came as small comfort to those GIs and Marines facing the endless, crushing waves of determined infantrymen who seemed indifferent to the massive casualties the CCF was suffering.

The Marines and GIs ringing the Chosin Reservoir quickly found themselves *on their own*, as *Gunny* Ramsay had feared:

This fucking brutal weather has slowed traffic on the MSR to a trickle. Right now, we don't have the fuel to drive any farther north into those damn mountains, and we ain't likely to get it any time soon, either. Just as well...my tanks will never make it through those mountains, anyway.

So we're stuck here. Like sitting ducks...

Or maybe frozen ducks.

General Smith, our division C.O., has established our perimeter up on three peaks overlooking the Chosin and the road north. It's good that our infantry's on that high ground...

But there's not a damn thing my tanks can do to support them up there, so the armor mission is to provide security for the airfield General Smith is trying to build at Hagaru and make sure no chinks slip behind us to cut off the MSR. Because that one damn road isn't just the only way we'll get supplies—it's the only way we can back out of here if we have to withdraw.

The CCF is already coming up the back side of those mountains for tonight's attack—the side my tankers can't even see from down here. The radio is alive with reports of contact and calls for mortar fire. It'll be another bloodbath. Mostly theirs, but plenty of ours, too.

Our guys are holding their ground, at least for now.
But if we can't get resupplied with enough ammo,
fuel, and food...
We won't be able to hold those mountains for long.

*****

Twenty-Fourth Division's withdrawal plan was a simple one; it had to be, because night movements when in contact with the enemy were among the most risky maneuvers a unit can undertake. The potential for confusion, chaos, and deadly errors was monumental.

As it would be this night.

Jock's regiment—the 26th—would lead the division column south toward Pyongyang, setting the pace for a major vehicle movement that would last all night and into the following morning. Once on the road, the motorized units of 24th Division had little fear of pursuing Chinese. Without vehicles to transport them, the CCF couldn't keep pace. Only able to march at night due to the threat of American aircraft, they'd have to walk for two nights to reach Pyongyang. By that time, the GIs could be well dug in on flat terrain that would deny the Chinese the concealment to infiltrate American positions they'd enjoyed in mountainous terrain. That flat ground would become a killing field for the CCF's mass attacks.

Ten minutes to the scheduled time for 26th Regiment to start rolling, frantic radio traffic began to spill from the CP van's speakers. It painted a picture of a plan already falling apart. "Seventeenth Regiment jumped the gun, sir," Patchett told Jock. "They're already on the road, and it's the wrong road, to boot. Near as I can tell, they got panicky that the ROKs on their left had cut and run, so they did the same."

Jock asked, "And where's the Seventeenth now, Top?"

"They're already *behind* us on the Pyongyang highway, sir."

Jock kicked a tire of his jeep in frustration. "Dammit, that means our left flank—hell, the whole Eighth Army's flank—is wide open."

"What do you reckon we oughta do, sir?" Patchett asked.

Spreading the map on the hood of his jeep, Jock told his driver to hold a flashlight on it. Tracing a secondary road that fed into the highway just south of Sunchon, he asked, "Is this the road the Seventeenth took to get behind us, Top?"

"Has to be, sir."

"All right, we're going to drive south down the highway and plug that road junction. It's only two miles from here, and we're all ready to roll. Second Battalion will go in first with a company of tanks as a blocking force until the rest of us can get there. That should put the brakes on any chinks that might be running after the Seventeenth...and stop them from getting behind the whole damn division."

"Amen to that, sir," Patchett replied. "I reckon you want a staff meeting right here?"

"Yeah, Top. Right here, right now. We've got to get everybody on the same page real quick."

Chapter Four

Sean Moon led the company of tanks supporting 2nd Battalion. Once they'd gotten the order from Colonel Miles, it had taken twenty minutes for the combined arms team to drive to the road junction that would become their blocking position.

"I hope we're not too late getting here," Major Harper, 2nd Battalion's C.O., said as he struggled to get his rifle companies emplaced in the darkness. "I'd hate to think some chinks have already slipped past here."

"Not likely, sir," Sean replied as he and Harper studied the map on the hood of the major's jeep. "They can't run too fast with all the shit they carry with 'em. They ain't got trucks, remember?"

"Do you think we ought to use the flare ship?" Harper asked.

"Why not, sir? It's supposed to be way better than shooting illum rounds. We just gotta get that ship to drop those babies in the right place. Where the hell is that damn ASO who's supposed to be with us? It's his job to get that stuff on target."

A voice replied, *"That damn ASO* is right here. I've been trying to find you, Major. Good thing that big noisy tank decided to find you first. I just followed the sound."

An Air Force captain—the *air support officer*—appeared out of the darkness and joined the two. He asked, "So what can I do for you, sir?"

Harper told him they wanted the flare ship to deliver the *deluxe* illumination package. "I want it so bright that I'll be able to look through a chink to see the one behind him," he added.

"*Firefly* is five minutes out," the ASO replied. "She can start dropping immediately."

"Whoa, not so fast, sir," Sean said. "We gotta time the drop for when the chinks are in the open. Otherwise, we'll spook 'em."

The ASO didn't see the problem with *spooking* the Chinese. "Wouldn't that be just as good, Sergeant?"

"Negative, sir. *Negative.* They'd still be out there somewhere. We gotta get rid of 'em before they start popping up all along this damn highway. We don't need no fucking ambushes tonight."

"Okay," the ASO said, "but how will we know when the chinks are coming?"

Harper replied, "I've already got listening posts set out. The second they hear anything, they'll pull in and we'll light up the fireworks like it's the Fourth of July."

"I got a question," Sean said. "How do we get this flare ship oriented in the dark?"

"They fly intersecting radio beams out of Pyongyang and a mountaintop near Yankdok," the ASO replied. "They'll guide her close enough to us that I can signal the crew with my blinker light. That way, they get positive ID of your unit's position, too. Just tell me how far out you want the light sticks. The wind's going to make the flares drift toward us, so we'll have to compensate for that."

"Sounds like a plan, sir," Sean said. "Just do us a favor and have the ship loiter about a mile east of here so the drone of her engines don't mask any sounds for the guys on the LPs."

"What about the noise from your tank engines, Sergeant?" the ASO asked.

"Once my vehicles are in position, we shut 'em down. I hate doing that—you never know if the damn things are gonna start again, especially in this icebox we're in—but the chinks will hear 'em, too, if we keep 'em running before it's time to engage. Kinda ruins the surprise, you know?"

*****

Twenty minutes later, the first LP reported the unmistakable sound of many footsteps crunching through snow. Within thirty seconds, the other two LPs reported the same thing.

"Let there be light, Captain," Major Harper told the ASO.

The flare ship—a C-47 transport with a cabin full of parachute flares, each flare capable of providing several million candlepower of illumination—began her run. Night became day as her crew hurled the canisters from the ship's open cargo door at an altitude of 2,500 feet. The blanket of snow covering the ground heightened the flares' effect, reflecting and enhancing their brilliant light. Her pass complete, the ship headed back to the holding pattern, safely away from the bedlam that was about to erupt.

A surreal scene appeared to the GIs: in their puffy white uniforms, the approaching Chinese—still about two hundred yards away—appeared to be ranks of snowmen trundling toward them. Though their usual procedure if caught in the light of flares was to freeze, the CCF soldiers began to charge the American positions on the dead run. Perhaps they realized that even if they stood stock-still, the shadows they cast while being backlit by the flares would give them away.

Or perhaps they started running because they were terrified.

"They got two choices," Sean said. "Run away or run straight at us. Looks like they picked the wrong one."

Within seconds, hundreds of Chinese were cut down by the interlocking fire of dozens of machine guns. Even those who tried to crawl under the bullets grazing the earth found no safe haven; airbursts from mortar rounds showered them with deadly steel, the sizzling hot, razor-sharp fragments slicing through flesh and bone like paper.

"They didn't play that one real smart," Sean said. "But we'd better get another flare drop lined up real quick. It ain't like a chink unit that big to quit after only one try."

The American gunfire began to taper off; there was little to shoot at anymore. Nothing was moving in the dimming light as the first drop of flares began to burn out.

Then the GIs heard the bugles sounding the call they'd come to associate with an impending attack. Sean said, "See? What'd I tell you? Get ready for round two."

*****

The Marines at the Chosin Reservoir could hear bugles, too, echoing through the mountains, announcing that another attack by the CCF was on the way. It would be the second of the night; the first had been repulsed by the skin of their teeth.

As they fired great volumes of lead into Chinese

troops assaulting up the steep slope, the men of the platoon holding the south face of the peak were startled to find enemy troops among them, seeking out their fighting holes, trying to kill the unwitting Americans in those holes with bullets, grenades, and even bayonets.

When his squad leader was shot dead from behind, a Marine PFC named Morton grabbed the .30-caliber machine gun the sergeant had been firing. Pulling the weapon from its tripod, Morton stood, turned around, and laid down a deadly curtain of fire behind his platoon's position on the peak.

"GRAB ANOTHER BELT," he yelled to the closest Marine.

The man didn't move. He just hunkered deeper into the fighting hole. It looked like he was trying to disappear into his helmet.

"FUCK YOU, THEN," Morton said as he grabbed the ammo belt and slung it over his shoulder. He climbed from the hole and started walking across the peak, firing the machine gun from the hip. The only illumination was from the flashes of weapons firing all around him. There wasn't enough light for him to see where he was going or who he was shooting at.

Then Morton tripped over something.

As he scrambled back to his feet, the obstacle that had taken him down began to groan. He reached out to the man, telling himself, *Please don't tell me I shot one of my own guys.*

But just a touch of the man's rough clothing—the brittle feel of cotton stiff with ice—told him this was no Marine. He felt no need to shoot the man again. Bullets were precious.

Then he continued to stalk the peak of the mountain,

firing at the many silhouettes still darting about in the darkness.

Anything running around like that gotta be a chink.

Morton was almost out of ammunition when something struck him in the midsection and knocked him off his feet.

He didn't remember falling.

*****

Despite the freezing weather, the Marine Corps engineers at Hagaru were making steady progress on the runway General Smith so desperately wanted. Their bulldozers and graders were turning the frozen, rocky turf into a surface long enough, smooth enough, and flat enough for large transport aircraft to takeoff and land. Within the next twelve hours, the engineers felt confident an R4D—the Navy and Marine Corps designation for the C-47—could land there. "She might be a little weight-restricted on takeoff," the engineering officer told General Smith, "but she'll have a good twenty-five hundred feet of runway."

The work was too important to be delayed by darkness, so they toiled through the night in the glare of floodlights, hoping—*praying*—the enemy didn't possess artillery powerful enough to fire over the mountains at the well-defined targets they were.

But even without artillery, Chinese infantry could still infiltrate and attack. Every engineer kept his weapon close as he labored; they couldn't forget that every Marine, whatever his specialty, was an infantryman first.

Gunnery Sergeant Jim Ramsay had a hunch: *This airfield is more an insurance policy to get our wounded out of here than a supplemental way to bring supplies and reinforcements in. It's no secret we can't advance any farther than the Chosin without decimating First Marine Division...despite the bullshit the Army generals are trying to peddle.*

And there sure as hell isn't much point in our Marines dying just to hold this useless piece of ground.

Ramsay had another hunch, too: *If the chinks are going to try to overrun the airfield, they're going to come from the east, infiltrating around that route-step Army outfit on the east side of the reservoir...and those GIs won't even have a clue they did it.*

The Marines on the west side of the Chosin won't let that happen.

That second hunch was proved right when, on the airfield's darkened eastern edge—beyond the glare of the engineers' floodlights—the startling flash from the main gun of his *Number Three* tank lit the night like a lightning bolt. In that brief moment of illumination, the tankers could see the squads of CCF sappers running toward them. Some had already made it to the tanks, climbing onto their decks.

"Dust them off, Marines," Ramsay commanded. While his lead tank and *Number Two* trained their machine guns in the direction of the sappers still approaching, the other three tanks turned their machine guns on each other, firing into the Chinese who'd already clambered on board with their grenades and satchel charges.

Within seconds, the decks of all the Pershings had been swept clean. But for *Number Four*, it was too late; a sapper had managed to wedge a satchel charge against the grate covering her engine inlet. Though a stream of bullets quickly found him, he'd done his damage. The explosion tore into the engine's inlet duct and dual carburetors. It was still running but only at an unsteady idle; any attempt to accelerate made it sputter to the point of stalling.

But her crew could—and did—keep firing, imprisoned in the immobile steel cocoon that had just saved them. They all shared the same thought: *Just so she doesn't start burning.*

A voice from the airfield's CP boomed from Ramsay's radio: "Do you need illumination and support from the engineers?"

"Affirmative on the illumination. Negative on the engineers. They don't need to get caught in the middle of this."

Immediately, several floodlights were turned the tankers' way. The harsh light left no doubt the fight was over. A ghastly scene surrounded them: by Ramsay's rough count, there were thirty dead Chinese littering the ground, a few more on the decks. If there were survivors among those sappers who never reached the tanks, they had vanished into the night.

"Correction my last transmission," Ramsay radioed the CP. "Tell the engineers we need a bulldozer to dig a real big hole. Maybe a padre to say some prayers over these dead chinks before we throw them in, too."

*****

At sunup, Ramsay's tank platoon was relieved from patrolling the Hagaru airfield construction site. It was the first chance for the crews to talk face to face. Ramsay had a question for *Number Three's* commander:

"Dave, how come you fired your main gun instead of your MGs when you first spotted the chinks? I mean, it was a hell of a way to get everyone's attention, but why'd you waste the round?"

"I didn't waste the round, Gunny. I had a chink swinging from my tube. I couldn't shake him loose, so I blew him off with the muzzle blast. You said never open a hatch to take a shot at somebody trying to pull shit like that, right?"

*****

Ramsay's platoon of tanks—minus the one still disabled on the edge of the airfield— had one more job to do before catching their brief daytime sleep. The four Pershings drove five miles to the Toktong Pass at the base of Hill 1451—one of the three peaks the Marine infantry held on the Chosin's west side—to serve as ambulances for the wounded being brought down off the mountain.

Damn, there are a lot of them, Ramsay told himself. *Looks like a company's worth, at least...*

And Lord knows how many dead are still up there.

With eight wounded Marines crammed across his aft deck, Ramsay's vehicle started rolling slowly toward the field hospital at Hagaru. They hadn't gone more than one hundred feet when he saw a Marine sitting on the side of the road. He was staring into the brightening sky as if in some sort of trance. Ramsay told his driver to stop.

"Are you okay, Marine?" he asked the man.

"I'm just resting before I go back up for another load."

Ramsay replied, "You mean there are more wounded still on the mountain?"

The man nodded. But the gesture seemed otherworldly; Ramsay felt sure there was something not right with this Marine. He climbed down from the tank for a face-to-face talk.

As he approached, the man saw the stripes stenciled on the sleeves of Ramsay's tanker's jacket and rose unsteadily to his feet. Once standing, the gunny could see the dried blood staining the front of his unzipped parka. It didn't take much of an inspection to realize the man had a serious abdominal wound.

"What's your name, Marine?"

"My name's Morton, Gunny. PFC. Charlie Company, First of the Seventh Marines."

Ramsay called out for a corpsman. A corporal walking nearby replied, "Ain't no corpsmen down here, Gunny. They're all too busy up the mountain."

As they talked, Ramsay checked Morton's wound. Pushing the front of the open parka aside, he could see the woolen shirt and long johns had been torn apart just above the belt line. Beneath lay a jagged tear in his lower abdomen several inches long...

But there was no blood flowing from it. And this private seemed oblivious to the grievous wound.

When Ramsay touched the area around the wound, he understood why: *This blood is frozen! It's sealed the puncture.*

He resisted the urge to zip up Morton's parka. The man didn't show any signs of hypothermia...

And if this wound gets warmed up, the blood'll thaw, and he'll probably bleed to death before I can get him to Hagaru.

"C'mon, Morton, you're coming with me. I'm going to get you up on the deck of this tank."

"No, Gunny...I'm okay. The other guys up there...they need me. They need all the help they can get."

"Maybe so, Morton, but that help won't be coming from you, at least not until a doc fixes you up. Now climb up on the vehicle. That's an order, Marine."

*****

A mile from Hagaru, three men jumped into the road in front of Ramsay's tank-turned-ambulance, waving their arms frantically for her to stop. They were obviously not Asian and wore American uniforms, but he could tell from fifty feet away they weren't Marines.

Two of them weren't carrying weapons. All of them looked like they were running for their lives. As the Pershing rolled to a stop, they tried to climb onto her bow.

Ramsay yelled down from the turret hatch, "WHAT THE HELL ARE YOU ARMY PUKES DOING ON THIS SIDE OF THE RESERVOIR?"

They started babbling like crazy men, rambling about how the Chinese had attacked *by the millions*, and how they had no interest in *committing suicide* by actually trying to fight them.

"WE AIN'T THE ONLY ONES WHO FEEL THAT WAY, EITHER," a weaponless GI said, as if offering justification for their flight.

"SHUT UP FOR A SECOND," Ramsay said. "JUST HOW THE HELL DID YOU GET ALL THE WAY OVER HERE? WHAT'D YOU DO? RUN

RIGHT THROUGH HAGARU WITHOUT STOPPING?"

"NO, WE RAN ACROSS THE LAKE," the GI still with a weapon replied.

"ACROSS THE RESERVOIR? ARE YOU SHITTING ME?"

"NO! NO SHIT! IT'S FROZEN. WE JUST RAN ACROSS."

"WELL, YOU SHOULD'VE FUCKING FELL IN," Ramsay replied. "ANY OF YOU DESERTERS WOUNDED?"

Their blank expressions told him none of them were.

"THEN GET OFF MY TANK, YOU CHICKENSHIT ASSHOLES. IT'S FOR WOUNDED ONLY, NOT BUG-OUT BASTARDS LIKE YOU."

Chapter Five

The only good thing the GIs of 24th Division could say about their sudden nighttime withdrawal to Pyongyang was that it incurred very few wounded and none killed. But two days later, the chaos resulting from that botched motor march in darkness still hadn't been completely sorted out. Twenty-Sixth Regiment had arrived at its designated sector only to find the battalions of 17th Regiment clogging the area; this was the same unit that had panicked and withdrawn too early, precipitating that unnecessary night battle beneath the *Firefly* ship's brilliant flares. The demoralized and apathetic troops of the 17th milled around as if establishing a defensive line was somebody else's problem. The lack of direction in that outfit wasn't rectified until General Bishop—the 24th Division commander—relieved the regimental commander on the spot during a rare visit to his frontline units.

That change of command, of course, brought its own disorder as the new commander tried to quickly reforge the unit to his liking. But at least it moved the 17th Regiment troops out of 26th Regiment's way.

A few other outfits—both American and ROK— still hadn't fully regrouped, with platoons and even entire companies not yet accounted for.

"The sad thing about all this confusion," Jock Miles said, "is that we created it ourselves by not sticking to plans. We haven't seen *Joe Chink* since that night fight at the crossroads south of Sunchon."

But every man in the 26th knew the absence of

Chinese couldn't last long. Patchett summed it up this way: "Even if them chinks are on crutches, them bastards'll be here by tonight."

The relief of a regimental commander wasn't the only administrative change suddenly disrupting the division. General Bishop informed Jock, "Say goodbye to your Australian battalion, Miles. They're to become part of the newly formed Commonwealth Brigade."

"Effective when, sir?" Jock asked.

"Today, Miles, today. You can manage that, can't you?"

"That depends, sir. Who am I getting to replace the Aussies?"

"You're getting an outfit from Third Division, fresh from the States."

Great, Jock thought. *A battalion that's green from head to toe.*

"Can I at least assume they're at full strength, General?"

"Yes, Miles, you can."

I'm afraid they won't be for long. Not until they get their feet wet...or frozen, as the case may be.

Then Bishop said, "I'm doing you another favor, too, Miles. I'm giving you an additional battery of one-oh-fives."

"That's good news, sir. Who are they?"

"Baker Battery, Fifty-Third Artillery."

*****

As soon as Bishop drove off, Patchett asked Jock, "You know who Fifty-Third Artillery is, don't you, sir?"

"No. You'd better tell me, Top."

"They're them colored boys from Second Division. A lot of people are saying their fire support was so piss-poor that Eighth Army ain't got no choice but to break that battalion up." Lowering his voice, he added, "Before they get lynched."

"From what I've heard, Top, the performance of the entire Second Division wasn't so hot. Got themselves way over their heads and never came back up."

"Be that as it may, sir, but you know as well as I do that shit flows downhill...and them colored boys are always gonna be at the bottom of the hill."

"Ain't that the truth," Jock replied. "But right now, I'm more worried about this new infantry battalion we're inheriting to replace the Aussies."

"Me too, sir. They won't be worth a bucket of warm spit for a while. I reckon you wanna make them regimental reserve as soon as they get here?"

"Yeah, we've got no choice, Top."

Jock looked pained as he settled gingerly onto a camp stool, his bad leg stretched stiffly before him.

"It's acting up bad, ain't it, sir?" Patchett asked.

"Yeah. It's hurting like a son of a bitch today. But I've got to get out there and inspect how the *digging in* is coming along, so—"

"Negative, sir. Let me take care of it."

Jock started to protest but thought better of it. "Okay, Top. I'd appreciate you doing that."

*****

The *digging in* was going better than Patchett expected, considering the challenges Mother Nature was throwing at them. *This ground's frozen like a sumbitchin' rock,* he told himself, *and so is that damn Taedong River that's supposed to be the moat to this castle of ours. It's just too narrow around these parts. Iced up like it is, it won't be stopping no chinks all by itself, that's for damn sure. We already figured out it's thick enough that a deuce won't even fall through, since one of our drivers got hisself lost and drove right out onto the damn thing. A horde of chinks in tennis shoes sure as hell ain't gonna fall through, neither.*

But Sean Moon, with a little help from the engineers, had figured out how to dig into the rock-hard turf.

"You infantry-types don't stand a prayer trying to dig into this frozen shit," Sean said, "so on this flat stretch along the river, we took a dozer tank and dug out some nice big trenches for you. Then the engineers got a coupla deuce-loads full of wood and framed up some forms down in those trenches for the heavy weapons, like they was gonna pour cement. Then we filled the dirt back in around the forms...and you have yourself a dug-in firing position. As a bonus, your riflemen are using the leftover dirt and wood to make bunkers for themselves with overhead cover. No digging required, just some toting."

"Well, don't the sun rise outta your asshole, Bubba," Patchett replied.

"Only on certain days, Top, this being one of 'em. The only trouble is, we can't do this trick everywhere, like in the thickly wooded areas or on the steeper hills."

"I wouldn't worry about it much. That's where your tanks and the reserve battalion's gonna be, anyway."

Sean asked, "Speaking of reserves, did that new battalion show up yet? They got big shoes to fill. I got a bad feeling we're gonna miss them Aussies like crazy."

"Amen to that, Bubba."

*****

Just after 1500 hours, the new battalion commander reported to Jock's CP, a lieutenant colonel named Mike Beemon. He breezed in as if making a social call. His field uniform and boots looked immaculate, like he'd just stepped off the parade ground. He wore a big class ring on his finger, but it wasn't from West Point. After the usual round of introductions, Jock began to take Beemon's measure. "What's your combat experience, Mike?" he asked.

His long and rambling reply couldn't mask one simple fact: Lieutenant Colonel Beemon's combat experience amounted to zero. He'd spent his overseas time in the last war as a paper-pusher in Omar Bradley's European headquarters, living in hotels and mansions across England, France, Belgium, and Germany.

I figure this guy's biggest hardship was when his laundry didn't show up on time, Jock told himself.

"Have you ever commanded a rifle company, Mike?"

"Of course, sir."

"Where?"

"Fort Benning."

"In Georgia," Jock said. "Not exactly a war zone. When was that?"

The answer was just what Jock expected: prior to December 1941.

This man never heard a shot fired in anger in his entire career, let alone led men who were in harm's way. Somebody told him if he wants that star on his shoulder, he'd better get some combat command time, so here he is.

Lucky me.

Jock asked, "Where'd you go to school, Mike?"

"VMI, sir."

Virginia Military Institute, the alma mater of General George Marshall...I would've put money on that. No wonder he's had nothing but cushy staff jobs— he's a Marshall minion.

He noticed Beemon examining his own ringless finger.

Anticipating the question, Jock said, "I went to the Point. Lost the ring somewhere in the jungle during the Papua campaign."

"Ah, that's too bad, sir. Papua...that must've been tough duty."

"It was." The throbbing of pain in his leg seemed to intensify as he said it, as if the old wound didn't need to be reminded of that ordeal, either.

"So you've worked for MacArthur before, sir?"

Jock didn't think he could sound any less enthused as he replied, "Yeah, I've had the pleasure."

Then Beemon said, "I've been told the other battalions in this regiment are all commanded by majors. Is that the case, Colonel?"

"Yes, it is, Mike. So what?"

"Well, sir, it means I'm your senior commander." He said it like that entitled him to some sort of privilege.

"We've had light colonels commanding battalions in the past, Mike...and all of them either died or got relieved. I hate to break this to you, but your seniority doesn't mean shit around here. You may be my highest ranking commander, but you're also my least experienced commander. You and your men have a lot of learning to do, and school's going to start right now."

Jock explained how Beemon's 3rd Battalion was to be the regimental reserve, where their assembly area would be, and how the other units of the regiment were emplaced. He finished with, "My staff will fill you in on all the other details. Meet with them here at the CP in thirty minutes."

Beemon checked his watch, as if that schedule was somehow inconvenient. He said, "My men haven't had hot fresh chow since this morning, sir."

"Sorry to hear that, Mike, but the rest of this regiment hasn't had a hot fresh meal since Thanksgiving. And we're not likely to have one in the next few days, either. Right now, the priorities for our supply trains are ammo and fuel, not perishable food. My supply people will set you up with all the C rations your people need. Heat up the cans with the main courses any way that works."

*****

Baker Battery—the colored artillery unit—arrived at 26th Regiment's position just as that night's Chinese assault began with the usual blare of bugles. There was a fire mission waiting for them before the wheels of their trucks had stopped turning.

But after a few minutes went by, Baker still hadn't fired a shot. Jock's artillery battalion commander had no choice but to shift the mission to another, already engaged, battery, which quickly split itself into two 3-gun platoons to fire the different missions simultaneously. He prayed that the delayed and reduced fire support wouldn't be a case of *too little, too late* for those who needed it.

A 105-millimeter howitzer battery like Baker should've been able to pull off the road and start firing within two minutes, even in the darkness of night. Their first round might not have been accurate, but once the forward observer had it as a reference point, the next round would be.

When Baker finally got off its first round some ten minutes later, its impact was hundreds of yards from the mission's coordinates.

Seething, the artillery battalion commander drove to Baker Battery, but they weren't in the *goose egg* they'd been assigned. Guided through the darkness by the sound and flash of the guns, he found them almost half a mile away.

When he finally located Baker's battery commander, he told him, "You're off to a pretty shitty start, Captain. You'll be damn lucky if the infantry doesn't come back here and murder all of you when this fight is over. Now let's see if we can get this godawful mess of yours sorted out."

The captain said nothing, but the sullen look on his face meant he'd heard menacing words like those many times before and assumed their subtext remained the same:

You useless niggers can't do anything right. And you never will.

*****

To the men of 26th Regiment holding the Taedong River line that night, there seemed no end to the Chinese soldiers trying to race across that frozen river beneath the glare of illumination rounds. No matter how many the Americans killed, more took their place. Even with the temperature hovering around zero degrees Fahrenheit, their machine gun barrels were overheating and wearing out from the continuous firing. All along the line, it wasn't uncommon to see tracers lazily corkscrewing through the air, the sign of a ruined barrel. It would need immediate replacement if the gunner expected to hit what he was aiming at.

Sometimes, the several minutes it took a machine gun crew to change that barrel resulted in a unit being overrun.

The GIs even tried to shatter the thick river ice with artillery rounds, but it held together well enough for the CCF to keep coming. Worse, the surface impacts of the HE rounds were affecting surprising few of the onrushing enemy, since they passed mostly through the ice cap before detonating. Once they'd fired two dozen ineffective rounds, Jock ordered, "Call off the ice-breaking. We need those rounds to be airbursts so they'll actually knock down some chinks."

From Jock Miles on down, every man in the 26th expected the 17th Regiment on their right flank to collapse beneath the weight of the Chinese assault. As Patchett put it, "They're still fucked up from that bug-out of theirs up at Sunchon, and that change of command needs a little more time to straighten things out, if they're gonna get straightened out at all."

But to everyone's surprise, it was elements of 33rd Regiment on their left flank that collapsed under repeated pressure from the Chinese. By 2330 hours, swarms of CCF had broken through the 33rd and were moving to get behind the 26th.

"Coming from that direction, the chinks will be in the dark and blind, so keep them that way," Jock said as he and his staff pieced together fragmentary bits of intel on the breakthrough. "They'll have the best reference points if they follow the railroad tracks and cross the airfield. We've still got armor on the airfield, don't we?"

"Affirmative, sir," Patchett replied. "Bubba Moon's got a company in place over there."

"That's good," Jock replied. "Now it's time to commit Colonel Beemon's reserve. They'll work with the tanks to stop the breakthrough while everyone else holds the river. Do not—repeat, *do not*—shoot any illum rounds west of the airfield unless requested by Beemon's people or the tankers. Keep the chinks in the dark. They don't know exactly where they're going, and without radios, they don't improvise well. Let's not make it easier for them."

Chapter Six

On Pyongyang East Airfield, Sean briefed his tank commanders—his *TCs*—on Regiment's plan to block and defeat the CCF breakthrough. He told them, "It's a pretty good bet the chinks'll try to use the railroad embankment for cover, so we gotta be able to hit both sides of it as well as the tracks on top. Rocky, I want your platoon to handle that. Set up at that road junction near that village on the north side of the airfield. You see it on the map?"

"Yeah. Got it covered, Sean."

"Good. Now, Jimmy and Frank, put your vehicles in line across the airfield. Set up as far east as you can so you get the widest fields of fire and give yourselves room to move."

Both tankers acknowledged with a nod.

"Colonel Miles thinks it's better to keep it dark, and I gotta agree with him on that. Don't make it any easier for the chinks to see what's around 'em by shooting illum. It's open ground, so we should see their movement real easy with all this snow reflecting the moonlight. But if you absolutely need illum rounds, you got the green light to call for it."

"No flare ship tonight, Sean?"

"Afraid not, Rocky," Sean replied. "Them flyboys musta had a hot date or something. Now let's get back to the plan. Joe, your platoon comes with me. We'll go south and meet up with the reserve battalion. Colonel Miles just committed them, and we're gonna keep 'em straight. They're greener than hell, so they'll need a lot of *direction*."

Joe asked, "Do they have any idea how to work with tanks, Sean?"

"Probably not, but they'd better learn real fast."

*****

Finding Colonel Beemon's 3rd Battalion proved harder than Sean imagined. There was no trace of its CP at the village of Pin-ni, the location he'd been given. They weren't answering his radio calls, either.

That burns my ass, Sean fumed silently. *I clutter up my turret with this walkie-talkie just so I can talk direct to the infantry, but they ain't even listening. I wonder if they even know what the command net frequency is?*

On the west side of Pin-ni, the tanks came across four American three-quarter-ton trucks parked in an alley. Hesitantly, a GI left the alley and walked to Sean's tank.

"You with Third Battalion?" Sean asked.

"Yeah, Sarge. We're the ambulances for the battalion aid station."

"So where's the rest of the battalion?"

The GI pointed west. "They went that way."

"I'm Moon from Regiment. Who's in charge here, Corporal?"

"I guess I am, Sarge."

"You *guess*? You better decide real quick, pal. If it ain't you, get the real honcho out here on the double."

"Well, there's a Lieutenant Hammond with a rifle platoon on the back side of the village."

It didn't take much driving around Pin-ni to find the lieutenant. He looked relieved to be in the presence of the five tanks and greeted Sean enthusiastically.

"We're supposed to be your infantry support," Lieutenant Hammond explained, "but they must've given me the wrong frequency. Then my radio died."

"A platoon? That's all I get? It was supposed to be a fucking battalion."

Hammond just shrugged. Those decisions weren't his to make.

"You got four full squads, at least?" Sean asked.

"Affirmative, Sergeant Moon."

"That'll have to do. Let's get 'em moving."

Reluctantly, the GIs of Hammond's platoon left the small warming fires they'd been huddled around and sidled toward the tanks. Despite their brand new cold-weather gear, they shivered in the biting cold. Their hesitation was evident in every movement. Sean knew what he was looking at:

These greenhorns are one step away from cutting and running...a bug-out waiting to happen. They need a couple of size-twelve boots up their asses...

Or maybe they just need to haul some of their dead buddies away all wrapped up in ponchos. Nothing tightens up a slack unit like having to do that.

Sean asked, "Lieutenant Hammond, do you have any idea where the rest of your battalion is?"

"I'd be lying if I said I did."

"Do your men have any idea what they're supposed to be doing?"

"I was hoping you'd tell us, Sergeant."

Yeah, no shit. I kinda figured that.

Sean gathered the platoon around him and explained the mission: "We're going to stop a bunch of chinks from surrounding the regiment. My tanks'll do the hard work. All you ladies gotta do is keep 'em off our decks. Now don't be afraid to shoot at the tanks...those peashooters in your hands won't hurt us inside one little bit. But a sapper stuffing explosives down our vents is another story entirely. It's your job to make sure that don't happen. So stay right behind us, cover our asses, and cover your own while you're at it. Use the handsets on the back of the tanks to talk with us if you get in Dutch or see something we need to take out. Any questions?"

Lieutenant Hammond asked, "Aren't we supposed to ride on the tanks?"

"Absolutely fucking not, Lieutenant. When we're in the fight, you're in the worst place you could possibly be riding a tank's deck. If the bad guys don't pick you off or my muzzle blast don't blow you away, I'll probably knock you off and run you over when I spin the turret. The only exception we'll make is if we gotta extract wounded who can't walk. Am I making myself clear?"

*****

Sean led his platoon of tanks west, searching for Colonel Beemon and the rest of 3rd Battalion. They rumbled slowly through the darkness, intent on not outrunning Lieutenant Hammond's platoon trailing them.

But precious time was being wasted; his platoon's firepower would be far more effective if massed with the guns of the other tanks.

After they'd driven about half a mile, Sean brought the tanks to a halt. He told his loader, who was manning the tank's radio, "Try to raise Third Battalion one more time."

When that attempt still brought no response, Sean said, "Call Regiment. See if they got any idea what's going on with Third Battalion."

Regiment's reply: "Negative contact with *Omaha Green Six.*"

Sean knew he was getting off track trying to chase down 3rd Battalion. Properly employed, Beemon's unit—with a platoon of armor support—should've been able to crush the CCF breakthrough.

Even if it's as much as a CCF battalion that's come through our lines, we would still have a big advantage in firepower...and we've had a couple of days to get familiar with the terrain around here. The chinks are strangers to this turf.

But I can't play the lone cowboy out here much longer. I gotta do whatever Colonel Miles wants me to do.

On the radio, it was Jock Miles' voice that provided the answer: "Do not pursue *Green Six.* Repeat—do not pursue. Return to your blocking position at the airfield. Give me maximum firepower there."

With a wave of his arm, he called Lieutenant Hammond to his tank. "I'm gonna break one of my own rules here, Lieutenant. Get your guys up on the tanks. We're gonna cover some ground real fast."

*****

Racing down a road that led back to the airfield, Sean considered how best to use this mere platoon of infantry to provide security for a company of fifteen tanks. They'd be stretched thin. As far as he could tell, Hammond's platoon had little, if any, radio communication between the squads; he hadn't seen more than one walkie-talkie between them.

Maybe we should just put a squad with each tank platoon. Keep it simple and hope for the best, right?

*****

Sean's platoon of tanks was still several hundred yards from the airfield perimeter when the fight erupted. He could see tracers streaking through the darkness and then muzzle flashes from the Pershings' main guns. The radio channel—which had been dead silent—came alive with the agitated voices of tankers under fire.

A TC on the airfield—Rocky Micelli—was one of those voices. "The chinks are getting behind us, Sean," he said. "We're slicing them up on the railroad tracks pretty good, but they gotta be coming some other way, too. There's just too many of them around here. We need help. Where's our fucking infantry?"

"Anybody on your decks yet, Rocky?"

"Don't think so. But if we stay put and don't get help, it's just a matter of time."

Sean knew Lieutenant Hammond was on his deck with some GIs. But when he turned in the turret hatch to yell instructions to him, he was talking only to the night. The infantrymen were gone.

Son of a bitch, he told himself. *They probably bugged out the second they saw all the shooting up ahead.*

His tank on the airfield now, he could see the silhouettes of men running from the south, toward the Pershings and 26th Regiment beyond...

And they sure as hell ain't GIs. Like Rocky said, the

chinks gotta be coming from some other way...and there they are. But they're coming from the same direction I did. How come I didn't see 'em sooner?

Then it came to him: *That streambed! I didn't see 'em because they're duck-walking down that fucking streambed.*

While the other tanks of his platoon started cutting down the runners, Sean's Pershing doubled back to the streambed. Reaching it less than a minute later, the tank was immediately swarmed by Chinese.

"BACK UP," Sean told his driver. Then he ordered, "PUT UP A CANNISTER ROUND, RIGHT FUCKING NOW."

"WHAT AM I SHOOTING AT?" the gunner asked.

"PUT THAT SHIT RIGHT DOWN THE STREAMBED."

"I CAN'T SEE IT, SARGE."

"JUST TRAVERSE RIGHT. I'LL TELL YOU WHEN YOU'RE ON IT."

The loader yelled, "UP."

The canister round transformed the 90-millimeter tube into a giant shotgun. Its steel pellets swept away those Chinese still creeping down the streambed.

But it didn't do anything to those who'd already made it to Sean's tank. He could hear them on the deck and turret, trying—and failing—to pry the hatches open.

And then another wave of Chinese emerged from the streambed.

"MORE CANNISTER," Sean ordered. "KEEP THEM ROUNDS COMING."

The loader replied, "WE ONLY GOT FIVE, SARGE."

"TELL ME SOMETHING I DON'T KNOW, PAL.

JUST DO WHAT I SAY. THIS AIN'T NO FUCKING DEBATE."

Then he told his driver, "GIVE ME SOME QUICK SHIFTING BACK AND FORTH. THROW THE BASTARDS OFF, THEN RUN 'EM OVER."

It went on like that for what seemed a small eternity, the tank bucking to and fro, blasting its canister rounds into the night until there were no more. Chinese still swarmed her deck, but they hadn't breached her. Many died trying.

And then, with the cruel snarl of machinery in revolt, the tank lurched to a stop as the driver attempted one more violent change of direction. Although her engine was still running, the Pershing wouldn't move an inch. Her transmission had failed catastrophically; any attempt to engage that transmission only resulted in a sickening grinding of gears that could no longer mesh.

She'd become just another immobile bunker in the midst of battle, a stationary target awaiting the one blow that would destroy her and kill the men within. They could hear the laughing voices of Chinese soldiers on her deck and the clanking of pry bars being levered against the hatches.

When Sean tried to call for help, the radio was dead.

*****

The battle on the Taedong River kept raging, even at sunrise. The Chinese didn't melt away at dawn's first light as they usually did. This morning, they were still trying to force 26th Regiment's lines when American fighter-bombers swept in, the low-flying F-51s dropping their loads of napalm with impressive accuracy. Air power proved the tipping point; the CCF finally broke off the attack.

But where they went, nobody was sure.

Throughout the morning, the regiment regrouped. No unit had been overrun, but casualties were fifteen percent or better among 1st and 2nd Battalion.

Too damn many, Jock told himself.

Colonel Beemon's 3rd Battalion, which nobody had heard from since just before midnight, suddenly popped back on the radio at sunrise, as the fighter-bombers were beginning their work. An hour later, Beemon proudly marched into the regimental CP with three CCF prisoners in tow. He announced, "I'd say my men did one hell of a job cutting the chinks off, and here's the proof."

Jock led Beemon outside, behind the CP's motor park, where he could berate the man in private. "As fuckups go, Colonel Beemon, your performance last night pretty much takes the cake. Not only couldn't you navigate your way out of a paper bag, your radios went silent because you neglected to change frequencies at midnight, as the ops plan dictated."

Beemon seemed shocked he was being reprimanded. He started to say something, but Jock cut him off. "*At ease*, Colonel. I'm not interested in your excuses or your delusions of success. Getting back to the list of things you fucked up, you were supposed to work in conjunction with a company of armor to cap the CCF breakthrough, providing them with security while they provided you with firepower. Instead, you left those tankers high and dry…and while they did an unbelievable job holding off the chinks on their own, we lost four tanks out of fifteen, and this is to a force that's shown us little in the way of anti-tank weapons so far. You're damn lucky none of my tankers were killed."

"But we took prisoners, sir, and—"

"Save it, Colonel. Your prisoners are useless. They're North Korean peasants impressed into the CCF. They don't know shit about anything…and they were probably as lost as you were out there and more than glad to be captured. Their intel value is zero. And since your battalion never fired a shot, I strongly doubt you cut off any Chinese forces at all."

Jock waited a moment to see if Beemon was going to smart off again, but he didn't.

"Now, I'll cut you just a little bit of slack, Beemon, because you're brand new to the outfit, brand new to the country, and a combat virgin. But that slack is going to tighten really quickly. I'll expect a complete debrief of your botched operation, with accurate map overlays of where and how your companies were deployed, in one hour."

"Sir, that's hardly enough time to—"

"Nobody ever has enough time, Colonel Beemon. One hour. Not a minute more."

*****

When Colonel Beemon had first arrived at the CP, Patchett thought for sure Sean Moon was going to assault the man. When Sean dropped what he was doing and stormed in Beemon's direction, Patchett blocked his path.

"Take it slow, Bubba," he said. "He ain't worth no court-martial over."

"I'm gonna knock that useless son of a bitch on his

ass, Patch."

"No, you won't, Bubba. We ain't losing you that way. We came too close today as it is."

Sean's fight drained out of him as his anger turned inward. "I fucked up, Patch. Real bad."

"Are you outta your ever-loving mind? You did what you was supposed to do. More, in fact...and that ain't no damn lie."

"No, Patch, you don't understand. I shoulda never gone off on my own like that. I lost the vehicle, coulda got my whole crew killed. Couldn't even communicate...all my antennas got snapped off somehow. And that walkie-talkie I lugged around so I could talk to the infantry don't work worth a shit if you're in a buttoned-up tank. We just got lucky no sappers set us on fire."

"Maybe so, Bubba, but in the process, you musta stopped a regiment of chinks all on your own. Them canister rounds you fired...shit, did you see what that ground around your tank looked like? A goddamn butcher shop, that's what. Nothing but little chunks of raw meat all over the place, and every inch of ground painted red. Couldn't hardly find a whole body nowhere."

"Yeah, Top...and those are from the fucking canister rounds nobody upstairs thinks we need. I was lucky to find the ones we had."

"We got any more of 'em in stock?"

"A handful scattered around in a couple of vehicles, maybe."

"So why can't we get more, Bubba?"

"The brass seem to think it ain't a tank's job to get into short-range shotgun fights, so they don't give us no canister. You know the old story—the pencil-pushers think it's *uneconomical*. Burying GIs is cheaper, I guess."

*****

Mid-afternoon, a grim-faced Jock returned from the commanders' meeting at Division. The news he had to give his exhausted regiment was disheartening.

"General Walker is certain that significant numbers of Chinese penetrated Eighth Army's lines in a number of places during last night's attack," he began. "He considers our positions around Pyongyang—and all across North Korea—to be untenable. We're stretched too thin, our supply lines are too long, and the weather isn't likely to cut us a break anytime soon. The latest estimate is that the Chinese outnumber us two to one, and a significant number of them may already be behind us. To make matters worse, in the last two days, Eighth Army's lost twenty percent of its manpower due to cold-related injuries alone. This damn winter is causing us more casualties than the chinks."

He paused, knowing his next words would raise a collective groan: "So Eighth Army's pulling back to positions along the Thirty-Eighth Parallel immediately."

The sound that rose from his assembled cadre was more a howl of pain than a groan. They knew that *pulling back* wouldn't be just another motor march; if the Chinese really were behind them already, it would be running a gauntlet.

His S2—the intelligence officer—had a question steeped in skepticism: "Is MacArthur going along with General Walker's decision to withdraw back to the

Thirty-Eighth, sir?"

"I suspect he's not," Jock replied, "but it'll be interesting to see what Tenth Corps does in the next few days. If they start withdrawing as well, then we'll know that MacArthur is on board."

"And if he's not," the S2 said, "I suppose that means we can say goodbye to General Walker?"

"Let's not waste time in speculation, Major. Focus on keeping our men alive."

As his commanders and staff trudged off to share the bad news with the troops, Jock pulled Patchett aside. "Top, there's a planning meeting at Division headquarters at 1800 hours today. It'll be to lay out plans for the defense of the Parallel. I'm sending the S3, and I'd like you to go with him. Snoop around as only an ace recon man like you can. Try and dig up any useful information they haven't felt like divulging to us lesser mortals. The chopper will pick you up around 1630 hours."

Patchett replied, "It'll be my pleasure, sir. And I could sure use that *eggbeater* ride to catch me a little nap."

Chapter Seven

Tommy Moon couldn't remember ever being so cold in an airplane's cockpit. As he guided the Douglas B-26 *Invader* through the brilliant blue skies above the Japanese home island of Kyushu, he cursed the US Air Force for not including a cockpit heating system in the model's specifications.

Dammit, he thought, *my old P-47 didn't have a cockpit heater, either, but at least that big radial engine right in front of you sent a little warmth back your way, even in the coldest European winter. And the cockpit of that F-84 jet had heat! You could keep it nice and comfy in there. But in this ship, with her two engines sitting out on the wings and no heater, you'd better wear a couple pairs of long johns.*

And over Korea, it's below zero even down on the deck.

Why'd I let Pete talk me into this?

The *Pete* in question—Major Pete Newsome—was relaxing in the right seat as he mentored Tommy through his first flight in the new ship.

"For a guy with hardly any multi-engine time, you're handling her just fine," Newsome said. "But it shouldn't be that big a deal for you. I mean, it's the same Pratt engine we had in the *jug*…there are just two of them now. And an airplane's an airplane. You fly one, you fly them all. A couple more check rides like this and you'll be good to go."

"I figured with all this power, she'd be faster," Tommy said, his gloved finger tapping the airspeed indicator.

"C'mon, man...she's a ground attack ship, not a racer. And she's a natural fit for ground attack guys like you and me."

Tommy could find no argument with that statement. He and Pete Newsome had known each other since 1943. Back then, they were both young, novice P-47 pilots based in England, flying ground attack against the Germans in France and the Low Countries. A year later, after the Normandy Invasion, they'd performed that same mission from bases on the Continent. Though they flew in different sections of the 301st Fighter Squadron, no pilot in that squadron was a stranger to any other.

They hadn't crossed paths since the last war until they bumped into each other in the officers club bar at an airbase near Tokyo. Tommy had just been through the long and grueling debrief of his shoot-down, bailout, and solitary trek to safety through North Korea. Though he felt he'd acquitted himself well in front of the interservice brass, answering with clarity every question they'd thrown at him, he had little doubt he'd earned himself a new distinction, a dubious one he might wear around his neck for the rest of his Air Force career: *Looks like I'll always be the jet jockey who was the first to get knocked down by a MIG.*

It hadn't helped that when he'd checked back in with his F-84 squadron after the debriefing, his commander informed him the squadron's flights had been reorganized, there was no flight leader slot open for him, and it had far more pilots than aircraft at the moment. He could stay in the unit as a relief pilot—a very senior one, at that—but as far as *bumping* a less senior flight leader out of his slot, the commander left no doubt he wasn't interested in doing that.

Bad news travels fast, I guess. Looks like the boss already got the word from on high that I'm to be treated as a pariah.

Later that night, after he'd lost count of how many beers he'd drunk, Pete's offer to join the B-26 squadron sounded like salvation.

"We're real short on pilots, Tommy," Newsome told him. "Most of these ships were in mothballs when Korea kicked off, and hardly anybody in the Air Force is still qualified to fly them. We're getting some reserve units that actually fly the old girl over here in a couple of weeks, but it'll be a while before they're fully ready for combat operations. You should come over…you're a natural for the ground attack role, and you've already got a lot of hours over Korea. You'd fit right in."

"But I've only got three hours of multi-engine time in my book, Pete…and it's all in C-47s, for cryin' out loud. Not exactly a hot ship."

"That's okay. I had zero hours when I came over. You'll be up to speed in no time. I'll give you the check rides myself. How's that for a deal?"

Tommy stamped his boots on the cockpit floor, trying to get the circulation back in his feet. He'd need those feet to function properly for the next—and most crucial—part of this check ride. He asked, "I guess we should go out over the water for the engine-out stuff?"

"Yeah," Newsome replied, "and bring her up to *angels ten*, okay? Let's get a couple of mistakes high."

Once level at 10,000 feet, Newsome said, "Okay, before we get into it, I'm going to pull back the power on the *good* engine just a little bit."

"So it'll feel like she's got a full load on board?"

"Absolutely right, Tommy. That's what I like about you…you catch on fast. Just remember—she's got a real big rudder. You won't need to stomp on the pedal very hard to keep her straight once we kill an engine. Just a couple of units of trim will do it, actually."

"How easily will she spin if you overdo it with the rudder?"

"You'd have to push it to the stops. She's real forgiving, believe me. You can even turn into the dead engine as long as you keep her speed up."

"So Mister Douglas really knew what he was doing when he built this baby?"

"You got that right, Tommy."

Newsome adjusted the throttles for the exercise and then asked, "Ready?"

"Yeah, Pete. I was born ready."

"Okay, hotshot…you just lost number two."

The B-26 quickly slowed and yawed as Newsome shut down the engine. With sure, deft motions, Tommy feathered the windmilling propeller and cranked in rudder trim. But he never lost focus on his primary job: *fly the airplane*. The ship lost only a few hundred feet of altitude in a smooth, controlled descent. With his gentle power corrections, her airspeed settled into the optimum single engine speed of 150 miles per hour.

"That's real good, Tommy," Newsome said. "I'll say it again…you're a natural. Now let's try a few turns."

"Do you mind if I turn into the good engine first? I'm still trying to get used to the idea that it's okay to turn into the dead one."

"Sure. Give me a one-eighty to the left."

When that turn was done, Tommy steeled himself

and began a gentle right turn. Much to his surprise, the ship showed no tendency to spin even as he tightened the turn into that dead engine.

"I think I could learn to like this girl," Tommy said.

*****

Once all the engine-out maneuvering was done, Newsome said, "Excellent. Now go ahead and restart number two."

Easing the ship into a gradual descent, Tommy engaged the starter as he prepared to unfeather the prop and bring the shut-down engine back to life. Looking through the right side of the windshield, he watched two blades slowly pass as the big radial engine cranked...

And then the propeller stopped dead.

Newsome's calm shattered like a glass bottle being used for target practice. He straightened up in the seat and said, "Dammit, Tommy, hit the starter again."

"No joy, Pete. I think it's sheared. I'm getting some current draw but no rotation."

"Can't be! This ship is so low time it still smells of Cosmoline."

"Tell that to our busted starter."

"Here...let me do it," Newsome said, his finger pressing the starter button.

Nothing happened.

"Told you," Tommy said, still calmly flying the airplane. "But I didn't figure I'd get the bonus of an engine-out landing on a check ride. You ever done one?"

"Hell, no."

"You want to change seats?"

Newsome thought about it for a minute. Then he

replied, "Are you okay with doing it?"

"Sure. And if I make the landing, you'll sign me off right then and there as *good to go*, right?"

"Man, you're pretty eager to get back into the fight, aren't you?"

"You'd better believe it."

"Okay, then...not only will I sign you off, I'll buy the beer for a solid month."

"You've got yourself a deal, Pete. Dial up Itazuke. Tell them we've got a little emergency."

*****

Five miles from the runway's threshold, Tommy noticed that despite the cold in the cockpit, Newsome was sweating bullets. His face looked as white as a ghost.

"Are you going to make it, Pete?"

"Yeah, yeah...just land the damn airplane, okay?"

Tommy smiled, remembering the old airman's truism:

Takeoffs are optional. Landings are mandatory.

*****

The planning meeting at 24th Division Headquarters dragged on well into the night. Patchett used the time to do some of that *recon* Jock had requested. But the only interesting details he could uncover had nothing to do with the treacherous tactical situation the Americans and ROKs faced.

First, there was a sealed communiqué from the States addressed to Jock Miles and stamped *eyes only* in big red letters. From the routing information on the envelope, he figured out it had come from the Inspector General, 6th US Army.

Hmm...Sixth Army. California's in Sixth Army's region. That's where Miss Jillian's having that problem that's got Colonel Miles all riled up.

I wonder if the IG has something to do with all that? I reckon he wouldn't have no business with us otherwise. We sure as hell ain't part of Sixth Army.

He didn't have to wonder much about his second discovery: experienced combat officers were being pulled from the inactive reserve for duty in Korea. An old friend in the Adjutant's section had shown him a list of the activated officers assigned to 24th Division. Two names practically jumped off the page:

GROSSMAN, LEON A., MAJ, INFANTRY
PAPADAKIS, THEO M., CPT, INFANTRY

As I live and breathe, Patchett told himself, *two of the finest fighting officers who ever served with Jock Miles and me are putting on the Army green again.*

He told his friend, "Bucky, Twenty-Sixth Regiment got dibs on these two. Where are these fine gentlemen, anyway?"

"Probably on a plane headed for Kimpo, Patch."

"How about cutting them orders for the Twenty-Sixth right now? I'd like nothing better than to deliver that news personally to Colonel Miles. He could use some cheering up."

"No problem, Patch. Everybody's gotta be someplace, so they might as well be at the Twenty-Sixth. Nobody else around here is gonna give a rat's ass where they go."

"Damn right, Bucky. Now get those fat little fingers of yours banging on that typewriter."

*****

By 1000 hours the next morning, 26th Regiment had already covered twenty-five miles on the road bringing them south to the 38th Parallel. The helicopter carrying Patchett and the S3 intercepted the column near the city of Hwangju.

"Any problems with the chinks on the road?" Patchett asked Jock.

"Nothing serious. It's daylight, you know?" No sooner had he said that than a flight of F-51s streaked overhead. "The CCF knows that if they show themselves, they're going to get burned by those flyboys."

That wasn't just a figurative use of the word *burned.* Every prisoner they'd interrogated—both Chinese and North Korean—had said their armies were terrified of napalm. A few GIs who'd been captured were promptly released with instructions to relay this message: *Tell your airplanes to stop firebombing us, or else.*

Nobody could imagine what *or else* might entail, except, perhaps, attacks by even vaster human waves.

Or, perhaps, Russian divisions suddenly showing up on the battlefield.

As Patchett handed the *eyes only* envelope to Jock, he said, "Before you open that, there's something I just gotta tell you."

"Go ahead, Top."

"I pulled a few strings to get us Lee Grossman and Theo *Pop* as replacement officers."

At first, Jock thought he might have misunderstood. It didn't seem possible.

"Did I hear you right, Top? Grossman and

Papadakis are coming our way?"

"Affirmative, sir. Ain't that good news?"

"The best I've heard in a long while. When do they show up?"

"They're in Seoul now. They'll meet up with us once we're on the Parallel."

"Outstanding," Jock replied. Then he examined the envelope in his hand, hesitant to open it.

"You want some privacy, sir?"

"I'd appreciate it, Top."

The communiqué read more like a personal letter than a military message. Its sender was Major General Dick Molloy, Jock's regimental commander during the Southwest Pacific campaigns of the last war and a good friend. He was now 6th Army's Inspector General.

Jock,

I'm told you've been made aware of an effort by US immigration authorities to deport Jillian back to Australia. I found out about her situation while members of my IG staff were investigating a possible case of criminal activity by military personnel at Fort Ord. Since that action is intertwined with the criminal matter my people are investigating, I've persuaded some people in Washington to put the brakes on the deportation while that investigation is ongoing.

She's being charged with falsifying the intent of her entry into the United States. They claim she acted as the agent of a foreign corporation, which is not an authorized activity for someone residing in the US on a spousal immigration visa. The issue is far more complicated than that, however, and involves possible malfeasance by Army personnel and their associates.

Due to the legal nature of the investigation, I cannot reveal further details to you at this point.

I'm afraid the delay of deportation may only be temporary, but I'm doing all I can to get the deportation order rescinded, if possible.

I'll keep you posted on what develops.

Dick Molloy

Jock stuffed the piece of paper into his pocket. Then he walked over to Patchett, who was in a discussion with the artillery battalion commander, a lieutenant colonel named Hector Sanchez.

"Good news, sir?" Patchett asked.

Jock replied, "Let's just say it's not bad news, Top."

"That's encouraging, sir, because I'm afraid the colonel here's got some *bona fide* bad news."

Sanchez laid out his problem. "It's Baker Battery, sir…the colored battery. They're just not working out. They dragged their feet badly this morning, nearly missing their slot in this motor movement. I practically had to lead every officer and NCO in that outfit by their noses just to get them on the road."

Jock asked, "What do you propose to do about it, Colonel?"

Having to ask that question worried him; it sounded like the man had already given up trying to solve the problem. It was surprising, too: of all his officers, Hector Sanchez would, in all likelihood, be the man who could best understand and direct the motivations of those troopers immersed in racial and ethnic prejudices. As a Hispanic officer who'd grown up the son of migrant farm workers in the American West, he'd suffered—and overcome—the institutional xenophobia of American society in general and the Army in particular. Surely, Sanchez would, at least, have an idea how to improve the morale and motivation of the Negro troopers under his command.

And he did. But Patchett didn't like the idea. Not one bit.

"I thought we'd exchange battery commanders," Sanchez said. "Swap a white man for Captain Little and vice versa. But Sergeant Patchett tells me he's dead set against it."

Here's another surprise, Jock thought. *Melvin Patchett may be from Alabama, but when it comes to the GIs standing before him, he treats everybody the same regardless of race, with malice toward none. Off the top of my head, I'm not sure I'm crazy about Sanchez's idea, either, but I want to hear Patchett's reasoning before I say anything...and make this bad situation even worse.*

"Tell me why, Top," Jock said.

"Because we're gonna ruin two outfits in one shot, sir. Everybody's gonna feel like they're getting punished, the colored and white boys alike."

That's exactly what I was thinking, Jock told himself.

But Patchett wasn't finished. "And it's typical of *this man's army* to think that officers are gonna be the ones to solve all its damn problems. Now I got no qualms mixing the races—shit, I think the Army fucked up when it resegregated itself last summer—but expecting officers to make it happen is a big mistake. What's worse, it's a mistake we keep making over and over again, too."

"So what do you suggest we do, Top?"

"Exchange the first sergeants, sir. That'll get Baker

Battery back on its toes real quick because they'll want to show their new white top kick that they know their shit. And it ain't gonna hurt whatever white unit got itself a colored top kick one little bit, neither. Some good ol' boys will gripe, but the outfit'll still perform just fine. Let 'em get settled in a little while, then swap a section chief or two. Before you know it, you'll be able to mix white and colored personnel all you want...but let us sergeants take the lead on this. I guaran-damn-tee we'll make it work, because we *live* with the men. No offense, gentlemen, but you officers don't."

"None taken, Top," Jock replied. Looking to Sanchez, he said, "What do you say we give that a try, Colonel?"

The artilleryman knew it wasn't really a question.

Chapter Eight

On the east side of the Chosin Reservoir, there was no doubt the Army's 31st Regiment would collapse soon. It was just a question of *how* soon.

In five nights of intense Chinese attacks, scores of panicked GIs had fled across the frozen reservoir and stumbled into the Marines fighting for their own lives—and stubbornly holding their ground—around Hagaru-ri. By the GIs' frantic accounts, many more of their number on the east side had been killed or were missing, probably captured.

Yet General Almond, commander of X Corps, wasn't interested in talk of withdrawing. He didn't even want to consider the prospect of defending in place. He seemed hell-bent on continuing this fool's errand to reach the Yalu and seize all of North Korea...

Even though six CCF divisions now stood in his way, grinding his greatly outnumbered forces steadily to dust.

On this frigid morning, Almond's helicopter brought him to the command post of 31st Regiment. The pilot didn't dare shut her engine down; it might never start again in the brutal cold, and it wasn't very likely the general planned to stay long at *the tip of the spear.*

Lieutenant Colonel Don Faith was now commanding the regiment. He'd been thrust into the position just the day before, when the previous regimental commander was wounded and presumed captured by the Chinese. Faith had only one question for the general: "When do we begin our withdrawal, sir? If we wait much longer, there won't be any of us left."

Almond replied, "The Chinese you're facing are nothing but disorganized remnants of a shattered division. You're not telling me that a bunch of *laundrymen* are going to stop you from pushing north, are you, Colonel?"

There could be no answer to a question as ungrounded in reality as the one the general had just asked. Even if the Chinese forces were, in fact, remnants, Faith knew all too well that there were many thousands of them against his dwindling hundreds.

Reaching into the pocket of his parka, Almond produced a Silver Star and proceeded to pin it on the dumbstruck Colonel Faith.

Then the general began walking toward the aid station a short distance away. Seemingly oblivious to the scores of wounded—and the stacks of dead GIs wrapped in ground sheets piled behind the station's tent—he approached two exhausted soldiers who'd taken a moment to rest on some crates. Seeing the man with the stars on his winter cap striding in their direction, the soldiers dragged themselves to their feet. They couldn't quite manage to remain at rigid *attention*, though. After spending an entire day and night carrying the dead and wounded down from Hill 1221, their aching limbs simply wouldn't allow it. The best they could do was sway like frail saplings in the icy wind.

"You men are doing a fine job," Almond told the two as he pinned a Bronze Star on each of them. His voice brimmed with the bravado of one fortunate enough to be well-rested, well-fed, and not under fire.

The bizarreness of it all stunned one of the GIs to silence, just as it had Colonel Faith. The other soldier, however, coolly appraised the medal on his chest. Then he pointed to the stacks of dead men and told Almond, "With all due respect, General, those are the guys you should be pinning medals on."

Without saying another word, Almond marched like an automaton to his helicopter and flew away, back to a world where the delusions of his commander in Tokyo—delusions he'd parroted so proudly on that frozen helipad—didn't have to compete with harsh realities.

From his airborne perch, he couldn't see Faith and the two GIs hurl the medals he'd just bestowed on them into a snowdrift.

*****

Later that night, the question of *how soon* until 31st Regiment collapsed received its unequivocal answer. With over two-thirds of its manpower lost, including many of its officers and NCOs, the 31st was finished as an effective fighting force. They'd managed to hold off the enemy for five days—and protect the right flank of the Marines on the other side of the reservoir—but they could do no more. To prevent what was left of his shattered unit being engulfed and destroyed by the swarming Chinese, Colonel Faith led hundreds of survivors in a fighting withdrawal across the frozen reservoir to the Marines' base at Hagaru-ri.

Even in retreat, they suffered heavy casualties and lost all their vehicles and heavy weapons. By survivors' accounts, however, Colonel Faith's judgment, heroic actions, and strong leadership—even after being grievously wounded—saved their lives. For those qualities, he'd receive one more medal, but it wouldn't be pinned to his chest by a foolish sycophant wearing stars on his collar.

This medal—the Medal of Honor—would be awarded posthumously to his family by the President of the United States, for Don Faith never made it to Hagaru-ri. He died of his wounds that very night.

*****

The Marines on the west side of the reservoir were suffering mightily from Chinese assaults, as well. Most companies were down to half or one-third of their fighting strength.

Yet, with the help of Marine Corps and Navy air support during daylight hours and prodigious amounts of artillery fire around the clock, they were holding on to the terrain they'd claimed while inflicting catastrophic casualties on the attacking CCF divisions.

Gunnery Sergeant Jim Ramsay saw it this way: *It all boils down to the air support... not only the fighters shooting rockets and dropping napalm but all those transport planes bringing in supplies and ammunition: the C-47s that can land here at Hagaru, the Air Force's big C-119s that can't land on this short runway but drop their big loads on parachutes. Without those drops from the Air Force guys, the Marines up at Yudam-ni would've been overrun days ago.*

But let's not kid ourselves...if we try to hold on much longer here, we'll get decimated just like the GIs on the other side of the reservoir.

It's simple arithmetic. There are just too many chinks.

We'll never kill them all.

*****

General O.P. Smith, the Marine division commander, could do the math, too:

If we don't get out of here real soon, our only escape route—the MSR—will be overrun with Chinese. We'll be completely cut off.

His attempt to keep the MSR clear had been a dismal failure. A mixed convoy of Marine Corps, Army, and British Royal Marine companies—with sixteen US tanks—was hastily assembled from units around Koto-ri, a town ten miles to the south. Known as Task Force Drysdale after the group's British commander, Lieutenant Colonel Douglas Drysdale, they rolled north from Koto-ri toward Hagaru, intent on sweeping away the CCF roadblocks.

They were ambushed and mauled in the process. Only a few hundred of the 1,100-strong task force made it to Hagaru. The rest were dead, captured, or trapped in enclaves surrounded by Chinese. As Smith put it, *The ones who made it here are no more a fighting force than the GIs who fled the east side of the reservoir.*

We're going to have to fight our way out of here. It'll be twenty miles of murderous hell in those mountains before we hit the more favorable terrain of the coastal plain.

Smith stared at the message in his hand from X Corps Headquarters. When he first read it, he was surprised it wasn't another of Almond's exhortations to *push on to the Yalu.* Instead, it instructed his 1st Marine Division—with the survivors of those ravaged units from other services now under its wing—to conduct an orderly withdrawal to the port of Hungnam. The message went on to say that all available air support would be at Smith's disposal.

Yeah, all available air support…in daylight only. At night, we're screwed.

*****

In the briefing room at Itazuke Air Base, Kyushu, the operations officer began by saying, "You're not going to believe this, gentlemen, but the United States Marine Corps is actually asking for help from the Air Force."

He let the assembled B-26 pilots and crew smirk for a few moments. Then he said, "That might sound amusing to us, since those guys run their own show without bothering to tell us what they're doing most of the time. But the request actually comes from MacArthur himself. It seems the chinks are about to destroy First Marine Division, which is a real big chunk of his boy Almond's Tenth Corps, and that would make *the man in Tokyo* look worse than the Chinese have already managed to do."

There was another round of snickering as they imagined the *great man* himself wandering the halls of his headquarters in the Dai-ichi Building, down in the dumps and muttering to himself for being so dead wrong about the Chinese not daring to intervene in Korea. According to reliable sources, there had been actual sightings of him doing just that.

One of the pilots sounded disgusted as he asked, "We're not going to be flying missions with *gyrene* and *squid* pilots, are we? You know what a disaster that'd be."

He was right; the Air Force rarely worked with Marine and Navy squadrons for a very good reason: the various services shared very few standard operating procedures—*SOPs*—which were necessary for coordinated actions in combat. Without those SOPs, the pilots faced the potential for confusion, redundancy of missions, and the likelihood of accidentally killing each other in the air or friendly troops on the ground.

"We're all aware of that potential for disaster, Captain," the ops officer replied as he aimed his pointer at the big situation map on the wall. "So here's the deal: First Marine Division's got itself between a rock and a hard place at this place called the Chosin Reservoir. They're going to try to pull out of there and head to the coast for evacuation by ship. The trouble is, there's only one way out—one stinking road called the MSR—"

One of the pilots interrupted, asking, "What does MSR stand for? Marines Swiftly Retreating?"

Nobody laughed this time. The seriousness of it all was making its impression.

"As I was saying," the ops officer continued, "MSR stands for *main supply route*, and the first twenty miles or so of that road will be *ambush city*, with high ground towering over it on both sides. It's a gauntlet they just might not survive without a whole lot of help."

The pilots listened intently, but they were still wary. Their point of view: they'd all had to deal with time slots for attacks when coordinating with other USAF units, and those fragile schedules usually disintegrated promptly, leading to off-the-cuff improvisations that had a good chance of causing mid-air collisions and fuel exhaustion while diminishing the chances of an effective strike on target.

"Now here's the good news," the ops officer continued. "We won't actually be sharing airspace with those guys at all. They'll handle all day missions…"

The pilots groaned en masse. They knew what the rest of the sentence would be.

"And we'll employ those night tactics we've been developing so diligently, working with the *Firefly* ships."

That didn't stop the groaning. If anything, it got louder. There wasn't much enthusiasm for flying around mountains in the dark, with or without the illumination from the flare-dropping ships.

Then he announced that the squadron would fly its first *Firefly* mission that very night. Takeoff time was less than four hours away.

*****

The setting sun was dropping into the sea west of Itazuke as Tommy began the preflight inspection of his B-26. He was taking his time; it was still a new ship to him, with quirks yet to be learned. He'd amassed a grand total of five hours at the controls since joining the squadron just two days before. The last three hours he'd been solo, just boring holes in the sky over Japan to sharpen his feel for the powerful twin-engined machine.

The squadron commander hadn't balked when Pete Newsome signed him off after he'd executed the engine-out landing on his first—and only—check ride. As the C.O. put it, "If you can do that on your first time in the seat and not so much as blow a tire, I'd say you're good to go. Welcome to Fifty-Third Bomb Squadron, Major Moon."

Having multiple engines wasn't the only new thing Tommy needed to get used to; this ship had two other men in her crew, as well. Staff Sergeant Bob Allen was his gunner, a veteran of B-25 bombers in the last war. Lieutenant Hank Roth, a rookie on his first squadron assignment, was the navigator.

Tommy took one last look at the front of the ship before climbing the boarding ladder. She was a *hard-nosed* model: eight .50-caliber machine guns protruded from the nose in a tight group stacked four to a side. Smiling as he thought about the last eight-gun ship he flew—the P-47; the *jug*, they called her—he told himself, *Man, you won't have gun convergence issues with these babies like you had with those wing-mounted guns on the jug. With this ship, it's just point and shoot. I like this type a hell of a lot better than the glass-nosed "B" models, with the bombardier's position up front...and no nose guns.*

The ship's name—*Moon's Menace VI*—had been painted on each side of the nose earlier that day by his crew chief. Hopping on top of a servicing cart so his outstretched hand would just reach the characters, he touched a finger to the paint and was relieved to find it dry.

That's all we'd need...to come back from the mission with her name obliterated and paint streaked down the side of the fuselage. If I'd known we'd be flying tonight, I would've put the artwork off a day or two.

When Tommy slipped into his seat in the cockpit, Bob Allen was already tucked into the gunner's compartment in the rear of the fuselage. He wouldn't be able to get to the cockpit until the napalm canisters had been dropped from the bomb bay, clearing the passageway forward.

But he'd need a good reason to leave his position. "Better I stay on the guns, sir," he told Tommy. "Never can tell when some clever bastard's gonna try to jump us."

Seated to Tommy's right was Hank Roth, the navigator. He looked wonderfully organized, with his marked-up charts, *whiz wheels*, sextant, and frequency cards neatly arranged around his station—the picture of preparedness. But Tommy could tell the young man was nervous.

He's got every right to be. He doesn't have a whole lot of combat time, and this is his first night combat mission.

Hell...this is technically my first night combat mission, too.

"I've got to be honest with you, Hank...I find it a little strange flying with a navigator. Never had one before."

He decided not to mention all those times he wished he did have one.

"We've got an updated takeoff time, sir," Roth said. "Nineteen-oh-seven hours."

"Great, they're throwing changes at us already. What's the reason?"

"The *Firefly* ship is going to be a little late getting airborne out of Kimpo. They didn't say why."

"Let's just hope he lights up the right place," Tommy said. "We're still number four in the conga line?"

"Affirmative, sir."

Tommy had one more ritual to perform before beginning the pre-start checklist. Reaching into his flight bag, he pulled out a photo of Sylvie Bergerac and affixed it to a corner of the instrument panel.

"Your wife, sir?" Roth asked.

"Nope. Close as we can get to that, though, considering she isn't the marrying kind. I guess you could say I'm not the marrying kind, either."

Roth had no idea what that meant. But he didn't think it was his place to ask for an explanation.

"Known her ever since Forty-Four, back in France," Tommy added. "In fact, she's the one who thought up the name that adorns our ship."

"She sure is pretty, sir."

"Pretty isn't the half of it, Hank. Now start reading me that checklist."

Chapter Nine

The Marines gave up trying to measure the progress of their withdrawal down the MSR in terms of miles. In the two hours since the lead element rolled out of Hagaru, it had traveled roughly seven hundred yards— less than half a mile—through the gauntlet of Chinese in the hills to either side of that narrow road.

They'd come up with a name for that stretch of the MSR, too: *Hellfire Valley.*

Gunnery Sergeant Jim Ramsay and his tankers were spending more time acting as bulldozers than fire support, shoving the burning and disabled vehicles off the road. The valley was so narrow in most places that a disabled truck or tank blocked the path completely, bringing every vehicle behind it to a standstill...

And making everybody better targets, dammit. Once the column is stopped, Chinese come out of the hills and try to swarm all over the vehicles. Tanks, trucks...it don't matter to the chinks. A lot of them die trying...but plenty are getting through.

I'm seeing too many Marines die because their weapons won't work right in this godawful cold. The carbines, especially. They won't fire more than one shot on auto or semi-auto, like some damn bolt-action hunting rifle. You're not going to hold off a wave of chinks one shot at a time, that's for damn sure.

Without the Marine and Navy Corsairs dumping load after load of napalm onto those hills, we'd all probably be dead already.

But once the sun goes down and they go home,

we're on our own.

The other day, before we set out, some reporters were stupid enough to show up at Hagaru, wanting to know all about our coming retreat. General Smith had it right when he told them, "We are not retreating. We are merely advancing in another direction."

Those reporters laughed, like it was all just some bullshit fantasy.

But it ain't a retreat when you're surrounded. You've got to attack to break out.

And that's what we're trying to do.

*****

Moon's Menace VI was *tail-end Charlie* of *Switchblade Green Flight*, the last ship of four B-26s in trail stretched out over several miles. Behind them was *Switchblade Blue Flight*, another four-ship formation some five miles behind. The night mission would last nearly five hours. If all went well, they'd return to Itazuke around 2300 hours.

Although it was technically a formation—a loose *follow the leader*—each ship was on her own. The route was mostly over water, skirting the east coast of the Korean peninsula on a northerly heading until going *feet dry* near Hungnam, North Korea. From there, the Chosin Reservoir—and the rendezvous point with *Firefly*, the C-47 flare ship—was a twenty-minute flight inland.

Navigator Hank Roth nudged the dial of his *whiz wheel*—the circular slide rule that was the backbone of aerial navigation—and told Tommy, "Winds aloft are giving us a little drift, sir. Bring the nose two degrees left."

"Two degrees, huh? That's really getting it down to a gnat's ass."

"Well, sir, if you'd rather run out of gas on the way home and go swimming in the Sea of Japan..."

"No, that's fine," Tommy replied, squinting at the tiny, one-degree increment marks on the directional gyro's scale. "Anything you say, *Sinbad.* Two degrees, coming right up."

There wasn't much to see outside the cockpit windows. Cruising at 5,000 feet, they'd passed the lights of Pusan and a few other coastal cities on their way north. But mostly, there was the blackness of the ocean, the slow transit of the moon and stars, and the twinkling white taillight of *Switchblade Green Three* almost a mile in front of them.

A little over an hour into the flight, they crossed the 38th Parallel. Tommy asked, "How are we doing on fuel?"

"A little better than the flight plan, sir," Roth replied.

Then he called to Bob Allen in the gunner's compartment, asking, "Everything okay back there, Sarge?"

"Peachy keen, sir, except my electric socks quit working. I'm losing feeling in my feet from this damn cold. You mind if I stamp them a little to get some circulation going?"

"Sure, go ahead." He wondered why Allen had bothered to ask.

A moment later, he realized why: the stamping of feet could be felt in the rudder pedals, vibrations strong enough to get the pilot's attention. If he didn't know what was causing those vibrations, he'd think there was something breaking loose in the tail.

Okay...mark that off as another lesson learned about this ship.

Almost thirty minutes later, lights began to appear dead ahead over the ship's nose. "That must be Hungnam," Tommy said.

"It is *absolutely* Hungnam, sir," Roth replied. "In three minutes, on my mark, begin the climb to seven thousand feet."

Tommy was beginning to realize how much he liked working with a navigator, and Roth in particular:

This kid's precise as a fine machine. I'm glad to have him, even if he is a little green.

The climb to 7,000 feet—the minimum safe altitude, or *MSA*—would ensure they were higher than any of the invisible mountain peaks lurking in the darkness. Doing it now, after the fuel burned so far had made the ship lighter, used less gas in the climb than if they'd done it earlier in the flight.

They were just short of landfall when Roth completed a star shot with the sextant. After a few moments of calculation, he plotted the computed position on the flight map. Then he said, "You'll be happy to know, sir, that we were exactly where we were supposed to be a couple of minutes ago."

"Outstanding. Let Bob know we're officially in *bad guy* territory now. Not likely we'll run into any of those *night MIGs* this far east, but if the North Koreans have any *Yaks* or *Lavs* left..."

Tommy looked into the darkness all around, marveling that once past the lights of Hungnam and those of Hamhung a few miles inland, he could make out absolutely nothing of the Earth below. *It's strange, considering that on a clear day at this altitude, you can*

*see all the way across Korea to the other coast. It's only
a little over a hundred miles away...*

*And in between are all those mountains sticking up
into the sky, invisible now in the darkness. If it was
daytime and the peaks were hidden in clouds, we'd call
them Hardcore Cumulus.*

At night, we call them Black Death.

Tommy asked, "Any word from *Firefly* yet?"

"Negative," Roth replied. "That's a little
concerning."

Yeah, Tommy thought. *This mission is a real closely
timed thing. If we've got to hold for the flare ship more
than a couple of minutes, we won't have the gas to make
it back to Itazuke. That'll mean a diversion to Pusan or
Taegu. Or if we're really low on gas, Kimpo.*

*And if Firefly doesn't show, this has all been for
nothing.*

They were ten minutes from the Chosin Reservoir
when Tommy said, "I don't see the guy in front of us
anymore. Where the hell did he go?"

Looking up from his charts, Roth said, "Check to
the right, about two o'clock."

Tommy took a look in that direction. "I still don't
see him. What makes you think he's over there?"

"I've got a hunch the other three ships from *Green
Flight* all went that way," Roth replied. He was now
scanning that quadrant with binoculars.

"There they are, sir," he said, pointing through the
right side of the windshield. "You can't see the taillights
anymore, but I can make out their red nav lights."

"Okay...so we're looking at their left wingtips.
Which one of us is in the wrong place?"

"I believe they are, sir. I'll bet the navigator in the

lead ship is still using two Japanese radio beacons to establish position. That was great for when we were over water, but once you get back over land, those beams crossing the water will bend, and your position will be off a little bit. *Green Two* and *Three* must be playing *follow the leader*."

"And we're not using those same stations, Hank?"

"Negative, sir. Once we made landfall, I switched one of my vector plots over to the Kimpo beacon. Since that signal doesn't cross water, it doesn't bend."

"So we're on course...and they're not?"

"Affirmative," Roth replied. "And every second they fly that heading, they're getting even farther off course and wasting more precious gas. You want to tell them?"

"Nah. You know the rule...no chatter unless it's an emergency so the gooks' direction finders can't track us."

"Roger, sir."

By the time *Moon's Menace VI* was at the Chosin Reservoir waypoint, the lights of *Green Flight* had vanished into the blackness. "We'll orbit here," Tommy said, "and wait for *Firefly*. How long can we hold?"

Roth tweaked the *whiz wheel* and said, "Ten minutes, and I'm rounding down a little."

*****

Two minutes later, *Firefly* was on frequency.

"Look south," Roth said. "The lights should be on in about ten seconds."

They couldn't see the flare ship; it was several thousand feet higher and a few miles distant, flying away from their orbiting B-26.

And then, as if someone was walking down a long, dark corridor, switching on light after light every few seconds along the way, the valley nestling the MSR was illuminated as if bathed in incredibly bright moonlight. The harsh radiance of the flares lit everything in a monochromatic silver, from the mountain peaks, to the treed slopes, to the long column of vehicles that didn't seem to be moving. Some of those vehicles were burning, their billowing smoke climbing the valley walls like glittering vines.

They were too high to see human forms.

An *ASO*—air support officer—on the ground began to identify the most urgent target. From his call sign, *Tripoli Three-Five*, Tommy was fairly sure he was a Marine.

"Southernmost burning vehicle is at head of column," *Tripoli* said. "Enemy troops with heavy weapons are just south of that vehicle. Put your stuff as close as you can beyond it."

Switchblade Green Leader replied, "Unable to identify target at this time. Too far out. Expect on station in four minutes."

"They've got to be at least twelve miles away," Roth said. "He sees the glow from the flares but that's about it."

"A lot of guys down there can die in four minutes, Hank," Tommy said. "So we're going to cut the line, since we're the only game in town right now. There are no other ships close enough to worry about mid-airs, so here we go."

He flipped the switch that opened the bomb bay doors and pushed her into a steep descent. In just over a minute, they were deep in the valley, below the peaks of the hills rising on either side of them. Hank Roth's entire body tensed; he could see the skeletal outlines of trees on those slopes that were higher than *Moon's Menace VI*.

The altimeter read 1,000 feet and was still spinning down.

Roth couldn't help it; he was so unnerved he blurted, "Oh my God!"

"Something wrong, Hank?"

"We're so low…"

"Yeah, because we only get one shot at this. I want that flaming *goo* on target."

"But we're way below MSA…"

"Hank, I can see the ground, for cryin' out loud. Not likely I'm going to fly into it. Okay, on my count: *three, two, one, DROP.*"

The ship lurched upward, having shed the weight of the napalm canisters. Tommy pushed the throttles forward and put her into a steep climb, seeking that minimum safe altitude Roth was so nervous about. It would take a climb of almost five minutes to reach it.

He asked Roth, "How much time before we've got to head for home?"

The navigator already had the answer. He'd been working that calculation ever since entering the target area.

"Two minutes, sir."

Tommy began some mental calculations of his own. *That flare drop's going to burn out before the rest of the squadron gets to make their pass. It's going to take Firefly a good couple of minutes to get into position for a second round of flares.*

How much you want to bet that Switchblade Leader

*is going to abort before the new flare drop, claiming low
fuel? He'll bring the rest of the squadron back to Itazuke,
dumping their junk into the Sea of Japan instead of
helping out those Marines.*

*That's a crying shame. But it's SOP for bomber
jockeys. If they can't see the target, they abort and go
home. Add in a critical fuel situation, and I'm betting
there's no way they stay around.*

As they passed through 5,000 feet, Tommy told his
crew, "We're going back to the target area, just in case
the rest of the squadron doesn't make it. We've got
enough fifty cal on board for several gun runs. Hank,
start working up time limits for diverting to Kimpo,
Taegu, and Pusan. Bob, put your lower turret guns
straight down. You're going to get to play, too."

Roth had the answers in a matter of seconds. Then
he asked, "Why are we doing this, sir?"

"Because those poor bastards down on the ground
have no one else, that's why."

He didn't expect his young navigator to understand;
he'd never been under fire with the ground troops...

But I have.

As Tommy suspected, *Switchblade Leader* was on
the frequency now, announcing the squadron would
abort the mission and return to Itazuke. Tommy radioed
he was staying and would divert to a South Korean field
as fuel allowed.

"That'd be your call, *Green Four*," came the reply.
"You're on your own. Best of luck."

The second flare drop began, once again bathing the
valley in brilliant light.

Tripoli asked, "*Green Four*, was that you who
unloaded the napalm?"

"Affirmative."

"Excellent work. Dead on the money."

"Glad to hear it, *Tripoli*. I can give you a strafing run before the flares die again. Just tell me where you want it."

Where he wanted it was on the slopes of the hills just west of the MSR. They were thick with Chinese.

"We're going in even lower this time, Hank. Hold on to your hat and keep your eyes peeled. If you see any kind of movement at all on these hills, call it out, because that'll be chinks."

Then he advised Allen, "Bob, when I open up with the nose guns, you open up with the lower turret, too."

"Roger, boss."

Then they seemed to be brushing the treetops, streaking along the hillside at over 200 miles per hour.

"I SEE MOVEMENT," Roth shrieked. "COUPLE OF DEGREES RIGHT."

Tommy nudged her nose right and fired a long burst from the nose guns. Bob Allen opened up with the lower turret. Tracers bounced crazily off the ground well ahead of the ship.

The stench of spent gunpowder in the cockpit was almost overpowering.

It was all over in a split second. Tommy nosed her up sharply again, clawing for altitude.

Trying to catch his breath, Roth asked, "Did you see them?"

"Nope. Good thing you were here."

"Do you think we hit them?" Roth asked.

"I hope so."

"Do you think anybody's shooting at us?"

"Probably," Tommy replied.

Bob Allen's voice crackled over the interphone. "Make that *definitely*, sir. I saw some tracers whipping along behind us. I don't think the chinks have had much practice shooting at airplanes, though. They ain't figured out how to lead a target yet."

Firefly was on the radio now. They were game for one more pass, but they only had a few flares left. *Tripoli* said, "Lay them out from the head of my column to as far south down the road as possible. Can you locate the head of the column?"

"Roger," *Firefly* replied. "Can't miss that napalm barbecue going on."

With fewer flares falling, the illumination wasn't as bright this time. In their scant light, Tommy couldn't get a good view of the surrounding hills.

"For all we know," he told his crew, "there could be one right in front of us that we won't ever see. We'll have to make this pass a little higher."

But there was enough light on the MSR itself to see groups of people scuttling about. After quick confirmation from the ASO that no *friendlies* were forward of the napalm blaze, *Moon's Menace VI* riddled those groups with her .50-caliber machine guns.

As she began her final gas-guzzling climb to the MSA, there was a moment of sheer terror as Tommy saw the silhouette of a peak looming suddenly out the right side of the windshield.

"SHIT," he yelled, banking the ship violently left, waiting for the impact that would snuff out their lives.

But nothing happened. *Moon's Menace VI* kept right on flying.

Roth was looking at him strangely. Tommy asked the navigator, "Did you see that?"

"See what, sir?"

"That peak. We were headed right for it."

"No, sir. Didn't see a damn thing."

He asked Allen if he could see a peak off the tail, much too close for comfort.

"Nope," was the gunner's response. "Looks like empty sky to me."

I could've sworn, Tommy told himself. *Am I seeing ghosts?*

If that was really a mountain, I would've hit it for sure.

They were leveled off now, headed south. Tommy asked Roth, "Call it, Hank. What's the closest we can get to home without swimming?"

"Taegu, sir."

"Okay, pit stop at K-2, it is."

"You've been there before, sir?"

"Yep. Plenty of times. A charming little place."

During the hour of cruise flight it would take to reach Taegu, Tommy kept thinking about the phantom mountain peak. He remembered all the guys he'd known who'd had close encounters with terrain and thought they'd gotten away scot-free. Some of them ended up bringing home a tree branch or a piece of roof jammed somewhere in the lower surfaces of the ship.

I wonder…would I rather that peak was just a hallucination? Or find that tree branch stuck in her after we land?

As they prepared for landing at K-2—with mountain peaks nowhere near—Tommy saw his apparition in the windshield once again. But this time, he realized it wasn't his imagination at all. It was a reflection of the dim cockpit lighting off Roth's shiny metal clipboard.

"Do that again, Hank."

"Do *what*, sir?"

"Move the clipboard up to your lap."

He did as asked. For a brief moment, its silvery reflection shimmered on the windshield once more. The sharp corner of the clipboard made it look just like a mountain peak.

*****

Gunny Jim Ramsay couldn't tell what type of aircraft had come to their aid in Hellfire Valley. Or who was flying it. But he knew one thing: *That guy had balls, God bless him.*

Or maybe it should be God bless them. Who could tell how many planes and pilots were flying around in the dark?

But the unexpected help from the night sky had been fleeting. It did break one roadblock and allowed the battered column to start creeping toward Koto-ri again. For the next few miles, the Chinese threat was reduced to little more than sniping, usually silenced by a healthy dose of tank fire.

The casualties, however, kept mounting.

An hour before sunrise, they hit the next roadblock.

The chinks ain't dumb, Ramsay thought. *They gotta get their licks in before the day fighters show up again.*

That night strike was the cat's ass...but where the hell are they now?

It was a great little show, but it ended way too soon.

And nobody seems to know if we're ever going to see another act, either.

Chapter Ten

Twenty-Sixth Regiment's assigned sector along the 38th Parallel seemed like a gift; its terrain greatly favored the defense. An east-west ridge several miles long paralleled and dominated the valley of the iced-over Imjin River. Through that valley ran several major roads that led to Seoul, just thirty-five miles to the south. Units emplaced on that ridge could easily command those roads, the river, and the frozen marshland that defined the valley.

As an added bonus, Kamak-San, a mountain 3,000 feet high, stood behind the ridge, providing a vantage point to detect any Chinese advance from the north. Even if its peak was shrouded in clouds, an OP only halfway up its front face would provide excellent fields of vision to a distance of almost fifty miles.

"Too bad you can't spot chinks walking at fifty miles," Patchett told the team of observers about to scale Kamak-San. "But as long as the sun shines, you'll be able to give us plenty of warning of anybody headed our way."

The only drawback to the regiment's area of responsibility was its width; Jock's GIs would be forced to defend almost five miles of the ridgeline. There'd be no regimental reserve; all the rifle battalions would be on line and spread very thin. As a result, communications across the 26th would be difficult and easily disrupted. If those communications broke down, so would command and control.

It was late in the afternoon as the individual

battalions moved into their assigned sectors of the ridge. Briefing his battalion commanders, Jock said, "Keep laying your commo wire even after it gets dark, duplicate lines wherever possible. I won't tolerate any excuses for not doing so. We've got plenty of wire, for once, and our ability to stay in touch with each other is going to depend on it. We know damn well that most of our radios won't cover the distance from one end of the regiment's position to the other...if they keep working at all."

As the briefing adjourned, Lieutenant Colonel Beemon, commanding 3rd Battalion, asked for a moment of Jock's time. "Any chance of reconsidering your edict on sleeping bags, sir?" Beemon asked.

"Negative," Jock replied. "We're sticking with one bag for every two men. That's the only way to ensure that the people who are supposed to be on duty will be awake and not snoring in the warmth of their bag."

"But what about the officers' bags, sir? Why should we get punished, too?"

"Nobody's being punished, Beemon. Unless you consider trying to keep your troops alive is a form of punishment, that is."

The sleeping bag *edict* had been Patchett's idea, after he found two entire platoons burrowed into their warm cocoons one frigid night, including the men who were supposed to be manning the perimeter.

"If I'd been a chink, I woulda just bayoneted every last one of you stupid sons of bitches," Patchett told them. "Now get your heads out of your asses...and your asses out of them fart sacks."

Then he personally *reamed the asses* of the two platoon sergeants—both of whom he'd had to wake up while cozy in their sleeping bags—and assured them their stripes would be gone the next time their platoon was caught with their guard down, adding, "Assuming, of course, *Joe Chink* ain't already murdered y'all in your sleep."

The formal *reaming* of the officers involved would have to be performed by their battalion commander. But that didn't stop Patchett from needling those lieutenants: "You do realize, gentlemen, that out here, the expression *sleep like the dead* takes on a whole new meaning, right?"

*****

Apathy among the GIs was fast becoming as great a threat to their survival as the Chinese. The extreme cold, exhaustion, and hunger were taking their toll. Even a man eating the official combat minimum of daily calories burned far more than that number just trying to stay warm. Once that indifference to his and his fellow soldiers' well-being took hold of a man, the decline in his physical and mental condition came with alarming speed. When it took hold of a squad or platoon, it could spell death to an entire company.

Surprisingly, the worst cases of apathy could be found in Beemon's 3rd Battalion, a unit that had been in Korea less than a month and in combat with the 26th for only a week. The men weren't caring for themselves and no officers or NCOs were forcing them to do so; frostbite and dysentery had already taken fifteen percent of the battalion's manpower out of action in a period where they'd incurred only two combat casualties, neither of them serious.

When Jock had been mapping out the regiment's position, Patchett asked, "Where do you want to put our weak link, sir?"

"We'll put Third Battalion on the right flank," Jock replied. "The strongest threat will be from the left, where the Imjin bends south at our boundary with Seventeenth Regiment. Over on the right, it should be easier. Beemon's boys will have a sweet position up on the ridge. My grandmother could defend that turf."

Patchett was still skeptical. "And you ain't worried about the boundary they'll share with the ROKs on that side?"

"Negative. I'm not worried. Having ROKs from their Second Division over there is probably a good thing."

It was true the Korean 2nd Division had fought well during the latest Chinese onslaught. The GI tankers and artillery who'd supported them had been impressed with the ROKs' aggressiveness and tenacity. And since the ROKs weren't shy about executing prisoners, the Chinese POWs Jock's men had taken recently were more than glad to be in American hands.

"As you wish, sir," Patchett said.

Jock knew from long experience that those words meant his trusted advisor was not convinced.

"Oh, and by the way, sir," Patchett added, "some good news just came in. Major Grossman and Captain *Pop* will be here first thing in the morning."

"I'm sure looking forward to that, Top."

*****

Perhaps Lieutenant Colonel Beemon didn't

appreciate the degree to which apathy was festering in his command. Or perhaps it infected him, too.

In either case, he hadn't bothered to check that his plan for occupying the ridgeline was being properly executed when the sun was still up. Now that darkness had fallen, it would be difficult, if not impossible, to determine compliance with that plan and make the necessary corrections.

Instead, he elected to believe the reports of his junior officers who, like him, had not bothered to check. They had little idea where their men were emplaced.

The result: only a handful of GIs from the three-hundred-strong 3rd Battalion were on the ridgeline. Most of them hadn't—and wouldn't—bother to dig in or establish wire communications with company or battalion CPs. Few had working radios.

The rest were encamped along the road at the base of the ridge, more a bivouac than a tactical disposition. To the annoyance of the tankers, groups of 3rd Battalion GIs kept trying to ride the decks of the armor patrolling the road, seeking the warmth of their engines.

Just past midnight, when the squad-sized CCF patrol slipped along the boundary between the ROKs and 3rd Battalion and scaled the ridge, no one knew they were there.

*****

The Chinese division commander shared Jock's tactical assessment: the most likely route of CCF advance would be where the Imjin River changed direction from west to south. There, the terrain was mostly hilly, with little of the flat, open swampland that lay in front of 26th Regiment's position.

That terrain is far more suitable to our style of warfare—infiltrate unseen through your adversary's lines, then block their escape to the rear while cutting them to shreds.

He was stunned when the patrol that had ventured into the right side of 26th Regiment's area returned to report no American or ROK presence on the ridgeline just north of Kamak-San, the mountain providing a crucial vantage point for anyone who occupied it.

Oddly, reconnaissance hadn't even been that patrol's mission. What would be the point? Without radio communications, any information it might uncover would be worthless by the time they could relay it.

But instead of accomplishing their assigned mission—the capture of an American officer or two— they'd found intelligence that, if it could be acted on quickly enough, might give us a breakthrough we never imagined possible.

Perhaps I'm not facing the same tough American commander I've been up against these past few weeks. This one seems woefully stupid.

By 0300 hours, the Chinese commander still hadn't organized more than a battalion to infiltrate through the undefended ridgeline and get behind the American forces. But if he waited any longer, the opportunity would disappear with the dawn.

He decided to launch the infiltration force immediately.

*****

When the CCF battalion scaled the icy ridge in the

predawn darkness, they couldn't help making a tremendous amount of noise. Men slipped and fell, equipment clattered. The ROKs to the east heard it but thought the source to be just clumsy Americans on the ridge. The GIs to the west—men of 1st Battalion—heard it, too, and thought the same thing...

Until two lost Chinese soldiers, separated from their unit, stumbled into a GI wire team. In the shadows, the big wire-laying reel mounted on the truck bed looked just like a heavy machine gun to them. They immediately threw down their weapons and surrendered.

The quick-thinking wire team sergeant spliced into the line they were laying from 1st Battalion and told that headquarters, "We've got chinks everywhere."

The word spread in seconds through the battalion's wire network. "Light them up," Major Appling, 1st Battalion commander, told his mortar section.

Exposed in the glare of 81-millimeter illumination rounds, the Chinese infiltrators were cut down in a hail of fire from GIs on one side and ROKs on the other.

When the sun came up, they found the bodies of over one hundred CCF soldiers littering the ridge. None of the Chinese had succeeded in getting behind the American positions on the ridgeline.

It didn't take long to figure out how the infiltration attempt had been possible. Colonel Beemon's battalion, still camped on the road beneath the ridge, had failed to follow orders, leaving a huge gap in the regiment's line. That failure had nearly resulted in an encirclement of the regiment.

"You're relieved, Beemon," Jock told him. "Report to Division Headquarters for reassignment."

"You're not giving me a chance to explain, sir. My

command was—"

Jock cut him off. "It's not *your command* anymore, Colonel."

Scanning the 3rd Battalion troops moping along the road, he added, "I've got all the explanation I need."

As Beemon walked off, Patchett asked, "Who you gonna replace him with, sir? Not his XO, I hope. The man's looking pretty weak, too."

"Actually, Top, I was thinking of Lee Grossman."

"I was hoping you might say that, sir."

*****

Switchblade Green Flight was in the air again to support the Marines on the MSR. But this time they were operating in daylight, flying flak suppression for a very special mission. *Moon's Menace VI* was lead ship in *Green Flight* as it hurried north in a tight, four-ship formation. Tommy and his crew had earned the honor of leading this mission after their stellar performance in the otherwise unproductive *Firefly* fiasco of a few nights ago.

All the credit goes to Hank Roth for that one, Tommy told himself as they cruised toward Koto-ri, *but you don't get any medals when the mission was officially considered a failure. The squadron wasted a lot of gas for next to nothing that night. Our Japanese bases are just too far from just about anything north of the 38th Parallel. We had hardly any time at all on station to coordinate with the Firefly ship before we went fuel critical. Throw in all that gas wasting with the navigation mistake the rest of the flight made, and the whole thing went straight into the crapper.*

Actually, I'm kind of surprised I didn't get in Dutch for going it alone and then diverting to Taegu. But since we brought the ship home in one piece—even though our return to Itazuke was about ten hours behind schedule by the time we refueled and caught a quick nap—nobody made much of a stink that the squadron's combat effectiveness was down by one ship during that time. These days, having the unit readiness look good on paper is more important than fighting the war, dammit.

The brass say we won't be doing any more coordinated night missions like that one until we move to South Korean bases, but that's still a month or two away, supposedly. They just don't have the equipment and people in place to support us there yet.

Until then, we'll do what we can flying out of Japan. But it's going to be in daylight only...

Which brings us to today's mission.

*****

The Marines on the MSR were as good as trapped, their withdrawal from the Chosin Reservoir stalled. At Funchilin Pass south of Koto-ri, an essential bridge across a river gorge had been sabotaged for the third time in a week by the Chinese. The first two times, the damage had been minor; Army and Marine Corps engineers had managed to repair it under fire so it would be available to the troops withdrawing from Hagaru. But the third time, the Chinese succeeded in blowing a bigger gap in the concrete span. It would require prefabricated repair sections to span this new gap, but the engineers didn't have any of the cumbersome components on hand.

Nobody had to tell Gunny Ramsay what that meant: *If we don't have that bridge, we'll need to abandon all our vehicles: no tanks, trucks, artillery, or heavy weapons. We can keep trying to walk out, but without our fire support, we're not a fighting force anymore. We'll just be target practice for the chinks in the surrounding mountains who haven't frozen to death yet.*

But there's a rumor the Air Force has a plan to bail us out. Let's hope it's a damn good one.

*****

Switchblade Green Flight had just gone *feet dry* over the North Korean port of Hungnam. Visible through the scattered clouds below were four cargo planes—C-119 *Flying Boxcars*—headed in the same direction, at a speed fifty miles per hour slower than the B-26s. Each of the big transports carried two Treadway bridge sections which they'd drop via parachutes into the valley at Koto-ri. The engineers on the ground knew they needed two sections to repair the bridge at Funchilin Pass; eight would be delivered to improve the chances of two being recoverable and serviceable after the drop.

What the engineers didn't know: there'd been one practice parachute drop of the Treadways. It had been a dismal failure; the sections were destroyed on impact with the ground. But there was no time left to experiment further. With each bridge section now rigged with larger parachutes in pairs, the C-119s were dispatched to Koto-ri with nothing but the hope that this untested improvisation would work.

Tommy said to Roth, "Give me the numbers, Hank.

How much time will we have on station?"

"Twelve minutes, sir. The winds are helping us out a little today."

They were able to raise the ASO at Koto-ri when they were still five minutes out.

"Sounds like the same guy as the other night," Roth said. Then he went to work plotting a vector to the target coordinates the ASO had called.

"Okay, sir, bring it right to heading zero-one-four. Target is anti-aircraft guns on a mountaintop. Open bomb bay doors now."

Tommy ordered the rest of *Green Flight* to form in trail behind him. They'd drop their napalm when they saw *Moon's Menace VI* drop hers.

"I'm hoping these clouds don't thicken up," Roth said. "As it stands now, we should be able to see the target pretty well. I'm still wondering how they got heavy flak guns up on top of a mountain, though."

"Chinks are clever bastards who aren't afraid of hard work, Hank."

A Corsair appeared out of nowhere and raced diagonally across their flight path, just a few hundred feet below.

"Whoa! I'm a little surprised to see that guy," Tommy said, "and a little worried, too. I hope those Marine and Navy pilots know we're up here...and that the *Boxcars* are going to be right behind us. If these clouds start socking in, though, people could start bumping into each other real easy."

Roth nodded and said, "I'm surprised the brass didn't just let Marine air handle the flak suppression for this drop."

"Just like the Marines, Hank, the Air Force prefers

to take care of their own, especially when the game's on the line. We could do a better job of it if we were able to stick around a little longer, though."

They both knew the rest of that story: they *could* stay longer if they diverted to a South Korean airfield for fuel on their way home to Japan. But the brass had made it crystal clear after the failed *Firefly* mission: diversion was not authorized for anything other than emergencies, since those airfields weren't equipped to handle a sudden surge of *drop-in* aircraft. The squadron was to perform its mission as well as possible and then return— intact—to its home base. No freelancing. Period.

Thirty seconds passed in tense silence before Roth said, "On my mark...*five, four, three, two, one, DROP.*"

Climbing away from the target, *Moon's Menace VI* had to avoid a flight of Corsairs streaking through the clouds from the east. The evasive action—a hard roll to the left—was so violent that gunner Allen's helmeted head struck his canopy frame, leaving white streaks on the aluminum and glazing.

He was stunned and annoyed but not hurt. He asked Tommy, "A little warning might be nice, sir, if you can spare the time."

"That's the problem, Bob. There was no time."

"I figured. No big deal. I've been knocked around a lot worse. My helmet's ready for the trash can, though."

"I'll buy you a new one when we get back," Tommy said.

The ASO's voice filled their headsets now, announcing, "Good strike, *Switchblade*. Excellent job."

"Glad to hear it," Tommy replied, "but how about clearing the airspace for the *Boxcars*? There are Corsairs all over the place, and those lumbering girls won't be able to dodge them like I can."

"Working on it right now, *Switchblade*. Clear the frequency, please."

As *Moon's Menace VI* completed the 180-degree turn to exit the area, her crew could see the C-119s lining up for the drop, now just seconds away.

"I can't believe how low they are," Roth said. "Anybody with a peashooter can hit them."

"They don't want to miss, Hank. There won't be another chance for them."

*****

The *Flying Boxcars* vanished as quickly as they'd appeared, their job done. Of the eight Treadway sections they'd rolled out of their cavernous fuselages, six were serviceable after their brief parachute rides to the ground. Of the remaining two, one was damaged on impact; the other fell too far outside the Marines' perimeter at Koto-ri and was conceded to the Chinese. Two good sections were quickly hoisted by crane onto the engineers' heavy-duty Brockway trucks and, under escort from Gunny Ramsay and his tankers, began the four-mile drive to Funchilin Pass. It would be treacherous; not only would the Chinese be shooting at them, but the Brockways—top-heavy and unwieldy with their loads— could easily slide off the road and tumble down an embankment.

Yet they made it.

The emplacement of the Treadway sections encountered many technical challenges, and the Chinese harassing fire was continuous. But twenty-four hours later, the first tank rolled across the repaired bridge. His

Pershing standing guard on the far side of the improvised span, Ramsay shook the hand of an engineer officer and said, "Lieutenant, if you told me yesterday we'd be across that damn gorge today, I'd have told you that you were out of your ever-loving mind."

*****

Three days later, the survivors of 1st Marine Division—still a fighting unit despite being reduced to a third its size from the combined battering by the enemy and the cold—marched into the port city of Hungnam. In their wake, they left six shattered Chinese divisions who'd suffered far more catastrophic losses while failing in their mission to destroy them.

*****

Boarding the LST that would take them back to Pusan, Gunny Ramsay and his tankers had plenty of company: there were an equal number of Korean civilian refugees being rescued from the Chinese. As the flotilla of transports set out to sea, those grief-stricken refugees wailed as they watched US Navy ships bombard the deserted port city—and their homes—to dust.

"Can't let the chinks use the harbor facilities," a deck officer explained.

As Ramsay watched the sobbing Korean civilians, it brought back a bitter memory:

Watching those people cry reminds me of our so-called victory at Seoul back in September, when we had to watch as MacArthur paraded his triumphant little motorcade through the ruins of the city. He even brought the missus along. But he never so much as looked to see the suffering his mistakes had caused those Korean civilians. He couldn't have cared less that they were crying, too.

I bet he expected them to throw flowers at him.

We Marines wanted to throw something at him, that's for damn sure.

I said it then and I'll say it now: we didn't liberate these people. We slaughtered them.

Chapter Eleven

As much as he might want to, Jock Miles couldn't greet every replacement joining his regiment the moment they showed up. He was just too busy, the burdens of command simply too great. For Lee Grossman and Theo Papadakis, though, he'd make the time. So would Patchett. The bond they shared fighting the Japanese in the jungles of Papua and the islands off New Guinea made any less of a welcome unthinkable.

Papadakis was first off the truck, having ridden in the back with the enlisted men even though he wore the *railroad tracks* of a captain. He saw Jock and Patchett before his boots hit the ground. Not even bothering to scoop up his duffel bag, he marched directly to them and snapped to attention in front of Jock. In a booming voice straight from the streets of New York City, he said, "I hear you could use a little help, sir. Where do you need me?"

Then he turned to Patchett and said, with mock surprise, "You still here, Top? I figured you had the good sense to get out after the last one, you old goat."

"Nah, I reckon any damn fool can do two wars," Patchett replied, "so I went for three. But little did I know it would give me a chance to serve with *The Mad Greek* one more time. As I live and breathe, sir, them chinks gonna be damn sorry they pulled you into this fight, I tell you what."

Jock searched the crowd of arriving soldiers milling around the trucks. "Where's that other damn New Yorker who's supposed to be with you, Theo?"

"Lee? He'll be along in a minute," Papadakis replied. Lowering his voice, he added, "Be gentle with him, sir. He ain't in the best of moods at the moment. In fact, he ain't been since we got on the boat back in Frisco."

Major Lee Grossman emerged from the crowd of GIs and approached slowly, almost reluctantly. There was a look of disgust on his face that finally dissolved to a tepid smile once he drew close.

Jock and Patchett both wondered if he was mad at the world. Or mad at his present circumstances, at least.

"It's good to see you, sir," Grossman said, "but I can't say it's good to be here."

"None of us can say it's good to be here, Lee," Jock replied. "But it's damn good to see you, too. Why don't we all go over to the CP and have some hot coffee? We've got a lot to talk about."

Grossman seemed surprised, asking, "You mean you've actually got something *hot* in this godforsaken icebox? We haven't had a hot meal since we got off the boat at Pusan. Couldn't even eat the damn C rations they gave us. They were frozen solid."

Patchett asked, "They didn't have no immersion heaters to heat up them entrees back in the rear area?"

"Fuck no, Top," Grossman replied. "The only immersion heaters I saw were being used to keep the plasma at some field hospital from freezing."

"By the way, sir," Patchett said, "they call them field hospitals *MASH* units now. Mobile Army Surgical Hospitals."

Grossman scowled; he didn't much care what they were called. But he asked, "What else did the Army change on me in the last five years?"

"Not much, I'm afraid," Patchett said. "All the individual and crew-served weapons are pretty much the same ones we used back in the jungle, except we got better rocket launchers now. They'll actually stop a tank if you hit it right. They upgraded the M1 carbine to an M2 with full auto, but they don't work worth a shit in this cold. And the radios still stink."

Jock added, "You'll have to get used to working with armor, though. We didn't have to do much of that back in the jungle. Take my word for it…you'll learn to appreciate those tankers real quick."

Lee Grossman didn't seem to be appreciating much of anything. But that first sip of hot coffee seemed to perk him up a little. He seemed positively eager to hear the answer when Papadakis asked, "By the way, how's Miss Jillian, sir?"

Jock assured them that she and the kids were fine. He didn't get too deep into the possible deportation. This wasn't the time or place.

"But Colonel Molloy's working on it, right?" Papadakis asked.

"Yeah, but it's *General* Molloy now."

"Even better. He'll straighten things out, for sure."

"Let's hope so, Theo."

Then Jock and Patchett gave them a down-and-dirty overview of the struggle with the Chinese, the regiment's successes and failures, and dealing with that other enemy—the Korean winter. The avalanche of details drove Grossman back into a funk. Jock told him, "Let's you and I have a talk, Lee. Step into my office."

The *office* was a field desk and some crates used as tables and chairs in a corner of the big CP tent. "Something's on your mind, Lee," Jock said. "I need to hear it."

"This is a screwing and a half, sir," Grossman began. "It doesn't seem fair. Guys like me and Theo…we did our bit already, in spades. There are plenty of others out there who haven't." He went on to explain that since he'd left the Army back in Forty-Five, he'd finished law school, gotten married, and finally landed a highly competitive position at a good Manhattan firm. But two months after being hired, he was recalled to active duty from the reserve officer pool for service in Korea.

"I can pretty much kiss that job goodbye now," he said, his eyes downcast, staring at the dirt floor, which was frozen as hard as concrete. "With any luck, I won't have to kiss my marriage goodbye, too. At least we don't have any kids yet. Rachel and I were focusing on our careers for the time being."

He took a long swallow of coffee before continuing. "When I got to in-processing, I tried to pull a transfer to JAG, considering I'd been accepted to the New York Bar. I thought the personnel officer was going to laugh in my face. He told me they'd take my transfer request but not to hold my breath. They wanted officers from the combat arms"—he tapped the crossed rifles of the infantry on his shirt collar—"and they got me hook, line, and sinker, dammit."

Jock let him fall into self-pitying silence as he thought, *Lee Grossman was one fine warrior, tough as nails and smart as a whip, with a year's experience as an exceptional battalion commander in tough jungle combat.*

But the man sitting before me doesn't sound like the same Lee Grossman.

Maybe I should reconsider giving him Third

Battalion?

After a few moments, Grossman broke the silence, asking, "So what kind of job do you have in mind for me, sir?"

"Actually, Lee, I was considering giving you a battalion."

His answer, delivered without a moment's hesitation and almost upbeat, floored Jock. "Okay, sir. That's fine with me. It's not like I haven't done the job before when the shit was flying. But what happened to the last battalion commander?"

"I relieved him a few hours ago. He was a total disaster. I moved up his XO to keep the seat warm temporarily...but he's not the right man for the job."

"Okay," Grossman said. "When do I start?"

"How about right now, Lee? I know it's a little sudden, but that'll give you a whole half a day to settle in...because once the sun goes down, there's a real good chance the chinks will start coming out of the woodwork."

*****

While Jock and Grossman were having their private chat, Patchett and Papadakis—*Captain Pop*, as GIs had always addressed him so as not to mangle his actual surname—did some serious catching up.

"When I got home in Forty-Five," Papadakis said, "I got a job with the New York City Department of Sanitation right away. But I couldn't see myself hanging off the back of a trash wagon the rest of my life, picking up other people's crap. I guess I had a pretty big chip on my shoulder from being an officer and all. In fact, the other *can smashers* on the crew started calling me *The General*...and not in a respectful way, either. One day, some *wop* union steward started breaking my balls about how I was working too fast, making it hard on everyone else who just wanted to *go along to get along* and *put in their eight.*"

Patchett smiled. He had a hunch where this story was going.

"It got kinda heated," Papadakis continued, "and then the jerk-off throws a punch at me..."

"And?" Patchett asked.

"And I beat the ever-loving shit out of him, Top. He wanted to press charges, but too many guys saw him throw that first punch. When the cops heard that, they decided that maybe it wasn't worth their time getting involved. I figured I'd get my ass fired, but the next thing I knew, the department moved me to a different garage and made me a foreman. By Forty-Eight, I was assistant manager of the place. And then, a coupla months ago—"

"Uncle Sam sent you his greetings, right?"

"You got it, Top. I didn't take it hard like Lee did, though. To be honest, I needed the change. It was a *two birds with one stone* sorta thing. There was this woman breaking my balls to get married, see? I didn't want any part of that....and I'd kinda gotten to the point where I was looking forward to breaking a few heads again like we did back in the jungle."

"You're gonna get your chance, sir. You can bet on that. But if you missed *this man's army* so damn much, why'd you stay out? It woulda took you back any ol' time."

"Hey, let's not talk crazy, Top. Not everybody's got

Government Property stamped on his ass like you and Colonel Miles. But if you're gonna *order* me back in, well..."

His voice dropped to a whisper as he asked, "But what the hell is the colonel still doing here, anyway? Ain't he a millionaire now or something?"

"His wife is, not him."

"Yeah, but ain't that the same thing?"

"No, it ain't like that, sir. The colonel's got a special bond with the US Army. Miss Jillian understands all about it. She always has. Jock Miles ain't hanging it up until he's good and ready. And that's an outstanding break for us, as far as I'm concerned."

"And his leg's holding up okay?"

"His leg's doing just fine, sir," Patchett replied.

He considered it just a small fib.

*****

Lee Grossman wasted no time assuming command of 3rd Battalion. Within an hour of his heart-to-heart discussion with Colonel Miles, he convened his first meeting with the battalion's cadre. He expected to be met with skepticism, even hostility. Jock had pulled no punches about how screwed-up the battalion was. But Grossman wasn't concerned.

When I took over the battalion from Jock Miles on Biak back in Forty-Four, it was a tough transition, too. Not because that battalion was dysfunctional like this one is—far from it—but Jock's a tough act to follow. The men loved him. After having worked for him for so long, I loved him, too. Still do, I guess. A lot of us wouldn't be alive today if it wasn't for him.

This transition's going to be a lot different. But I've got a plan that's going to work for me...and if the men in this outfit are smart, it'll work for them, too.

"My name's Grossman," he told his assembled officers and senior NCOs. "By the time the sun goes down, I'll know all of yours, too. This is not the first battalion I've commanded in combat, and I'm going to tell you right now that I'm not here to win any medals. I've already got all I need from the last war. Some of you old hands might feel that way, too, and that's fine."

Then, as if addressing a jury, he continued, "But I don't want to be here any more than any of you, and I'm going to keep my time in this stinking country as short as possible. Here's how I plan to do that: as you've already heard, your rotation home is contingent on accumulating the necessary points. You all know the math involved—the speed at which you collect points depends on what type of unit you serve in, whether or not that unit is in contact with the enemy, and for how long it's in contact. A man in an infantry outfit like ours, positioned here on the front line and remaining in that position, will leave Korea in a little less than a year. I plan to keep this battalion on the front line for as long as I'm here, because that's my quickest ticket home. Yours, too. In fact, most of you already have a month's head start on me."

A captain asked, "What happens if we were to go into reserve, sir?"

"Then your time in Korea will increase proportionally. It could add as much as fifty percent to your stay."

Then a skeptical master sergeant asked, "Interesting plan, sir...but ain't it a little risky? I mean, it sounds like a whole lot of ways to get dead as fast as you can."

"You're as good as dead from the moment you were born, Sergeant. But you don't get to pick the time, so there's no point worrying about it. Your job will get a hell of a lot easier once you realize that."

Just like reading a jury, Grossman could tell that about half of the officers and NCOs before him found his argument appealing, although most were guarded about showing it. But there were enough small, tell-tale gestures—chin rubbing, positive eye contact, gentle nods, relaxed posture—to indicate their agreement.

Then he added, "But let there be no doubt that when we have to fight, we will fight and fight well. Some of you may already know that Colonel Miles and I go back a long way. I served under him in the Southwest Pacific during the last war...and I'm proud to serve under him again. You should be, too."

He paused and then asked, "Are there any more questions?"

When no one raised his hand, Grossman said, "Okay...I've got a couple more things. I understand your last commander was real big on creature comforts and not so big on command and control. I assure you that I'm not afflicted with either of those diseases. If any of you are so afflicted, I suggest you take the cure immediately, or you and I will be having serious problems very shortly. And yes, it's cold here...cold enough to hurt you, even kill you, if you're not smart. But the last place I fought was hotter than a blast furnace, with deadly snakes as big as telephone poles, crawling insects the size of taxi cabs, and squadrons of mosquitoes intent on giving you malaria, which you either came down with or turned yellow as a Jap from the drugs that supposedly prevented it. So in other words, get your heads out of your asses about how miserable you are here, button up real good, and start counting your blessings. You could be in worse places."

*****

Theo Papadakis asked Jock, "What'd you tell Lee to turn him around so quick, sir?"

"I didn't have to tell him much of anything, Theo. I think he just liked the idea of being in command again."

"I can go along with that," *The Mad Greek* replied. "So what've you got in store for me?"

"Able Company in Second Battalion has no officers," Jock told him. "It's yours, Theo."

"No officers? What happened to them, sir?"

"Two dead, the rest wounded and airlifted to Japan. The company took a beating a couple of nights ago, but the NCOs did an outstanding job holding the unit together under heavy pressure from the chinks. Major Harper is your battalion commander. He's waiting for you with bated breath."

*****

On the jeep ride to drop Papadakis off at 2nd Battalion's CP, Patchett drove past Baker Battery, the regiment's Negro artillery unit. When he caught sight of all the colored GIs busy around the howitzers, *Captain Pop* said, "Pull over, Top. I ain't believing my eyes."

"What's the matter, Captain? You never seen a colored outfit before?"

"Actually, no, Top. I thought the Army was

supposed to be integrated now."

"Technically, it is, sir. But practically speaking, we still got a long way to go. To be accurate, though, it ain't an *all colored* unit no more. The first sergeant's a white man."

"Really? Whose dumb idea was that?"

"*Mine*, sir," Patchett said, not bothering to hide his annoyance. "Let's just say we were having a little *morale* problem when it was all colored. A lack of motivation to excel, plain and simple."

"And swapping out the first sergeant fixed the problem? You're kidding me, right?"

"No, I ain't kidding you," Patchett replied. Then he added, "In all fairness, it's only been a week but...well...so far, so good."

*****

As the sun set and the men of the 26th braced for another night of probable Chinese attacks, the ASO at the regimental CP received an unusual radio call. It came from an F-82 *Twin Mustang* pilot on night patrol, flying some twenty miles north of the Parallel.

"Be advised, bandits in the air," the pilot said. "I picked them up on radar near Chorwon but lost them right away in the ground clutter when they ducked into the Imjin valley. Couldn't ID the type ships, but they're pretty slow. Looks like they're headed your way."

Sean Moon was the duty NCO at the CP. He asked the ASO, "What the hell is that flyboy talking about, sir? Did the chinks finally get themselves an air force?"

"Not likely it's the Chinese," the ASO replied. "They're probably remnants of the KPA Air Force."

"The North Koreans? I thought we'd seen the last of them."

"Maybe not, Sergeant."

"I'll raise Colonel Miles on the horn," Sean said. "He's helping the new Third Battalion C.O. get settled in. Should be a piece of cake, considering they're old buddies and all."

*****

At 3rd Battalion CP, Jock scanned the darkening night sky. There would be no moon tonight; low clouds were gathering to dump more snow. It was a perfect night to bounce the powerful beams of the searchlight company off the cloud deck, illuminating the probable Chinese attack routes in the reflected glow. Jock would give the order shortly: *Let there be light.*

He told Lee Grossman, "I just got the word that we might have some enemy planes headed our way, too."

"Do we see a lot of activity from enemy aircraft, sir?"

"No. The most action we've seen—believe it or not—is from PO-2s, those old Russian biplanes. They'll glide in with their engines off and dump some small bombs on you, then crank back up and vanish before you know what hit you. As low and thick as these clouds are getting, that's going to be risky business for them tonight. Lots of high ground to smack into."

Grossman asked, "Should we hold off the illumination until we get rid of the planes? Those searchlights would be pretty easy targets when they're all lit up."

"We can switch them off if planes actually do show

up," Jock replied. "But believe me…the chinks on the ground will be a lot more trouble than a couple of planes in the air."

Chapter Twelve

Theo Papadakis was used to Japanese *banzai* charges. He'd seen plenty of those attacks, where an entire unit—be it a platoon, company, or battalion—would hurl itself at you like a suicidal herd of snarling animals.

But once you cut enough of them down so they knew their attack was gonna fail, it'd be all over. The survivors would withdraw and start popping knee mortars at you, making it hard to chase them.

But these fucking chinks don't know when to quit. They just keep coming. I swear, half of them in the second rank didn't even have weapons until they took them off the dead guys from the first rank.

And those damn bugles...

God, I hate that sound.

Now where's that fucking artillery I asked for?

It had been almost a minute since he'd called in the fire mission. Ten seconds in combat was a lifetime. A minute was an eternity.

The CCF had launched their attack that night undeterred by the floodlights that spoiled the cover of darkness. From Able Company's perch on the ridge, the advancing Chinese became visible to *Captain Pop* and his men when they were still hundreds of yards away, exposed as they ran across the iced-over Imjin River and the frozen marshes on its banks. At that distance, in the soft, reflected light of the searchlights, they looked more like a viscous, flowing mass—something akin to a spreading oil spill—rather than individual human forms.

He'd phoned in the fire mission to the artillery thinking, *This is too easy, all those chinks in the open. Or maybe they're just cutting me a break my first night on the line.*

More seconds ticked by, but there were still no rounds in the air. He spun the crank on the field telephone again.

"What's the holdup, dammit?" he said to the voice at the artillery battery.

"We're still checking the data. Stand by." The sonorous tone of that voice left little doubt he was speaking to a colored man.

"Hey, pal, I'll be checking the goddamn data when I see the rounds land. Step on it, will ya? I need fire support *on the double.*"

The first wave of Chinese was now just a hundred yards away, scaling the steep slope to the ridge. They were no longer an amorphous mass but hundreds of individual soldiers in silhouette. His men were already inflicting grave punishment on them with rifle and machine gun fire.

But they kept coming.

Another fifteen seconds passed before the voice on the line reported, "*Shot,* over."

Captain Pop figured the time of flight of those rounds should be about fifteen seconds.

If those airbursts pop where they're supposed to, this first wave of chinks will already be past 'em and right in our damn faces.

He was right on both counts. The airbursts showered their steel rain right on target, cutting down a good number of the attackers in the second wave who hadn't reached the slope yet. But as Papadakis feared, the first wave was well past that deadly downpour. It didn't seem possible, but the numbers of Chinese seemed to be growing.

"Captain," his RTO said, "First Platoon says one of their thirty cals just went out of action. They say they can't cover the highway and hold off the chinks at the same time without it."

"Tell them to pull back to the top of the ridge," Papadakis replied.

His first sergeant—an old hand named Grundy— shook his head and said, "If they pull all the way back up the ridge, Captain, that leaves the road wide open. The chinks will be behind us before we know it."

"Not if I can help it, Sarge. We're going to shift the artillery left, putting it right on the road while First Platoon repositions. That'll give us a coupla minutes until the tankers can move up and help us plug the gap."

First Sergeant Grundy replied, "I don't know, sir...that sounds a little too complicated with all this shit flying. And you're gonna depend on those nigger cannon-cockers to cover our asses?"

"You got a better idea?"

"Yeah. Tell First Platoon to move behind Second Platoon. Then when the chinks try to get up on the ridge, both platoons mass fire on them."

It was Papadakis' turn to shake his head. "Negative, Sarge. That's the best way I know to have our guys shooting each other. This illumination's good, but it ain't that good. Second Platoon won't know First Platoon from the chinks. Everybody's staying in their own sector. And we ain't giving up this ridge to nobody."

Then he called in his corrections to the artillery: "New target. From last coordinates, shift left two hundred, drop one hundred..."

When finished with the call for fire, he turned to Grundy and said, "Now get First Platoon up that ridge on the double, before that artillery lands so close it scares the shit outta them. Then get the tankers moving to Checkpoint One-Three."

And pray the radio and phones don't crap out.

It still took too long for the next volley of artillery airbursts to arrive, well over a minute this time. It did its job on the Chinese still on the road. But 1st Platoon was now in a point-blank fight with those who'd managed to scale the ridge.

Grundy said, "We've got to shift that artillery farther up the ridge."

"No time," *The Mad Greek* replied. "They're taking too fucking long to get rounds in the air as it is." He picked up the handset and told the artillery, *"Repeat, over."*

Grundy didn't understand that request at all. "You want them to shoot the same damn thing again?"

"You bet," Papadakis replied. "No computation involved, so there shouldn't be any delay. I'll take rounds *right now*—even if they ain't exactly on the money—over rounds that are too damn late."

He was right. Less than twenty seconds elapsed before the rounds burst along the road, erasing another wave of Chinese about to scale the ridge.

He told the first sergeant, "Keep doing that until there's no more chinks at the base of this ridge. In the meantime, I'm going over to First Platoon. If that fight turns hand-to-hand, I wanna be there."

Grundy said, "You real sure you want to do that, sir?"

"Yep. I gotta know what kind of fighters I got here."

*****

In the searchlights' muted glow, hurrying over terrain he'd never set foot on before, Papadakis hadn't found 1st Platoon yet.

Did I miss them completely?

He was about to tell his RTO to call the platoon leader for a status report when he heard a voice cry out, "GRENADE!"

Four men were running in his direction—they hadn't seen him yet in their panic—and after a few more steps threw themselves on the ground ten yards away. At least five seconds had passed since that initial cry of panic.

Papadakis walked up to them and crouched above a man wearing sergeant's stripes. Calmly, he asked, "Thanks for not shooting me. Now, what's the problem over here, Sergeant?"

The man raised his head hesitantly, as if afraid lifting it another inch off the ground would make it an easy target. There was no glimmer of recognition when he looked into *Captain Pop's* eyes, only shock that this crazy captain he'd never seen before was making himself an even easier target.

"I'm Papadakis, your new company commander. Call me *Captain Pop*. Now I believe you said something about a grenade?"

The man pointed back in the direction from which they'd run. Breathlessly, he said, "One just fell into our hole, sir. We gotta get out of here. *Joe Chink's* right behind us."

"Is that so?" Papadakis replied. Then he stood up and started walking toward the fighting hole they'd just abandoned, his rifle on his hip and ready to fire. With mock cordiality, he asked the four GIs, "Join me, won't you?"

But they didn't move.

He pressed on, anyway, until he saw the hole. When he heard the sizzling sound coming from it, he dropped to his belly and crawled to the rim.

Shit, it's a dud...like cheap Chinese fireworks.

Sliding into the hole, he picked up the smoking grenade and hurled it down the slope.

He saw long, faint shadows moving toward him. *Ah, crap. Don't tell me those are more of my guys straggling up here...*

Five of them...but five of who? Gotta hold my fire until I know for sure.

Wouldn't that be hot shit? First day with the outfit and I shoot my own men.

I'm thinking they're GIs because they look kinda tall. I thought all chinks were short.

They were only ten yards away now.

Still can't see their faces...but I can hear them breathing real hard. I'd yell the challenge word, but I don't remember what the hell it is.

Say something, you bastards.

The distance closed to ten feet, and he got the clue he needed:

Ain't no GIs wear snowman hats like that.

Papadakis shot the closest four before the last man had a chance to raise his weapon. But he never got to fire that submachine gun. The Chinese soldier went down in a hail of gunfire, dealt by the four GIs who'd finally followed their new company commander back to the fighting hole.

"Nice shot group," *Captain Pop* said, his voice as cold as the air engulfing them. "Even if it did take you like a fucking year to get back here. You do understand that when somebody gives you an order, that means *do it now*, right?"

"Yes, sir," the sergeant replied, "I understand. But we didn't…that grenade…and our lieutenant got killed yesterday, so—"

"No time for sob stories, Sergeant," Papadakis said as he climbed from the hole. "Can I assume you've got your sector back under control now?"

"Yes, sir, we've got it."

"Outstanding. Now all I gotta do is figure out why everything takes so damn long around here."

As he made his way back to his CP, he called Battalion on the radio, complaining to Major Harper about the slow response of their artillery support.

"I know all about it," the major replied. "Working with Regiment now to get it sorted out. Keep it together down there."

*****

At Regiment, Sean Moon was concerned about slow responses, too, but not from the artillery. From the CP's perch on high ground, he'd been the first to spot the aircraft loitering near 3rd Battalion's sector, three PO-2 biplanes that were, most likely, being flown by North Koreans. They'd been hard to see, even with the searchlights working their magic, due to their slim silhouettes and being painted a dark green that blended into the shadows. When the biplanes first appeared, they seemed to be making a beeline for the source of that light on the backslope of Kamak-San. Several belated bursts from the *quad 50s* on that mountain's front slope had driven them away, their streams of tracers pointing to the ships like angry fingers. But the *quads* hadn't knocked any of them down.

Even though the PO-2s made their escape by ducking low into the Imjin valley, Sean continued to track the planes, knowing that if he looked away, he'd never pick them up again. He watched as they passed in front of the regiment's sector from west to east, probing for a target of opportunity on which to drop their meager bomb load.

"You've got two bandits about a mile due north of your position, low and orbiting," he told 3rd Battalion's CP over the landline. "A coupla good squirts of fifty cal from an ace gunner should put 'em out of their misery."

"We can't see them yet," the voice at 3rd Battalion replied. "They must be blending into the background real well from this angle. Do you still have eyes on them?"

"Affirmative. I'm looking down on them, actually, with a pretty good view. I'll tell you when and where they turn into you."

"Roger. Standing by."

It didn't take long; in less than a minute, Sean reported, "Okay, they've turned south, directly toward the junction of Highways One-One and One-Xray. I can be your spotter if you still can't see 'em."

"Negative. The XO says we'll handle it."

But they didn't seem to be *handling* anything. The PO-2s roamed at will over 3rd Battalion's sector for several minutes, searching, apparently, for a choice target to bomb. Lee Grossman had been busy checking on his emplaced companies, roving his defensive line in a jeep; he hadn't heard any of the landline conversations about the intruding aircraft. But when one of the planes passed directly over his head—seemingly close enough to touch—he headed directly to his quad 50 section.

He found the gunners in a relaxed state of readiness, keeping tabs on the PO-2s without bothering to engage them. When Grossman asked why they hadn't knocked the planes out of the sky yet, the section's sergeant seemed amused. "Those little pieces of shit ain't gonna hurt us, Major," the sergeant said. "No sense aggravating them."

"I don't want you to aggravate them, Sergeant. I want you to kill them."

"It don't work that way, sir. Didn't you get the word? If we don't bother them, they won't bother us."

Grossman relieved him on the spot. He'd take two of the man's stripes as soon as there was time to process the paperwork.

Then he told the next ranking GI in the section, "Corporal, you're in charge now. Shoot down those aircraft."

The gun crews stayed idle, shuffling and smirking, like this wasn't to be taken seriously. Their eyes shifted back and forth from their ex-chief to their new battalion commander, waiting indifferently for the next move in a negotiation they'd eventually win, like all those they'd had with their officers before. Colonel Beemon might've been gone, but the culture of indiscipline he'd allowed to fester in 3rd Battalion was still alive and well.

As a few seconds passed in ominous silence,

another thought began to cross their minds: *This new guy—this Major Grossman—just one look at him and you can tell he's a tough son of a bitch who'd just as soon coldcock you than play nice. He doesn't seem to care if he makes waves. And he sure as hell doesn't care whether you like him or not, unlike that apple-polisher Beemon.*

"I mean *now*, Corporal," Grossman reminded the man he'd just put in charge, "unless you're ready to get busted, too."

No one took it as an idle threat.

"But...but they're out of range, Major," the corporal said.

"The hell they are. You ever fire this thing at a fucking aircraft before?"

The corporal didn't answer, but his body language left no doubt he hadn't. Though the quad 50 was conceived as an anti-aircraft weapon, there had been few enemy aircraft to shoot at in Korea.

If this crew was even trained as anti-aircraft gunners at all, the only thing they ever engaged was a target sleeve that didn't shoot back, Grossman felt sure.

"There...the leader's turning left," Grossman told the gunner. "He's giving you a perfect broadside shot. Just lead him and walk the tracers back onto him."

"I can barely see him in this crappy light, Major."

"All you've gotta see is the movement, Corporal, and those planes are the only things moving in the sky. Let her rip. Those flimsy things will come apart like wet paper bags."

*****

Major Harper's call to the regimental CP about the late artillery came as no surprise to Sergeant Patchett. He'd been following the requests for fire on all the commo nets, radio and telephone; he already knew the response time of Baker Battery—the Negro 105-millimeter battery—was much too slow.

"Let me see if I can fix this, sir," he said to Jock Miles. "I got some skin in this game, seeing how the first sergeant swap was my idea and all."

"Negative, Top. I need you here."

Jock's reason why: nobody brought order to the chaos of battle reports like his top sergeant. *It's almost like having a savant in your CP*, he thought. *He understands what every trooper is going through because he's done it all.*

Patchett wasn't happy being refused, but he understood a *no* when he heard one. "As you wish, sir," he said. "But who's gonna handle it?"

Jock looked to Sean Moon, who had a phone in one ear and a radio handset in the other. "Can you break free, Sergeant?" he asked.

"Well, sir, now that Third Battalion took out those rinky-dink airplanes and the tankers got Second Battalion's left flank covered, I guess the S3 can do without me for a little while."

"Good. Now go find out why that battery is so damn late with their fire support."

*****

It took Sean only a few minutes to drive to Baker

Battery. The illumination from the searchlights was brighter there, since those powerful beams were being generated from a position only a few hundred yards away. That light allowed him to see that something was obviously wrong; the gunners were poised with rounds in the tubes, ready to fire. The firing lanyards were taut, waiting for that quick pull that would ignite the propellant and send the round on its way.

But these gunners were waiting for a command to fire.

It ain't supposed to work like that, he told himself. *They ram in a round...and once the gunner levels his bubbles and yells "Ready," the assistant gunner jerks the lanyard. That's all there is to it.*

So what the hell's the holdup?

As he approached the fire direction center tent, he could hear the battery's white first sergeant—an old-timer named Fritz Waltzer—shouting angrily into a field telephone.

"No, goddammit, *you're* the ones who fucked up," Waltzer was saying. "The elevation's all wrong. Either your chart operator's got his head up his ass or that *whiz-bang* you've got doing the computing's been hitting the bottle."

Captain Little, the black officer commanding Baker Battery, explained the situation to Sean. "Battalion doesn't trust my FDC to do the firing computations. Their FDC has to double-check all of my guys' work before we have permission to fire. That takes a lot of unnecessary chatter back and forth on the landline, and it's slowing everything down. So if you're asking why it's taking so long to get rounds on target, there's your answer, Sergeant. We're trying to do our job, but they've got us handcuffed."

"Whose big idea was that, Captain? I know it didn't come from Regiment, that's for damn sure."

"It comes from Colonel Sanchez, the artillery battalion commander," Little replied.

"Sounds like he fucked up, then," Sean said. "You use one FDC's numbers or the other. You don't waste time looking over each other's shoulder."

"I agree, Sergeant, but he won't listen to reason. And *orders are orders*, you know?"

"Well, sir, I believe I can get you a different set of orders right quick. You got a line to Regiment?"

"Affirmative. We'll ring them up for you."

Jock Miles was on the line within a minute. In that time, the battery had fired only one volley. They could've easily fired three or four if not slowed down by the roadblock at Battalion FDC.

Three minutes after that, Colonel Sanchez was on the landline to Baker Battery, lifting the requirement for their computations to be checked by Battalion.

"Sounds like a certain gentleman just stepped into a pile of shit," Waltzer said.

Captain Little smiled, adding, "The man earned it."

Sean stayed on for a few minutes to watch the battery's FDC function. It ran as well as any he'd ever been in, the five-man computation team working together like clockwork. Rounds were in the air within seconds of receiving the firing data at the guns.

"That's more like it, Fritz," Sean said to Waltzer. "But tell me, one top kick to another...did Battalion have a reason to think your guys were, shall we say, *error-prone*?"

Waltzer laughed and shook his head. "Sure, they've

got a reason, Sean...but it ain't a *good* reason. My guys know their shit. In fact, did you hear me yelling at those idiots up at Battalion? *They* just made a mistake. If we'd fired their data, we would've dropped rounds into our infantry, for sure. And it ain't the first time Battalion's fucked up, either."

They stepped outside the tent to watch the gun crews in action.

"You like what you see, Sean?"

"Yeah, Fritz, they look good. Real good."

"Like I said, buddy...my guys know their shit."

As Sean headed back to his jeep, Waltzer called after him: "Tell that redneck Patchett he owes me one, big time."

*****

There were many close calls that night, but 26th Regiment held the line against the Chinese onslaught.

The same couldn't be said for some other units in 8th Army.

"Twenty-Fifth Division to our west got torn up pretty bad," Jock told his commanders and staff at sunrise, once the CCF facing the regiment had melted back into the wooded landscape to the north. "The Chinese have broken through their line in a couple of places. That'll put them on the other side of the Imjin, headed south for Seoul...and racing to get behind us."

Every man in the CP tent knew what was coming next.

"So it won't come as any surprise to you that we're pulling back again," Jock continued. "Start getting used to a new term Eighth Army just coined to identify where we're going to dig in and hold the Chinese: the MLR, or *main line of resistance*. Our MLR will be the Han River, and that means Seoul."

A staff officer asked, "So that's where we're going to spend Christmas, sir? In Seoul?"

"That's the plan, gentlemen," Jock replied.

Once the briefing was over, Jock called Colonel Sanchez aside and led him to a corner of the CP tent, where what he was about to say wouldn't be overheard. Ass-chewings needed to be done in private.

"Colonel," Jock began, "did you have any good reason for the restrictions you put on Baker Battery?"

"Well, sir...my staff just didn't feel we could trust them to—"

Jock cut him off. "I'm not interested in what your staff felt, Colonel. They're your problem. I asked about *your* decision as commander. What basis did you have for not trusting them?"

The artilleryman started to blather about their *record of unreliability.* But Jock wasn't buying it.

"That's all bullshit and rumor, Sanchez. Despite any past issues they had, there have been *no* instances of fire direction errors at Baker Battery while supporting this regiment. The only problem they exhibited last night was delayed delivery of fires, which was entirely *your* doing. By my calculation, your bad judgment was singularly responsible for about half the casualties this regiment took before Sergeant Moon alerted me to what was going on. That adds up to roughly twenty-five men who needed that fire and didn't get it in time."

"But sir, I was concerned that if I'd let them fire unchecked, we might have had even *more* casualties, and they'd be due to friendly fire."

"That's pretty weak, even for a hypothetical excuse, Hector. Now I'm only going to tell you this once: as far as this regiment is concerned, the color of a man who puts his life on the line is irrelevant. He's entitled to the same treatment and respect as any other soldier. If you don't agree with that, you and I have a big problem. So tell me...do we have a problem here, Colonel?"

"No, sir, we don't have a problem."

"And in your opinion, has swapping first sergeants between the white and colored batteries had the desired effect?"

Hesitantly, Sanchez replied, "Yes, sir...it seems to be working."

"Outstanding. We're all in agreement, then. Do you have any other questions, Colonel Sanchez?"

When he had none, Jock said, "You're dismissed. But a word of caution, Colonel... don't ever fuck my men over like that again."

Chapter Thirteen

Eighth Army wasn't the only mass of humanity traveling south to Seoul; civilian refugees fleeing the approaching Chinese clogged the highways, greatly slowing the GIs' withdrawal to the MLR on the Han River. Jock Miles' 26th Regiment had been the rear guard for 24th Division's motor movement, fighting small, sporadic skirmishes with advance elements of the CCF all along Highway 33 for the past week. They were still fifteen miles from Seoul and the Han.

Jock and Patchett watched their column crawl through the mass of refugees from high ground overlooking the highway. "With any luck at all, it'll only take us one more day to reach our destination," Jock said.

"Amen to that, sir," Patchett replied, "but I'm getting to feel real bad for these people. I wish now I'd shot that son of a bitching ROK lieutenant we caught beating on them old men and women yesterday. There was no call for that. A Korean just can't get enough of pissing on anybody he thinks is lower than his sorry ass."

"I'm glad you didn't shoot him, Top. That wouldn't have helped a damn thing."

"At least we made that bastard give 'em back the rice he stole from 'em. But I swear, as I live and breathe, sir, if he'd mouthed off one more time…"

They could see the trucks of the regiment's medical section parked in a circle off the road, creating an ad hoc aid station. A column of refugees waiting to enter that circle for treatment stretched back almost a half mile. A platoon of GIs stood watch over the refugees, keeping the line orderly.

Patchett said, "Kinda ironic that since we pulled back from the Imjin, the docs ain't had hardly nobody to treat but civilians. You still think it was a good idea to start taking care of 'em like we're doing, sir? They're causing a big drain on our supplies."

"Yeah, I still think it's a good idea, Top. From what our surgeon tells me, something like twenty percent of them were unlucky enough to get wounded in crossfires. Another ten percent got hit by our vehicles."

"Is he talking about the ones that didn't get themselves run over and killed?"

"Yeah, Top."

"It ain't like we don't warn 'em to stay outta the way, sir. And all the rest are just plain sick, I reckon?"

"They get dysentery and frostbite just like we do," Jock replied, "and a lot of other diseases we're not used to seeing."

The muttering of a helicopter caught their attention. It was flying toward them from the direction of Seoul.

"You expecting company, sir?" Patchett asked.

"That's all we need. Let's take bets who's in that *eggbeater*."

"My money's on General Ellis, sir."

"Ah, that's who I was going to bet on, too. Or maybe Santa Claus bringing our Christmas presents a week early."

The Sikorsky orbited twice before selecting a landing spot on the opposite side of the highway from the medical section.

"I guess I'd better go meet him," Jock said, steeling himself to the task.

When he drove up to the idling helicopter, he was startled to see the man emerging from the aircraft was not General Ellis, the assistant division commander, but General Bishop, the division commander himself. A crewman had to help him exit the ship. Once he was on the ground, he walked slowly and unsteadily toward Jock's jeep.

This is one guy I never expected to see out here. Arthritis, severe cold, and the numbing vibration of aircraft don't go together well. The shape he's in, I can't believe he's still in command.

Reaching the jeep, Bishop settled wearily against the passenger's seat. The exertion of the walk had him breathing heavily; each exhalation blew great clouds of condensation into the air. It took almost a minute before he could speak.

Pointing to the column of refugees lined up for the aid station, Bishop said, "Just what in blue blazes do you have going on over there, Colonel? Are we running free clinics for the gooks now?"

"We were told by Eighth Army to provide medical care to civilians *as required*, sir. I don't believe that directive has been rescinded."

"That doesn't look like you're dispensing *as required* care, Miles. In fact, you're being taken advantage of. I'd venture a guess that most of those people don't have a damn thing wrong with them. And there are probably a good number of KPA and Chinese infiltrators among them."

Bishop's comment seemed ridiculous on its face, considering that everyone queued up for treatment was either a woman, child, or elderly man. While the regiment had rounded up a few communist infiltrators along the way—always men of military age with bogus or no papers and unlikely stories—no one who appeared to meet that description could be seen among this crowd.

"I'm afraid you'd be incorrect on all counts, sir," Jock replied. "If there are any young men in that line, they're probably ROK deserters."

"There you go, quibbling again, Miles. Good lord, you West Pointers just love to do that, don't you? If you ask me, those people are running a scam to get free medical supplies. And you're playing right along. I'm ordering you to disband that little operation right this minute, Colonel."

"That would be going against Eighth Army's directive, sir. Are you telling me to disobey orders?"

Bishop began to sputter, his irate face nearly vanishing in a cloud of breath turned white in the frigid air. It took him a few moments to calm down. Once he had, he turned strangely philosophical: "These Koreans...they really are *the Irish of the Orient*, aren't they? So mercurial. Either they're reveling in murderous glee when they've bested someone, or they turn into sniveling victims when things don't go their way, like this sorry rabble before us."

He paused, looking quite pleased with his little sermon. Then he continued, "But that's not what I'm here to discuss, Miles. I've been going over the after-action reports from the fight on the Imjin. I see you took advantage of having the only searchlight company in the division to give yourself an easy night. In the meantime, the rest of the division—in fact, the rest of the whole damn Eighth Army—was taking a beating."

"Begging your pardon, sir, but my men took quite a beating, too. And am I not supposed to use all the tools available to me to get the job done?"

"That's not the point, Miles. You've been hogging those lights for months."

"They're not *my* lights, sir. They were *delegated* to me by your staff after nobody else wanted them. And since there isn't much of an aircraft threat, they've been fairly useless except on the few totally overcast nights we've been able to use them for indirect illumination. The rest of the time, I've been using the searchlight crews as utility manpower. And to my knowledge, no other regiment has expressed a desire to have the lights."

"Be that as it may, Colonel, but I'm giving that searchlight company to Seventeenth Regiment. Their sector on the MLR will be perfect for them, since it looks out on miles of flat terrain."

"So you're planning on using them for *direct* illumination, sir?"

"Of course, Miles. Isn't that their primary purpose?"

"They won't last a night, sir. They'll be exposed and get shot out the first few minutes of operation."

"We'll just see about that, Colonel. Have the searchlight company report to the Seventeenth at Uijonbu by 1500 hours."

*****

Twenty-five miles north of the 38th Parallel, *Moon's Menace VI* was alone in a crystal blue morning sky as she cruised the North Korean coast near Yangyang. She was standing by to provide air support to a ROK division that was slowly withdrawing to the south. She'd been on her own since her sister ship turned back to Japan an hour ago with engine trouble.

Hank Roth, Tommy Moon's navigator, said, "Too bad *Blondie* had to abort the mission. We could've used a glass-nosed model with a bombsight, letting us drop our *liquid fire* from much higher up."

Bob Allen, the gunner in the rear of the fuselage, chimed in with, "Yeah, it's a hell of a lot safer that way. Altitude is your friend, right?"

"Can't have everything, boys," Tommy replied. "It was nice of that Navy Corsair to escort her back, though. Let's stay on station...and maybe do some good for these ROKs."

Roth said, "And if something else goes wrong with *Blondie* and she has to ditch, at least that Navy guy can guide the *Dumbo* bird to the spot so those guys get picked up ASAP. Did you ever have to go in the drink, sir?"

"I thought I'd have to a couple of times...but I always managed to make it home."

"Where'd they happen?"

"The first time was way back in Forty-Three. My jug outfit was coming back from a *rhubarb* over the Low Countries—"

"Rhubarb...that's what you called a mission that looked for targets of opportunity on the ground?"

"Exactly right, Hank. The visibility was lousy and I got separated from my flight. I was still pretty green, just a *second louie* with low hours..."

"Like me."

"Yeah, just like you. Anyway, coming back across the Channel, my gyro started acting up. I got all turned around for a little bit. While I was preoccupied trying to sort out my heading on the wet compass, I forgot to switch tanks and the engine quit when I was only a couple of thousand feet up. I swear I was skimming the waves before I got her started again. And, of course, I had no idea where I was."

Trying not to sound too flippant, Roth said, "That's because you didn't have a navigator in those P-47s to keep you straight, sir."

"Yeah, I could've used you, that's for sure. But luckily, England's pretty big, and I managed not to miss it. Had to *scud run* like crazy to find an airfield, though."

"What about the other time?"

"My ship got beat to hell over the North Sea. This *E-boat* I was strafing blew up in my face. There was so much crap in the air...it was worse than any flak I'd ever been in."

"What year was that, sir?"

"Forty-Five, a little while after VE Day. Our friends the Russians were driving those German boats, looking to stir up some mayhem at the Kiel Canal...but that's a real long story we'd better save for the bar." Then he asked Allen, the gunner, "What about you, Sarge? You went for a swim once, didn't you?"

"Affirmative, but that's another real long story."

"All right, we'll save it all for another time," Tommy said. "How're we doing on gas?"

Roth spun his *whiz wheel* and replied, "We've got another twenty-three minutes of loiter time. If they want our help today, the ROKs better hurry up and ask for it."

"We may never get that call," Tommy said. "You remember what they said in the briefing...those units in the eastern third of North Korea haven't taken the same beating the rest of the UN forces have. They're only withdrawing to keep our line of defense straight and continuous so nobody gets flanked."

No sooner had he said that, an American ASO was on the air with a mission for them. When he got to the target description, they turned to each other, dumbstruck. "Tanks? I thought the chinks didn't have tanks," Tommy said. "And I thought we saw the last of the North Korean armor, too."

"Maybe not," Roth replied. "How should we attack them?"

"We'll douse them with napalm first. Whatever's still moving, we'll hit with rockets. Just confirm that the ROKs don't have any tanks supporting them. All armor looks alike from up here."

The ASO confirmed there were no friendly tanks in the area. He added that the T-34s—most likely North Korean vehicles—were attacking in line formation.

"Outstanding," Tommy told Roth. "Give me a vector to an IP two miles north of the target. We'll pass through that IP on a westerly heading, then do a one-eighty to the left and come across the tanks laterally for maximum coverage. They should present us with a fairly straight line."

"Roger," Roth replied. "What altitude do you want over the IP?"

"Eight hundred."

"No problem. It's flat as a board along the coast. Fly heading three-one-two. We're two minutes out from the IP."

As they bore down on the target area, Roth could feel his stomach tightening to a knot. Try as he may, he couldn't hide his uneasiness, either. Picking up on it, Tommy asked, "You okay, Hank? You're not going to puke on me, are you?"

Now the young lieutenant was mortified. This

wasn't their first mission together, and he'd never exhibited a case of the jitters before. In vivid contrast, Major Moon looked as relaxed at the controls as if he was on a Sunday drive:

The major's done this a lot. It doesn't faze him much.

He could think of only one explanation for his nervousness: *It must be the tanks. Maybe there's something extra scary about a big rolling bunker with all that firepower...and we're taking them on in this flimsy thing whose skin you can push a screwdriver through by hand.*

When he conveyed that explanation to Tommy, he got this reply: "Think of them as snakes, Hank. They're more scared of us than we are of them. A lot of the Kraut tankers used to abandon their panzers and run like hell as soon as we showed up. Since they couldn't really fight off aircraft very well, they figured they were safer on foot than inside those rolling deathtraps."

Roth asked, "But isn't your brother a tanker? How does he feel about *those rolling deathtraps?*"

"He loves them. Of course, my brother's a lunatic...but he's a *good* lunatic. You want him on your side when there's a fight on."

Pushing the ship lower as they reached the IP—the *initial point* of the attack run—Tommy began a tight left turn, standing her on a wingtip as she reversed direction. Halfway through that turn, they could see the cloud of snow and dirt being thrown into the air behind the T-34s. Rolling level with the turn complete, the six tanks came into view dead ahead. Their line wasn't perfectly straight, but Tommy figured he could spread the *liquid fire*—the napalm—across at least half of them.

"Open bomb bay doors," he told Roth.

He put the bombsight's pip on the tank that was second closest to his aircraft. Then he watched as the distance closed quickly and the sight's indices converged on the target vehicle's image. When they touched it, he pressed *release*.

And then they were climbing away, their load of napalm canisters hurtling down on the North Korean armor. They were passing through a thousand feet when Allen reported, "Excellent spread, sir. We've got four of them covered in flames."

Tommy asked, "Can you tell what the other two are doing?"

"At the moment, they're stopped dead, just like the burning ones."

"Good," Tommy said. "They're easier to hit with rockets when they're not moving."

Roth asked, "Are we going to attack from the rear?"

"Yep."

"Did you ever use fifty cal against a tank, sir?"

"Yeah, Hank, I have. And my advice on that is don't waste your time and ammo, unless you're only interested in shooting the baggage off their decks or busting some antennas."

"So all those stories about bouncing bullets under the tanks so they go through the soft belly skin aren't true?"

"Affirmative. They're total bullshit. That only works in the movies."

As he brought the ship around for the rocket attack, Tommy said, "Tell me when we've got fuel remaining for five minutes on station, Hank."

Now aligned with the targets, he said, "Dammit,

they're turning. It's going to be a deflection shot."

Roth asked, "Can we shoot at both on one pass?"

"We could...but we'll probably miss both of them. I'm going to take the trailing one first." He asked Allen, "Hey, Sarge...are we taking any fire?"

"Can't see any tracers, sir. And I don't hear anything hitting us back here, either."

"Keep your eyes peeled, Bob. We're going down on the deck."

He got no argument from Roth or Allen; they both knew it was much harder for gunners on the ground to track and hit a fast-moving aircraft flying at low altitude. Any rounds coming up at them would be random and poorly aimed. A hit would be by pure chance...

But to say it wasn't possible would be kidding yourself.

Moon's Menace VI was a thousand yards out, with Tommy's finger resting lightly on the firing button for the rockets.

Get just a little closer...

But before he could press that button, the T-34 in his gunsight blew up...

And he had no choice but to fly right through the explosion's debris-laden cloud.

Tommy braced himself; just like that jug in the North Sea story he'd told just a few minutes ago, this plane had just as good a chance of being taken down by all the junk suddenly in the air.

He gripped the control wheel for dear life.

In an instant of obscuring darkness, she passed through the forbidding cloud...

And emerged, still flying. Tommy had heard or felt no impacts. There were no vibrations signaling an airframe suddenly in distress. Her engines still hummed like clockwork. The only change was the stench of burning diesel, incinerated flesh, and cooked-off ammunition that permeated the cockpit, the horrific aroma of an armored vehicle on fire.

"Give me a damage report," he told his crew.

"All okay on the aft fuselage and tail," Allen said.

"All good on the right wing," Roth added.

Tommy would have to survey the left wing himself; he was the only one who had the field of vision to see it. It, too, looked okay.

Damn, we got lucky.

"But what the hell just happened, sir?" Roth asked. "We didn't even shoot that tank."

"The ROKs did. They hit it with something…a rocket, an anti-tank gun…who knows? But the one thing I do know is they're putting us in jeopardy, shooting like that when we're in the target area. It's not like they can't see us. They just don't have any fire discipline."

He guided the ship out of the target area, saying, "Tell the ASO that we're done here. I'm not getting taken down by friendly fire if I can help it. Watch the fuel gauges real close, Hank." Then he asked Allen, "Bob, are we trailing a fuel stream?"

"Negative, sir. Not that I can tell."

Roth said, "But we've got self-sealing fuel tanks, sir. Doesn't that pretty much guarantee we won't lose gas, no matter what?"

"True, but we don't have self-sealing fuel *manifolds* to the engines. A little leak for a long time means we lose a lot of gas, Hank. Give us a course for home."

But Roth persisted, asking, "Shouldn't we hang around and see if the ASO can get the ROKs to knock it off and give us another chance? We've got a couple of minutes of loiter time left, and we could still divert to Taegu if we think we're losing fuel."

"Negative. Nobody's going to fix some ROK's itchy trigger finger in just a couple of minutes. We're getting out of here. Just do what I'm asking, Hank."

*****

They'd flown five miles east when Tommy spotted a column of eight trucks moving south along a road paralleling the coast. *Moon's Menace VI* was still low enough to make out the white stars adorning the hoods of the vehicles.

"More GIs headed to the Parallel," he said, "from Seventh Division, probably." Then he turned his attention back to the instruments, especially the fuel gauges.

Roth kept his eyes on the column. Just before it would disappear from view behind the aircraft, he saw the attack on the American trucks begin.

"They're getting hit, sir," he told Tommy. "They're stopped dead on the road."

But there was no call for help on the air-ground frequency.

As Tommy turned the plane to keep the roadway in view, they could see enemy soldiers—maybe Chinese, maybe North Korean—swarming the column like ants, clambering onto the beds of vehicles, pulling the drivers from the cabs.

With the combatants mingled as they were, there was nothing Tommy and his crew could do to help the GIs. They would only kill them.

There must've been gunfire, but from this distance, the airmen had no sense of it. Men would run and then they'd fall, never to stand again. It made the mortal combat going on below them look like a game of cowboys and Indians.

It was all over so quickly. The enemy wreaked their havoc and then scattered into the woods, careful not to mass and become an easy target for the aircraft orbiting above. The trucks were ablaze, the plumes of gray and black smoke like thick brushstrokes trying to paint over a canvas filled with dead men.

Tommy asked his crew, "You boys see any place the bad guys might be using for an assembly area?"

Neither Roth nor Allen could give an answer. But they kept searching, hoping that somehow they could avenge the massacre they'd just witnessed.

But even if they could, it wouldn't matter anymore. Tommy said, "We just ran out of time. Fuel's gone critical."

Roth protested, "But it doesn't look like we're losing any gas, sir. Maybe we can squeeze a couple more—"

"No, Hank. It's time to go home. Can you pinpoint the location of that ambush?"

"Yeah, I've got it."

"Good. Report what we just saw on the air-ground *freq*. Maybe there are survivors they can rescue."

Allen's voice came over the interphone: "You really think anybody survived that mauling, sir?"

"Stranger things have happened, Bob."

On the flight back to Itazuke, the crew maintained a dejected silence, speaking only when operationally necessary. Even then, they used as few words as possible.

Only once, when Tommy's finger had lingered on the push-to-talk switch after a brief exchange over the interphone, did they hear him mutter, *"What a fucking waste..."*

Chapter Fourteen

Twenty-Sixth Regiment's sector of the MLR was on the northern outskirts of Seoul, centered on a small civil airport they called Northeast Airfield. It had been heavily damaged in the fighting last September, when US Marines took the city back from its North Korean occupiers. Due to the poor condition of its runway, the US Air Force had little use for it. Jock Miles didn't have much use for the airfield, either: "It makes it too easy for the brass in their helicopters to drop in whenever they feel like it," he told his staff.

On the morning of 23 December, another frigid day that threatened a snowstorm before nightfall, General Walton "Johnnie" Walker, the 8th Army commander, used Northeast Airfield—and Jock's CP—for a meeting of his senior commanders. The gathering was marred by tragedy before it even began.

A helicopter bearing Brigadier General Ellis, 24th Division's assistant commander, crashed just outside the airfield's boundary, falling into an infantry company's defensive position. Two of Jock's GIs on the ground had been killed and six injured.

The helicopter's three crewmen escaped with only minor injuries. But their passenger, General Ellis, suffered head trauma and died instantly.

Before details of the crash had reached the CP, General Bishop was already telling Jock, "If that aircraft was shot down over your area, I'll see to it that you're court-martialed for dereliction of duty, Miles. Whether it was your own men or the chinks who did it won't matter.

It's on your turf. You're responsible, one way or the other."

Bishop didn't realize General Walker had just arrived from the crash site and was standing behind him, able to hear every word.

Softly, Walker said, "I need a word in private with you, General."

Then he led Bishop outside the CP tent.

"You're making an ass of yourself, Ted," Walker told him. "That helicopter went down for mechanical reasons. I spoke with the pilot myself. He lost power and couldn't keep the damn thing in the air. It's a cryin' shame what happened to Ellis. He was a good man. But before you go threatening other good men, you'd better get your facts straight first."

He left a stunned Bishop just standing there with his mouth wide open. Then he walked back into the tent and convened the meeting.

After a brief eulogy for the late General Ellis, Walker said, "I need to fill you in on the facts coming out of Tokyo and Washington. You'll need the straight scoop to stamp out the rumors that will be running wild throughout Eighth Army any day now. Yes, I'm afraid it's true that General MacArthur has *publicly* stated he wants to bomb Red China, preferably with nuclear weapons. He's also put forth a plan to *invade* Red China using Chiang Kai Shek's Nationalist Army."

He let the surprised murmurs die down before continuing.

"Now, even though there are some politicians in Washington who think that sounds like the greatest thing since sliced bread, I can assure you Mister Truman will allow none of it to happen. Never forget, gentlemen, that our nation is involved in *two* wars at the moment, one being here in Korea, the other in Europe against the Russians. The only difference is that we and the Russians are not expending any ammunition at each other *at the moment.*"

Standing at the back of the tent, Sean Moon couldn't hide his amused look as he thought, *I'm sure glad the general specified "at the moment." I guess he knows full well there've been a bunch of "other" moments.*

Walker added, "The president is well aware that any provocative escalations here in Korea could have catastrophic repercussions in Europe, where the Allies are outnumbered by Soviet forces five or more to one. Therefore, gentlemen, it's important for you and the men under your command to understand that they, and they alone, will be holding the line against the Chinese in Korea. The path home will not be lit by Nationalist Chinese lanterns or glowing mushroom clouds. Do I make myself clear?"

Their silence was all the acknowledgment he needed.

As the meeting moved on to tactical and logistical matters, Patchett whispered to Sean, "Ain't MacArthur not supposed to be saying things like that out loud? Sounds like he's skating on pretty thin ice."

"I got a hunch the guy's running for president, Patch."

"You gonna vote for him, Bubba?"

"Fuck no."

"Me neither."

Walker's G4—the bird colonel who was 8th Army's supply and logistics chief—had the floor now. He had the unfortunate job of telling the commanders that Christmas dinner would be nothing special. "If you're expecting another feast like we put on for Thanksgiving, you can forget it. It's just not logistically possible right now, I'm afraid."

Patchett's expression turned more sour than usual. He resisted the urge to spit on the dirt floor. Fighting a similar reaction, Sean said, a little too loudly, "I guess *the man in Tokyo* is only a sport with the holiday food when he thinks he's winning. Now that the chinks called his bluff, the rest of us can suck on C rations. But who knows? Maybe they'll come with a candy cane stenciled on the fucking box."

"Betcha MacArthur's gonna eat pretty damn good on Christmas Day, though," Patchett added.

*****

Another tragedy would mar the day, as well. Driving back to his Seoul headquarters, General Walker's jeep would be accidentally struck by a ROK vehicle that had swerved from its lane. Thrown from the jeep by the force of impact, Walker was mortally injured. He would die a few hours later.

*****

Master Sergeant Warren Orr was pretty sure he was wasting his time. An investigator with 6th Army CID, he'd made the long trip from San Francisco to Seattle to interview a man being held at that city's jail. The prisoner was charged with a local armed robbery and was reported to be an AWOL soldier from Fort Ord, a buck sergeant who'd vanished from that post two months ago. The name on the arrest report was *Willis, Steven M.*

The only damn reason I'm even up here is because this shitbird's spinning some fantastic story about being hired by a general's wife to rough up some colonel's wife. That story caught the eye of General Molloy, the Sixth Army IG, who thinks this Willis character has got something to do with a case that's got his balls in an uproar. The general considers the timing of this guy's AWOL as concurrent, suspicious, and potentially implicating in the assault on that colonel's wife.

My guess is this clown Willis thinks he can leverage that bullshit story into the Army smoothing over this armed robbery charge the Seattle PD has on him...and maybe putting a big dent in any time in the stockade he's going to do for being AWOL.

In other words, he's just another scumbag who thinks he's got the goods to get himself off the hook.

Orr displayed his credentials at the jail's front desk. Several jailers—a lieutenant, a sergeant, and a man with no stripes at all—studied the documents and then gave him a thorough once-over.

"How come you're not in uniform?" the lieutenant asked.

"CID doesn't wear uniforms when working cases off post. It's SOP."

"How do I know you're from the Army? You could be anybody with phony credentials, Mr. Orr."

"It's *Master Sergeant* Orr...and I'm not *anybody.* I'm the man on that ID. Now, are you going to let me do my job? Or do I have to get a federal court order? Because I can lay one on you inside of an hour."

"It's the Friday before Christmas, *Sergeant* Orr. I don't think anybody's going to be in a hurry to give you a court order."

With cold confidence, Orr replied, "You want to test that presumption?"

The lieutenant took the credentials to another desk and made a hushed phone call. Just watching the body language, Orr could tell the man was being scolded by the person on the other end of the line. He hung up the receiver with a repentant, "Yes, sir. I understand."

"Take him inside," the lieutenant told the sergeant.

As they walked down the hallway to the interview room, the sergeant said to Orr, "Sorry for that, buddy...but we don't get you Army dicks around here too often."

Orr just nodded. He'd assume the use of *dicks* referred to his being a detective and nothing else.

Willis was already seated at the table when the CID man entered the room. "You can take the cuffs off him," he told the jailer. "We're just going to have a friendly little chat."

A look of disappointment spread across the prisoner's face as Orr introduced himself. "I thought they'd send a *JAG* lawyer for something as juicy as what I've got," Willis said.

"Whether or not you see a JAG lawyer anytime soon depends on whether I think your story's full of shit or not, son."

"What I'm gonna tell you is one hundred percent on the level, Sarge. But maybe we can talk about getting me out of this shithole before Christmas first?"

"Not likely you'll be going anywhere quite that fast, sport, even if you've got a story that solves every mystery in the universe."

"Maybe not *every* mystery, but I've got enough to get a crooked general and his wife in Dutch."

Willis launched into a tale about the night he and another soldier—a buck sergeant named Riddle—were sent to the home of a Colonel Miles, who was in Korea, with instructions to *deliver a message* to his wife.

Orr knew who Riddle was. The man was languishing in the Monterey County Jail down in California, awaiting trial on a variety of civil charges stemming from the attempted home invasion at the Miles house. To date, he'd said nothing about the motivation behind the crime. At every court appearance, however, he'd whined about how Jillian Miles should be the one in jail, "Because it was *her* that shot *me*, not the other way around."

"You said you were *sent*," Orr said to Willis. "Who sent you?"

"The post commander's wife, Mrs. Whitelaw."

"Seems kind of unlikely a yardbird like you would make the acquaintance of a general's wife."

Willis then related how Mrs. Whitelaw had been quietly searching for a few *handymen* to do some *miscellaneous* tasks, men who *weren't afraid to get their hands dirty*. Only one company commander on post suspected she was talking about something other than household chores. Eager to curry the general's favor and not caring what he had to do to gain it, he figured Riddle and Willis, two of his men with checkered records and a loose grasp on propriety, were just the *handymen* she was looking for.

Orr asked, "Did you ever actually meet Mrs. Whitelaw?"

"Just once. Me and Riddle were invited to her house, like for a job interview. Apparently, she'd seen a whole bunch of *goody two shoes* deadbeats before us, and she rejected them all."

"The interview...is that when she told you to go rough up Mrs. Miles?"

"No, she didn't tell us nothing specific at the time. She just slipped me a key to a safety deposit box at a Wells Fargo bank in Monterey. Just me, not Riddle. He didn't get one. Said we'd be told when to check the box for instructions."

"Who told you when to look in the box?"

"No idea. One morning, a note got slipped under the door of my barracks room."

"When did you go to the bank?"

"That very morning. Thought I'd get gigged for going missing for a couple hours, but when I got back, nobody said shit to me."

"What was in the box, Willis?"

"A map to this Colonel Miles' place—it's some spread, let me tell you—with written instructions what we were supposed to do and when. There was also a set of keys for the vehicle we were to use for the job, since neither of us had POV."

Orr looked up from his notebook and asked, "For the record, you mean *privately owned vehicle*, correct?"

"Yep."

"Do you know why Mrs. Whitelaw would want to terrorize Mrs. Miles?"

"No. All I know is we were told to give her a message: *Quit the real estate business.* Whatever the hell that's supposed to mean."

"Were you paid for this job in advance?"

"No. The money—five hundred bucks apiece—was supposed to be in that same safe deposit box within twenty-four hours of the job being done."

"But the job never did *get done*, did it?"

Willis shook his head. Then he said, "That Miles dame...she could shoot like nobody's business. I'm lucky to be alive. I read in the papers that she nailed Riddle, though. Is he dead?"

Orr remained poker-faced and didn't answer.

"You ain't gonna tell me, are you?"

Look at him, Orr told himself as he watched Willis squirm. *He doesn't even know if his partner is dead or alive. And he doesn't know what a live Riddle might've told investigators, either, which is exactly nothing.*

"I've got one more question, Willis. Can you prove any of this?"

"Yep."

"How?"

"I've got that map, the keys to that car—I grabbed them when I started running after that crazy woman blew the shit out of it with some elephant gun—and the key to that safe deposit box."

"Where's the stuff now?"

"I left it at my sister's in Portland when I was on the lam. She ain't gonna get in any trouble, is she?"

"Not if she hands the stuff over without a fuss," Orr said. "Let's have her address." He wrote down the reply and got up to leave.

Willis called after him, "Hey, Sarge...you *are* gonna get me outta here, aren't you?"

"Have a Merry Christmas," Orr replied.

*****

A thousand-foot-tall mountain sat on the boundary between 26th Regiment and 17th Regiment to its east. It was the perfect place for an OP that would provide both units with excellent fields of vision to the north. The only problem was getting to its peak and the unobstructed visibility it offered. Steep-faced at the top and without switchback trails, no vehicles had, so far, found a way to climb it. A helicopter had tried to place an observation team on the peak, but treacherous winds had prevented a safe landing on the narrow summit.

"We already lost one whirlybird today," the pilot had radioed as he aborted the attempt, referring to the crash that had taken General Ellis' life. "I'm not looking to make it two."

"I got an idea how we can do it, sir," Sean told Jock. "Give me a three-quarter-ton radio truck with a winch on the front bumper and I'll get her up that mountain. There's just a couple of spots where she'd need a little help. That's when we use the winch. There are plenty of trees up there we can use as anchor points."

As Jock thought about it, Patchett said, "That's all well and good, Bubba. But how're you gonna get her down when you have to?"

"You ever heard the expression *disassembly is the reverse of assembly*, Top?"

"Of course I've heard it, but it's the other way around, Bubba. Any swinging dick who ever got shown how to tear down a weapon knows it."

"Well, the same applies here, Top. We come down the reverse of how we got up—using the winch to lower the truck."

Jock had made his decision. "As far as I'm concerned, if we can get a team of observers up there right now with long-range radios, I don't care if we leave the truck up there indefinitely." Then he told Sean, "But don't make a major project out of it. Especially one that might get somebody accidentally killed. If it doesn't work out on the first try, forget it. We'll wait for the wind to die down and let the helicopters do it."

"I understand, sir. But one thing...let me pick the driver. I can put a guy behind the wheel with a set of balls big enough that he won't shit his pants halfway up."

"Approved," Jock replied. "Do whatever you have to."

*****

The driver Sean had in mind was a corporal in the tank battalion maintenance section named Jacob Barefoot, the only man in the regiment taller and burlier than he was. When told he'd been tapped for the job, Barefoot just shrugged and replied, "Sure, Sarge. Why not? But do I have to stay up there? I don't know anything about calling for fire, and I can't fix any tanks up on that mountain."

"No, Jake...all you gotta do is drive a three-quarter-ton with a big radio to the peak. Then you come back down with me."

To Barefoot, it sounded like an adventure, a brief but interesting change of pace. "Great. When do we leave?"

"How about in ten minutes?"

*****

Gathering the forward observation team, Sean briefed them on his plan to scale the mountain. "We'll go up the south slope. It ain't quite as steep...only the top hundred feet or so. That's where we'll use the winching gear on the radio truck to pull it to the peak."

Five sets of wary eyes from the FO team stared at the mountain as he spoke.

"Another reason for going up the south face is there ain't much snow on that side, not like the other slopes," he continued, "and we won't have no line-of-sight problems with the radios talking to Regiment, either. If for some reason we can't get it all the way to the top, we'll just anchor the truck with the winch line as high as she'll go and use a landline relay from the peak. I see you guys already packed the wire reels and phones, so we're all set on that score. But we only do that as a last resort. It'll be much better if the truck's right up there with you, especially if you gotta start fiddling with the radios."

A Negro lieutenant from Baker Battery named Edgar Thackery, the lead FO and ranking man technically in charge of this operation, asked, "Are you sure we can get that radio truck to the peak, Sergeant? Have you ever done something like this before?"

Sean replied, "Let me tell you something, Lieutenant. I spent the closing days of the last war in the fucking Alps. You better believe we had to winch vehicles—and bigger ones than a stinking little three-quarter-ton—up all kinds of mountains. It ain't no big thing. You just gotta know how."

After a final check of their gear, they were ready to

go. Sean led in a jeep with Lieutenant Thackery in the passenger's seat. Behind them followed Jacob Barefoot at the wheel of the radio truck, with a four-stripe sergeant from 17th Regiment up front and three RTOs in the back with the radios. The climb up the south slope was exactly as Sean predicted; in four-wheel drive, the vehicles clambered up the steep slope along dangerously narrow ridgelines that led to that final, undriveable incline. Once they reached it, they parked the jeep and got down to the serious business of winching the truck the last hundred feet uphill.

"Let's get this right the first time," Sean said. "We're gonna use that biggest tree *waaaay* up at the top for an anchor point."

Lieutenant Thackery shook his head. "That won't work, Sergeant. There can't be enough cable in that winch to reach it."

"Sure there is, Lieutenant. Just watch."

It took almost fifteen minutes, but in that time, Sean played out the winch cable, fastened a pulley block to the tree with a woven strap used to lift heavy tank components, and still had just enough cable to reach back to the truck and be hooked to the shackle on her front bumper.

"There you go, Lieutenant," he said. "All hooked up. Now let's make the vehicle as light as possible—take all your baggage outta the back and lug it up the hill. Me and Jacob here will bring the truck up to you."

As they unloaded the gear from the truck, the sergeant from 17th Regiment, a Carolinian named Combs, told Sean in hushed tones, "It ain't bad enough we got ourselves a nigger leading this goat-rope, but we brung that big dumb Indian along, too. This Army's going to hell in a handbasket, Sarge."

"I ain't got time to read you the riot act right now, Combs, but just in case you're confused, a guy with a shiny bar on his collar gets to be top dog, period. And as far as *that big dumb Indian*, didn't they ever tell you peckerwoods that Indians ain't dumb…and they ain't afraid of heights, neither?"

The mention of heights made Combs turn to look down the mountain. Immediately, he had to grip the truck's fender to steady himself; shivers of fear went through him far greater than any the cold might've been causing. From this dicey vantage point, he felt sure he was looking down into the yawning mouth of death.

Then Combs pivoted to look at Barefoot, who was casually urinating while precariously balanced on his feet against the howling wind on the icy, forty-degree slope.

"That's what I'm talking about," Sean said. "That Indian's got balls, and that's why I want him behind the wheel, not some chickenshit who'll get all panicky and fuck up the whole show. Now get your ass up that hill, Sergeant."

The winching operation didn't run into trouble until the truck was halfway up that final incline. Tight as a bowstring while scraping along the ground, the cable had picked up a tree branch and fed it into the pulley block, causing a jam before Sean could prevent it.

"HOLD IT, HOLD IT," Sean called to Barefoot behind the wheel.

He tried to free the branch with his bayonet, but the cold blade just splintered the dead wood, leaving the fragment jamming the pulley firmly in place.

"I'M GONNA HAVE TO BACK OFF THE

WINCH JUST A LITTLE AND GET SOME SLACK,"
Sean said as he hurried back to the truck, hanging onto
the taut cable to keep from falling. "GIMME YOUR
STEEL POT, JAKE."
　With Barefoot's helmet and his own, Sean chocked
the truck, one helmet wedged behind each rear wheel.
Then he said, "Now Jake, I need you to stand on those
fucking brakes with your right foot like your life
depended on it, because it kinda does. Pull the throttle
lock out all the way when I tell you so she'll rev up
enough to power the wheels and the winch without your
foot on the gas. Then you can ride the clutch with your
left foot if she starts to go backward, because you only
got two feet, right?"
　"No problem, Sarge. I've got it." Barefoot didn't
seem at all concerned that he and an untethered truck
were about to confirm the laws of gravity while poised
above a thousand-foot drop.
　Sean said, "Okay, I'm gonna go to the front bumper,
disengage the winch, and put some slack in the cable.
Stand by to kick up the throttle."
　In one quick motion, Sean pushed the lever that
disengaged the winch and then gave Jacob a *rev it up*
hand signal, whirling a finger above his head.
　The winch disengaged; the cable suddenly fell slack
as if it had been severed.
　The truck slid slowly backward just a few inches. It
hit the chocks—the GI helmets—and began to force
them down, each becoming less and less of an obstacle
as they cracked their way through frozen turf. With the
winch disengaged, the cable offered no resistance to the
downhill slide. It remained slack, playing out a few
inches at a time to accommodate the truck's rearward

motion.

Sean could hear nothing but the wail of the engine at high rev. He couldn't hear Combs screaming as he tumbled head over heels down the steep slope, having lost his balance hurrying back to the truck. He bounced off Sean before they could grab hold of each other, spun off him like a top, and continued his plummet along the left side of the truck...

Until Jacob Barefoot stopped him by holding open the door with his left foot. Slamming into that door slowed Combs long enough for the strapping Indian to reach down and grab him by his web gear.

All four wheels of the truck were spinning rapidly, tractionless against the frozen ground, the rear ones bouncing against the helmets. With each bounce, those wheels came closer and closer to skimming right over those chocks.

Sean had worked his way back to Combs at the driver's door. For a moment, he wondered just how many feet Jacob Barefoot actually had: *One foot on the brake, one on the clutch, one out the door stopping this idiot from falling to his death...*

The truck was now bouncing up and down against the chocks with a ferocity guaranteed to send them all hurtling off the mountain in a second or two.

Then it all stopped. The screaming of the engine calmed to a high idle; the wheels stopped spinning. Jacob had pushed in the throttle lock. The truck was no longer trying to bounce over the chocks. She was clinging to the mountainside on her own.

There'd been no need for Barefoot to keep his left foot on the clutch. Once it was engaged, he'd been free to use that foot to break Combs' fall.

"There's a bunch of chinks coming up the north face on foot," Combs said, his trembling voice an octave higher than usual. "We gotta call in a fire mission on them, right fucking now!"

Sean pointed to the back of the truck. "There's the radio. Get to it."

When Combs had trouble climbing over the tailgate of the steeply inclined truck, Sean gave him an *assist*: a boot against his backside. But as he clung to the radio rack, Combs got the fire mission call through to Baker Battery.

Sean checked his watch: *Let's see how long it takes 'em to get the rounds where we need 'em this time.*

Forty-six seconds later, the first adjustment round crashed into the north face of the mountain.

Now we're talking, Sean told himself.

An RTO on the peak shouted down the correction, capping it with *fire for effect.* Barefoot relayed it to Combs.

Sean told them, "Okay, you guys got this. I'm gonna go free that pulley."

Now that the tension was off the cable, it took no time at all to fix the jam. The truck winched herself to the peak while the fire mission was still in progress.

Lieutenant Thackery told Sean, "It looks like the chinks have the same idea we do—use this mountaintop for an OP. We stopped them for now, at least."

"It's a good thing, too, Lieutenant, because they could see plenty of both regiments' positions from up here. Could you tell if they had radios with 'em?"

"They were lugging something heavy, that's for sure. It probably was a radio."

"Shit," Sean replied. "They coulda been putting fire

on our guys in a coupla minutes. Their main force—and their artillery—must be a lot closer than we think."

He repeated, "Shit."

*****

There had been rumors prior to his accidental death that General Walker was soon to be sacked from his job as 8th Army commander. His sudden passing hastened the selection of a replacement.

In a suburb of Washington, D.C., the phone rang at the home of Lieutenant General Matthew Ridgway. A celebrated commander of airborne forces in the last war, Ridgway would board a USAF transport in just a few hours. Staffed for a long journey with two complete flight crews, that plane would fly through the night, into the next day and the night after, stopping for fuel three times as it crossed the Pacific and the International Date Line. It arrived in Tokyo late on Christmas Day 1950.

Matt Ridgway was unaware that somewhere in the darkness over that ocean, his plane had crossed paths with the one carrying home the body of Walton "Johnnie" Walker, the man he was about to replace as 8th Army commander.

Chapter Fifteen

Christmas in Korea came and went like any other day. The cooks tried to make it seem festive, somehow; mess officers bartered in Seoul, trading cigarettes for sorghum to supplement the wheat flour ration, hoping to have enough fixings to bake holiday cakes without cutting down on the amount of bread their field kitchens needed to produce. But without enough eggs or cornstarch to properly bind the sorghum, everything they baked with it came out dry and crumbly.

A slice of fresh-baked cake fell apart in Patchett's hands as he tried to spread jam on it. Tossing the remains to a scavenging dog lurking near the mess area, he said, "I coulda closed my eyes and pretended it was holiday sweet cake like my mama used to make. But it might as well be dog food now."

Jock wasn't paying attention to him. His face was buried in a letter he'd received from Jillian. The message it contained was a Christmas present, of sorts.

"The deportation decision has been postponed until after the New Year," he told Patchett. "She and the kids are still in Monterey."

"Well, the minute you saw that US postmark and not some Australian one, you knew it had to be good news," Patchett said. "Ol' Dick Molloy must be working overtime straightening that mess out for y'all."

"Yeah. But it doesn't sound like we're out of the woods yet, Top. Not by a long shot. I wish to hell I knew what was really going on. Maybe I could do something to help."

But they both knew the painful truth: whatever was going on half a world away was totally out of his hands.

Jock stuffed the letter into his pocket, intent on returning his focus back to fighting the Chinese. "It's disappointing the Air Force hasn't found that artillery that's trying to plaster us every night," he said. "I can't believe our target acquisition people haven't nailed down their location yet, either."

"I bet them chink guns are moving around a lot, sir. I'm thinking maybe there are two batteries. One fires while the other moves. That's why we're having so much trouble finding 'em."

Jock had to concede the point. Like all of his top sergeant's tactical assessments, it seemed like a good possibility.

Patchett continued, "It's a good thing we hold that mountaintop over yonder and not the chinks. They ain't got no FO up close, that's for damn sure. They're throwing out a lot of rounds and counting on luck to hit something, but they ain't doing much damage to us at all."

"Still, we need to find them and finish them, Top. I want to start patrolling farther to the north. Throwing seventy-six millimeter at us like they are, they can't be more than ten miles away. The squad patrols we've been sending only a mile or two out haven't run into one damn chink, day or night."

"So this long-range patrol you're thinking of…how big do you want it to be?"

"Platoon-sized."

Patchett wasn't crazy about the idea. "A platoon's too big to be quiet and too small to fight their way out if they get into serious trouble, sir," he said.

"So what do you suggest, Top?"

"Recon by fire, sir. In daylight. A small FO team walks the fire in front of them into likely areas for a battery to be hiding out. They'll know for damn sure when that fire scores a hit, something we can't always tell from way back here."

He knew he'd made his point with Jock. He watched as the wheels turned inside the colonel's head, formulating a plan, weighing the pros and cons.

"Why in daylight, Top?"

"Because nobody's gonna walk that far out at night, sir. When you can't see nothing, your brain gets spooked and lies to you, making you believe you've gone a lot farther than you have. It's just natural. In daylight, a man can't kid himself so easy. But you know that as well as I do."

"I can't argue with you there," Jock said. "But it's going to take someone with a set of balls to lead it. Who do we trust to run a patrol like that?"

"I can only think of two sons of bitches I'd trust to do it, sir: me...or Captain Pop."

"Then that makes my decision real easy, Top, because it's not going to be you. I'll give it to Theo."

The quickness of the decision shook Patchett just a little; he hadn't expected to be passed over for the job so effortlessly. But he knew there was a long list of reasons why he shouldn't be the one to go, starting with *It ain't my damn job.*

Still, he asked, "Any special reason, sir?"

"Just that I need you here, Top. Every man in this regiment—starting with me—depends on you to keep the *big picture* straight. Theo is more than capable of handling the recon mission. And from what Major

Harper tells me, he's made a big hit with his men. They're ready to follow him to hell and back."

Patchett replied, "You didn't expect no different, did you, sir?"

*****

After his arrival late on Christmas night, General Ridgway spent three days in Tokyo with MacArthur and his staff, absorbing their version of the situation facing 8th Army in Korea. He didn't see eye to eye with them on most issues:

These people confuse fantasy with strategy.

One thing on which he did agree with them: the tendency of many 8th Army units to immediately retreat when threatened even slightly, only to turn around and gain back the ground they'd surrendered, had to be curbed. MacArthur referred to it as *accordion war.*

Matt Ridgway kept this reply to himself:

You built that accordion, General MacArthur.

But I don't know how to play it…

And I'll do my damnedest not to learn.

Looking at the positioning of the Seoul-Han River MLR, Ridgway formulated the first strategic imperative for his new command: the MLR was in the wrong place.

"It needs to be south of the city—let's say about thirty miles south," he told MacArthur's operations chief, the G3. "We shouldn't be trying to defend Seoul. That's an urban brawl in which we'll be unable to bring our superior airpower and artillery to bear. I won't sacrifice my men in pointless house-to-house fighting."

"It won't come down to that, sir," the G3 replied. "The Chinese have exhausted themselves and their feeble supply lines. They haven't been able to mount a serious attack for a week."

There they go again…confusing fantasy with strategy, Ridgway told himself.

Then he asked, "Has it occurred to anyone here in Tokyo that the CCF may be simply regrouping? Sure, they may be exhausted. But they'll rest…and then come at my boys again."

They offered no reply. He watched their doubting faces, thinking, *It's not that they don't believe it. It's that they don't want to believe it.*

The G3 protested, "But holding Seoul has enormous symbolic meaning in this conflict."

"To hell with *symbolic meaning,*" Ridgway replied. "I prefer a sound plan of battle instead."

MacArthur ended the discussion by saying, "The Eighth Army is yours now, Matt. Do with it as you wish."

Then MacArthur left the room. Ridgway would never see him again.

*****

General Dick Molloy would've preferred his meeting with General Jarvis Whitelaw, the Fort Ord post commander, to be at one of their offices, preferably his own. But Whitelaw had asked it be held at his quarters on Fort Ord. Preparations were underway for a big New Year's Eve bash at that house. "*Somebody* has to be here to accept all the deliveries, Dick," Whitelaw had said over the phone. "You understand, of course."

What Molloy understood was that Mrs. Whitelaw wouldn't be at home for his visit. It was unusual for her to be absent on this particular day, considering that preparations for social functions invariably fell to an officer's wife.

Unusual...unless she's making a point of avoiding me, Molloy told himself as he pulled into the circular drive of the Whitelaw house, weaving the car through vans unloading party supplies. *Technically, it doesn't matter whether she's there or not. I can't question her, anyway, since my authority as inspector general pertains only to military matters and personnel. The general, on the other hand...I can pump him for all he knows. Or at least try.*

"Ah, come in, Dick," General Whitelaw said. "It's cold out there, isn't it?"

"This is Northern California, General. It's always cold."

Whitelaw cocked his head inquisitively and asked, "Aren't we on a first-name basis, Dick? We've certainly known each other long enough. And we both wear the same two stars."

"This isn't a social call, General."

"Well, then...if this is business, perhaps we should retire to my study." He sounded snippy as he added, "But I can't imagine what this is all about."

They settled into plush chairs in the small but well-appointed room. Whitelaw poured *two fingers* of Scotch into a glass and handed it to Molloy.

"No, thanks, General. I'm on the clock."

"Suit yourself, Richard," Whitelaw replied, keeping the Scotch for himself.

"Let's get right to it," Molloy said. "Are you aware the civil authorities in Seattle are holding the alleged *other man* in the attempted assault on Jillian Miles, Jock

Miles' wife?"

"Yes, I heard. Willis, I believe his name is?"

"That's correct, General. Willis, Steven M, Sergeant, US Army. AWOL from this post since 20 October of this year."

"I'm well aware of that, Richard." Whitelaw's annoyance was plain to see now.

"And are you aware that he's implicated your wife as the instigator of the assault?"

Whitelaw forced a laugh. "That's absolute nonsense. You're not telling me that Sixth Army IG is going to consider as gospel the word of some AWOL shitbird who's just trying to cover his own ass...and besmirch the good name of my wife in the process?"

"It's not just your wife's name, General. It's yours, too. Willis' accusation suggests a possible pattern of corruption on this post that could fall squarely into your bucket. No matter who's actually doing the dirty work, the responsibility would ultimately be yours."

"I don't need you to lecture me about responsibility, Richard." Then, with a smirk on his face, Whitelaw added, "So, should I expect the MPs to arrest me at any moment?"

"Negative, General. Consider my visit a courtesy. I'm simply here to advise you that the Monterey County District Attorney is going to be taking a long, hard look at your wife's business dealings, and you'll probably find yourself dragged through the mud in the process."

Whitelaw fell silent. Molloy knew what was on his mind: *He's got retirement coming up in a little over a year. Even if he doesn't get formally charged with anything, the taint of a criminal investigation could lead Washington to retire him at a lower grade than major general. Maybe all the way down to bird colonel.*

To a man used to wearing stars, that's as good as a dishonorable discharge.

Pouring himself another drink, Whitelaw said, "You do realize, Molloy, that the IG cannot investigate my wife?"

"I know that, General. But the civil authorities certainly can."

"Not likely. My wife's family—the Kerns clan—they're *old California money*. They trace their lineage all the way back to John C. Fremont. You know who he is, don't you?"

"Of course I do. I studied the same history you did."

"Good. Just know this: the Kernses and their ilk *think*—no, they *know*—that they own this state. No pissant jailbird, no matter how enticing his song, is ever going to change that."

He downed the rest of the glass.

"Now, unless you've got some actual Army business to discuss, you'll have to excuse me. I've got a celebration to organize."

As Molloy walked to his car, Whitelaw called after him: "Save yourself some trouble and get on the right side of this, Richard."

"I believe I already am, General."

"Bullshit. You're wasting your time. You'll never lay a glove on her."

Driving away, Molloy told himself, *I've got a nasty feeling he may be right.*

*****

Later that day, Dick Molloy met with Jillian Miles, her lawyer Mark Pitney, Master Sergeant Orr from CID, and Fred Peters, the district attorney for Monterey County, at Peters' office. The DA made it clear from the outset it would be a tough slog implicating Priscilla Kerns Whitelaw in the attempted assault at the Miles home.

"I want to thank Sergeant Orr for working through the Christmas holiday to gather evidence," Peters began. "I wish I could say we've processed that evidence into something useful in the very limited time allowed. Mrs. Miles' deportation judgment is supposed to come down on the third of January, I'm told?"

"That's correct," Jillian's lawyer said. "But we're not asking you for an indictment in the assault case by then. Just help us raise the possibility of a related concern—a criminal conspiracy to harm Mrs. Miles—so we can hopefully delay the judgment and buy more time for her defense before the immigration court. It's important to recognize the avarice toward Mrs. Miles by Mrs. Whitelaw and the company on whose board she sits, Guidon-Pacific. As you know, Mr. Peters, this avarice was the result of a real estate transaction in which an Australian firm—Forbes-Weipa Company, in which Mrs. Miles is a major shareholder—prevented Guidon-Pacific from continuing its predatory pricing of housing for military dependents around Fort Ord by buying property out from under it."

"You've made me well aware of the matter," DA Peters replied, "but since no laws of the State of California were broken in any aspect of that transaction, my office has no interest in it. My sole concern is successfully prosecuting the attempted assault on Mrs. Miles."

Pitney asked, "And seeing that Mrs. Miles is the prime witness in your case, you'd have no problem petitioning the Immigration Court to put the deportation proceedings on hold so she can testify?"

"No, of course not," Peters replied. "But I can make no guarantees what the Immigration Court will decide. And bear in mind this trial will last only a few days, at most."

Sergeant Orr asked the DA, "May we ask, sir, exactly what your office has done with the evidence I secured from Willis' sister in Portland?"

"Sure," Peters replied. "First, the words on the piece of paper containing the map to the Miles house, and the vague instructions what to do once on that property, are all typewritten, with no names listed. There's not a trace of handwriting or identifying quirks, like a damaged character on the machine. It could've come from anywhere or anybody. The document would never stand up as evidence in court. Any first-year law school student could easily demolish its credibility.

"Second, the car used in the assault. As you know, we determined the morning after the incident it was registered to a man in Salinas, who'd just sold it two days before to a used car dealer in Monterey. The car dealer hadn't yet transferred the registration or displayed the car for sale at the time of the assault. In fact, he claims he didn't even know the car had been stolen from his lot until the sheriff informed him. At the moment, we have no reason not to believe him. The only link between the car and the Whitelaws we've been able to uncover so far is this: the sister of the original owner was a secretary in General Whitelaw's office for a few months last year, not even close to the timeline for the crime we're investigating. She lives in Texas now. I'm not sending an investigator to Dallas—at great expense—to do a pointless interview."

"But Willis claims he didn't actually steal the car," Orr said. "The keys were passed to him through the safe deposit box."

The DA replied, "Can we prove that?"

When no one had a response, Peters continued, "Third, let's talk about that safe deposit box. The key does, in fact, open a box in the bank specified in Sergeant Willis' statement. Bank records indicate it's being rented to a Canadian national named John Arthur Mills, who supposedly resides in Vancouver, British Columbia. The phone number listed in the bank records is non-working at the moment. We've asked the Canadian authorities for their help in locating the man. They got back to us this morning with this information: there are over five thousand people on the Canadian tax rolls with that name. None of them reside at the address listed on the bank records, which is a commercial building in Vancouver. No one by that name has an office or is employed there."

Orr said, "The Whitelaws could've used a pseudonym and phony passport to rent the safety deposit box."

"That could very well be, Sergeant. But again I must ask, can you prove it?"

"Isn't that your job?"

"Only if I choose it to be," Peters replied.

Orr protested, "But Willis had the damn key..."

"Willis is a known thief. He could've stolen the key," the DA replied.

"That'd be kind of curious, wouldn't it?" the sergeant asked.

"Curious? Yes. Solid evidence against Mrs. Whitelaw? Not at present. Again, any first-year law student..."

They all settled into their chairs in frustrated silence. DA Peters finally broke it, saying, "For the foreseeable future, the only case I have is against Riddle for criminal acts against Mrs. Miles—trespassing, making terroristic threats, and assault with a deadly weapon. He's remained silent since his arrest, so his motives are still known only to him. Even though Willis claims to be Riddle's accomplice, I'm not sure I could present evidence to even get him indicted for that crime, let alone convicted. We only have his word, and he'll probably recant that confession of his the minute a public defender gets ahold of him."

He paused, steeling himself to deliver the summation. "So, to repeat...as far as implicating General or Mrs. Whitelaw in a conspiracy to harm Mrs. Miles, I have nothing that I'd feel confident taking into court. If I can't present solid evidence of a conspiracy, I'm afraid I can't help you there. I'm sorry, Mrs. Miles. Truly, I am."

Dick Molloy said, "Well, thank you for your time, Mr. Peters. If we could ask one favor, could we have some privacy for a few minutes?"

"Certainly, General. Use the room for as long as you need to." He closed the door behind him as he left.

"Well, what do you think?" Sergeant Orr asked. "Is the DA under the Whitelaw woman's thumb, too?"

Molloy had been asking himself that same question. Jarvis Whitelaw's blunt statement—that his wife's family was among the people who *owned* California— kept echoing in his head. He replied, "It's crossed my mind, Sergeant."

Pitney dismissed the notion with a shake of his head. "I don't buy it. I get the runaround from prosecutors all the time, and it doesn't look like this when it happens. The fact that he agreed to meet us on such short notice tells me he's on the level. And, unfortunately, I have to agree with his analysis of the evidence Willis provided. It's useless, at least for now."

Jillian asked, "So what's my next move? Or do I even have one?"

"Yes, you do, Mrs. Miles," Pitney replied. "Two moves, actually. We can still implicate Guidon-Pacific—the corporation run by Kenneth Kerns, Mrs. Whitelaw's brother—as the instigator of the deportation case. She sits on the board of that corporation. We have Kenneth Kerns himself on record saying it was his *patriotic duty* to report Mrs. Miles for the visa violation. Of course, all this happened immediately after your company—Forbes-Weipa—trounced Guidon in that real estate deal. That's very curious...and very vindictive."

Jillian said, "True, but the judge bloody well knows I initiated that real estate deal. How else would my company have known to get involved?"

"Also true," Pitney replied, "but it's your company that purchased the property, not you personally. Your name or signature doesn't appear on any of the contracts."

Jillian shook her head. "I didn't get the impression the judge cared a whit about the difference, Mark. To him, I violated the terms of my spousal visa, plain and simple, by conducting company business while in the United States."

"Ah, but I think he can be made to care. Our Judge Riggs is a hard case, but he's a little gun-shy at the moment. Some senators in Washington got in a lather about a case he was about to rule on last week. A Swedish steel tycoon looking to set up a business in the States entered the country on a six-month tourist visa, which would prevent him from conducting business or seeking employment. He wasn't here a week when he closed a deal purchasing some industrial properties."

Jillian asked, "How'd the authorities find out about the visa violation?"

"A competitor snitched on him."

"That doesn't sound any different from my case," she said.

"It's different because he actually signed contracts in California, a clear violation of his tourist visa."

"Why didn't he just get a business visa in the first place?" Jillian asked.

"Because the opportunity presented itself suddenly, and getting a business visa can be a long, slow process, with lots of red tape. Time was of the essence, as the saying goes, and a tourist visa could be obtained fairly quickly. He wasn't worried about the technicalities, because he knew he had friends in high places to smooth out any problems."

Molloy asked, "Friends in high places...you mean the senators?"

"Exactly. Some of their constituents were very interested in seeing that deal go through, apparently. Our Judge Riggs was all set to issue the deportation order...and then the senators began to make his life—and his supervising justice's life—miserable, suggesting they might be out of jobs if they didn't toe the line. I'm guessing he doesn't want to go through that again...and your case just might present that possibility."

"But I don't have any senator friends, Mark."

Dick Molloy smiled. "But I might, Jillian."

Chapter Sixteen

Theo Papadakis and Patchett had a bet: *Captain Pop's* money was on finding the Chinese artillery within one day of patrolling, returning the same day he departed. Patchett placed his wager on a two-day patrol.

"You got too much walking to do, too much distance to cover, for a one-day *out and back*, Captain," Patchett said. "And bundled up like you gotta be, you ain't gonna be moving fast, neither."

"We'll see, Top," Papadakis replied. "We'll see."

What Patchett didn't know was that Pop had another deal going, as well. He'd called in a favor granted to a helicopter pilot who'd lost big to him at the Christmas night poker game, temporarily letting that pilot off the hook for the payout. The pilot would pick up the captain and his eight-man patrol at the village of Wondang-ni an hour before sunset, saving them a night in *the icebox*. Successful accomplishment meant that his gambling debt would be forgiven.

"If I can't find the chink guns in an afternoon," Papadakis told the pilot, "I'd better turn in my bars."

The pilot asked, "But what happens to you guys if I can't get to you for some reason?"

"Then we unroll our sleeping bags and spend a very cold night in some Korean pigsty. And you still owe me two hundred bucks, pal."

As the pilot walked away, Captain Pop told himself, *If this works out, it's a hell of an expensive way to win a sawbuck off Top, ain't it?*

*****

As darkness fell, the dull, distant boom of Chinese artillery signaled its nightly appearance. The gunners proved no more accurate this night than any before it; their rounds were falling short of the regiment's perimeter.

Last night, they were long, Papadakis thought. *Give them a week and they might actually start dropping some right on us.*

But when it came time to sleep, he'd do it in the deep, covered bunker the men of his company had dug for him.

Can't be too careful, you know? Those chinks could get lucky tonight.

He made one more stop before turning in for the night: the tank park. There he'd pick up the handle Sean Moon and his mechanics had fabricated for the patrol; it made lugging the .30-caliber air-cooled machine gun a less exhausting job. Made from a section of broom handle and some thin steel tubing, the handle was lightweight and allowed the gunner an additional firing position: from the hip.

"You used one of these handles before, Captain?" Sean asked.

"Hell, yeah. I'm gonna do the same damn thing with it that I did in the jungle—give it to the shortest son of a bitch in my patrol so when he's running and shooting in a panic, we get that nice, knee-high grazing fire that no chink can crawl under."

"Outstanding, Captain," Sean replied. "Hey…what borough you from, anyway?"

"Queens, Rego Park…and I figure you for Brooklyn,

right?"

"Damn straight, sir. Sheepshead Bay. Us New York bastards can smell each other a mile away, right?"

"Fucking *A*, Sergeant."

*****

Papadakis had handpicked five of his eight-man patrol: the machine gunner and his assistant gunner, two riflemen, and an RTO. The other three men were assigned to him and comprised the artillery FO team: a lieutenant named Dorman, a recon sergeant named Carsey, and their RTO.

"Do we really need *two* RTOs, Captain?" Sergeant Carsey complained over breakfast at 0430 hours. "Couldn't we replace that extra radio with a BAR or something? You know...a little more firepower?"

Pop snarled, "Why don't I just bring a fucking tank along, too, Sergeant? Now hear me good: I want the second radio for backup. If we only got one—and it craps out—we're stuck in the woods with our dicks in our hands. You read me?"

Carsey figured it might be better not to ask any more questions.

But Lieutenant Dorman, the FO, had one: "Are we really going behind Pukhan-san, sir?"

"That's the plan, Lieutenant. Colonel Miles figures the reason we can't get a bead on those chink guns is their flash is masked by that mountain. You looked at the map, right?"

"Yes, sir. I did."

"Then you see that the valley north of Pukhan-san looks to be a pretty likely place to hide artillery batteries.

And your own target acquisition people say the incoming rounds are at a pretty high trajectory, so they're probably firing over something, right?"

"Yes, of course, sir."

"So do you have any more questions, Lieutenant?"

Hesitantly, Dorman asked, "Well, sir...you do realize that once we've gone that far, we'll be out of range of the one-oh-five batteries?"

"That's why I asked for the one-*five*-fives to support us, Lieutenant. They'll reach."

"Very good, sir," Dorman replied, "but you realize the rate of fire for the one-five-fives will be about half of what the one-oh-fives can shoot?"

"Kind of a moot point if we're outta their range, ain't it, Lieutenant?"

Dorman figured maybe it was time for him to stop asking questions, too. Captain Pop seemed to know exactly what he wanted from his artillerymen, to include what weapons they'd carry. Eyeing the lieutenant's carbine, Pop said, "Get rid of that piece of shit M2. Same for your men, if they're carrying one. Those things'll let you down in the cold." Patting the Thompson by his side, he added, "Carry a Tommy Gun. And if you can't trade for one of them, get an M1. At least it'll keep working."

The order flustered Dorman for a few moments. Before he could recover, Papadakis piled on with, "You did range check your radio, right?"

"Ah...no, sir. I'm not sure how to go about it, considering we're supposed to keep radio chatter to a minimum."

"Commo checks ain't chatter, Lieutenant. And they're real simple. Just get on the command net and ask

Third Battalion CP for a signal report. They're at least two miles from here. If you're banging in loud and clear with them, your radio's working fine."

Intent on these new directives, Dorman began to dash away, leaving his breakfast unfinished. Captain Pop stopped him and said, "You'd better eat that chow first. You're gonna need the energy. It'll be nothing but the C rations we carry once we move out."

*****

As the rising sun began to backlight the eastern mountains, Captain Pop's patrol set out on foot to begin their *recon by fire* mission. They'd parallel Highway 3, walking north in the semi-concealment of a treed ridgeline just west of the highway. Pop figured they'd reach the first waypoint—the village of Munemi, where a secondary road branched off to the north-northwest—in about ninety minutes.

He was only off by a little; it took one hundred minutes to get there. The village was deserted.

They began to follow the secondary road, still staying in the concealment of the woods off to the west. Carsey, the artillery sergeant, complained, "I don't see why the hell we can't stay on the roadway, sir. We'd make much better time."

Papadakis replied, "And every chink up in the hills will be able to lay eyes on us. This is a recon mission, remember? The point is to not be seen…and to not get into fights with anyone."

"I don't know, sir," Carsey said. "This still seems like a long walk to nowhere."

"You're right, Sergeant. It is a long walk, so save

your breath. You're gonna need it."

In two more hours, they'd reach Wondang-ni, where Pop had arranged for the helicopter pickup later that afternoon. If there was still no visible trace of the CCF artillery once they were beyond that village, the *recon by fire* would begin along the valley separating Pukhan-san from the next mountain about four miles farther north.

If those guns are anywhere, it's there, Papadakis told himself. *I'd put money on it.*

Oh, wait...I already did. I'm gonna take that ten bucks off Top tonight.

*****

Wondang-ni seemed deserted, too. Captain Pop called a halt so his men could rest and eat. He told Lieutenant Dorman, "Set up a perimeter while I go scout this place out. Don't let any of these shacks ruin your fields of fire."

Dorman asked, "Where are you going, sir?" He didn't seem comfortable being placed in charge so suddenly.

"I'm gonna find that eggbeater a good place to land so we don't have to go looking for one later. It looks a little congested around here. I don't want to give that flyboy an excuse to abort the mission." When that didn't seem to comfort the lieutenant, Papadakis added, "Don't worry. Just keep your eyes and ears open and you'll do fine."

He reached inside his parka, pulled out a candy bar, and handed it to Dorman. "Eat more chocolate," Pop said. "You'll feel better."

On the west side of the village, Pop found a clearing

with more than enough area for a helicopter to land. He found something else, too: *Two sets of track marks, chiseled into the frozen ground, sitting parallel to each other...just like what two self-propelled artillery pieces would make if they'd been set up to fire from here.*

He followed those track marks as they skirted Wondang-ni through the woods and joined the road just north of the village.

Top was right. These guns are moving around, he told himself.

And we must be getting pretty damn close to them now.

*****

By noon, beneath a lowering sky that threatened to unleash a fresh carpet of snow, Captain Pop's patrol was three miles north of Wondang-ni. Looking down on the valley road from a low ridge, they could see the tell-tale remnants of vehicle tracks leading into the woods on the far side of the pavement. Someone had done a poor job trying to obliterate them.

But if the Chinese gun carriages were still in those woods, they were perfectly concealed.

"They may be under camo nets or something," Pop told Lieutenant Dorman. "That'd explain why the recon planes never see them. Everything on this terrain looks white or gray. How hard is that to blend into?"

Papadakis scanned the woods with binoculars once more, hoping for some clue of what might be hidden within. But he could see nothing, just dense stands of skeletal trees and snow.

"Lieutenant, it's time to crank up the fire mission,"

he told Dorman. "You know where we are, right?"

The FO pointed to a spot on the map. "We're here...I think."

"You think? Or you know?"

"I'm not exactly certain, sir. I don't want to—"

"Hey, an FO's supposed to be the navigator, Lieutenant...*my* navigator. So what's it gonna be? Is that the spot or not?"

Dorman glanced at the map one more time, hoping, perhaps, that the answer would jump up and smack him between the eyes. But it remained just a piece of paper full of uncertainties. He thought about how it had been back in training, when map reading was just a simple game.

Out here, though, it could be a deadly one.

But he had to make a decision. Sucking his courage up, he drove his finger into the map again and replied, "Yes, sir. This is where we are."

"I'm glad you think so, Lieutenant, because I agree with you. Now give me a round one hundred yards into that tree line."

"They'll impact pretty close to us, won't they, sir?"

"Not if you're right about where we are, Lieutenant. Just call the fucking mission."

Dorman was visibly relieved when the 155-millimeter battery's FDC replied instantly, reporting his signal weak but readable.

About what I figured, Papadakis thought, *considering there's this big mountain in the way of those radio waves.*

The lieutenant's confidence bolstered, he called in the fire mission. Before transmitting the final segment, he stopped to ask, "Should we request *splash*, sir?"

"Might as well."

When the call for fire was complete, Pop added, "But if we don't hear those rounds fly overhead and then hear them impact, we'd better re-evaluate our map reading skills, Lieutenant. If they don't land on our heads, that is."

Papadakis began the mental calculation: *Okay...we're about nine miles from the battery. From the time they tell us "shot," it should take about forty-five seconds for the round to get here, shooting high angle.*

Thirty seconds later, the battery reported, "Shot, over."

Start the clock. In forty seconds, they should tell us "Splash."

He tried to keep his eyes on his wristwatch, but something down by the road caught his attention. A solitary man—a Chinese soldier by his quilted uniform—had materialized from the depths of the woods and was walking casually toward the edge of the tree line. He stopped, looked around, and then squatted against a tree, fumbling at the waist of his trousers.

As Pop said, "Joe Chink picked one hell of a time to take a crap," the voice from FDC spoke the hurried words, "Splash, over."

Seconds after that, the 155-millimeter adjustment round smashed into the edge of the woods, shattering trees and erasing the Chinese soldier from the face of the Earth.

Lieutenant Dorman cried out softly. It could have been surprise, shock, or glee; Papadakis wasn't sure which one. He told the FO, "Add one hundred, fire for effect."

"Are you sure we're ready to do that yet?" Dorman asked.

"Yeah, we are. Something's back in those woods. Gotta be."

The fog of uplifted snow and flying debris was still settling as the FDC reported once again, "Shot, over."

As those six *fire for effect* rounds were whistling toward their destination, Papadakis and his men thought they saw ghostly movements deep in the woods.

"They're running for their holes like rabbits," Captain Pop said. "This oughta be rich."

When those rounds landed seconds later, there was no doubt they'd struck more than trees. There were large, jagged objects in the air—torn metal, no doubt—tumbling through the roiling cloud of snow, tree fragments, and dirt thrown up by the explosions. Something round tumbled through the sky like a tossed coin, finally falling to the roadway: a vehicle's wheel. It bounced several times before coming to rest just off the pavement.

"Told you there's something back there," Pop said to Dorman. "Let's shift it around now. Move it left."

"How much, sir?"

"One hundred yards."

As the RTO called in the adjustment, a chain of new explosions thundered from the woods. Each one launched a fresh cloud of airborne debris.

"Ammo cooking off?" Dorman asked.

"Damn right," Pop replied. "I believe we found ourselves one of those chink batteries."

They kept shifting the rounds to the north until the *fire for effect* volleys had covered a line through the woods almost a mile long. But none of those subsequent volleys had produced the pyrotechnic effect that announced a hit on military vehicles and ammunition. If the rounds were shifted any farther, the GIs wouldn't be able to see their impacts anymore. They'd have no idea if they'd hit anything.

Papadakis checked his watch. There was still about an hour before they needed to start back toward Wondang-ni and the helicopter that would—hopefully—pick them up there. He wanted to walk the *recon by fire* rounds farther north, toward a road junction suspected of being a major conduit for the Chinese moving south in the darkness of night. If they were using that road, there might be large numbers of troops bivouacked in the hills and woods around it, hiding in daylight from the American aircraft.

I'd love to move up that way and take a peek, Pop told himself. *But we couldn't go far, because then we're putting more distance between us and that eggbeater.*

But this is recon by fire, right? So what the hell...let the fire do the work.

He told Dorman, "Give us one more shift left."

"But we won't even see the rounds impact, sir. That ridge over there will block our view."

"I don't give a damn if we see it or not," Pop replied. "Just do it, for cryin' out loud."

Dorman was right; they didn't see the rounds impact, just heard the distant roar as they exploded beyond the obscuring ridge. They waited, hoping to hear secondary explosions, too. But there were none.

"All right, let's get outta here," Papadakis called to his machine gun team.

But the team didn't move. The prone gunner gripped the bipod-mounted gun tightly, sighting on something down the road. The assistant gunner was waving frantically for Captain Pop to join them.

"Whaddya got, Trent?" Pop asked the gunner as he lay down next to him.

"There's something moving over there, sir," PFC Trent replied, cold fear in his voice. "There's *lots* of something moving."

Papadakis could see it now: Chinese soldiers were spilling onto the road. It wasn't an organized movement. They were fleeing the artillery fire in panic...

And there were *hundreds* of them. Maybe more. He knew all too well from the last war that in close combat you rarely saw more than a handful of your adversaries. But you could usually bet that if you saw five, there were probably fifty. If you saw ten, it could be a hundred.

But I'm already seeing hundreds, so there could be thousands of them around here.

And they're headed right for us...the nine of us.

Dorman and his FO team had already started walking south, their backs turned, oblivious to the threat swarming onto the road. Pulling gunner Trent and his assistant, Bova, along by their web gear, he hustled after the artillerymen.

"We ain't done," Pop told the FO once he caught up to him. "Keep moving, but shift the fire to the road. Make it airbursts this time. Try to put it about fifty yards south of where the Chinks are now, because that's where they'll be in about a minute." Then he told Trent and Bova to lead the patrol south.

Moving briskly down the ridge, they all watched over their shoulders as the first airbursts exploded over the road. But they'd detonated much too high. Very few Chinese were cut down by shell fragments.

"The battery doesn't have any VT fuzes left," Dorman told Captain Pop. "They're shooting time fuzes, so I'll have to adjust them in myself."

"Okay, it looks like we should start with *down fifty*, Lieutenant. You agree?"

Dorman didn't argue. He called in Pop's correction verbatim.

The jogging RTO was halfway through the transmission when he tripped and sprawled onto his stomach. The long whip antenna on his backpack radio snagged a tree as he went down, snapping the slender metal tube in half. His radio was now useless for long-range communication.

Sergeant Carsey—the man who'd questioned the need for taking two radios on the patrol—immediately understood the look Captain Pop was casting his way: *Now do you see why we took more than one radio, numbnuts?*

The other RTO—Papadakis' personal radioman—continued the interrupted call for fire. Carsey pulled the artillery RTO back onto his feet, and the GIs continued trotting along the ridge as fast as they could.

They all glanced back when they heard the *crack* of the next airburst volley exploding. These bursts were lower and much more effective, sweeping a section of the road practically clean of CCF soldiers.

But there were still so many more, swarming like ants, running away from the artillery fire.

Something else Papadakis had learned in the last war: the tendency to overestimate your adversary's numbers. But he didn't think he was exaggerating now: *There's thousands of Chinese down there.*

*****

They were still two miles from Wondang-ni. A light snow was falling, and the men of the patrol weren't running anymore; the hordes of CCF soldiers in their wake were either dead along the road or had fled into the hills. The GIs could no longer see the area where *recon by fire* had become *slaughter by fire.*

But they were all sure that many more Chinese soldiers were still very much alive. An urgent intel report needed to be radioed to Regiment immediately, and SOP required it be sent in code so an enemy listening in on the frequency wouldn't be aware what you knew of their disposition and react accordingly. Papadakis had given up trying to encode the report, though. He wasn't able to turn the pages of the codebook without removing his gloves. His hands, on the verge of frostbite, couldn't take it anymore. The gloves would have to stay on; the message would have to be broadcast in the clear.

At least we've got the coordinates of the CCF assembly area pretty damn close. The big stuff from Division Artillery—the eight-inchers and one-five-five Long Toms—can pound it all they like now. We did our job...we took out their artillery.

Now all we gotta do is get the hell outta here.

They were almost to the place where they'd have to leave the ridge, drop into the valley, and parallel the road into Wondang-ni. Machine gunner Trent was still leading the way. Suddenly he stopped and dropped to the ground. Despite the soft blanket of fresh snow, his machine gun clattered loudly as it came down with him. Pop felt sure that racket could be heard all the way to

Seoul.

Crawling up to his gunner, Pop asked, "What the hell's the matter?"

"Look," Trent replied, pointing to the road below. "Chinks. They didn't spot us. Not yet, anyway. They must be deaf or something."

There were four CCF soldiers visible. They were standing in the middle of the pavement, gesturing wildly as they spoke.

"Ah, they're fucked up," Papadakis whispered. "They don't know what the hell they're supposed to be doing."

"Maybe they're a patrol, sir," Trent said, "and they're looking for us. If the chinks were paying attention a little while back, it had to be obvious *somebody* was adjusting those rounds down on their heads."

"Nah, these clowns just look lost," Pop replied. "And the word on the chinks is *they don't patrol, they just probe in force.* From what I've seen so far, I think that's true."

But lost or not, those Chinese soldiers were blocking their path to Wondang-ni. There was no way around them without being seen.

"So what're we going to do, Captain?" Trent asked.

We've got thirty minutes before that eggbeater's supposed to show up, and we're still about fifteen minutes from the pickup point.

If we start a shooting war around that village, that pilot's gonna scram and we'll all be dead before the sun sets.

And those damn chinks are still standing there, arguing. The dumb bastards...

Dorman low-crawled up to Pop. He repeated Trent's question: "So what're we going to do, Captain?"

"We're gonna wait fifteen minutes right here," Papadakis replied. "You got the coordinates for where we are, *navigator?*"

"Yes, sir."

"Outstanding. Call in an *at my command* mission. Target it right on the road down there. Have the rounds in the tubes, but don't fire unless we give them the word. Got it?"

"Yes, sir...but you really want to use artillery fire against four guys we could hit with rocks?"

"It ain't those four I'm worried about, Lieutenant. It's the ones I can't see that got my knickers in a twist. They could be waiting for some of their buddies. Maybe *a lot* of their buddies."

"Affirmative, sir," Dorman replied. "But aren't we...a little close? I mean, the rounds might be off a little and—"

"Just pick out the biggest tree you can find, get your ass behind it, and roll the dice, Lieutenant."

Fifteen minutes passed. The four Chinese had stopped arguing but hadn't moved.

"Give them three more minutes," Papadakis said.

"Why's that, sir?" Trent asked.

"Just humor me, Private."

Captain Pop crawled among the men of his patrol, giving each a personal briefing; eight times he repeated, "If the chinks are still there in a couple minutes, Trent's gonna cut them all down before they know what hit them. Then we all run like hell straight down the road to the village. Understood?"

They were down to the last minute. Papadakis

watched the second hand of his watch sweep toward twelve. It was on the nine when he heard the distant murmuring of a helicopter.

He told himself, *Don't you love it when a plan comes together?*

His eyes met Trent's. They both took a deep breath. "Now," Pop whispered.

A two-second burst from the machine gun knocked down three of the Chinese. The fourth started to run for the cover of the trees. But he didn't escape Trent's second burst.

Then Papadakis and his patrol were running for their lives down the road to Wondang-ni. He knew it was tactically a dumb move; if there were more Chinese on the hills to either side, they'd be easy pickings. And if the helicopter pilot saw flashes of gunfire, he'd probably turn and fly away.

But we ain't staying out here in this icebox tonight. Not if I can help it.

They reached the village unscathed. As far as they could tell, nobody had fired on them. Carsey set off a red smoke grenade in the clearing Captain Pop had designated earlier, marking the landing zone for the pilot.

The wheels of the Sikorsky didn't even touch the ground. It hung inches above the frozen turf while the men of the patrol hurled themselves into her cramped cabin.

As the helicopter started to climb away, a string of green tracers arced across her nose, trying to find her range. They seemed close enough to touch. Every GI who could point his weapon out the door of the cramped cabin began firing wildly toward their point of origin on a hillside, without effect. Then Trent elbowed them out of the way. Grasping the machine gun by its jury-rigged handle, he began to spray the hillside with .30-caliber bullets, sweeping the weapon back and forth until the Chinese stopped firing. The Sikorsky hadn't been hit.

Trent shouted to Captain Pop, "Next patrol, can I load tracers? Would've been a hell of a lot easier to hit those chinks if I'd had them."

"Negative," the captain replied. "Not for a mission like this. Remember what I told you?"

"Yes, sir. You said *tracers work both ways.*"

"Damn right…and you just taught that to the chinks, too."

The helicopter didn't fly directly to 26th Regiment's CP; instead, she flew east a few minutes before turning south for home.

"We've got to get clear of this artillery box, pronto," the crew chief told Papadakis. "There's big stuff in the air. Don't want to get knocked down by friendly fire."

"Yeah, I know all about the big stuff," Pop replied. "I'm the guy who called for it."

Fourteen minutes later, the helicopter deposited the patrol next to Jock Miles' CP on Northeast Airfield. They even had time to clean themselves and their weapons before the supper meal.

Later, as darkness fell, Theo Papadakis stretched out in his covered bunker, stoking the fire in the makeshift oven that struggled to keep the temperature inside above freezing. Nestled in his sleeping bag, he waited for the shriek of incoming Chinese artillery.

But it never came. He went to sleep with a smile on his face.

When he awoke a few hours later, he found ten $1

bills stuck in the strap of his Thompson submachine gun. Patchett had paid off their bet.

Chapter Seventeen

By next morning, the snow had stopped and the skies had cleared to only scattered clouds. With airborne visibility restored, the ground support planes of the Air Force were in business again. At 26th Regiment's CP, the sights and sounds of tactical airpower pummeling the mass of Chinese just ten miles to the north were most welcome.

But it didn't change the fact that 8th Army was preparing to pull back once again. "With all those flyboys knocking the hell out of them chinks, you'd think that maybe we'd be staying here a while," Patchett said.

"Our new boss has a different idea, Top," Jock replied. "General Ridgway thinks this MLR is in the wrong place. He's afraid we're going to end up in a street fight in Seoul...and he's probably right. It'd be another pointless bloodbath, just like the Marines got into after the Inchon landings, and we'll end up withdrawing south of the city, anyway."

Patchett added, "I'm kinda liking the way this General Ridgway thinks, sir. It seems like he's making plans based on what's actually going on...instead of some fairy tale they cooked up in Tokyo."

"You'll get to tell him that in person, Top. He's visiting all the frontline regiments today, before we all hit the road south. I figure he wants to give everyone a chance to hear his game plan from the horse's mouth."

Then Jock addressed the staff manning the CP: "Has anybody ever worked for General Ridgway before?"

Nobody had.

But Sean Moon said, "Never worked for him, but I heard a lot about him when we were all fighting the Krauts. Tough son of a bitch—a paratrooper. Commanded the Eighty-Second Airborne until Ike gave him the whole damn airborne corps."

"I don't reckon he'll be doing a lot of parachute jumping in these parts, Bubba," Patchett said.

"Yeah...but he'll still be a tough son of a bitch, Patch."

*****

General Ridgway's visit to 26th Regiment was scheduled for 1300 hours. He'd arrive by helicopter; if he tried to come by jeep, he'd be bucking the traffic jam of GI vehicles already headed south to the new MLR. If he planned to visit every line regiment on this day—his first on Korean soil—he'd have to fly.

"Let's take bets," Patchett said. "Our good ol' division C.O. will be showing up, too, no doubt. Is he gonna be in Ridgway's chopper or his own?"

Jock laughed and replied, "Are you still a betting man after Captain Pop cleaned you out of ten bucks?"

"Hey...how'd I know that pilot was in hock to him? Besides, I can't really say it wasn't fair if it got the job done, right?"

"No, you can't," Jock replied. "I'll put a buck down that General Bishop shows up in his own helicopter. And he'll get here well before General Ridgway does."

Patchett shrugged. "That'd be my bet, too." He called to the others in the CP, asking, "Last call...anybody else want a piece of this action?"

There were no takers. Nobody doubted that Bishop would show up first, if for no other reason than to make sure nobody cast him in a poor light with the new 8th Army commander.

They were all correct. At 1225 hours, Bishop's helicopter pilot was on the radio, announcing an imminent arrival at Northeast Airfield and 26th Regiment.

Patchett asked, "Should we mess with him? Tell him don't land because there's live fire in the area?"

He might've been kidding. Then again, maybe he wasn't.

Jock—who definitely wasn't kidding—replied, "Tempting, but no."

Three minutes later, Bishop's helicopter touched down. Grimacing with arthritis pain, he ambled to Jock's CP in the dilapidated structure that was once the field's operations building.

The first words out of Bishop's mouth: "Have you begun disciplinary proceedings against that idiot of yours who radioed an intel report *in the clear*?"

"Yes, sir, I have," Jock replied. Somehow, he managed to keep a straight face as he said it. "It's taken care of."

"Share with me what that action was, Colonel."

"He received a verbal reprimand, sir," Jock replied. He didn't elaborate that the reprimand consisted solely of the words, *Try not to do that again—if you can help it, that is, Theo.* Then he told the general, "And while his actions were against SOP, sir, they did make this leisurely withdrawal possible. Otherwise, we'd be fighting tooth and nail to retreat right now."

"Negative, Colonel. Negative. What he did was a negligent act that could have put the tactical situation of your regiment, my division, and the entire Eighth Army in jeopardy. When General Ridgway gets here, I'll expect you to inform both him and me that you'll be taking more severe action against that man. What's his name, again?"

"Captain Theo Papadakis, sir."

Bishop tried to repeat the name but couldn't. His best attempt came out sounding like *Papa-doppa*.

Jock offered, "Maybe you should call him what we do, sir: Captain Pop."

"His name's going to be *mud* when I'm finished with him," Bishop said. "Now I want you *personally* to show me your plan for this withdrawal *in detail*, Colonel."

As annoying as that request was, fulfilling it kept Bishop from bothering Jock's staff. They had more than enough to do without having to put up with his second-guessing. As Patchett put it: *Some officers sharpshoot you just to see what you really know. They'll never ask a question they don't already know the answer to. But with General Bishop, he don't know the right answer in the first damn place.*

General Ridgway's helicopter settled onto the snow-covered ramp at 1257 hours, three minutes ahead of schedule. The moment her wheels touched down, he was out of the aircraft and striding toward the welcoming party.

First impressions of a commander were important, though, and Jock's people all thought the same thing: he looked like a soldier, ready to fight. Most generals looked like they were on the parade field, with no intention of getting their uniforms dirty or their shiny boots scuffed. Matthew Ridgway looked just as sharp as any other general, yet still gave the distinct impression he was ready to jump into a fighting hole with his GIs and take on Joe Chink. He wore web gear with suspenders like a common soldier, and taped to those suspenders was a live hand grenade.

There was a story spreading like wildfire that some fool back in Seoul had asked the general if that grenade was real or just an inert prop.

He'd replied, "Why don't you pull the pin and find out, son?"

Bishop raced forward to greet his commander, but Ridgway looked surprised—and a little displeased—to see him. He asked, "Haven't I already spoken to you twice this morning, General Bishop? Surely, you must have something better to do than bird-dog me." He'd spoken the words quietly so nobody else would hear them over the rumble of the helicopter's engine and the pulsing *swish* of her whirling blades.

Then Ridgway brushed past Bishop and walked up to Jock. "You must be Miles," he said. "I've heard a lot of good things about you and your regiment, Colonel."

Out of the general's earshot, Patchett muttered, "All true, too."

"Damn straight," Sean added.

But Jock was thinking, *Can't imagine from who. MacArthur's no fan, Bishop thinks I'm a West Point troublemaker, and I doubt General Ridgway ever got to talk to General Walker.*

"Show me your situation map, Colonel," Ridgway said.

*****

They spent almost thirty minutes at that map, going over everything 26th Regiment had learned about the Chinese forces facing them. General Ridgway followed along in rapt attention as Jock described the *recon by fire* patrol led by Theo Papadakis. When he was done, the general said, "It does my heart good to see that at least one regiment in Eighth Army is patrolling effectively…and not just pretending to be doing so."

General Bishop jumped up and said, "Sir, *every* regiment in my division has been actively patrolling."

Ridgway scowled as he replied, "But no other regiment has done it with any measure of success, General. Not like the Twenty-Sixth. Thanks to the patrol Colonel Miles just described, we've finally figured out where the Chinese Fortieth Army is. We knew they'd crossed the Yalu into Korea. But until now, we didn't know where they were headed." Then he asked Jock, "You are going to decorate the men of this patrol, aren't you?"

"Absolutely, sir."

Dismay was written all over Bishop's face as he said, "I don't think that's such a wise move, sir. The leader of that patrol violated communications SOP by broadcasting crucial intel in the clear."

"I don't see the problem there, General Bishop," Ridgway replied. "With the Chinese troop dispositions we're looking at, do you really think it would've made a rat's ass worth of difference if that intel had been coded? The CCF is not exactly known for its ability to rapidly adjust to a changing situation."

"But sir," Bishop bleated, "if we don't adhere to

procedures, we—"

Ridgway interrupted him, saying, "I'll take a man who can think on his feet over one who's just a slave to procedure any day, General."

Turning back to Jock, Ridgway asked, "By the way, where do you stand on the promotion list, Colonel?"

Although it had been a straightforward question with no hidden agenda, General Bishop took it to have one:

He wants to give Miles a star and replace me with him. He'll slide him into the vacant assistant division commander's slot, and then before you know it, he'll quietly push me out. That's how those West Point bastards work. They take care of their own.

Feeling humiliated, Bishop skulked into a corner of the CP.

Jock was surprised by General Ridgway's question. He hadn't given promotion to brigadier general a moment's thought since he'd arrived in Korea. He'd been far too busy trying to keep his regiment fighting and his men alive. Any time for thought he had left over went to pondering Jillian's deportation predicament and what it meant to their lives, their marriage, and their children.

And in all honesty, I have no idea exactly where I stand on the promotion list. Definitely not near the top, that's for damn sure.

But Jock needed to say something, and honesty would be the best policy: "I haven't had a chance to look lately, sir."

Ridgway smiled. "I understand, Colonel. Tell you what…I'll take a look for you and let you know."

Nobody was watching General Bishop. If they had

been, they'd have seen the daggers he was shooting Jock's way.

*****

When planning the withdrawal to the new MLR south of Seoul, Sean Moon had advised Jock to hold back most of the regiment's armor, keeping it in position on the old MLR until the very last minute. "We're not gonna run into any chinks on the road south," he'd said, "and the main column won't have 'em on their ass, neither, if we got the tanks playing rear guard."

Jock had accepted the idea immediately, with one proviso: "Let's make sure the Chinese can't flood through any gaps that might develop between us and Seventeenth Regiment. I'd like two tank platoons to serve as a fast-moving patrol along that boundary between the regiments, with a platoon of infantry in half-tracks to keep the chinks off their decks."

"Sure, we can do that, sir," Sean replied, "and we better, too. From what I've heard, the Seventeenth sent most of their tanks south already. Dumb move, if you ask me."

"I agree," Jock replied. "Set it up, will you? How soon can the tankers be ready?"

"Give me two hours, sir. Is it okay with you if I go with them?"

"By all means, Sergeant. I was just about to suggest it, anyway."

Then Jock added, "I want the entire regiment across the Han by nightfall, your tanks included."

*****

Sean had tactfully suggested to the armor battalion commander that the two tank platoons he'd take on the patrol be commanded by sergeants rather than lieutenants. That way, Sean would be the ranking man and there'd be no question who was in charge of the detachment. It wasn't a hard request to fill; of the battalion's twelve platoons, eight were led by sergeants but only four by lieutenants. Combat attrition had—as usual—been brutal on junior officers. As Sean put it, *By the time those louies learn enough to stay alive, they're already dead.*

He had the four Pershings of one platoon patrolling the boundary with 17th Regiment within an hour. The second platoon, consisting of four Shermans, was having trouble getting on the road. They were stuck—literally—in their holding area, locked in the grip of treads frozen to the ground.

Sean fumed as he told the platoon sergeant, "Didn't I tell you whipdicks not to *laager* in no gulleys? They don't freeze hard on top, so you sink in and get trapped. Now we gotta spend precious time bumping you all free, one by one."

"Ain't my fault, Sean," the platoon sergeant whined. "It was dark when we got here. Who the hell could tell it was a gulley?"

"You're supposed to be the one who could tell, numbnuts. If you got your ass outta the turret and your head outta your ass every now and then, you might actually be able to do it."

Sean climbed back into the unstuck Sherman he'd commandeered as his command vehicle, telling her driver, "We're gonna go play *bumper cars*, Sully. You know the best way to tap 'em, right?"

"Yeah, Sarge. Nose to nose."

With the roar of engines and clouds of exhaust smoke, the brutal ballet to jar the frozen tanks loose began. Two of the vehicles required multiple blows to crack the ice holding them fast. But within thirty minutes, the four Shermans were free and joining the patrol.

"All that slamming gave me a headache, Sarge," Sully said.

"Do I look like someone who gives a shit? Stop bitching, take a coupla aspirin, and drive the damn vehicle."

*****

Sean's patrol hadn't traveled more than a mile when they came across a discouraging sight: the remains of the searchlight battery the 26th had been ordered to turn over to 17th Regiment. The lights were devastated, blown apart by direct-fire weapons of large caliber, in all likelihood. The trailers on which the lights were mounted were overturned; the cylindrical lamp assemblies, each four feet in diameter, were nothing but empty rings now, resembling multi-pointed crowns lying on their sides.

I'll bet the GIs manning these things got chewed up pretty good, too, Sean told himself. *Colonel Miles told that dumbass general who wanted to use these things for direct illumination that this would happen right quick if he did.*

And Colonel Miles was right. Dead right.

But Sean sensed another problem far worse than the loss of the searchlights: *Only one type of gun can survive all the artillery we've been dumping on them and still do something like this: the main gun of a Russian T-34.*

Them bastards got tanks again.

Shit.

Chapter Eighteen

The patrol along the regimental boundary took Sean and his tankers through the eastern outskirts of Seoul. "Keep your eyes wide open," he'd briefed them before setting out. "We're used to the chinks hiding from the Air Force during the day, but inside the city, they won't have to worry about planes much. Plenty of places for them to operate in broad daylight but still be invisible from the air."

It didn't take long to encounter one of those places. Driving along a road that passed a row of what appeared to be warehouses, one of the half-tracks carrying GI infantry came under machine gun fire. Sean's tank was only fifty yards behind the half-track; he had a clear view of what was happening.

"If this is a chink ambush, it's the dumbest one in history," he said to his crew. Then he told his gunner, "Put an HE round right through that building where the MG's firing. Knock the son of a bitch down."

Sean had meant that last sentence only as a figure of speech. The tank round, however, did knock the building down. Its impact collapsed the near wall; seconds later, the rest of the building fell like a house of cards. The hostile fire from within was silenced. But there were six more warehouses in the row, and each looked like a good place for more Chinese soldiers to be lying in wait.

"Drive around back," he radioed the Pershing platoon sergeant. "Cover the infantry while they check that there's no chinks inside. The Shermans will do the same from the front side."

The first five buildings proved to be large empty spaces offering no hiding places inside. They were searched and found vacant within a matter of minutes. But when a squad of GI infantry entered the sixth and final warehouse, they never came out. There had been no gunfire, no sound of anything gone wrong.

The lieutenant leading the infantry platoon was hesitant to investigate. "I don't want to lose any more men," he told Sean, who'd climbed down from his tank to speak face to face.

"How do you know you lost anybody, Lieutenant? Maybe they just found a broad or two in there."

But the lieutenant still wouldn't—or couldn't—make a decision. Grasping for an excuse to justify his inaction, he said, "Look, Sergeant, we had a real rough time on the line the past few nights. I'm not going to risk any—"

Sean cut him off. "With all due respect, Lieutenant, knock off the crap. I've been having a *real rough time* since North Africa in Forty-Two. Are you gonna check on your men, or what?"

When it was obvious that his choice would be *or what*, Sean mumbled, "Ah, for fuck's sake," and then called to his bow gunner: "Swenson, grab your weapon and come with me."

As they walked to the warehouse entrance, Swenson asked, "Is that lieutenant making us do this, Sarge?"

"No. *I'm* making us do this. Something screwy's going on in there, and the lieutenant can't find his ass with both hands right now."

At the doorway, Sean peeked inside from a low crouch. This warehouse wasn't empty like the others; it was full of boxes, stacked high. He recognized the markings on those boxes right away.

"This place is full of GI field rations," he told Swenson, "and it ain't like the G4 to be stashing stuff like this and then forgetting about it."

"How do you think it got here, Sarge?"

"My guess? The ROKs are hoarding it."

"Hoarding? I'll bet it's more like they're stealing it."

"You might have something there, pal," Sean said.

Then, with weapons cradled at their sides, ready to fire, they stepped inside.

At first, it seemed there was nobody there. Then they heard someone speaking; the words echoed around the warehouse, making their origin difficult to detect. But as they rounded a wall of stacked boxes, they found the source right on the other side: the GIs who'd first gone into the building—all five of them—were being held at gunpoint by an equal number of ROK soldiers. The petrified GIs had been disarmed, their hands up, their weapons stacked out of reach against another wall of boxes.

One of them was mumbling the *Hail Mary*. Sean told him, "The Blessed Virgin ain't gonna help us, pal…not unless she's got some heavy hardware trained on these clowns."

"You'd be wise to drop your weapons," one of the ROKs—a lieutenant—said in perfect English. He started to say something else, but his voice faltered. He looked like he'd seen a ghost.

"Well, I'll be a son of a bitch," Sean said. "I know you. I bailed your ass outta some big trouble about a month ago up at Sunchon, didn't I? So what've you been up to, *Lieutenant Moon*, besides guarding all this food

you ROKs swiped? Oh, and by the way, we ain't
dropping our weapons until you drop yours."

There was talk in Korean among the ROKs, angry
words none of the Americans understood. Lieutenant
Moon said something that silenced his men.

But no weapons were lowered.

"The last time we met," Sean said, "you were about
to get bumped off by your own guys, weren't you?"

The Korean lieutenant said nothing in reply, but his
expression gave him away: the memory was an
uncomfortable one.

Sean continued, "All my guys thought it was so
fucking funny that you and me were both named Moon,
remember?"

The lieutenant nodded.

"And maybe you remember that last thing you said
to me? Something about *you owing me*?"

After a moment's hesitation, Lieutenant Moon
nodded again.

"And maybe you owe me *double* now, seeing how
we just took care of a bunch of chinks who were set to
confiscate your pile of swag here."

The lieutenant pointed to some boxes scattered on
the floor near the captive GIs. "Your men were trying to
steal, too, Sergeant."

"Now how could that be, *brother*, considering you
ROKs swiped it from Uncle Sam in the first place? They
were just taking back what's rightfully theirs." Sean
paused before adding, "So what's it gonna be with the
weapons? I mean, if it comes right down to it, between
my Thompson and Swenson's *grease gun*, we could
probably knock you all down with a burst apiece. Maybe
you'd get off a shot with one of them M1s...but I

guaran-damn-tee it'd be your *last* shot."

The Korean officer still couldn't seem to make a move, one way or another.

"What is it with you lieutenants today?" Sean said. "You and that *butter-bar* outside...neither one of you can make a fucking decision. Let's try this again...on my count of three, we all lower the weapons. Agreed? I'll even give you a little extra time to explain it to your boys so we don't get no misunderstandings."

Lieutenant Moon held out his open palm to Sean, a signal to *wait*. Then he said something to his men. Whatever it was, it started a new flurry of harsh words.

One of the ROK soldiers, his face red with anger, was being particularly vocal. The lieutenant pointed his pistol at him, speaking something the Americans figured must've been a death threat even though they had no idea what was actually said.

Sean thought, *Ain't this interesting? Go ahead...start shooting each other. That'll make it real easy for me.*

But no one fired. Lieutenant Moon turned to Sean and said, "Begin your count, Sergeant."

When he reached *three*, the lieutenant barked an order, and the ROKs' weapons were lowered. Sean and Swenson did the same.

"So we're even now, Sergeant?" the lieutenant asked.

"Almost," Sean replied. "Now that we ain't gonna shoot each other, I got one more condition to lay on you."

"And that would be?"

"My men are gonna leave here now. But on their way out, each man's taking a coupla cases of C rations with him."

When the lieutenant began to protest, Sean added, "If I had my way...and we had the time...I'd back some trucks up to this place and take the whole damn stash. But in a coupla hours, it's all gonna belong to the chinks, so there ain't no time."

"You say the Chinese will be here in *a few hours*, Sergeant?"

"No, I said they're gonna lay their grubby little paws on this food in a few hours. As far as being *here*"—he pointed toward the leveled building at the other end of the row—"they already are."

Lieutenant Moon said something to his men. Then, without so much as a *goodbye and good luck*, the ROKs fled the warehouse.

*****

General Ridgway's location for the new MLR had been well chosen. Thirty miles south of Seoul and the Han River, it was anchored in the west by the city of Ansong and stretched east all the way across the peninsula. Along that line, terrain favored the defender like few other locales in Korea; even if the CCF chose to continue avoiding the highways and advance clandestinely across the mountains, staging an attack would mean having to traverse the several miles of open, flat marshland in front of 8th Army's positions. The Chinese would be terribly exposed when they did attack—even at night—and pay a heavy price at the hands of the American artillery and air power.

The new MLR had a new name too: *Line D*.

Even before he'd left Tokyo, Ridgway had directed

his 8th Army engineers to dig defensive positions at critical points along Line D. As the men of 26th Regiment spilled south to occupy the line in front of Ansong, they were delighted with how little digging they had to do; the bulldozers and earthmovers of the engineers had done most of the work for them. Once Jock's men constructed overhead cover for the deep and roomy fighting holes, the fortifications would be complete. It wouldn't take long; the engineers had provided plenty of lumber to frame the roofs and mountains of loose dirt to fill the sandbags that would serve as the shingles.

Even the critical eye of an old hand like Patchett— an eye that could find genuine fault in almost anything a GI tried to do—couldn't help but be impressed with the engineers' work. "Most of these holes they dug are even in the right place, sir," he said to Jock. "Given how hard it is to get our boys to dig any damn thing, this just might start off the New Year right for us."

*****

General Ridgway was happy with the defensive positions along Line D, too. He only found a few places where the fields of fire didn't make as good a use of terrain as they might have. When he told his engineering officer those mistakes were to be corrected by sunset, the colonel replied, "That's impossible, sir. There's not enough time."

"It's your job to make it possible, Colonel," Ridgway replied. "Are you telling me you can't do your job?"

"But sir...that gives us only four hours, and my men

have already worked their tails off doing what you asked. It's not fair to—"

"*Fair* doesn't apply in matters of life and death, Colonel. Now I've already given you a big pile of *attaboys* for the great work you've done so far. Don't let one *aw, shit* wipe them all out."

The engineer noticed Ridgway seemed to be speaking not to his face, but to the insignia of rank—the eagle—on his fur-lined cap. Withered by the general's unwavering gaze at that eagle, he became quite certain that the silver bird could quickly regress to the silver oak leaf of a lieutenant colonel, or even the gold leaf of a major if that one *aw, shit* came to pass.

"Sunset, Colonel," the general reminded him.

*****

In those days before he stepped off the plane at Kimpo Airfield, days he spent in Tokyo wrestling with the delusions of MacArthur and his staff, Ridgway had been sending dispatches to the division commanders of 8th Army. While the orders in those dispatches were many and varied, one theme was constant throughout: *there was to be no more talk of retreat.*

He'd made it clear that the repositioning to Line D was a strategic move *dictated by him, not the Chinese*, to put his forces into a more advantageous stance for the resumption of offensive action by 8th Army. Once on the new line, further moves to the south were not to be contemplated. When they moved again, the only direction they'd be going was north.

But as in all large organizations, somebody never gets the message.

As Ridgway toured General Bishop's headquarters at 24th Division, he stopped to watch the G3—Bishop's operations chief—drawing a series of long red lines on a large-scale wall map. The lines traced a southward progression from Ansong, to Taejon, to Taegu, ending at Pusan.

"What are you working on, Colonel?" Ridgway asked the G3.

"A withdrawal plan for the division, sir."

"May I ask why?"

The G3 seemed stunned by the question, as if the reason was painfully obvious. He replied, "Well, in case we have to *bug-out* again, sir, of course. I thought it—"

"You thought wrong, Colonel. You're relieved. No, make that you're *fired*."

Then Ridgway led Bishop, the ashen-faced division commander, from the room. Once they were alone, he asked, "Are there any other men on your staff who don't understand what *no retreat* means, General?"

"No, sir."

"How about you, Bishop? Do *you* understand what it means?"

"Yes, sir. I understand completely."

"Outstanding. I'll be sending you a new G3 within twenty-four hours. I can guarantee you that the term *bug-out* is not in his vocabulary."

"But sir, I already have someone who can take over as my G3," Bishop said.

"No, you don't, General. I'll be providing the suitable replacement."

*****

Ridgway's next stop was Jock's CP at 26th Regiment. "I thought we'd talk for a little bit," the general said. "Have you got the time?"

Jock fought the urge to smile. You *always* had time for a general. He offered Ridgway a seat on a camp stool and began to pull over a field case to use as a chair. The motion was awkward; without warning, Jock's bad leg gave way.

It could have been worse; he hadn't fallen on his face, just gone down on one knee. Still, the impact of that damaged leg with the floor hurt badly. His grimace of pain left no doubt of that.

Patchett raced across the room, saying, "My apologies, sir, I told those jackasses not to load them cases so darn heavy. You're lucky you didn't throw your shoulder out trying to drag that *sumbitch*."

Then he made a great show of struggling to push the field case into position across from General Ridgway, keeping a straight face the whole time.

If this son of a bitch weighs more than five pounds, I'll eat my steel pot, Patchett told himself. *The colonel's leg couldn't've picked a worse time to flare up.*

But maybe we'll get away with it.

"Are you okay, Miles?" the general asked. As Jock rose gingerly and took a seat on the field case, he added, "I know about your injury. I'm not concerned about it if you're not. I've had airborne officers working for me who broke a leg or an ankle on a combat jump but kept right on leading their men brilliantly."

Patchett excused himself, leaving the two officers to talk. Once he was gone, the general said, "NCOs like him are the backbone of *this man's army*, Miles."

"I couldn't agree more, sir."

"And he's loyal to a fault, I see…but that's a wonderful thing in my book. Have you two served together long?"

"Yes, sir," Jock replied. "We go back to 1942. He was first sergeant for the company I took to Australia and then Papua. Later, he was my *sergeant major* when I got a battalion."

Ridgway smiled. He understood just how essential and priceless the bond between fighting men was.

"I'm finding it amazing, Jock, how *jungle rats* like you and Sergeant Patchett have excelled in this frozen hell. It certainly isn't the type of war you were used to fighting. But the thing that really galls me is that so many officers who served with distinction in the European theater, where it got pretty damn cold, too, can't seem to function in Korea at all."

Jock just nodded, wondering where this talk was going.

"But those same officers think that just because they stepped off the boat at Pusan, they'll get their tickets punched for promotion. That might've been the way it used to be in Eighth Army, but those days are over, Jock."

He should've been uneasy with the general calling him by his first name. It had always been his experience that when a superior who didn't know you well lapsed into first name usage, he was buttering you up for a real screwing.

Somehow, though, he had the feeling that wasn't the case this time.

"I've looked at the promotion list for brigadier, Jock,

and to be honest, you're in the upper half, but just barely."

I'm not sure if I should be disappointed or relieved, Jock thought.

"But based on your performance in this theater, I'm confident I can get you bumped well up the list. I can see you commanding a division—with a second star on your shoulder—in a year's time."

So we're still planning on being in this mess a year from now?

Promotion to general officer had been the furthest thing from Jock's mind. It had never seemed in the cards, considering the enmity MacArthur held for both him and his wife, an enduring product of the last war and all that ugly business in Australia.

"I'm sure you know, sir, that I'm far from being MacArthur's favorite officer."

Ridgway dismissed that thought with a shake of his head. "I wouldn't worry too much about what MacArthur thinks. He's not a soldier anymore, just a politician. He's got his sights set on running for president in Fifty-Two. I don't know how much of the politics back home you've been able to follow, but he's the darling of the right wing now. If he's going to run, he needs to get as far away from this mess he's made in Korea as he can."

"Are you saying he's going to be relieved, sir? Or resign?"

"Who knows, Jock? That's for him and the president to decide...and ol' Douglas certainly hasn't gone out of his way to endear himself to Mr. Truman lately. You'd think those public statements about attacking Red China would've ended his career right then and there, but he's still got a lot of powerful supporters in Washington, people who still think the sun rises out of his rear end."

Ridgway leaned forward, his expression serious and probing. "But you are aware, I'm sure, of the rotation policy Washington's stuck us with, right?"

"Yes, sir, I am."

And Jock knew he would be up for rotation home by the end of April, just four months away. If he took a promotion before then, he'd go to the bottom of the rotation list for generals, where the clock would be reset for another full tour in Korea of approximately one year.

Would that be fair to Jill? It's bad enough already I haven't been able to do a damn thing to help her with this deportation nonsense that's turning her life—our life—upside down.

But add another year to that helplessness?

What kind of husband would do that to his wife and children?

He was terrified of one possible answer to that question: *the kind who's lost his family forever.*

*****

There was nothing to celebrate as the clock struck midnight on New Year's Eve. The last of 8th Army's units to withdraw to Line D were now crossing the Han River, leaving Seoul an open city.

"Gotta feel sorry for them poor civilian bastards still trying to live there," Patchett said. "This makes the third time that place has changed hands in six months, right?"

Sean Moon nodded in agreement.

"That's some sorry state of affairs," Patchett

continued. "All them Marines that died so MacArthur could have his little parade through that city back in September...it was all for nothing, wasn't it?"

Sean asked, "You ain't blaming General Ridgway for giving up the city, are you?"

"Hell, no, Bubba. That's about the smartest thing I seen a man with stars on him do since I got to this godforsaken country. Glad to hear he ain't no fan of house-to-house fighting, because I sure as hell ain't, neither."

He paused, looking at the bottle of whiskey from which they'd planned to drink a New Year's toast. But no drinks would be poured that night, for they knew the Chinese wouldn't be celebrating. Their New Year— which would begin *the Year of the Rabbit*—was still a few weeks away.

Both sergeants had no doubt what tens of thousands of Chinese soldiers would be doing instead: they'd be marching through the night, drawing ever closer to Line D.

Chapter Nineteen

Theo Papadakis let the binoculars fall on their strap against his chest. "All I gotta say is *Happy Fucking New Year*, Top. Where the hell are all these damn chinks, anyway? We been on this Line D for a coupla days now...and nothing's happening. Don't get me wrong...I ain't complaining or nothing. But still, how long can this last?"

"Not too long, I reckon," Patchett replied. "But don't you worry none...they're out there. I'd bet you money on it, but you already took me for all I got right now. Like Colonel Miles said, though, their supply lines are getting a little on the long side. They may be able to march their asses over mountains, but their artillery and ammo trains still gotta stick to the roads and railways...and pretty long stretches of 'em, at that."

"Let's hope the Air Force is cutting those stretches to ribbons," Papadakis said.

"Yeah, let's hope. But the thing I want most outta the Air Force right now is that ammo resupply that's overdue," Patchett replied. "When the chinks do come, we only got us enough illum rounds for a night or two at the moment."

"Why the hell is it so damn hard to keep us supplied, Top? It's not like Uncle Sam's fighting in more than one part of the world...not like in the last war. The G4s don't have to choose anymore between supplying the guys in Europe or the guys on those stinking Pacific islands. All the fighting's going on right here in this frozen crap hole."

"I hear you, Captain…but them airplanes and supply trucks don't like this cold any better than we do," Patchett replied. "I hear-tell they got breakdowns all over the damn place."

*****

He wasn't sure he could keep her in the air much longer.

The right engine on *Moon's Menace VI* was already shut down. It'd started backfiring right after takeoff. Major Tommy Moon had elected to shut that engine down and return to K-2 at Taegu, South Korea, the airfield from which the heavily armed B-26 had departed just moments before.

But now—at an altitude of only 600 feet—the left engine was acting up, too. Steadily losing power, its usual steady drone had decayed to a spasmodic growl, like the warning an injured dog issued if you tried to approach it.

This is a hell of a way to start the first flight from our new Korean base, Tommy thought. *Too low to bail out, no place to jettison the load.*

If it was just one engine acting up, I could come around and land, no problem. These babies don't even drift down with an engine out.

But that's assuming the other one's running good.

Now the left engine's dying on me, too…and I've got three choices:

Do I crash into the mountain dead ahead?

Or do I try to turn right—into the dead engine—and smack into that mountain?

Maybe I turn left…and risk going down in the city of

Taegu?

He took a quick look at the photo of Sylvie Bergerac tucked into the corner of the instrument panel. Silently, he asked her smiling face, *What do I do, baby girl?*

A voice in his head—*her* voice—replied, *Turn left, silly. There's plenty of open space between you and the city and nothing but flat ground if you have to belly her in off the field.*

Mon Dieu, Tommy! Keep her away from the mountains!

He was grateful that Lieutenant Hank Roth, his young navigator, didn't need to be told what to do. He'd already taken the initiative on the radio, calling the control tower to declare an emergency and receiving priority clearance to land in the direction of their choice. Then, command of *Switchblade Green Flight* was passed from Tommy to Captain Price in *Green Two*. As he checked that the gun, bomb, and rocket switches were all still in the *safe* position, Roth asked Tommy, "What else do you need me to do, sir?"

"You can pray, Hank. And tell Bob in the back he'd better do the same."

The voice of the gunner, Sergeant Bob Allen, was in their headsets now, speaking a terse, "Already got that covered, gentlemen." Sitting between two gun turrets loaded with hundreds of rounds of .50-caliber ammunition and right behind a bomb bay full of five-hundred-pounders, he'd seek help from any quarter if it got him a landing he could walk away from.

The ship had managed the 180-degree turn back toward the field, but she'd sunk to 400 feet in the process. The left engine was only giving them half power.

"Try to restart number two," Tommy told Roth.

"We've got nothing to lose."

"Okay, sir. Are we going straight in, downwind?"

"That's the plan."

"Roger," Roth replied, sounding just a little relieved. He was sure Tommy had long since figured out they'd run out of sky if he tried to fly the normal pattern and land upwind. But it felt better to hear him say it. He eased the prop lever out of *feather* and engaged the starter.

He watched the silver blades of the propeller begin their slow rotation. Relieved to see them come out of their streamlined feather and bite the air again, he switched on the ignition. The engine came to life reluctantly, surging and then dying with each backfire. With Tommy nursing the throttle and mixture levers, it settled into a faltering rumble.

Still a half mile from the runway threshold, she'd sunk to two hundred feet.

"Need more speed," Tommy said, "or this tailwind's going to pancake us."

Inching the throttles forward, he told Roth, "Give me another notch of flaps."

The engines still refused to cooperate. With each momentary surge of power, Tommy clawed for every inch of altitude she could hold. But when they sputtered, he had to drop her nose to maintain speed just barely above a stall. One way or another, this *seesaw* was going to end on contact with the ground in a few seconds; whether that ground would be the firm concrete of the runway or the muck short of it remained to be seen.

Moon's Menace VI was still three hundred yards

from the runway's threshold, with the altimeter reading a needle's width from zero, when Tommy told Roth, "Gear down." Neither man in the cockpit could quite believe the props had not yet struck the frozen marsh below them.

They felt the first bump of tire contact with the pavement before any of the landing gear indicated *down and locked.* Normal landing procedure for a B-26 was to land flat on all three gear simultaneously. But this was no normal landing; with the nose slightly down to keep her speed up for one last, crucial second, the nose gear had hit first. Mercifully, it didn't collapse, but the nonstandard attitude at touchdown tossed the ship back into the air—her nose up—inviting a stall she had little power to counteract.

She was still in mid-bounce when Roth called out, "Main gear down and locked."

"Nose gear?" Tommy asked.

"No joy," Roth replied.

"Oh, well...nothing to lose now," Tommy said. He pushed the throttles to the stops.

And just that one time, the engines responded with a reassuring burst of power. It lasted only a second, but it was enough to maintain flying speed, allowing him to control the ship to a level touchdown.

They both expected the nose gear to fold and the airplane to slide to an undignified stop in a shower of sparks as metal scraped across concrete.

Got to kill the engines before the props hit the ground, Tommy told himself. *And if there's a fire, maybe we can get out before she blows up.*

But despite the *unsafe* indication, the nose gear held. As he steered her off the runway with gentle taps of differential braking, the right engine coughed and died on its own in a cloud of white exhaust smoke.

A few seconds later, the left engine died, too.

Roth jotted the time down in the flight log: 0907 hours.

He told Tommy, "You sure know how to cram a lot of excitement into a six-minute flight, sir."

*****

It took the maintenance team about an hour to sort out the problems on *Moon's Menace VI*. "The nose gear's okay," the crew chief told Tommy. "That bounce you took bent a switch bracket. It's already replaced. We'll swing the gear in a little bit to confirm the fix."

Tommy knew that the trouble with the engines had to be fuel related: *There's not too many other ways multiple engines can act up together unless you've got fuel problems.*

"So what's wrong with the gas, Sarge?" Tommy asked.

A brief smile crossed the crew chief's face. Pilots who understood the *nuts and bolts* of the planes they flew were few and far between. There was a pretty good chance that Major Moon was among the ones who did, so he wouldn't have to dumb the explanation down for him.

"Water contamination, sir," the chief said. "Lots of it. It's this damn freezing weather. Some of that *avgas* has been sitting out in the open in barrels here at K-2 for months. Snow's been piled up on them most of that time, and the melt off the bottom layer has been seeping in. We're still sumping the water out of your tanks, and your fuel filters are full of ice. That's why you were losing power...clogged them right up."

Tommy said, "I thought we religiously sumped the fuel trucks after they filled up. What happened today?"

"We're still looking into that, sir...but somebody dropped the ball real bad. When the maintenance officer figures out who it was—and there aren't too many to choose from—that man's going to be real sorry, I can promise you."

"How long until my ship's ready to fly, Sarge?"

"Give it a couple more hours, sir. Let us get all that water out. We've got to keep heating up the sump drains, because they want to keep freezing. That's been slowing my guys down."

The squadron operations officer was part of this discussion, as well. Tommy asked him, "What about the other ships in the flight? Did they get fueled from the same truck I did?"

"Apparently not. There were half a dozen fuel trucks working this morning, and yours looks like the only ship unlucky enough to get the dregs. The rest of *Switchblade Green Flight* took off right behind you and kept on going, headed to those rail yards on the south side of Seoul. Hell, they should be on their way back already."

*****

By 1300 hours, the mechanics had completed the work on *Moon's Menace VI's* engines and were doing a retraction check of her nose gear. If that went well, she'd be rearmed and ready to fly again.

When Tommy returned to the operations shack to

prepare a new flight plan, he could tell something was wrong right away. The place had contracted the stale, almost funereal atmosphere typical of when ships didn't return from a mission.

"Price and Levenson went down," the operations officer said. "Flak over the rail yard got them."

Tommy asked, "What about Hobart?"

"He's in the landing pattern now. He radioed in the bad news as soon as he was in range."

*****

Tommy found Lieutenant Hobart's debriefing sickening to hear. In his absence as flight leader, *Switchblade Green Flight* seemed to have done almost everything wrong, breaking nearly every rule of bombing from medium altitude.

As the story was pieced together, it became clear that sloppy navigation caused the three bombers to not locate the target—the railroad marshaling yard at Yongdungpo—on their first approach. They had to backtrack along the Han River, exposing themselves to every anti-aircraft battery in a fifty-square-mile area. The reflection of the late morning sun off the snow-covered ground made it hard to find the tracks that led to the yard, so they'd descended to 3,000 feet for a closer view of what lay below. But the lower altitude limited the visibility of what lay ahead; they didn't see the rail yard, which was nestled in a bowl of shallow hills, until they were right on top of it. By then, it was too late to set up for a bomb run. They'd have to climb and circle back to the target. In doing so, they became excellent targets themselves, because their objective and path had now become predictable to the gunners on the ground.

If I'd been there as lead ship like I should've been, Hank would've gotten us to the target on a beeline. We could've dumped the bombs from eight thousand, like we were supposed to, and been perfectly oriented on the target area. Then we could've dropped down and come over the hills at low altitude for the strafing run.

Those anti-aircraft gunners wouldn't have had much of a chance to track us.

As it was, it's lucky Hobart didn't get knocked down, too.

The squadron commander sat in silence throughout the debrief, letting Tommy and the operations officer handle the questioning. When there was nothing more to be asked, the commander announced, "Gentlemen, the word's come down from Fifth Air Force: due to the alarming increase in the rate of aircraft and crew loss to anti-aircraft fire, Fifty-Third Bomb Squadron will no longer conduct daylight combat missions, effective immediately. All our efforts will now be at night, in conjunction with *Firefly* and searchlight-equipped aircraft. That's the main reason we repositioned our base from Japan to K-2 in the first place: so we'd have more time in the target zones to exploit the advantages those illumination ships give us. Night flying is our mission until further notice."

*****

Jillian Miles sat impatiently in a San Francisco federal courtroom with her lawyer, Mark Pitney. Her deportation hearing was supposed to have convened at 9 a.m., but it was already twenty minutes past that time and Judge Riggs was still in chambers. The government prosecutor seated at the table across from them seemed just as anxious as they were. Jillian asked Pitney, "Do you take this dawdling as a good or bad sign, Mark?"

"Well, we did give him a big pile of briefs to mull over," Pitney replied. "It must mean he's actually reading them, so I take that as a good sign, Mrs. Miles."

She forced a smile, hoping he was right.

It took another five minutes for Judge Riggs to finally make his appearance. When the bailiff called, "All rise," the judge shuffled from the doorway of his chambers and ascended the few steps to the bench. When he settled into his chair, Riggs nearly vanished behind the polished mahogany bulwark.

"Elfin old bugger, isn't he?" Jillian whispered.

Once the court was called to order and her case announced by the clerk, Judge Riggs said, "I've been informed by the Monterey County District Attorney that you are a witness to a criminal prosecution currently being pursued in that county, Mrs. Miles. Is that true?"

"Yes, My Lord," she replied, "but I'm also the—"

He cut her off before she could finish. "Mrs. Miles, I must remind you that we're not in the British Commonwealth. This is the United States of America, where we address justices as *Your Honor*, not *My Lord*. Do you understand?" He sounded as if he was scolding a child.

Unflustered and unapologetic, she replied, "Yes, *Your Honor*. I understand completely. My apologies…but may I finish what I was saying now?"

Pitney jotted something on his note pad and eased it across the table toward her. He'd written, *Be nicer*.

Jillian felt like telling her lawyer, *I'll bloody well*

NOT be nice to this petty little wanker, but decided that wouldn't help her cause one bit. Pitney's hand was on her arm now, as if reining her back.

"What my client wishes to say, Your Honor, is that—"

"I'm speaking to the woman, Mister Pitney, not you."

He said the word *woman* as if describing some inferior creature.

Riggs continued, "It seems to me the woman is quite determined to speak for herself. Please continue, Mrs. Miles."

Pitney tapped his pen against the words he'd just written on the pad, a silent plea to his client.

Jillian said, "I just wanted to point out, *Your Honor*, that I am not only a witness in the Monterey County trial, I am the victim of the crime being prosecuted."

Judge Riggs settled back in his chair, his face puckered as if he'd just smelled something foul. Then he said, "Whether you're the victim or not makes no difference in these proceedings, Mrs. Miles. Just like it makes no difference to this court that your husband is an Army officer serving overseas in Korea."

Pitney jumped in, adding, "A distinguished *colonel*, Your Honor, leading a regiment in combat."

"Again, Mr. Pitney, that matters not at all to this court. It has no bearing as to whether or not Mrs. Miles violated the conditions of her visa and is, as a result, subject to deportation."

"I understand, Your Honor, but as our brief to this court states, there remains the fact that Mrs. Miles is not the person who signed the transaction that precipitated this case. If she took no such action, how can it be claimed she violated the terms of her visa?"

"That's a smoke screen, Mr. Pitney. That may be how the law works in Australia, but not in this country. *Whoever* signed *what* document is immaterial when dealing with a corporate transaction such as the one Mrs. Miles is alleged to have initiated as a foreign officer of that corporation. It's *intent* that matters, and Mrs. Miles' *intent* to execute such a transaction constituted a violation of her visa once that transaction was, in fact, executed. And as your brief makes clear, that transaction was executed. Money and property changed hands. Is that not correct?"

"No, Your Honor, it is correct. The transaction was executed."

"I'm glad we agree, Mr. Pitney. And now we need to agree on something else. I just picked through your rather sensational yarn suggesting a conspiracy by business rivals exists to wrongly deport Mrs. Miles. Let me assure you that this court has already rejected that ridiculous and unsubstantiated suggestion out of hand."

"May I have a moment with my client, Your Honor?"

"Just so it *is* just a moment, Mr. Pitney."

Their heads close together, Pitney whispered to Jillian, "We suspected he'd reject the Whitelaw conspiracy allegation. After all, we don't have concrete proof...not yet, anyway."

"But all this *intent* rubbish has me very confused," she said. "How the bloody hell can anybody prove that my intent was anything more than to help military families who were being victimized?"

"That's exactly the point I'm prepared to argue," Pitney replied. "The only question is *when* to argue it."

He still hasn't told us if he's honoring the DA's request for postponement or not. There's no point right now trying to refute the *intent* issue if this isn't your actual hearing. We'd only be tipping our hand and giving the government time to devise counterarguments."

"Agreed," Jillian said.

Turning back to Judge Riggs, Pitney asked, "Your Honor, may I ask if the court will be honoring the request of Monterey County for a postponement of Mrs. Miles' deportation hearing?"

"I would have gotten to that a few minutes ago, Mr. Pitney, if you and your client hadn't engaged in all this pointless quibbling. I'm told the trial in which Mrs. Miles has been subpoenaed as a witness is scheduled for Monday, the nineteenth of April, and is expected to take less than a week. Is that correct?"

"Yes, Your Honor. That is correct."

"So you're asking me for a *four-month delay* in this deportation proceeding?"

"I believe it's the district attorney of Monterey County who's requesting the delay, Your Honor."

As soon as Pitney said it, he wished he hadn't; at least not in that patronizing manner. The judge was back to looking like he'd smelled a pile of shit again. The government prosecutor was on his feet, objecting to the delay. The only person in the court who was smiling was Jillian, who'd taken delight in her lawyer's comment...

And Pitney wished she wasn't doing that, either.

But Judge Riggs surprised them all when he said, "Very well. This matter is adjourned until Monday, the twenty-sixth of April. And not a day more." Then he asked the prosecutor, "I assume the government can live with that, Mr. Dayton?"

"With respect, Your Honor," Dayton replied, "the deportation case against Mrs. Miles is very straightforward. This delay seems totally unnecessary and, I suspect, intentionally exaggerated by Monterey County to stall this court. I would think a certified transcript of her testimony, which could've been taken down weeks ago, would serve the local prosecutor just as well as her being in court for some run-of-the-mill criminal trial."

"Your Honor, if I may comment?" Pitney asked.

"Just make it quick, counselor."

"Certainly, Your Honor. I would suggest that Mr. Dayton, as a federal prosecutor, has no business opining on how courts in the State of California conduct their affairs."

"Once again, we agree, Mr. Pitney," Judge Riggs said. "My decision to postpone remains as stated. We'll reconvene on this matter the twenty-sixth of April 1951."

He then gaveled the hearing to a close.

As they hurried out of the courthouse, Pitney said, "The DA did us one hell of a favor pushing the date of Riddle's trial as far back as he did. He didn't need to do that. By his own admission, the court backlog for a case like that is only about six weeks."

"Maybe he's hoping that extra time will somehow allow him to indict Willis, too," Jillian offered, "and maybe even General and Mrs. Whitelaw."

"Wouldn't that be splendid?" Pitney replied. "And it gives General Molloy more time to muster any help he can from *friends in high places*."

"I've got to get word of the postponement to Jock right away," Jillian said. "The poor lad has enough on his plate without having to worry about this, too."

"How will you notify him? Isn't the mail to Korea slower than molasses in winter?"

"Yes, it bloody well is. But General Molloy is standing by to send a radiogram through official channels. That should only take a day or two."

She fell pensive for a few moments before adding, "You know, with the hearing moved back to the end of April...that's about the time Jock is due to rotate home."

Pitney's eyes lit up like he'd just heard angels sing. "Now that would be wonderful, having him in the courtroom in full uniform. What a positive image he'd present for the case!"

She didn't share his enthusiasm. "I'm not sure it's going to matter a hill of beans to that judge, Mark."

Chapter Twenty

In all his combat experience, Sean Moon had never seen quite so much armor and artillery massed in one sector—and more was coming to 8th Army. He told himself, *Ol' General Ridgway's building us up for another big offensive. You can take that to the bank. But how much you wanna bet the chinks are doing the same damn thing?*

At the moment, Sean was *riding herd* on some drivers he'd detailed to pick up a shipment of new tanks at the rail depot in Ansong, just a few miles south of Line D. As their deuce rumbled through the ravaged city, he could see almost nothing had changed there since 26th Regiment took it from the KPA three months ago, back in early October. Before that battle, most of Ansong's civilians had fled south. Few had returned.

They passed the scorched hulks of ten T-34s Sean and his tankers had destroyed during that fight. He yelled to the GIs in the back of the deuce, "If any of you *jaboneys* ever wonder why I call them T-34s *rice cookers*, the reason's right before your eyes. Take a look at them burned-out sons of bitches. They look like they've been on the stove too long."

But the sight of the T-34s revived a stinging memory: *We only lost a few tanks ourselves that day*, Sean recollected, *but we didn't have to lose any. It was all that idiot captain's fault. Damn glory hound cost us vehicles and got good men killed for nothing. Couldn't talk sense to him. He saw too many war movies and believed all that gung-ho bullshit.*

He didn't last long himself, though. The next day, he decided to drive off on his own to do a little recon. What a dumbass move that was. The gooks left him and his crew laid out dead on the road and stole their Pershing...

And it left us down another tank and crew for no fucking reason.

At the rail depot, the deuce's driver, who wasn't a tanker, watched in bewilderment as strange-looking tracked vehicles with long-barreled, large-caliber guns—but no turrets—were being maneuvered off the flat cars. "What the hell kind of tanks are those, Sarge?" he asked. "Seem a little light in the armor department, ain't they?"

"Yeah, because they ain't tanks, numbnuts," Sean replied. "They're self-propelled artillery. You ain't never seen eight-inch SPs before?"

The driver shook his head.

"How long you been in *this man's army*, anyway?"

"Six months, Sarge. Just got to Korea a couple of weeks ago."

"Then you're gonna learn something new every day, my friend," Sean told him. "Those SPs come in real handy when armor's leading the way. They can keep up with tanks, go off-road with 'em if necessary without getting bogged down like towed artillery would. And they throw one hell of a big round, too." Pointing to a column of Pershings lined up on the road, he added, "Now fall in as *ass-end Charlie* behind those new tanks of ours."

"No can do, Sarge. The lieutenant told me to come straight back after I dropped you guys off. I'm not supposed to wait around or anything."

"What? The lieutenant told you wrong, pal. You and

me are gonna stay on the tail end of that tank column, sweep up any breakdowns, and corral anybody who's thinking about getting lost. And you are *coming straight back*, anyway. You're just gonna be doing it at a more leisurely pace."

"You're putting my ass in a sling, Sarge. The lieutenant's going to be pissed."

"Yeah, I know damn well what delicate little flowers lieutenants can be, but I'll help him get over it real quick. Now, follow them tanks…and do it with your mouth shut."

*****

Driving to Major Grossman's 3rd Battalion HQ, Patchett's jeep was flagged down by Ralph Shelnutt, first sergeant of a company in that outfit, and—in the absence of any officers to fill the slot—its acting company commander. He obviously had a load on his mind.

"I hear you know Major Grossman from way back, Patch," Shelnutt said. "Maybe you can help us talk some sense into the boy."

"He ain't no *boy*, Ralph…and I ain't liking the sound of this right off the bat. Not one damn bit."

"Hey, wait a minute, brother. Don't go making me the bad guy here."

"You're gonna have to prove to me you ain't, First Sergeant," Patchett replied, "and it better be a damn good story. Do me a favor, too…ain't neither of us in no Southern Baptist church right now, so don't be pulling that *brother* shit on me."

"Fair enough," Shelnutt said. "It's just that the

major—that *city slicker jewboy*—is trying to push these men too damn hard, Patch. He keeps wanting them to dig more foxholes and bunkers—"

Patchett interrupted him. "First off, they're called *fighting holes* in this regiment. A foxhole is where some green troop with his head up his ass hides, remember?"

Shelnutt nodded, his head down to avoid eye contact.

"Second," Patchett continued, "the major and me spilled blood together back in the jungle. I'm more his brother than I am yours. So I better never again—and I mean *never*—hear him referred to in the terms you just used. You understand me, First Sergeant?"

The way he spoke the term *First Sergeant* made it sound like a question in itself, one that suggested the pay grade and prestige it carried could be a fleeting thing.

"Okay, Patch, okay…I read you loud and clear," Shelnutt said. "But the engineers dug us some beautiful bunkers already. The men just don't understand why they gotta dig some more, especially up on that rock-hard ridge."

"I don't really have to tell you the answer to that, do I, First Sergeant?"

"Because the major likes to hand out *busywork*, right? So they don't have so much time to think about how miserable they are?"

Shaking his head, Patchett said, "No, you moron. It's because he wants to keep as many of their stupid asses alive as he can. You know, Ralph, it's a cryin' shame when an old infantryman like you forgets how he got to be an *old* infantryman. Rule number one: when you ain't moving, you dig your sorry ass in as deep as you can."

"So what do I tell the troops, then, Patch? They're still *pretending* to follow his orders, but I'm afraid we're just around the corner from them *refusing* an order. Help me out here, will you?"

"The first thing you're gonna do, First Sergeant, is remind those men they don't wanna get on your wrong side. Or mine, neither...because I could sure use some fresh *volunteers* for them night patrols."

Just the mention of *night patrols* sent a tremor of fear through Shelnutt's body. He knew they were personally supervised by Patchett or that other *city boy lunatic,* Captain Pop. Nobody ever volunteered for them—not in the literal sense, at least. They were instruments of corrective discipline as much as they were tools to gather information on the enemy. Those who'd tried to sandbag their way through one of those ass-puckering outings had been made very sorry about it in short order. There was never a mention of the stockade; they just found themselves assigned to the next night's patrol. And on that patrol, they'd be the point man, the first one in the column.

Unless he remained completely focused, he'd be the most vulnerable one, too.

It was an all-too-real example of what hardened NCOs always told recalcitrant GIs: *I can't make you do anything, boys. I can just make you wish you'd done it.*

Patchett decided his visit to 3rd Battalion's CP could wait a few more minutes. He needed to see with his own eyes what Lee Grossman's men were complaining about. He told Shelnutt, "I tell you what, Ralph...show me a place on your perimeter where your men think they know tactics better than their commander and don't have to pay him no mind."

*****

The section of the perimeter Shelnutt brought him to was on high ground at the eastern edge of the battalion's sector, a barren ridgeline overlooking a highway that paralleled frozen marshland. It was one of those areas 8th Army engineers couldn't do much to improve; climbing that steep slope was nearly impossible for bulldozers and earth-moving vehicles.

"This terrain's not exactly generous with natural cover and concealment," Patchett said. "I reckon it could use a little shovel work."

Nearly a mile away on the far side of that board-flat marsh lay a line of hills as barren as the ridge on which they stood. They seemed uninhabited, but Patchett was sure that if the GIs looked hard enough with binoculars, they'd get a hint of the well-dug-in fighting positions their Chinese adversaries had prepared.

Walking among the GIs manning the perimeter, he found only the crew-served weapons teams—those manning the machine guns and recoilless rifles—had bothered to dig any kind of fighting positions, though they appeared entirely inadequate. Low parapets of loose dirt, wood, and sandbags reduced the weapons' silhouettes but did little to protect the gunners. Overhead cover hadn't been constructed anywhere. Patchett collapsed one of the parapets with a shove from his foot.

"It don't look like this little fortress of yours is gonna stop shit," he told the startled GIs, "and surely not bullets, grenades, or shell fragments, that's for damn sure. If I was you, I'd get that weapon dug into the ground as far as she'll go, then use that lumber and sandbags to put a roof over your heads."

The other GI defenders—the riflemen—hadn't bothered to dig in at all. They were huddled in pairs behind the boulders that were strewn along the ridge.

"Now that's mighty fine cover in a pinch, boys," Patchett observed, "except, of course, if you want to shoot back. When you stick your head up to do it, you're gonna get a face-full of rock fragments from that incoming fire that'll cut through you just like shrapnel. You're better off behind a thick berm made of dirt or sandbags. They don't make their own shrapnel. Minimizes your risk, you know?"

Then Patchett walked behind the line of boulders about twenty paces, picked up a rock, and hurled it like a fastball ace. It split the air between two startled GIs and struck the boulder they were huddled against with a resounding *crack*.

"Hello, GI! Me Joe Chink," Patchett called out in a bad parody of an Asian accent. "Me sneak up behind you!"

Shifting back to his normal voice, he continued, "And he blows your asses to kingdom come."

A GI wailed, "But the chinks won't be coming from that direction, Sarge!"

"Son, you ain't paying attention to what you don't wanna hear," Patchett replied. "Or maybe you slept through that part of the briefing. But I'm here to tell y'all that the chink is gonna stand on his head to get behind you. More than half the GI units that got wiped out got themselves overrun *from behind*. And y'all look like prime candidates to be the next ones on that sorry list. So them rocks ain't doing you good like you figured, boys. They can't hold a candle to nice deep holes that'll let you fight in any direction you gotta."

A tall, cocksure corporal replied, "But who's gonna dig into this *concrete*, Sergeant? It's frozen fucking solid."

Pointing to the hills across the wide marsh, Patchett said, "Them chinks over yonder ain't having no trouble digging into it, son, and they ain't even got the top shelf pioneer tools y'all do. Shit, them Chinese are digging *tunnels* through this stuff, not just li'l ol' holes in the ground. And they do it all for a little bucket of spoilt rice a day. I reckon one of them tunnels might just pop up right in the middle of your position. Then they jump out and kill *all y'all*, just so they can steal your Hershey bars and canned peaches."

He paused to let them ponder in stunned silence for a moment. Then he added, "So what's it gonna be, soldiers? You gonna dig...or you gonna die?"

Patchett didn't have to look back as he walked to his jeep. He could tell what was happening just from the sound; dozens of shovels and pickaxes hacking into the frozen turf made a clatter that was unmistakable.

There was another sound, too: the muttering of griping GIs, blowing off steam but knowing they didn't dare cross this old sergeant who knew more about war fighting—and war *surviving*—than all of them put together.

Patchett couldn't decide which of those two sounds he found more pleasing.

*****

At 3rd Battalion CP, Patchett and Lee Grossman were having a long talk over canteen cups of hot coffee.

"Thanks for helping me out on the east ridge, Top," Grossman said. "I know I've got a big problem with Shelnutt's company. But believe it or not, it wasn't my most pressing one. That's why I hadn't paid them a visit in the last twenty-four hours."

"No problem, sir. Glad to do it. But you're right...that company's in sorry shape."

"What do you suggest I do, Top?"

"Get rid of Shelnutt, sir. Shitcan him...he's a weak sister. Maybe he's an adequate first sergeant, but he needs a real company commander over him to keep him straight."

"I figured that out already," Grossman replied. "I asked the colonel if I could have Theo, but he turned me down."

"I know. He and I talked about it. But we need Captain Pop right where he's at, and company officer attrition has been brutal across the board. But there's another six-striper coming in with the next batch of replacements who should be right up your alley. He don't need no captain or lieutenant telling him what to do."

"No officers in that batch, Top?"

"Nothing but a handful of green second louies, sir."

"Figures," Grossman said. "So when will my new master sergeant show up? We're going to be moving north again in a couple weeks. I'll need him in place before we start rolling."

"He should be here in a coupla days, sir. That should give you plenty of time to break him in."

"I'll hold my breath until he gets here, Top."

Patchett downed the last of his coffee and rose to leave. "You got the colonel's meeting at 1600 hours on your calendar, right, sir?"

"Wouldn't miss it for the world," Grossman replied. "I want to hear more about General Ridgway's plans to take back Seoul before the snows melt." He paused, making sure nobody else in the CP could hear. Then he asked, "What do you make of Ridgway, Top? At first glance, he seems like the right man for the job...but is he on the level?"

"From what I can tell, sir, we couldn't've asked for better."

"The rumor mill's saying he's going to hang a star on Jock Miles. Is that true?"

"Ain't my place to say, sir...but I reckon the star's there for the taking."

"That's great, but is he going to take it?"

"That depends a whole lot more on what happens back in the States with Miss Jillian than what's going on here, sir."

Recoiling in disgust, Grossman said, "I can't believe they're serious about deporting her back to Australia, Top. What the hell could she have done to deserve that? And after all she did for us—for MacArthur and his whole goddamn Army—when we were all back in the jungle? That's the thanks she gets?"

"You're preaching to the choir, sir."

*****

Taxiing out for takeoff from K-2 at twilight, the crew of *Moon's Menace VI* passed an unusual sight: in a run-down hangar built by the Japanese during the last war, a glass-nosed B-26 was having both gun turrets removed from her aft fuselage.

"That's going to be our squadron's first *SHORAN* ship," Hank Roth, Tommy Moon's navigator, said. "You should've come to the briefing, sir. They put out a lot of good poop about that system."

"I would've loved to be there," Tommy replied, "but giving check rides to those new pilots ran a lot longer than it was supposed to. I'm not worried about having missed anything, though. You'll tell me all the good stuff, right?"

Rear gunner Bob Allen's voice blared in their headphones. "I don't know what could be so *good* about it. It's putting guys like me out of work. Ain't no room for a gunner on a SHORAN-equipped B-26."

"Don't sweat it, Bob," Tommy replied. "I hear they're looking for B-29 gunners."

"That's all I need, sir…riding one of those lumbering beasts through MIG Alley. I always had the nasty feeling I should've gone to cooks' school. To hell with this *glory of aviation* shit."

"But if the system works like they say it should," Roth added, "SHORAN will let us bomb blind with pinpoint accuracy. It won't matter if it's dark or the target's socked in. We just line up those two little arcs in the scope and then *bombs away*. It's more than just a *short-range navigation* system. It's a precision bombsight, too."

"All that *Buck Rogers* stuff sounds great," Tommy said, "but save it for later. Read me the takeoff checklist, Hank."

*****

The two-ship formation was cruising north through

the night sky at 10,000 feet, en route to what promised to be a lucrative target area: fifteen miles due east of Seoul, two major highways intersected near the village of Chinjung-ni. Intelligence reports indicated heavy convoy traffic on those roads after dark as Chinese and resurgent North Korean forces massed to counter 8th Army's buildup along Line D. The two aircraft—the heavily gunned *Moon's Menace VI* and another B-26, lightly armed but equipped with a powerful wing-mounted searchlight—were the first relay in a series of attack ships flying an all-night interdiction effort against the enemy convoys.

They'd be limited to two directions of attack: from either north or south. Mountains jutted into the sky over two thousand feet on either side of the highways. Those mountains would be invisible in the dark, making low-level strafing attacks a hair-raising adventure. Fortunately, the highways were fairly straight and level for miles at a stretch. The one bringing traffic from the north—the most likely one on which to intercept multiple convoys before they disbursed onto the intersecting roadways—closely paralleled the Pukhan River, running through its valley. The river was partially frozen over; the crystalline surface reflected moonlight and searchlight beams well, providing the pilots with a visible reference for avoiding the adjacent mountains.

"We're five miles out," Roth told Tommy. "Time to drop down and have a look-see."

The navigator on the searchlight ship, call sign *Limelight One-Seven*, concurred. Her pilot initiated a straight-in descent toward the Pukhan River and its parallel highway.

"Bringing her down to five thousand," Tommy said.

"Just keep an eye peeled for that *hardcore cumulus*."

"Roger on avoiding those rocks in the sky," Roth replied as he watched the exhaust flare of *Limelight's* engines a few miles ahead. "We're in the light ship's sound mask now. Maintain this airspeed...that should keep us there."

Being in *Limelight's* sound mask was a tactical imperative for the attacking ship. When the Chinese and KPA convoys weren't pressed for time, they'd drive slowly with their headlights off, making them invisible to aircraft without the aid of searchlights or illumination flares. Lookouts in the convoy would search the skies for the blue-orange exhaust glow of American planes; they'd even use ear trumpets—primitive but effective tools—to discern the engine noise of distant aircraft from the rumble and snarl of their own vehicles. By staying behind *Limelight*, the engine noise of *Moon's Menace VI* would be difficult, if not impossible, to pick out.

If the convoys were pressed for time—which was their usual situation—they drove with headlights on until aircraft were detected overhead.

Once illuminated in the searchlight ship's beam, a convoy might—if terrain permitted—leave the road for the cover of trees. If terrain didn't permit leaving the road, they'd try to drive as fast as they could to escape the probable kill zone.

But there'd be those few moments after the searchlight ship flew past that the convoy might think it was in the clear. They'd resume their travel, sometimes even switching their headlights back on. By the time they realized there was another aircraft bearing down on them, it was too late. The convoy would be riddled by fire from the attacking ship.

Limelight's beam was illuminating a stretch of the road now, as well as the riverbed to its right and the base of the mountain to its left. Tommy's ship was still too far away to see the targeted area, but they knew the game was on when *Limelight's* pilot announced, "We've got a live one here. Lots of vehicles, headlights off, and nowhere to go. They're staying on the road, still moving."

"Okay, we're descending to five hundred feet," Tommy replied as he flipped the switch to arm the guns. "Report when you're clear."

Usually that announcement would come in just a few seconds. But instead of calling his ship *clear*, *Limelight* said, "Well, *lookee here*...we've got another bunch a few hundred yards behind them. Have a field day, Tommy. Got yourself a good visual reference?"

"Roger. Douse your light and get out of there. We're rolling in."

Then he told Roth, "You look left, I'll shoot."

Look left meant keep an eye on the looming mountain. The slightest hint that they were off course and headed for disaster—like a sudden, impenetrable blackness where there'd been the deep gray tinge of night sky just a moment before—would send *Moon's Menace VI* into the steepest climb she could achieve. That climb wouldn't end until the altimeter read 2,000 feet above the highest peak in the target area. Then Tommy would have to make the decision whether to try again or abort the mission.

They were swooping lower now, down to 1,000 feet and still descending. Tommy could see the satiny gray ribbon of the river fairly well. The less visible roadway was just a matter of yards to the ribbon's left. He couldn't make out any trucks; either they'd kept their headlights off...

Or I'm in the wrong place altogether.

Hank Roth's mantra was reassuring: "Clear left...clear left...clear..."

Tommy opened fire at 650 feet on the altimeter, aiming by probability tempered with a dose of intuition.

Within a few seconds, they'd descended to 500 feet, still firing.

"Not an inch lower," Tommy said as he released the trigger button, eased the throttles forward, and pulled her nose up into a brisk climb.

They weren't sure if they'd hit anything or not until Bob Allen, the only crewman who could see aft, gasped from the gunner's compartment, "Holy crap! We scored a big hit on something."

As he said that, there was a flash like a bolt of lightning beneath the aircraft. A second later, a shock wave rocked her like an earthquake's tremor.

Tommy asked, "What are you seeing, Bob?"

"Looks like we hit an ammo convoy. Nothing else blows up quite like that. Getting secondaries now, too."

From an orbit over the target area, *Limelight* added, "We've got major explosions going on down there. Nice shooting, Tommy. But I think there are still more vehicles needing some attention. Want to do another pass?"

"Affirmative," Tommy replied, "but I'm going to make my run out of the north this time. You stay high and keep the light trained on the road so I can see what I'm doing, since it isn't any secret anymore that we're here. Just don't light me up when I'm coming in."

"Roger," *Limelight* replied. "Did you take any fire?"

"Don't think so."

"Me either. Give 'em hell, Tommy."

With the first convoy element stalled and burning, the second element couldn't get through. Its trucks were now stationary targets, viewed from the night sky as tiny gray rectangles throwing long, dancing shadows in the searchlight's glare.

When they were raked with a few hundred rounds of .50 caliber from the guns of *Moon's Menace VI*, they erupted just like the vehicles of the first element.

Limelight's pilot was on the air again, saying, "Looks like there are going to be a bunch of chinks who won't be getting their ammo resupply tonight. If we can keep this up, they won't be able to do anything but throw rocks before long."

Chapter Twenty-One

In the Ansong schoolhouse that served as General Ridgway's forward headquarters, the corps, division, and regimental commanders of his 8th Army assembled on this last week of January 1951. There was one notable absentee: General Almond, still wearing the two hats of X Corps commander and MacArthur's chief of staff, was in Tokyo with the Supreme Commander. Ridgway found the situation intolerable: *Any man trying to do two jobs does neither of them well. But I can't fire him from MacArthur's staff...and if I dump him as Tenth Corps commander, I disrupt the command and control of a quarter of my forces for a while.*

At least I put a stop to Almond and his corps being an independent command that answered to Tokyo and not Eighth Army.

The roaring flames in the old building's fireplaces did little to warm the frigid air inside. The officers huddled in the briefing room were still swaddled in the parkas, fur-lined caps, and gloves they'd worn outdoors.

The only good thing anyone could say about the weather was that no fresh snow had fallen in the past week, leaving the skies clear for American airpower to continue their interdiction of the Chinese and North Korean supply lines. While that effort was greatly appreciated by the officers and men of 8th Army, they shared a collective wish for more:

If only those flyboys could actually locate and plaster those major CCF units that must be assembled somewhere near here, that would be even better. It's great that the Air Force is messing up their supply chain, but the chinks are still here.

For the past week, Ridgway's forces had been engaged in *Operation Thunderbolt*, a series of reconnaissance-in-force efforts conducted by individual infantry regiments and armored battalions. Probing north from Line D, the goal of these efforts was to locate where the Chinese and KPA forces were massing for their inevitable renewed assault. Ridgway's instructions to his commanders had made one thing clear: *First: no unit is to become so deeply engaged that it requires other commands to have to come to their rescue.*

If a unit had to be bailed out in that manner, it would result in a disruption of 8th Army's MLR, inviting a Chinese breakthrough and encirclement of American forces. Since its establishment, the MLR at Line D had been largely unchallenged by the CCF. Matt Ridgway wanted to believe that was due to its perceived impregnability; he didn't need a foolish or overzealous commander setting up an opportunity for the Chinese to prove him wrong.

"Gentlemen, we've learned a lot this past week," Ridgway said as he opened the briefing before a gigantic wall map. "As we suspected, the enemy forces we've faced in the area of Line D are fairly light. Operation Thunderbolt was envisioned as a reconnaissance effort, but because of this light resistance, we've been able to move our line north, cutting the distance to Seoul and the Han River in half. That city now lies only fifteen miles away."

He walked to the side of the platform, motioning for a towering major general with close-cropped white hair to stand. "Gentlemen, before we get down to brass tacks,

I need you all to meet somebody. As you know from dispatches over the last twenty-four hours, General Bishop is no longer in command of Twenty-Fourth Division. His replacement is General Blackshear Bryan," he said, pointing to that mountain of a man. "As you're probably thinking, General Bryan would make one hell of a football lineman. Well, rest assured that he was—a tackle at West Point back in the early 1920s. I've known him for quite a while, and he's worked for me before. He's an outstanding officer. Get to know him."

To some small degree, they had already gotten to know him, at least on paper. The minute the change of command order was published, gossip flowed in from all across Korea about Blackshear Bryan. The consensus: *The man's been a pencil-pusher his whole career. Never had a combat command in his life, not in this war or the last one, where everybody and his brother could get combat time if he wanted it. But his basic career was with the artillery, so at least he's from a combat arm.*

But most importantly, General Ridgway wants him. Based on what we've seen of Ridgway so far, that's good enough...for now, at least.

Rumors of Bishop's impending removal hadn't been surprising; the only question was why hadn't it happened long before Ridgway fired him. As Jock put it: *The man just wasn't in good enough physical shape for a combat command. He was a deskbound commander, and that just doesn't work out here on the line. His various ailments kept him from being where he was needed most of the time.*

And the few times he was around, he was a pain in my ass.

General Ridgway returned to the map, sketching a *goose egg* in grease pencil some twenty miles east of Seoul, anchored on the Han River's south bank. "In this area, gentlemen, is where we believe the Chinese Thirty-Eighth Army is massing."

Every man in the room noted that the area was directly across from 24th Division's current position on the 8th Army line. They were all thinking, *The Twenty-Fourth is directly in harm's way. And it's the one with the brand new, untested commander. If it folds, we all fold.*

"Now I want everyone to know that I have no intention of plowing headlong into this mass of Chinese," Ridgway continued. "And, of course, given the river, the mountains, and the presence of at least two other Chinese armies to the east and the potential bloodbath with the KPA in Seoul to the west, the Chinese Thirty-Eighth Army will be difficult, if not impossible, to envelop."

Then, in red grease pencil, he drew a large *U* whose lower curve plunged through the heart of 24th Division's position. His officers interpreted that *U* to depict a salient, a penetration of an enemy deep into your lines. That seemed to confirm their worst fears...

Until Ridgway said, "We're going to create a ruse, gentlemen. Twenty-Fourth Division is going to sucker the Chinese into an artillery trap here"—he placed the tip of his pointer at the base of the *U*—"roughly five miles north of the city of Kumnyangjang-ni along Highway Seventeen. Colonel Miles, I understand your regiment is well acquainted with that city from the drive north in October. That name is a mouthful, but I understand your men called it something else. Would you share with us what it was?"

"Yes, sir," Jock replied. "We called it *Come Yank My Chain*. Much easier to remember and say."

Smiling, Ridgway said, "Indeed it is. I suspect we'll use that name extensively in the planning and execution of this operation. If the Chinese take the bait, I'd like to see the trap sprung no later than 2359 hours on thirty-one January. That's tomorrow night, gentlemen. If our artillery succeeds in shattering CCF forces in that sector—and I have every confidence that they will— First Cavalry Division will immediately exploit through the gap we create in the Chinese line, split their forces, and send them reeling as the rest of Eighth Army presses north behind First Cav. General Bryan, I'll expect to see your division's operations plan for this action by 2000 hours today."

*****

As Jock and the other two regimental commanders from 24th Division were huddled with their new commander, General Ridgway approached and asked, "General Bryan, may I borrow Colonel Miles for a moment?"

In the privacy of what must've once been a classroom, Ridgway said, "I still haven't named an assistant division commander for the Twenty-Fourth, Jock. I'd like it to be you, but as I know you're aware, I'll have to fight to jump you up the promotion list and get you the star that comes with the job. I don't want to waste any time doing that if you're not interested. I sense you have reservations, so what's it going to be?"

Reluctantly, Jock explained the problem with Jillian

and her possible deportation back to Australia. The fact that he knew so little of the details of the case against her was incredibly frustrating, and it showed as he spoke.

During his long career commanding units at every level from platoon to corps and now an entire army, Matt Ridgway had heard all kinds of stories from subordinates about problems back home. He knew the effects those out-of-reach issues could have on men overseas, who were powerless to provide any assistance to their loved ones.

"I'm really sorry to hear this, Jock," Ridgway said. "I can understand how betrayed you must feel that such an action by our nation's government—a nation you defend with your life on a daily basis—is even possible. But why didn't you come to me sooner?"

"You've got more than enough on your mind, sir. I don't think I should be troubling you with my family's problems. I'll manage on my own, and I've done my best to keep it from affecting my performance."

"By all accounts, you certainly have, Jock. But you need friends in matters like this. You say your wife's case will be decided in April?"

"Yes, sir. The twenty-sixth of the month."

"And if she's allowed to stay in the States, you'd take a promotion as well as perform the extra tour it would entail here in Korea? That's awfully close to your rotation date, isn't it?"

"Yes, sir, it is close. But knowing my family wasn't about to be uprooted from the life and home we've chosen would make a world of difference in considering the promotion."

Ridgway was about to press him about his use of the word *considering*; it sounded as if he was still leaving himself room to refuse the star. He decided not to push the issue now, though, because regimental commanders who were considered *fighters* were in far shorter supply than one-star generals looking to punch their ticket for that second star...

And Matt Ridgway knew he needed *fighters* to push the Chinese back beyond the 38th Parallel and keep them there. But he also knew that domestic tranquility could keep a career soldier's morale high. Lack of that tranquility could destroy him.

"Let me see what I can do to help, Jock," Ridgway said. "Maybe a little more pressure to persuade Uncle Sam to do the right thing by your wife will make all the difference."

*****

The premise of the artillery trap was simple: lure a large enemy force into a relatively compact kill zone and then rain holy hell on them with every cannon you could muster. It was the *luring* that was the difficult part. They had to convince the Chinese that a portion of the 8th Army line had suddenly become exploitable.

The first ops plan devised by the G3 of 24th Division was anything but inspired. It depended on a small number of vehicles—mostly tanks—making a great deal of noise by driving back and forth along the division front, attempting to give the impression a much larger force was on the move. Then the decoy vehicles would retreat to the south, signaling this *larger force* was withdrawing.

Sean Moon was the only man in the CP who'd had experience in this type of operation. He told the G3,

"Begging your pardon, sir…and with all due respect…but that ain't gonna work. What you're proposing, we did plenty of times back in Third Army, but it wasn't to trick them into thinking we were pulling out. What it does do is it gives the impression that they're facing a much larger force than they really are. I can make a platoon of tanks sound like an armored battalion, no problem. But to make it sound like that battalion's *pulling back*? That takes a little something extra."

Quite annoyed, the G3 asked, "Like what, Sergeant?"

"Like this, sir. We gotta make it sound like there's been a huge fuckup in our line. For example, a big explosion you can hear for miles, capped off with a controlled fire you can see for miles. *Then* you can move around all the vehicles you want, making it sound like we're in a headlong *vamoose*."

His eyes wide with wonder, General Bryan asked, "You've done something like this before, Sergeant?"

"Yes, sir. And the Krauts fell for it just about every time. They'd come barreling into this big artillery ambush and get the shit blown out of 'em. We'd ring the kill zone with tanks, too, because the Krauts would always lead with lots of armor. The chinks won't have much in the way of tanks, though, so the artillery'll be blowing up personnel, mostly."

Anxious to regain the spotlight, the G3 blurted, "I've got it! Since the weather's going to be clear for at least the next few days, why don't we get the Air Force to *accidentally* bomb our lines? After we've pulled back from the targeted area, of course. When the Chinese see that, they'll say *Thank you very much* and come flooding in."

Not one of Jock's officers thought much of that idea. They all started to refute the G3 at the same time, creating a jumble of voices nobody could understand.

"Hang on, gentlemen," Jock said. "Sergeant Moon's been carrying the ball pretty well so far. Let him take it to the end zone." Then he turned to General Bryan and asked, "If that's okay with you, sir?"

"By all means, Colonel. I'd like to hear what the sergeant has to say."

"Very well, sir," Sean said. "Okay, here's the problem...you're giving the flyboys a little too much credit. The odds are pretty good they'll drop some bombs right on friendly heads. Accidentally, of course...but that don't make no difference to the casualties. Don't get me wrong...I love our flyboys. One of 'em is my little brother. But they're only human...and they'll all tell you the same thing: everybody looks pretty much alike from up there."

The officers thought Sean was finished, but then he added, "Do any of you gentlemen remember *Operation Cobra* back in Normandy in Forty-Four? Eighth Air Force managed to kill or injure better than a battalion's worth of GIs. Killed a three-star, too—General McNair. So if you're asking me, I'd say we stage our own pyrotechnics. The engineers got loads of explosives, and we got enough *foo gas* to make a fire the chinks'll see in Seoul."

*****

General Blackshear Bryan made Ridgway's deadline with an hour to spare. Twenty-Fourth

Division's ops plan was presented to the 8th Army commander at 1900 hours. The only thing that worried Bryan: *There's an old saying among those of us who've worked for the man that goes like this: there are three ways to do things: a right way, a wrong way, and a Ridgway.*

Let's hope we're in that latter category.

The 8th Army commander smiled as he read the name they'd chosen for the task: *Operation Chain-Link.* He asked, "I'm guessing it's inspired by *Come Yank My Chain?*"

"Affirmative, sir," Bryan replied.

"Good. I like it."

But Ridgway did have some questions. Circling an area on the wall map with his fingertip, he asked, "This fire we'll be setting...you're putting it up on a plateau near the village of Yubang-ni?"

"Yes, General," Bryan replied.

"Have you checked the wind forecast for tomorrow afternoon and evening?"

Bryan knew why he was asking, because Jock Miles had raised the same question. Joining his boss at the map, he began to illustrate his battle plan as he told Ridgway, "Yes, sir, we have. The wind will be from the west-northwest at fifteen knots. The staged fire and the explosion that precedes it will be on the plateau to the east of the village and Highway Seventeen. The wind will be carrying the smoke away from the trap area and our troops. Visibility of the battle area—even in the dark of night—should not be an issue."

Then Ridgway asked, "You'll be setting off this explosion and fire before the sun goes down. Why not wait until after dark?"

"In daylight, we can see well enough to be sure that their triggering is as spectacular as it needs to be, sir."

Ridgway nodded approvingly. "Good point, General. Now let me ask you something else. That fire—it'll be a great temptation for your troopers. They'll want to leave their posts and huddle around it to get warm. What did you say the forecast temperature for tomorrow night is?"

Bryan replied, "Minus ten degrees Fahrenheit, sir, with a biting wind we've already discussed."

"So how do you plan to keep your shivering troopers away from that fire?" Ridgway asked.

"My troopers will be well south of the fire, sir. Once the engineers set it off and rig the delayed fuzes for the follow-up explosions, they'll be gone, too."

Ridgway had no argument with that.

Then Bryan discussed the most critical aspect of the plan: how his forces would know, even in the darkness, when the Chinese were actually in the kill zone. He explained that there'd be a small tank force that would serve as an armored cavalry decoy, with the ability to make and then quickly break off contact with the approaching Chinese. Using hit-and-run tactics, these tankers would lure their foes deeper into the kill zone while still maintaining the mobility to escape once their quarry was in the trap.

This was the part that worried Ridgway the most. It was essential to sucker as large a Chinese force as possible into the trap and destroy them outright; otherwise, the exercise would fail to provide the void in the CCF lines he sought to exploit. The violent dance of deception the armored cavalry patrol would execute— amid the confusion of darkness and shots fired in anger—was not something to be left to anyone other than a proven combat leader. Without such a leader, it was doomed to failure.

When Ridgway asked who would be leading the patrol, Bryan replied, "We have very few experienced junior officers in our tanker ranks, sir...unfortunately, we have very few junior officers, period. But we're in luck—there's a very senior armor sergeant on Colonel Miles' staff who fought with Patton against the Krauts and has executed operations like this before. That sergeant was instrumental in putting this ops plan together, so he knows precisely what needs to be done and has the experience to make it happen."

Ridgway felt his worries melting away. "What's this sergeant's name?" he asked.

"Moon, sir. Master Sergeant Sean Moon."

Chapter Twenty-Two

Even though the GIs knew it was coming, the blast still scared them half to death.

It was just a few minutes past 1600 hours when the engineers set off that thunderous explosion on a cleared portion of the plateau near the deserted village of Tunjon-ni. It shook the snow-covered ground for miles in all directions. On the heels of the detonation came the planned fire: a huge, napalm-fueled blaze now flared near the blast site. As thick black smoke billowed into the late afternoon sky, there were high hopes this demonstration had been as attention-grabbing as the commanders planned.

"Look at that damn fire," Sean told the crewmen of his four tanks as they watched the flames leap over a hundred feet into the air. "The engineers said they'd make the base of that son of a bitch about fifty yards in diameter and set out enough *foo gas* drums, satchel charges, and combustible shit on delay fuzes all around the perimeter to keep the blaze going for hours. They even threw in that captured chink ammo we ain't got no use for…not until now, anyway. That shit'll be cooking off for a while."

His apprehensive loader said, "I hope to hell that fire don't spread and fry us all."

"Ain't likely," Sean replied. "Not with everything covered in snow and the wind blowing it away from us."

They could hear the roar of a hundred GI vehicles behind them. Trucks and tanks were beginning the next step in setting the artillery trap: creating the aural illusion of an American withdrawal. Those vehicles wouldn't travel far, just a few miles south to the empty village of Yubang-ni, where they'd join the rest of 26th Regiment in their prepared defensive positions at the base of the *U*-shaped trap. The division's other two regiments were already emplaced in the hills that paralleled Highway 17, the route of the anticipated Chinese advance. There, they'd form the sides of the trap; one regiment lay two miles east of the highway, the other two miles west.

The rumble and growl of the vehicles went quiet as the gray dusk darkened into night. Looking toward the low, frozen marshland the highway passed through, Sean and his tankers saw something neither they nor their commanders had expected: the decoy blaze, still burning ferociously, was casting a pale glow across the roadway. The flames showed no signs of subsiding.

"This is better than illum rounds," Sean said. "Let's hope it keeps up. But since they can see us as well as we can see them, let's give ourselves a bigger margin for error, like an extra hundred yards or so."

A gunner asked, "You really think they're just going to come strolling down this road, Sarge?"

"If they want to get here fast, they will," Sean replied. "And if all this noise and flames fooled 'em good enough, they'll definitely want to get here fast."

"But what if they don't come, Sarge?"

"Then all we wasted was a little time and a little gas, pal. All right, before we mount up, let's go over this shit one more time…"

Sean led his men through a final review of the plan: the four tanks would split into two pairs, each pair roaming its own side of the roadway while providing mutual protection from sappers. He'd picked Shermans for the task. His reasons: *They ain't so likely to break down, and they can haul ass a hell of a lot quicker than a Pershing.*

The crews were not rookies; they understood the goal of the exercise was not to engage but to lure the Chinese forward into the kill zone. This would require quite a bit of movement on their part—some of it at great speed—with a great deal of fire discipline.

Sean asked, "You've all got a canister round in the tube, right?"

The three other tank commanders nodded *yes.*

"Just remember, if they start swarming you, button up and spray that canister around good while you're getting the hell outta there. Use the MGs as emergency backup if you gotta, but don't waste your time firing HE from the main gun, because there ain't gonna be nothing out there but chinks on foot. It'd be like driving a pin with a sledgehammer. Wrong damn tool for the job."

It had been difficult to come up with the canister rounds. Army tactical doctrine considered using the main guns of tanks as gigantic shotguns a waste of tactical assets, so few of those rounds had been shipped to Korea. The division ordnance section claimed they had none on hand, but Sean wouldn't take *no* for an answer. He located twelve rounds in their dump that had been overlooked and never logged into inventory. Those crates were promptly loaded into his jeep trailer. When the ordnance officer tried to stop him on the way out, saying, "You've got to sign for them, Sergeant," Sean replied, "Sign for what, sir? You didn't even know you had 'em, so the way I see it, it's *finders keepers.*"

Sean was right. In the minds of Army *bean counters,*

you couldn't be charged for losing something you never had on your books in the first place. The flustered lieutenant decided not to argue.

Back at the tank park, Sean distributed three canister rounds to each of his four tanks.

A TC had a question: "What if the chinks got T-34s with them, Sarge? Canister won't do shit to a tank. I'd rather start out with HEAT in the tube."

Sean replied, "Negative. If you see a chink tank, don't engage the son of a bitch. That's not what you're here for. Just back off and don't make yourself a goddamn target. You read me, all of you?"

Again came the affirmative nods. But his tankers seemed more wary this time.

"Everybody keep talking to each other, too," Sean added. "Radio silence is only gonna get you cut off and in deep shit. Okay, let's mount up and move out."

*****

The night was only half an hour old when they saw them coming. In the faint glow the blaze on the plateau was still providing, the Chinese infantry moving toward the tankers materialized as a bizarre apparition: a moving graveyard, each man the shadowy silhouette of a walking tombstone.

I seen this movie before, Sean told himself. *The Krauts in the Ardennes looked like walking tombstones, too, trudging through fields of snow just like these chinks are doing right now. I put 'em about five hundred yards away...*

"All *Temptation* units, this is *Temptation Six*," he radioed his teams. " Let 'em close about half the distance to us, then we back up until they look about as small as they look now. If you can't dope out how far that is, set your gunsight for two-fifty yards and use its picture to guide you."

"*Six*, this is *Three*. Remember the T-34 we were wondering about? Well, she's here. Looks like she's trying to climb up the plateau and get to that blaze."

Temptation Three was Sergeant Rocco Micelli, the leader of the team on the east side of the highway.

"Just one, Rocky?" Sean asked.

"Affirmative. That's all I can see right now. I got a *five-spot* that says she don't make it. Too steep, too slippery."

"Keep an eye on her, Rocky," Sean replied as he fixated on the approaching infantry.

"If she shows me a soft side, you want me to take her, Sean?"

"Negative. What'd I tell you already?"

"Copy," Micelli replied.

Sean figured the approaching Chinese infantrymen were close enough to hear the Shermans' idling engines. Their pace seemed more rapid now...

And over that raucous clatter of his own engine, he could hear bugles, blowing a pattern that sounded like an *A* in Morse Code repeated over and over: *ta taaah...ta taaah...ta taaah...*

Looking up to the plateau, he could see the T-34 clearly; she was backlit by the flames. But she was having trouble scaling the slope. Like Sisyphus trying to roll that rock up the hill, the heavy tank would begin to slide backward every time she neared the top. Then she'd regain traction and begin the slow climb all over again.

"Why the hell does that chink even want to go up there?" Sean's gunner asked.

"Because if he gets on top, he can hit anything within a coupla square miles real easy, that's why."

"Including us, Sarge?"

"Yeah, including us. You got your scope on that infantry?"

"Roger," the gunner replied. "They're at three hundred yards."

"Close enough," Sean said. He keyed the radio and ordered, "All *Temptation* units, pull back now. Repeat, pull back now. Acknowledge, *over.*"

Temptation Two and *Four* replied. But after repeated attempts, there was still no acknowledgment from *Three*, Rocco Micelli's vehicle.

"Four, this is *Six,*" Sean said. "You got eyes on *Three?*"

"Negative. He was moving east last I saw him."

"Toward the plateau?"

"Affirmative. Toward the plateau."

Shit. What does that dumbass think he's doing?

Sean looked to the plateau again. The T-34 was sliding down the slope even farther this time, pivoting uncontrollably, presenting her vulnerable stern to the Shermans. He could guess what Micelli had on his mind: *He's gonna take a shot at her now that she's got her drawers down. Just like I told him not to.*

I gotta find him.

Sean told his driver, "Sully, shift to forward and turn hard right."

"Why, Sarge? That's going to put us awful close to the chinks, isn't it?"

"It might. Just do what the hell I tell you." Then he

told his gunner, "Tube left, toward the chinks."

The gunner was just as skeptical as Sully over what seemed a blatant disregard of Sean's own plan. But he did what he was told without saying a word.

There was a ripple of explosions from atop the plateau, like a barrage where each round impacted a split second after the one before...

And then the fire went out.

It had never seemed so dark.

"Musta been the chink ammo them engineers laced the fire with," Sean said. "When it went up, it blew the fire out, dammit."

As it rumbled east, Sean's tank crossed paths with *Temptation Four*, which was backing briskly away from the approaching Chinese, her engine turning high rpms in reverse.

"Still no Micelli?" Sean asked *Four's* TC over the radio.

"Negative," came the reply.

"Okay," Sean said, "but you better ease off the gas. You're throwing one hell of an exhaust flare with all them revs. That T-34 can see you from a coupla miles away. Make it a little harder for her to kill you, okay?"

"Roger...but how much farther back do we have to go until the trap gets sprung?"

"Another half mile," Sean replied.

"How far ahead of the chinks are we now?"

"Far enough, pal. Just keep it moving."

*****

Sean saw the flare from a Sherman's exhaust a few hundred yards ahead, but the vehicle producing it wasn't moving.

That's gotta be Micelli. What the hell is he doing so far east?

But there was still no answer on the radio.

He sensed the heavy round coming before he'd heard a thing. Its detonation shattered some trees just beyond Micelli's tank.

That son of a bitch chink in the T-34 musta seen that exhaust flare, too.

As Sean's tank got closer, they could see Micelli's problem: her right track was down in a ditch. Their attempts to drive her out were doing nothing but slinging clods of frozen earth behind the stuck Sherman.

There were more bugles. They sounded really close.

In the distance, he heard the dull *pop* of a Sherman's main gun.

Temptation Two is shooting canister at the chinks.

A quick radio check indicated *Two* was still okay and on the move.

Approaching Micelli's tank, Sean told Sully, his driver, "Pull up broadside to her."

They were still fifty yards away from *Three* when they saw the dark shapes of men clambering onto her deck.

"Dust 'em with canister," Sean said to his gunner. Then he told Sully to stop the tank.

"ON THE WAY," the gunner said and then fired the main gun.

Micelli's deck was swept clean.

"Put up another canister round," Sean ordered the loader.

"There's only one left after we shoot it," the gunner said.

"Tell me something I don't know, pal. Sully, get closer. Bump her so she knows we're there...she's buttoned up and something's wrong with her radio..."

Or her whole damn crew is KIA.

As Sully pivoted his vehicle next to the stricken tank, there was suddenly a voice on the intercom. It was Micelli; he'd exited his tank through the escape hatch in her belly and grabbed the phone on the stern of Sean's tank.

"I fucked up, Sean," Micelli said. "We're stuck. I think we threw a track. And the fucking radio—"

"No shit, Rocky. Get your guys in here right now. Your gunner goes last in case he's gotta fire some canister. Any rounds you got left, bring 'em with you."

"Okay. I'll be right back," Micelli said.

More bugles. They sounded like they were right inside the turret.

"Open the escape hatch," Sean told the bow gunner. "If some chink tries to crawl in, shoot him in the fucking face."

Another round streaked in from the T-34, still clinging, apparently, to the slope of the plateau. It landed short, maybe among a group of Chinese infantrymen...

Because the bugles stopped in mid-note.

Squeezing another full crew into the cramped interior of a Sherman was no easy task. But these were not easy times, so difficult things were done immediately.

Impossible things might take a little longer.

"CHINKS AT TEN O'CLOCK," the gunner yelled. He was already traversing the turret that way.

"Knock 'em down," Sean said.

The gunner did just that.

The last man from Micelli's crew was crawling through the belly hatch now. With only his torso inside the tank, there was no place for him to go. The other members of his crew were still struggling to make room for themselves and the one canister round they'd managed to bring with them.

"Hold on to him real good," Sean said. "Sully, get moving."

"We're going to drag his ass, Sarge," the driver replied.

"I could think of worse things right now," Sean replied. "I say again, *get moving*."

"MORE CHINKS," the gunner said.

"Take 'em," Sean replied.

"That's our last canister, Sarge."

"No, it ain't. We just got one more."

"WHERE IS IT?"

"Keep your drawers on. It's coming."

It took a clumsy bucket brigade of four tankers—one sitting in his seat, two kneeling between the driver and bow gunner, and one lying on his back on the turret floor—to pass Micelli's canister round through the crowded tank and up to the tube.

The instant it was loaded, the gunner fired it at a throng of Chinese who seemed to be less than twenty yards away.

Roaring away in reverse, they saw more dark shapes of men clambering over Micelli's Sherman. If there were bugles blaring, they couldn't hear them now over the screaming engine of Sean's tank.

"Put up an HEAT," Sean told the loader.

"You gonna shoot that T-34?" Micelli asked.

"I can't even see the fucking T-34, Rocky. I'm

gonna shoot *your* vehicle. Her gun'll work just as good for the chinks as it did for you, right?"

"Yeah, I see your point, Sean."

It took an awkward dance of the five men crammed into the turret to get the HEAT round out of its rack and clear its path into the breech.

"I've never shot a friendly before," the gunner said as he sighted on Micelli's tank.

"She ain't so friendly no more," Sean replied. "Put it right up her ass."

The gunner sighed, "If I must." Then he shouted, "*ON THE WAY*," and stomped on the foot trigger.

The turret's extra occupants clung to each other for support as the tank rocked and her main gun recoiled just an inch from their faces.

Temptation Three—Micelli's tank—erupted in a cataclysm of high explosives and burning gasoline.

Back on the radio, Sean checked with his other two tanks. Both reported they were crossing the trigger line for the trap, a culvert where a creek crossed under Highway 17, which was less than half a mile north of 26th Regiment's position at Yubang-ni.

Sean figured his tank could cross that line in three minutes...if they were in a forward gear. He told Sully, "Pivot one-eighty and make max forward speed."

"You sure it's safe, Sarge? That T-34 could still shoot us in the ass."

"She can't see much of us now...and in a minute, she ain't gonna be seeing much of anything ever again."

He called Regiment and gave the codeword *Calamity*, the signal to spring the artillery trap.

Sully started to protest, "But we're not at..."

"We're close enough. Just drive, Corporal."

*****

Temptation Six—Sean's tank—was still a hundred yards from 26th Regiment's line when the first rounds of the artillery trap crashed down close behind her. But there was little cause for her tankers to be alarmed; the trap would be like the jaws of a vise being cranked from wide open to fully closed, with several square miles of death and destruction resulting as the two long lines of impacting rounds—one north, one south—swept toward each other. The barrage would go on for twenty minutes, with seventy American guns firing over five thousand rounds as the vise opened and closed eight times.

From a ridge above the village of Yubang-ni, Sean and Rocky Micelli watched the impacts of the distant barrage from the turret roof of *Six*, the strikes twinkling like rapid-fire flashbulbs of manic photographers. The muffled *crump* of each explosion reached their ears like a drumroll seconds later.

As Sean finished a radio transmission to Regiment, Micelli asked, "What'd they say? Any chinks get through?"

"Ain't no reports of anybody walking outta that shitstorm yet, Rocky. But we better get our story straight about what the hell you were trying to do out there, because they're kinda curious about how I ended up having to destroy one of my own vehicles. So what's your story?"

"We're not in deep shit, are we?"

"Nah, not this time. But the colonel does a pretty good job of turning fuckups into learning exercises...and that's a good thing."

Relieved, Micelli launched into his tale. "The area to the east was in shadow, Sean. I thought the chinks might be slipping around us over that way, so I went to have a look."

"Without telling me about it over the radio?"

"I was trying to call you, Sean. I don't know exactly when the radio crapped out. But I musta tried ten times...and while I'm screwing with the damn radio, we ran a track into that ditch. She needed a tow to get out, but..."

"Yeah, I know...it wasn't the time or place to tow anything. But you were sure right about the chinks slipping around that way. That'll sound real good in the debrief. Might even get your sorry ass decorated. Anything else you wanna add?"

"No, that's about it."

"Good story," Sean replied. "Stick to it."

Chapter Twenty-Three

The artillery trap had accomplished its objective. When the sun rose on 1 February 1951, the better part of two CCF regiments lay dead along Highway 17. GIs of 1st Cavalry Division flowed through the new gap in the enemy lines, opening the way for the US 8th Army to push the rest of the Chinese 38th Army back against the Han River. General Ridgway had no doubts he still faced strong adversaries, with at least two Chinese armies and three North Korean corps south of the 38th Parallel. But he knew he had them reeling, at least for the moment.

"The Chinese have begun to shift more of their forces east, away from Seoul," Ridgway told his assembled commanders. "They're desperate to keep us from encircling the city. To do that, they need to maintain control of their Han bridgehead at Yangp'yong as well as the highway and rail lines that parallel the river in that area. Our job, gentlemen, is to cross the Han and get behind them before they can mass to stop us. Then we cut them off from their support in the north and east and choke off Seoul."

Like all audacious plans, it seemed a tall order, especially to those who'd be tasked with executing those plans. But his subordinate commanders had to admit that in the weeks since he'd taken command, General Ridgway's initiatives had achieved their goals decisively. As Jock Miles put it, *This guy knows how to win.*

"We've reached the final phase of *Operation Thunderbolt*, gentlemen," Ridgway continued. "I've ordered General Almond's Tenth Corps to advance north along Twenty-Fourth Division's right flank and become an eastward extension of our line, anchored on Chip'yong-ni. Since that town is a major highway and rail junction, denying it to the Chinese should put a big crimp in their transportation network."

There was another situation map hanging on the wall; it had been concealed behind a shroud to this point. Ridgway signaled his aide to uncover it and then told his commanders, "Gentlemen, once *Thunderbolt* is complete, this will be the next phase of our push to the Thirty-Eighth Parallel."

There was a moment of surprised silence when they saw the title of the map, printed in big letters across its upper border: OPERATION KILLER.

Jock told himself, *The man doesn't believe in mincing words, either.*

Of those present, only Ridgway knew how horrified Washington had been with the name *Killer*, as if the politicians believed that offending the enemy was somehow worse than destroying them. But he understood the desire of the Truman administration to seek a negotiated end to the fighting in Korea, the sooner the better. He considered Washington's revulsion at the term ridiculously overcautious and out of step with battlefield realities:

We're expected to fight from a position of strength. Shouldn't we be negotiating from one, too?

Ultimately, he'd held his ground and prevailed; the name would stand.

But *Operation Killer* wouldn't begin until Matt Ridgway had closed the book on *Thunderbolt*, and that closing was still one objective away.

*****

"Tenth Corps is dragging its feet," Ridgway told General Blackshear Bryan, commander of 24th Division. "General Almond's still fussing about where the boundary between your division and his Second Division should be. If he keeps screwing around, there's a good chance a gap will develop between your forces and his, and that could be disastrous. It's bad enough I had to drag his ass back from his playtime in Tokyo as MacArthur's chief of staff so he could do his job out here as a goddamn field commander."

Bryan replied, "I understand, sir. Do you have a preference where the corps boundary should be?"

"You bet your ass I do, *Blackie*. I want the entire length of Highway Twenty-Four from the Han crossing east of Yoju to Chip'yong-ni—the whole twelve miles—to be in Tenth Corps' zone of responsibility. None of this *you get one side of the highway and I'll get the other* crap. That's how we fuck up…nobody covers the highway itself because they assume the other guy's doing it, and the chinks come down the road like they're on a Sunday stroll. I've ordered Almond to cover the entire highway right up to the peaks paralleling it on both sides. But there's one part of that zone where coordinating the boundary is going to get tricky. Take a look at this…"

Using a grease pencil, Ridgway circled a spot on the map roughly three miles south of Chip'yong-ni. "Main line railroad tracks pass through two tunnels south of the town," he said. "If we don't stop them, the Chinese will use those tunnels to position troops who can block

Highway Twenty-Four. And we won't be able to see them doing it."

He traced the tracks running north toward Chip'yong-ni with his finger. "See how the tunnels sit on either side of the highway, about half a mile apart, connected by a bridge that carries the tracks over the highway? Have you ever seen better natural bunkers? We've already given the complex a name—*Twin Tunnels.*"

He paused until Bryan had finished making notes. "Aerial recon reports Chinese troops in the area of the Twin Tunnels," Ridgway continued. "We need to control every inch of the road and the tracks, especially at night when the chinks can move around best. I'm willing to bet that Almond's boys in Second Division will do a half-assed job of covering the western tunnel and the tracks beyond it, since it entails their going over yet another set of hills. I'll need you to pick up the slack there, Blackie. If you don't control that western tunnel, Almond's boys will be in for a tough slog on that highway. It'll be a bloodbath like the road out of Chosin Reservoir all over again."

*****

Picking up the slack fell to 26th Regiment, specifically Major Lee Grossman's 3rd Battalion, reinforced with a platoon of tanks. Jock Miles told him, "Lee, I'm giving you Sergeant Moon as your armor advisor. I know you haven't had much chance to work with the tankers yet, especially at night. He'll be a big help to you. There's no better teacher on the employment of armor than Sean Moon."

"I'll be glad to have him, sir," Grossman replied, "especially since it means I won't be the only boy from New York City when he's around." Casting a needling eye Patchett's way, he added, "And it'll be nice not having to listen to nobody but crackers for once."

"Begging your damn pardon, sir," Patchett said, switching to his histrionic Southern preacher voice, "but good ol' Bubba Moon might still sound like a city boy, but I been working on him for a long time now. I wouldn't call him a convert to proper living or nothing, but he's finally learned how to do some things right."

Grossman laughed, replying, "Like the way you worked on me back when we were in the jungle, Top?"

"No, it's better with Bubba...because I don't always have to say *with all due respect, sir* while I'm showing him the error of his ways."

"All right," Jock said with a smile, "let's knock off the walk down Memory Lane for now. We've got a lot to do."

As they returned to planning the mission that would coordinate the boundary with 2nd Division, Jock felt proud and blessed that these highly capable men, born of very different worlds, were still brothers linked by a warriors' bond. Even though that bond had been forged in a different time and a different hell, no adversity would ever break it.

*****

Task Force Grossman—the battalion-sized combined arms force of infantry and armor—encountered CCF resistance while still two miles from the western tunnel. A recon team out ahead of the main body had been badly mauled while scouting approaches to the tunnel's entrance in daylight. It had taken repeated air strikes by American fighter-bombers to drive off the Chinese and allow the team to escape decimation. During the fight, the Air Force ASO and his radio operator had been badly wounded in a *friendly fire* accident. A bomb that had hung up on an F-51 released belatedly as that ship pulled out of her attack dive. The late drop flung the five-hundred-pounder over a thousand yards farther than its intended target, impacting much too close to the ASO team. Both men were on a rescue helicopter within fifteen minutes of the incident. Two hours after that, they were on a medical evacuation airplane to Japan.

It was now late afternoon, and Division informed Lee Grossman that another ASO team would not arrive until the following afternoon. When he passed this on to his staff, Sean asked, "They're not pulling the night support aircraft, are they, sir?"

"No," Grossman replied, "but they're wondering who's going to call targets for them. Any ideas?"

"I can do it, sir, no problem," Sean said. "Done it plenty of times. Are we getting *Firefly* ships or birds with spotlights?"

"According to the ops order, we're getting both. But how are you going to talk to them, Sergeant? Didn't the ASO's radio truck get hit, too?"

"Yeah," Sean replied, "but we got the radio working again. Just had to fix an antenna cable that got tore up. The set's up and running, so let's make damn sure they don't welsh on that air support, sir."

*****

The Chinese forces at the tunnel seemed to be getting stronger as day rolled into night.

"They must be bringing reinforcements straight down Highway Twenty-Four," Grossman told Sean. "Chinks are just walking into the tunnel from the far end, and we can't see them coming, not with *Dog Bone Ridge* in the way. It doesn't look like Second Division's anywhere near controlling that highway yet."

Dog Bone Ridge: the name the GIs had given to the hill that housed their objective: the west tunnel. The hill was narrower in the middle where the tunnel passed through it—only half a mile wide—and then flared at its north and south ends. On the map, it was shaped just like a dog's bone that was three miles long.

The tank platoon hadn't been able to do much except lob HE shells at the tunnel mouth from two thousand yards away; they'd be too vulnerable to anti-tank fire if they moved closer across the open terrain. A few of the tankers' rounds had actually found their way inside, detonating to unknown effect. But most splattered against the hillside from which the tunnel emerged.

Grossman said, "The best we can do for now is stop them from going in and out of the tunnel on this end. But once it gets good and dark, they're going to come out to take us on. We won't see them until they're right on top of us. We'd have to fire illum all night long just to figure out what's happening, and you know Division's never going to buy that. Not with rounds in short supply like they are."

"Speaking of rounds, sir," Sean said, "these ammo

shortages are killing us. I'm still coming up empty on that white phosphorous I asked for. I'd really love to fire a couple of them *willy petes* straight into that tunnel and burn the shit out of the chinks inside. I could go back and rummage the ammo dump again, but you probably want me to stay here."

"Damn right I do," Grossman replied. "I need you to figure out how and when we're going to get your flame tank into that tunnel."

*****

Lee Grossman wished he hadn't been so right; once darkness fell, it seemed like half of China was probing the wooded high ground on which he'd positioned his task force. CCF forces hadn't broken through anywhere and were probably falling by the hundreds to American artillery, mortars, machine guns, and small arms. But in the dark of night, no GI could tell how many casualties he was inflicting. Old hands like Grossman knew it wouldn't be much different than daylight fighting: *Unless your target was standing right in front of you, you never knew who you shot, anyway...*
If you shot anybody at all.

All the GIs knew was that no Chinese had gotten close enough to hurl grenades into their fighting holes. Not yet, anyway.

GIs looked in awe at the tracers arcing through the sky, interwoven like stitches in a crazy quilt, desperate to believe that no living thing could possibly survive in their midst.

But the Chinese kept coming.

"They're feeding through that fucking tunnel,"

Grossman said as his frustration swelled. "Where's the goddamn Air Force?"

Sean was pressing the headphones tight against his ears, straining to hear every transmission from the aircraft through the bedlam all around him. "Five minutes out," he was finally able to tell Grossman.

The first aircraft overhead was *Firefly*, the C-47 that dropped strings of incredibly brilliant flares. Plodding across the sky at slow speed, she'd only released the first flare when several large-caliber anti-aircraft guns began firing at her, throwing bright green tracers that crisscrossed in the air as they sought their target.

"Those rounds are coming right from Dog Bone Ridge," a startled lieutenant said.

"No, they're not," Grossman replied. "The darkness just makes it seem closer. They're actually shooting from the other side of Dog Bone, probably right from Highway Twenty-Four."

"You mean where Second Division is supposed to be, sir?" the lieutenant asked.

"Yeah," Grossman snarled. "Exactly where they're fucking supposed to be."

"*Firefly's* bugging out," Sean reported. "*Too hot*, he says. One flare's all we're gonna get. And the damned thing's not even close to being on target."

Not even close: the flare was drifting down well to the east, casting only long, trembling shadows across the barren terrain in front of Task Force Grossman. Occasionally, a group of CCF soldiers were caught running through a sliver of the flare's silvery light, only to vanish back into darkness before weapons could be brought to bear on them.

Then Sean heard another voice on the radio. He

recognized it instantly.

"Hey, it's my little brother bringing in a flight of bombers," he told everyone in earshot.

"How the hell can you tell?" Grossman asked.

"Ain't no mistaking that Brooklyn mouth, Major. He's gonna know my voice the minute he hears it, too."

"That's great," Grossman replied. "So maybe they'll stick around and actually do something for us? Unlike that useless flare ship?"

"He better...or I'll beat his puny little ass black and blue, officer or not."

Then, thinking the officers around him might mistake his big brother bravado for insubordination, he assured Grossman, "With all due respect to present company, of course, sir."

"Don't worry about it, Sergeant. Just get him to kill some chinks...and quick, okay?"

Keying the mike, Sean said, "*Switchblade Leader*, this is *Cobra Five-One*. You wouldn't be Maggie and Paddy's baby boy, would you?"

"I might be," came Tommy Moon's reply, "but I'm only *Half* the Dodger fan you are."

"See, I told you, sir," Sean said to Grossman. "That's my little brother Tommy...eh, make that Major Tommy Moon. That business about *Half the Dodger fan*...that's code. *Half's* his nickname. Always has been."

"*Half Moon*?" Are you kidding me, Sergeant? How come?"

"Let's just say he ain't the biggest guy in the world, sir. But he makes up in brains what he lacks in size."

"Good," Grossman replied. "We could use a flyboy with brains right now."

*****

Moon's Menace VI was now a SHORAN-equipped B-26, the only aircraft so equipped in the four-ship *Switchblade Flight*. Besides Tommy in the pilot's seat and Hank Roth as navigator, the third crew member was the SHORAN operator, Captain Frank Martin, who was tucked into the old gunner's compartment in the aft fuselage. There was no longer any room on board for a gunner or his twin .50-caliber turrets. They'd been displaced by Martin and his electronic gear. A dome antenna for the system was installed where the upper turret used to be. The lower turret had been removed completely to save weight; the cutout where it once was had been faired over with sheet metal.

This was the ship's first combat mission utilizing SHORAN. The system's name was an acronym for *short-range navigation*, but its intended utilization was as a precision radio-guided computing system that allowed putting bombs on target in any condition of visibility, even blind. That was the intention, and it had been achieved with reasonable success during the several practice exercises they'd flown. But the training flights had all been under near-ideal conditions. On this first operational mission, however, Tommy and his crew were finding out the hard way that achieving the intention wasn't always possible:

SHORAN might be real good for dropping stuff on a fixed target from 14,000 feet, if we can even get a fully loaded B-26 up that high. But for a close tactical support mission at low altitude—like this one's suddenly become—it's useless.

"I can't give you the *due east* attack vector you're

asking for, sir," Martin insisted. "With the ground station alignment we've got here, *due east* isn't one of the four possible target vectors the system computes. We're off by forty degrees. Are you sure you can't use a vector of one-three-zero degrees?"

Tommy replied, "We're trying to drop an egg full of napalm into a tunnel mouth, Frank...in the dark, for cryin' out loud. It's straight in or nothing."

The use of the word *nothing* alarmed Hank Roth, the navigator. "You're not thinking of aborting, are you, sir? I mean...with your brother and all down there..."

"No, Hank, we're not going to abort...not on my brother or anybody else who asks for our help. Let's figure out how we can get this done. You know the exact coordinates of this holding orbit we're in, right?"

"Affirmative, sir. I've got it dead on the money."

Of course you do, Tommy thought. *You always know exactly where we are.*

"And the coordinates Sean—I mean my brother, *Cobra Five-One*—gave you for the tunnel mouth...do they make sense?"

"Yes, sir. They jive with the chart perfectly. We're holding eight miles north of the tunnel."

"Okay," Tommy said. "All we need now is two reference points in the sky guiding us in."

"*In the sky*, sir?"

"Yeah. Let's see if the ground-pounders can pull this off."

He called Sean: "*Cobra*, this is *Switchblade*. Can you give me *goalposts* with illum for a heading zero-niner-zero approach? I need two rounds...one at four miles from target and one at one mile. We'll give you their heights of burst in a second. Stand by."

Sean replied, "Can do on the goalposts. Standing by."

Roth was more than a little confused. "*Goalposts*, sir? What are we talking about?"

"It's a little trick we used to do against the Krauts, Hank. It helped guide us to a hard-to-see ground target. During the day, we'd use white phosphorous airbursts. The smoke from the burst would hang in the air for a couple minutes, the farthest one from the target high, the closer one low, marking a descending line of approach to the target. All you had to do was fly right over those puffs of smoke. Doing it at night—with parachute flares which'll be dropping constantly—that'll be a little tougher. But it's all we've got."

"Have you ever done this at night before, sir?"

"Nope," Tommy replied.

"Why can't the ground guys just mark the target with some burning white phosphorous?" Roth asked.

"Take a good look down there, Hank. You see all that shit exploding? Mortars, artillery, tank rounds...what do you think the odds are we'll line up on the right burst?"

He didn't need to add, *And what if we line up on our own guys by accident?*

As Hank took that long look, Tommy added, "But with a napalm fire...well, it's usually pretty easy to pick one of them out. Nothing else burns like that. And once we light it off, we've marked the target for the ships coming in behind us."

"Okay, I get all that," Roth said, "but how do *we* see the target on our run? Even with the goalposts, we're still going to be looking into a dark hole."

"You're right, Hank. That's why the searchlight

ship is going to fly on our left wing. When we pass over the one-mile illum flare, I'll tell him to switch on the light. We'll see that tunnel mouth clear as day, I'll bet."

"I understand, sir," Roth said. "How steep a descent do you want?"

"No more than three thousand feet per minute. Anything more than that will make aiming a real challenge. And figure in an additional two hundred feet of burst height to the far flare and five hundred to the near one. That should be about right to compensate for their drop while we turn to the attack run."

"Coming right up, sir."

While Roth whizzed through his computations, Sean came back on the radio, advising Tommy of the anti-aircraft guns' location.

Not missing a beat, Roth jotted the guns' coordinates as Sean spoke them. Transposing those numbers to his chart, he said, "That *flak* is down in a valley. If we come in low like you want, sir, they won't even see us until we pop up over the hill."

Tommy asked, "Once we clear that first hill, how far to the hill on the other side of that valley?"

"About half a mile."

"They probably won't have time to get a bead on us...or the ships coming in behind us, either. Our bomb release height...is it higher than those hills?"

"Affirmative, sir."

"Well, you can't beat that with a stick," Tommy said. "Give those burst heights for the flares to my brother while I get the rest of the flight into position. We'll turn to target over the four-mile flare."

Chapter Twenty-Four

The next ninety seconds would be brutally busy for the crew of *Moon's Menace VI*. The *goalposts* illum rounds were in the air; they'd pop their flares any moment. When they did, Tommy would fly the ship toward the highest flare, the one farthest from the tunnel mouth. From there, he'd turn toward the lower flare and begin the attack run.

"One more time," he asked Roth, "what's the highest terrain?"

"Eighteen hundred feet," the navigator replied.

With the ship at 3,000 feet, Tommy allowed himself a moment of confidence in his plan. But it was just a moment. Even though he'd learned to trust Hank Roth's skills, and the navigational data computed by both Roth and Martin—the SHORAN operator—had agreed precisely, there'd always be that shadow of a doubt, the tiny but nagging certainty that even the most experienced pilots and navigators can make mortal mistakes:

Nobody's perfect. We all screw up sometimes, especially when things are happening fast...

And the chances for those screwups increase astronomically in the dark.

He'd lost count of the pilots who'd crashed in darkness into terrain they'd known perfectly well was there. But for any number of mystifying reasons, they hadn't grasped that they were on a collision course with it.

Tommy had one more question: "No other point

along the bomb run is higher than six hundred feet, right?"

"Affirmative, sir," Roth replied.

The artillerymen had done their job splendidly; the high and low flares they'd fired popped from their shells simultaneously, three miles apart, providing a visible descending path to the low-level napalm drop on the tunnel mouth. *Moon's Menace VI* skimmed over the farthest flare just seconds after it deployed, turning hard left as she began a brisk descent—at 2,000 feet per minute—toward the lower flare, which marked one mile to the target. Maintaining the 185 miles per hour Roth had calculated as optimum for the attack, the ship was on course to overfly the lower flare in slightly less than sixty seconds. Once that point was reached, Tommy had ten seconds to acquire the tunnel mouth in the glare of the searchlight ship just off his left wing and make final corrections. Once those precious seconds were gone—whether he'd dropped her load of napalm or not—he'd have to pull up sharply to clear *Dog Bone Ridge* and a second hill a half mile beyond, which stood three hundred feet taller.

They were halfway to the lower flare when Martin, the SHORAN operator, said, "With all due respect, we're not supposed to be doing this with a SHORAN ship. This equipment is too critical to be put in jeopardy by—"

But Tommy cut him off, saying, "And you're not supposed to be talking right now, Frank."

When Martin tried to continue his protest, Tommy interrupted him again: "Shut the fuck up, Frank. I'm real busy right now."

Per the plan, the searchlight ship's beam switched

on when they reached the low flare. From a thousand feet up, the tunnel mouth and the tracks leading to it looked as if they were part of some elaborate model train setup, brightly lit yet colorless in the dazzling light.

The initial sight picture was better than Tommy had hoped. It took little in the way of adjustment to make it perfect. All he needed to do was jog her slightly left and raise the nose a few degrees...

"Two seconds," Roth said, the urgency in his voice impossible to mistake.

Tommy pickled the napalm canisters away in one.

Then the ship was climbing rapidly skyward. *Dog Bone Ridge* was already behind them.

"Anybody shooting at us?" Tommy asked Martin, the only man on board with a rear view. "We must be over those flak guns by now."

"No tracers coming at us," Martin replied, his tense voice raised an octave. He was new to combat flying. His anxiety confirmed it.

Tommy asked *Switchblade Two*—the next ship in the attacking column—if the napalm fire was giving a good visual of the target.

"You'd better believe it, boss," came the reply. "We won't be needing any searchlights to find this one. How's that flak on the other side?"

"Nonexistent, for now," Tommy replied. "Recommend you hold the easterly heading on your climb-out. That should give you the least time in the chinks' target box. If they figure out there are multiple ships, they'll start throwing up blind rounds. Don't try to turn until you're past that second hill. Use it for cover all you can."

Then he added, "If you can't make out that second

hill, wait twenty seconds into the climb-out after the drop before turning."

*****

Sean and Lee Grossman were well pleased with the napalm attack by the four B-26s. "Look at that," Grossman said. "They even got some of it a little way *inside* the damn tunnel. Was that your brother in the first ship?"

"I think so, sir."

"Well, he's got a set of brass balls on him, coming in low like that, spreading that flaming goo like hot butter. It sure took the wind out of the chinks' attack."

Sean smiled. "He always says that a flyboy can't hit nothing unless he gets right on top of it. I guess we just got the five-dollar show."

"Yeah," Grossman replied. "Now it's our turn."

"That blaze'll die down in a couple more minutes," Sean said. "Then I'll roll in with the flamer."

"You sure leading with the flame tank's the way to go, Sergeant?"

"Affirmative, sir. Chinks and gooks hate getting that burning shit spit at 'em worse than anything."

"I'm still worried, though," Grossman said. "Narrow as that tunnel is, once you're inside, there's no way out but to back up."

"Not necessarily a bad thing, sir. It stops us from having to show our weaker sides." Then Sean asked, "Do we have radio contact with them clowns at Second Division yet?"

"Still trying. But so far, no dice."

"That ain't good," Sean replied.

*****

The flame tank—a Sherman with the coaxial machine gun in the turret's mantel replaced by a flame-throwing nozzle—rolled through the dying flames from the air strike, clearing a path along the railroad tracks for the company of infantry behind her. Crossing the scorched earth, the foot soldiers took some small solace in not being cold for once; until the frigid night air regained its grip on the tunnel mouth and surroundings, their path into the tunnel was like walking across a toasty radiator.

"Just don't touch the rails with your bare skin," a platoon sergeant warned. "They'll be hotter than hell for a while."

A smart-mouthed GI replied, "You don't really think we're gonna take our gloves off, do you, Sarge?"

"It ain't your hands I'm talking about, dimwit. It's your face—when the chinks start shooting at you and you kiss the ground. You don't want to ruin that pretty puss of yours for the ladies back home, do you?"

Sean figured the flame tank was about as well-equipped for the task as he could make her: *We got a full tank of flame juice, so we can shoot liquid fire for a solid minute. We ain't seen or heard a chink tank anywhere around the tunnel, so I ain't real worried about having to go head to head with one unless it's been in there all along. And if they got an anti-tank gun or two tucked inside somewhere, they'll be shooting at our vehicle's thickest armor.*

So, again, I ain't real worried.

To cap it off, I still got those three canister rounds left over from the fight at the artillery trap. Tunnels are

natural-made shooting galleries for that shit. It'll tear
any poor bastards we come across to ribbons.
Just so our infantry behind us keeps sneaky ol' Joe
Chink off our deck.

Since the odds of communicating with *Task Force Grossman's* HQ while the tank was inside the tunnel were near zero, Sean had the commo section change the crystals in an infantry walkie-talkie so it worked on a frequency in the armor band. He'd station an RTO with that walkie-talkie just outside the tunnel mouth to act as a relay for Sean's onboard radio. The relay unit would then talk to a compatible radio at the task force's HQ.

Rolling slowly into the pitch-black abyss of the tunnel, Sean told the tank's driver, "Put the headlights on."

The horrified driver replied, "Are you kidding, Sarge? You wanna make us a better target than we already are?"

"No, numbnuts, I want you to be able to see where you're going so you don't drive us into a fucking mined barricade or something. And as far as being a target, it sure as hell ain't no secret we're here, lights on or not. Now get moving, nice and slow."

*****

At Task Force HQ, Grossman's RTO was getting frustrated. "I don't get it, sir," he said. "Even if those Second Division guys are still ten miles away, we should be working them on this frequency."

"Tell me something I don't know, Corporal," Grossman replied. "Somebody's screwed up somewhere, that's for damn sure."

Then it dawned on him what that screwup might be. He asked his commo officer, "Hey, Lieutenant...when did we do the *sig ops* changeover?"

Sig ops: the signals operating document, which contained, among other vital communications items, the list of assigned frequencies for all 8th Army units. When the current *sig ops* expired, all copies were to be destroyed and the superseding document put into effect.

"The changeover was at midnight on 1 February, sir," the commo officer replied.

"Hold it," Grossman said. "That could be an hour from now...or it could have happened twenty-three hours ago. *Midnight* is ambiguous. Did we change over already?"

"Yes, sir, twenty-three hours ago. Just like everybody else in Twenty-Fourth Division."

Grossman had seen this mistake before, back in the last war. It was the reason *midnight* was never to be the expressed changeover time. It was either published as *2359 hours* of a calendar date or *0001 hours* of the following day. Which of those two dates *midnight* fell on was too open to misinterpretation.

"Do we still have a copy of the expired sig ops?" Grossman asked.

The commo officer replied, "Well, I'm not supposed to have one anymore, but..."

He reached into a field box and produced the old document.

"Outstanding," Grossman said. "Switch to the old command net *freq*."

The RTO retuned his set and said, "It's dead air, sir. Nobody's home."

"That's good. Give Second Division another call."

A voice from 23rd Regiment—the 2nd Division unit moving up the highway on the far side of Dog Bone Ridge—replied immediately.

"Bingo," Grossman said. "Give me the mike."

He told the 23rd that there were *friendlies* in the tunnel headed their way, with a Sherman flamer in the lead. "Unknown at this time whether they'll be flushing enemy from the tunnel toward you," he added. "But be advised: any tank that's not backing out of the tunnel is friendly. Do not engage an armored vehicle moving in forward gear. Repeat—*do not* engage."

"Affirmative," the voice from 23rd Regiment replied. "Looking forward to making their acquaintance. We'll be at the tunnel very shortly."

Grossman turned to his RTO and said, "Advise Sergeant Moon there will be friendlies at the tunnel exit."

*****

Sean's tank was only a hundred yards into the tunnel when heavy automatic weapons fire began to *clang* off her hull and turret. GI infantrymen who weren't huddled directly behind the protection of the flamer threw themselves flat on the ground, each man making himself as small a target as he possibly could.

"Stop the vehicle," Sean said. "Just what I fucking figured. They got a barricade up ahead...looks like sixty yards, give or take." He asked his gunner, "You see it?"

"Yeah, just barely, Sarge. Should I give them a hot foot?"

"Affirmative. Just make it a short burst, though. It won't take much. Save the rest of the goo for later."

A four-second burst of liquid fire shot from the flame nozzle. It set the barricade ablaze and brought the automatic weapons fire to an immediate halt.

The driver sounded unnerved as he said, "I think the engine's going to stall, Sarge...and I think I'm getting dizzy. That fire's sucking the air out of here."

"No, it ain't. Calm the fuck down. It ain't that big an inferno."

Not reassured, the driver asked, "Then why are we stopped?"

"Because we're gonna let that fire die down a little before we plow through it. I don't want none of that sticky burning shit dropping off the ceiling and getting into the deck vents."

The gunner asked, "You think we just torched a bunch of chinks, Sarge?"

"Probably just a couple of 'em. Just enough to man that big machine gun. But I ain't gonna get out and look, okay?"

The infantry company commander was on the interphone now, asking Sean, "Are we going to be held up long here, Sergeant? We're sweating our balls off out here with that fire and all."

"Better you sweat, sir, than walk into chink twenty-three millimeter that's cooking off," Sean replied. "You hear it popping, don't you?"

"Can't hear much of anything over the racket that chariot of yours makes, Sergeant. Any more chinks up ahead?"

"Your guess is as good as mine, Captain."

It took five minutes for the napalm fire to subside to isolated puddles of flame. The cook-off of Chinese ammo seemed to be over, too.

"Let's get moving," Sean told his crew.

*****

The tankers could just make out the tunnel exit now, a dark gray arch of reflected moonlight a few hundred yards in the distance.

Suddenly, they could make out something else, too: silhouettes of men running toward the tank.

"Canister," Sean ordered. "Shoot it now, dammit."

The canister round had been loaded in the main gun since they'd entered the tunnel, a precaution on which Sean had insisted. The gunner stomped on the foot trigger without a moment's hesitation.

"Put up another one," Sean told the loader.

"I didn't even aim that last one," the gunner said, as if making an apology.

"Don't matter. We're in a fucking tunnel, remember? All them pellets are gonna bounce around and do the job, anyway."

There was no need to fire the second canister round. The first had made most of the silhouettes vanish. But a few were still running past the tank...

Into a hail of point-blank small arms fire from the GI infantrymen.

"You sure we don't have any chinks on the deck?" the gunner asked.

"I don't think they were trying to take this girl on," Sean replied as he scanned the limited view from his commander's cupola, looking for certainty in the disorienting darkness. "They just wanted to get the hell out of this tunnel. Second Division must really have the far exit all sewed up, just like HQ says they do."

When the infantry company commander's agitated voice came over the interphone, Sean asked him, "All you guys okay back there?"

"Yeah. No casualties, aside from ringing ears and brown drawers, that is. Pretty surprising, considering we just had a point-blank gunfight. Got a bunch of dead chinks lying around, though. A couple of wounded ones, too. We'll worry about carrying them out once we make contact with Second Division."

"I'm with you on that score, Captain," Sean replied. "We're almost there. Why don't your company hang back while I roll outside and link up with Second Division? That way, your guys won't be mistaken for chinks in the dark. I'll come back and get you once contact's made."

"I like that idea, Sergeant."

*****

The Sherman arrived at the threshold of the tunnel, rolling forward along the railroad tracks. Sean had started to open his turret hatch when the tank shook with a tremendous *THUD*.

Then there was another impact of startling violence.

"ROCKETS," the driver shrieked. He'd already thrown the tank into reverse, backing her into the tunnel.

The gunner was shrieking, too: "WHAT DO I DO, SARGE?"

"Start by getting your foot off the gun trigger," Sean replied.

"BUT—"

"But *nothing*, pal. You see that pile of rocks about forty yards in front of us?"

"Yeah, but—"

"Douse it with liquid, but don't fucking light it."

That confused the gunner even more, but he did what he was told. Lowering the elevation of the flame nozzle, he launched an arc of unlit napalm onto the rocks.

"Okay, that's enough," Sean said, confident the brief splash of liquid had done its job.

"Why don't you want me to light it off, Sarge?" the gunner asked.

"Because my money says they're GIs you just got wet. Fucked-up GIs. But that don't mean I wanna kill 'em."

"But they shot at us!"

"Like I said, they're fucked up. Probably green and panicky, too. And now they're scared shitless they're gonna catch fire. They won't be launching no more rockets our way."

"But what makes you think they're GIs, Sarge? We can't see shit outside."

"Let's just say I got a hunch, okay?"

Sean's hunch was right: it was GIs who'd fired two 3.5-inch rockets from two different launchers at the Sherman. Both had struck the thick armor of her glacis plate, exploding but not penetrating the hull, causing no damage other than chipped paint and headaches for her crew. Once the tank had drenched them and their launch position with the unignited napalm, they'd wisely lost interest in firing anymore.

An angry lieutenant approached the tank, the clingy, viscous liquid slowly dripping from his helmet and parka. Fortunately for him, his head had been down when the napalm was dispensed. That saved him from getting a faceful. His gunners hadn't been so lucky.

"What the hell did you do that for?" he said to Sean, who'd climbed down from the turret and was crouched on the foredeck.

"I coulda done a hell of a lot worse, Lieutenant," Sean replied, "and nobody woulda blamed me, neither. But the real issue here is why the hell you shot at my vehicle in the first place. Don't your men know a fucking Sherman when they see one? Especially after my C.O. told yours we were coming?"

The expression that came over the lieutenant's face made him look even more pitiful than the thick fluid dripping from him. "That's the problem," he said. "Every section on the perimeter acknowledged that friendlies were cleaning out the tunnel, but the wire to this rocket team's field phone must've got cut somehow. I couldn't raise them to say you were coming. As I was walking over to tell them in person, I heard all that shooting in the tunnel...I started running then...but before I could get to them, they'd already fired. I arrived just in time to get drenched with this shit."

"There's always somebody who don't get the word, eh, Lieutenant?" Sean said. "I kinda figured it might be something like that. But you and your guys better get that stuff off you before it starts stinging like a son of a bitch."

"Yeah, we'll do that." As the lieutenant turned to walk away, he stopped and said, "Hey, Sergeant...thanks for what you *didn't* do. And that's no bullshit."

"No problem, sir," Sean replied. Then he added, "But if I was you and your boys, I wouldn't be lighting up anytime soon. And that's no bullshit, neither."

Chapter Twenty-Five

Matt Ridgway was pleased the taking of *Twin Tunnels* had gone as planned. But he wasn't really surprised:

The Chinese forces in the area are weak, and a tunnel doesn't provide much of a tactical advantage to its defender when both ends can be accessed. They're like bridges, just harder to bombard to destruction. That western tunnel could've posed a real problem at the boundary between Twenty-Fourth Division and Tenth Corps' Second Division, but after a shaky start, the Second Division boys coming up the highway did a good job, and the Air Force's help was incredible...far better support than we can usually expect at night.

To cap it off, Jock Miles' people handled the follow-up on the ground in fine fashion.

I had no doubt they would.

But I'd really like to see all this bureaucratic silliness over his wife's immigration status put to rest, because I don't want to lose him, and I'd really like to pin a star on the man. He's head and shoulders above the rest of the field.

I don't think I could've made the recommendation for his promotion any more glowing.

Ridgway was well aware, however, that Twin Tunnels had been merely an obstacle, not a strategic objective. That distinction would fall to the vital transportation center of Chip'yong-ni.

*****

Praise for *Switchblade Flight's* action at the tunnel arrived at K-2 before the B-26s had returned. Eighth Army couldn't have been happier with the results of the Air Force's napalm attack.

"Now they'll be expecting us to pull something like that off *every* night," Tommy said at the debrief. He was only half joking.

But there was something else on his mind, and it needed to be dealt with immediately. He let it out as soon as the briefing ended and he could get the squadron commander's ear.

"I want Captain Martin off my crew, sir," Tommy told the colonel. "I don't mind my ship being one of the guinea pigs for this SHORAN system, but I won't fly with somebody who puts his fancy hardware over the men on the ground we're supposed to be supporting."

"Your request is a little late, Tommy," the C.O. replied. "Martin started crying to the ops people the minute his boots hit the ramp about how you refused to use the system properly. They told him he wasn't the mission boss, and if he didn't like it, he could take it up with me. He did, the dumb shit, and I fired him right then and there. No *sparky* second-guesses my mission commanders, especially a greenhorn who can still count his flight hours without having to use his toes."

"That's great, sir," Tommy replied. "Thanks a lot. I really appreciate the support. But who do I get instead?"

"There's a captain—a *mustang*—coming on board in a couple days who was on the SHORAN development team back in the States. I've worked with him before on some other radio projects back in the *Big One*, when he was still a tech sergeant. I think the two of you will hit it off just fine."

*****

Twenty-Sixth Regiment advanced slowly northward toward its final *Operation Thunderbolt* objective: the village of Hajin. It lay three miles west of the transportation crossroads at Chip'yong-ni, which was in the process of being occupied by 2nd Division's 23rd Regiment. Jock had hoped his regiment could move faster, but February had brought with it the full weight of winter, and that weight was bogging everything in 8th Army down. Vehicles and weapons of all sizes failed to operate as lubricants congealed, turning to glue. The scarcity of serviceable trucks to haul supplies to the front lines meant that food, ammunition, and fuel were frequently in short supply to those units in contact with the Chinese or North Koreans.

Men were failing to operate, too, as sub-zero temperatures stiffened joints and muscles worse than ever before, making even the slightest exertion exhausting. The bitter chill of the air they breathed tended to paralyze their lungs like poison gas. The food shortages resulted in the battered and exhausted GIs barely receiving enough calories to maintain their body temperatures. There wouldn't be energy left to perform the heavy labor of hauling, digging, clearing fields of fire, and incessant walking that defined a combat soldier's drudgery.

Huddled by one of the many warming fires the GIs had set as a matter of survival, Patchett told Theo Papadakis, "If we ever run outta shit to burn, all of us are sure as hell gonna freeze to death."

Casting a wary eye northward, he added, "I reckon we can hope them chinks are gonna freeze faster than us. How many you say you found stiff as boards in that half-assed bunker your guys overran the other day?"

"About a dozen, Top," Papadakis replied. "Looked like they'd been dead a coupla days. Can't believe how many bullets my guys wasted shooting at frozen corpses."

"Better safe than sorry, sir," Patchett said. "And at least it kept their damn weapons warm so that gun oil didn't gum 'em up. You'd think Uncle Sam would pay some genius to invent an oil that didn't turn solid in cold like this."

"Boy, you're sure asking for a lot, Top."

"If you don't ask, you don't get, sir," Patchett replied. "How you doing with that *other* morale problem?"

The *other* morale problem: as if the unbearable cold and the hardships it brought weren't doing enough to sap the GIs' will to fight, the rotation scheme Washington had put into place ensured that nearly half the men in 26ᵗʰ Regiment would be eligible to go home during the month of April, having earned enough rotation points by serving ten consecutive months in a combat zone. Motivating men who were *short* on time to put themselves at risk was a challenge vexing every commander in 8ᵗʰ Army. And it was still early February. The challenge would become more daunting as April drew closer.

"How am I doing? Not worth a shit, Top," *Captain Pop* replied. "I gotta bird-dog every damn patrol, especially the night ones, to make sure they're actually going out to where they're supposed to. I ain't got more than an hour's sleep a day since Operation Thunderbolt cranked up. Tonight ain't gonna be no different, I'm afraid."

*****

First Sergeant Grundy, the top kick of Theo Papadakis' Able Company, didn't like what his commander was telling him to do. "Top sergeants don't go on patrols, Captain," he growled. "That's not the way it's done."

"I'm not telling you to go on a patrol, First Sergeant. I'm telling you to *make sure* the NCOs assigned to lead those patrols actually execute them as ordered. That sounds like something a guy wearing six stripes and a diamond should be able to handle pretty easy..."

He considered saying this next thought out loud but decided not to: *Even if that guy doesn't want to stick his neck out because he's a short-timer.*

Instead, *Captain Pop* finished with, "And in case you forgot, First Sergeant, *I'm* the one who decides the way things are done in this company. *You're* the guy who enforces those decisions."

Grundy realized he'd overplayed his hand. He might be able to bluff some green lieutenant into surrendering his authority, but Theo Papadakis didn't fit that bill. He was a highly experienced combat leader who'd led companies under fire before. As a result, he was wise to all the ways a soldier might try to shirk his duty...

Or how a senior NCO might try to hide behind protocols and procedures he'd invented out of thin air to avoid the performance of distasteful tasks, like actually going out on a night patrol.

Patchett would have a shit-fit if he caught an NCO doing that, Papadakis knew for a fact. *He doesn't play that game.*

"Are you giving me a *die-rect* order, sir?" Grundy asked.

"I shouldn't have to give you an order to get you to do your job, Sergeant."

"That's *first sergeant*, Captain."

Papadakis said nothing in reply. There was no need; without a doubt, the look he gave Grundy got the message across loud and clear: *You won't be a first sergeant for long, pal, if you don't watch your step. Those stripes are only sewn on.*

*****

Able Company would send out two squad-sized recon patrols that night. The *easy* patrol—the one that covered the fairly open terrain along Highway 2 as it ran northeast out of Hajin—didn't cause Papadakis much concern as he drafted the patrol orders.

There's no mountain climbing involved, and the level, frozen marshland makes for good fields of vision, even at night. As long as the squad stays alert, there's little chance of them getting surprised by chinks coming out of the woodwork all of a sudden. It's more like setting up a listening post than walking around looking for trouble.

I'll tell Grundy to keep tabs on them. I couldn't care less how he does it, as long as the job gets done.

The other patrol was a different story. That squad would have to scale the heavily wooded ridgeline north

of Hajin. If the Chinese planned to infiltrate 26th
Regiment's area, there was little doubt those hills would
be the most likely avenue of approach. Visibility in
those dense woods at night would be almost nil. To see
or hear anything at all of an enemy's approach, the
patrol would have to climb to the highest point on the
icy ridge, a daunting task even in daylight. They'd be
doing it in near pitch dark conditions.

Even with a good sergeant in charge of the squad—
which Becker seems to be—the urge to fuck the dog is
gonna be real strong. I'll keep an eye on this squad
myself.

To aid in tracking the squads in the dark, Papadakis
had instructed his commo sergeant to rig two walkie-
talkies with a loop antenna rather than the standard whip.
A radio so equipped wouldn't be able to transmit, only
receive. But by panning the loop until maximum signal
strength was received, a radio operator could determine
a fairly accurate azimuth to the transmitter he was
tracking.

"Knowing that azimuth, you can usually tell right
off the bat if somebody's bullshitting you about where
he is," *Captain Pop* said.

Sounding skeptical, Grundy asked, "Have you done
stuff like this before, sir?"

"Yep. Came in real handy, too. A bunch of times."

"But now we've got to carry two radios...the RTO's
backpack set and this direction-finding nigger-rig you
cooked up. That's a lot of extra humping, Captain."

Papadakis just smiled and said, "Can't fool you, can
I, First Sergeant?"

"But word's going to get down to the patrol squads
real quick that their radios are being tracked," Grundy

complained.

"I don't see that as a bad thing, First Sergeant. Might help keep them on their toes."

"Negative, sir. They'll just clam up. Won't report in or nothing."

"They will if they want credit for the patrol," Papadakis replied. "There's a new rule that just came out, effective immediately: if you don't report in when required, you didn't walk the patrol. You stay at the top of the assignment list."

"What the hell are you talking about, Captain? What new rule?"

"The one I just made, First Sergeant. You'd better spread the word, too, so there are no misunderstandings."

*****

Captain Pop didn't find it necessary to physically track Sergeant Becker's patrol. He followed their progress by radio, easily plotting their transmissions as they scaled the ridge. To be certain of the plots, he and his RTO moved eastward along Highway 2, allowing the direction-finding walkie-talkie an ever-broadening angle to provide unambiguous azimuth readings. Those readings left him with little doubt that Becker's patrol was doing its job.

That eastward movement also allowed Papadakis to stay close to the *easy* patrol, the one First Sergeant Grundy was supposed to be keeping tabs on. Ordinarily, he'd never felt it necessary to bird-dog a senior NCO; a man with six stripes on his sleeve could usually get any job assigned to him done with no supervision whatsoever. But there was something about Grundy...

I don't trust the guy. He does what I tell him...but that's the problem: he never takes the initiative. I always have to tell him what to do. And even after I do tell him, I get the feeling he's scheming how to do as little as possible to get by.

I need to see what his idea of supervising this patrol comes down to.

To add to *Captain Pop's* uneasiness, the Chinese had begun to play their strange music over loudspeakers again, the sound drifting southward to the American lines in the stillness of night, reverberating through the valleys. The GIs had come to accept it as some sort of signal; broadcasting that signal in musical code made sense for an ill-equipped army that had little in the way of radio communications. Still, they found it unnerving.

It's gotta be pretty basic stuff they're trying to get across, like "attack at 0500" or "switch to plan B." I mean how much information can you get across by sticking messages in a piece of weird music that sounds like it's being played by drunken monkeys?

When you got as many people as the chinks do, though, I guess you gotta communicate by the old KISS rule: keep it simple, stupid.

There had been two transmissions from the *easy* patrol—call sign *Snowball Four-Six*—each transmission giving Battalion the name of a coded waypoint and reporting *negative contact*. Neither *Pop* nor his RTO recognized the voices.

"Those guys sound like they've never keyed a mike before, sir," the RTO said. "They're all kinds of nervous. Practically screeching, for cryin' out loud."

Scared, more than likely, Papadakis told himself,

probably outta their fucking minds. Night patrols'll do that to you.

"Where do they plot?" he asked the RTO.

"Funny thing, sir…it's like they're walking in circles. The azimuth is staying within the same arc…about twenty degrees." He held the map up so the captain could take a look.

"That don't look right," *Pop* said. "Get *Seven* on the horn."

Snowball Seven: First Sergeant Grundy's call sign.

When a voice replied—the same nervous voice that had been on the air as *Snowball Four-Six*—Papadakis said, "That don't sound right, neither. We gotta get over there. Gimme the azimuth."

"Zero-four-zero," the RTO replied, "toward some village called Maryong-ni."

*****

In a culvert halfway to the village, they found First Sergeant Grundy and six other members of Fourth Squad. They were nestled in their sleeping bags around the smoldering remains of a small fire that appeared to have been stamped out. In the glow of Papadakis' flashlight, the pools of frozen blood beside each sleeping bag glowed black like obsidian.

Grundy and the others were dead, gutted by bayonets in their sleep. Their sleeping bags, contorted in the postures of violent death, had been unzipped, no doubt to loot the weapons inside.

"I guess they wanted to keep their guns warm," the RTO said almost flippantly, as if slaughter like this couldn't affect him anymore.

"Fat lot of good that did them," *Captain Pop* replied. "It don't look like they even had sentries out. They all just crawled into the sack and went to sleep."

"Yeah, forever," the RTO added.

His eyes cast to the heavens, *Pop* said, "How the hell do I keep these idiots alive when being *short's* making them stupid?"

The radio squawked, startling them both. It was that same voice, the one who'd given the patrol's reports and also replied to the call to Grundy. But if that voice was tense before, it was absolutely terrified now.

"Help! Help!" the voice said, dropping any pretense of radio discipline. "This is Fourth Squad. We're lost. We hear chinks everywhere. Help!"

"Get an azimuth to him," Papadakis told his RTO.

"He's got to keep talking for me to do that, sir."

"I know. Tell him to say *The Lord's Prayer*—or any other prayer he remembers—while you get a bead on him."

The voice got to *Thy kingdom come* when the RTO said, "Got him."

"Outstanding. Now give him the reverse azimuth and tell him to start walking. He does have a compass on him, right?"

"Yeah, he says so, sir."

"Good. We'll wait for him right here."

*****

A few minutes later, a man materialized out of the darkness on the dead run, a radio strapped to his back. Behind him came another GI, encumbered only by an M1 rifle.

Papadakis asked the man with the radio, "What's your name, Private?"

"Pratt, sir, James C., PFC, serial number two-six—"

"Hold it, Pratt. You ain't been captured or nothing, so save the name, rank, and serial number stuff. What the hell were the two of you doing strolling around out there?"

Pratt and his partner—another PFC named Springer—began a convoluted tale of how the two of them, junior members of the squad and decidedly not *short*, were told by their squad leader to walk a circuit along Highway 2—ten minutes north and then turn around and do ten minutes south—reporting in to Battalion every thirty minutes per the new SOP.

"While the rest of them took a nap?" the captain asked.

"I don't know nothing about that, sir," Pratt replied. "Are they really...all..."

"Yeah, they're all fucking dead. Was *the late* First Sergeant Grundy with the squad the whole time?"

"Yes, sir. He was the one who picked out this culvert. Said it would make a nice, safe base of operations."

"Safe, huh? I guess he was wrong about that. Did his RTO have two radios with him?"

"Yes, sir. A *Prick-Ten* just like mine. And a walkie-talkie, too, with some weird antenna I've never seen before."

Shit. The chinks copped both radios, then...because they're gone.

Shaking from cold, fear, or both, PFC Pratt asked, "Can we go in now, sir?"

"Not a chance," *Captain Pop* replied. "You got

Battalion all stirred up with that *chinks are everywhere* shit. I had to calm them down from putting artillery fire all over us. Now tell me straight...did you really see or hear any chinks?"

"Well, sir...we were sure...well, pretty sure we heard something."

"You might've heard the handful of chinks who did this to your buddies," Papadakis said, "but my money says they're long gone by now."

"Do you really think it was just a handful of them, sir?"

"It don't take a lot of chinks to stab seven sleeping GIs to death, Pratt. But we're gonna get the drop on them now, because we ain't going to sleep. We're gonna form ourselves a nice little LP right here until sunrise...and finish the job you guys were supposed to be doing."

"We're going to stay here, sir? With all these...these dead bodies?"

"Yeah, with all these poor stiffs. But don't worry...they ain't gonna be no trouble."

*****

The fifth floor of Tokyo's Dai-ichi Building emptied as the bulk of MacArthur's staff left for the night, their nine-to-five paper war finished for another day. Just a handful of Americans remained to put in a few hours more, as MacArthur—the Supreme Commander—would be doing in his office on the floor above. One staffer who'd remained was a pencil-pushing aide to General Almond, the man who still wore two hats as MacArthur's chief of staff and commander of X

Corps.

The aide, a lieutenant colonel, was at his wit's end, not sure what to do with all the paperwork piling up in Almond's office. *This mess could be dealt with in just a few hours if only General Almond were here. But General Ridgway, the current 8th Army commander, won't let him come back to Tokyo, not as long as Almond still commands a corps in contact with the enemy. Without the chief of staff's guidance, I don't know how to handle some of these documents...*

And I don't dare ask anyone else in this headquarters for guidance. It would make me look indecisive. Unpromotable.

Almond always keeps a tight grip on what gets shuttled to the States in accordance with the Supreme Commander's wishes. Nothing leaves this office before it's been checked, rewritten as directed, and approved by him personally.

If it doesn't get that approval, it goes straight to limbo.

He picked up a thin manila envelope addressed to a US Senator in Washington and marked *URGENT— PERSONAL*. Its address of origin was *Commanding General, 8th US Army*. It wasn't sealed; the flap was just tied shut with the attached string looped in a figure eight around the cardboard buttons.

I don't imagine it would hurt anything if I took a look inside...

And who'd know, anyway?

He slid the envelope's contents onto his desk. It was a letter from General Ridgway in his own hand to the senator, who he addressed by first name, asking for his help in a deportation case. According to Ridgway, the

wife of a regimental commander was possibly being
railroaded by an immigration court in Northern
California and faced expulsion from the United States
within two months. Anything the senator could do to
clear this matter up would be greatly appreciated.

Deportation...what is she? A chink?

*Wait a minute. It says here her name's Jillian, so
maybe she's English? Eurasian?*

*Whatever she is, she's not an American, that's for
damn sure.*

The thrill of doing something illicit—and knowing
you wouldn't get caught doing it—inspired the colonel
to undo the string on another envelope from
Commanding General, 8th US Army. This one contained
paperwork endorsing a colonel's promotion to brigadier
general; oddly enough, it was for the same regimental
commander whose wife was in jeopardy of deportation,
as described in the first envelope he'd opened.

He'd recognized the regimental commander's name
from the first envelope into which he'd snooped: *Miles,
Maynard J...*

And he remembered seeing an *eyes only*
memorandum from Almond late last year. It stated that
Miles, Maynard J., Colonel, Infantry, was *not* to be
considered for promotion by this headquarters *under any
circumstances,* by order of the Supreme Commander.

He was quite certain that memorandum had not
been rescinded.

*That's a shame, too, because according to Ridgway,
this guy Miles walks on water.*

But *walking on water* didn't matter if the big boss
had already declared you *sunk.*

Jock Miles' promotion paperwork would go directly

into *limbo*: an unsorted drawer of random files in a storeroom cabinet, pending possible action at some later date...

Or, more than likely, no action at all.

Swept up in the heady exercise of power over the lives of others, the aide decided that the matter in Ridgway's letter to the senator didn't deserve the urgency the sender had attached to it: *It sounds like personal business, and that should never be transmitted through Army channels.* Righteously indignant that the military correspondence network was being abused in this way, he swept up the letter to the senator along with the promotion paperwork, took a brief walk to the storeroom, and filed them both in *limbo*.

Chapter Twenty-Six

By the second week of February 1951, Operation Thunderbolt had achieved its objectives. Eighth Army forces were now aligned east to west across South Korea some forty miles south of the 38th Parallel. Only the Han River separated the westernmost of those forces—an assortment of American, ROK, and Turkish regiments—from Seoul.

"We'll dig in along this line," General Ridgway told his commanders as they met at Hajin, "because there's no doubt the Chinese will be launching another of their *great offensives* any day now. The confluence of Highways 2 and 24 north of Hajin and Chip'yong-ni will be the most likely avenue for the main thrust of their offensive. They'll try to break through our line at one of those two places, maybe both. We'll be ready for them."

Since Hajin was occupied by 26th Regiment, Ridgway made a special point to visit with Jock Miles. Standing together outside the CP van, they looked toward the Chinese lines. The general asked Jock, "How far do you figure the chinks are from this ridge?"

"A mile, sir. Maybe a little more."

"Good," Ridgway replied as he took a few steps north. "That means they'll be watching while I make it clear what I think of them." He opened his parka, unbuttoned his trousers, and urinated in the direction of the Chinese lines.

A little surprised by the gesture, Patchett warned, "You know, sir, we do have ourselves a little trouble with snipers every now and then."

That news didn't seem to bother the general in the least. He leisurely put himself back in order.

Sean Moon was delighted by Ridgway's performance, telling the general, "You know, sir, I heard the stories about Patton pissing in the Rhine first time he crossed it. I'm sure you heard 'em, too, you being in the ETO and all. Wish I coulda seen it with my own eyes."

"Don't worry, Sergeant," the general replied. "You may get another chance when I cross the Han. So, you served with Patton?"

"Yes, sir. Fourth Armored, Thirty-Seventh Tank."

"Outstanding, Sergeant. Thirty-Seventh Tank...the best of the best. When are we going to get your old C.O. over here to kick some chink ass?"

"You talking about Colonel Abrams, sir? Hell, I was hoping you could tell me when he was gonna show up."

"Last I heard, he was real busy staring down the Russkies over in Germany. But be patient, son. Ol' Creighton Abrams never missed a fight yet. I'm sure you know that better than any of us, though."

*****

The biggest clue that the Chinese would be attacking soon was the constant daytime haze that hung in the valleys to the north. It was caused by CCF forces setting hardwood bonfires. Their bluish smoke remained low in the frigid air, shielding observation of Chinese assembly areas from aircraft or mountaintop OPs. But the ruse had its drawbacks; the predominant northwesterly winds of winter would carry the smoke along their route of attack, inhibiting their field of view just as much as it did the Americans'. When it blew strongly, as it often did in February, the windswept plumes became fingers pointing to the locations of the fires and the units who'd set them. Once those locations were observed by tactical fighters or spotter aircraft, an air strike or artillery raid was quick to follow. Unfortunately, those aircraft couldn't be everywhere at once.

The smoke and crazy music spilling from loudspeakers had started a spirited but fatalistic debate among the GIs about how the Chinese would come at them next. As a regimental staff meeting broke up, Sean Moon left no doubt what side of the debate he was on: "They're gonna come right outta the smoke like ghosts, dancing to that FUBAR music of theirs. We won't see 'em until they're right on top of us, so we gotta start sweeping our zones of fire the second we hear them bugles sound off."

"Negative, Bubba," Patchett replied. "When they're getting ready to attack, they're gonna let that smoke clear first and then paste us with some one-hundred-twenty-two millimeter so they can see where it's landing and adjust accordingly. That's why we been standing on our boys' heads to dig in so deep. If our counter-battery fire can't silence it, that barrage'll go on all day. Once the sun starts going down, they'll come with their human wave shit...and that'll go on all damn night. You mark my words."

They would've bet money on it if they hadn't both been broke.

Lee Grossman walked by on the way to his jeep. His head was down; he didn't even acknowledge the presence of the two senior NCOs. Patchett called out to him, "Hey, Major, me and Sergeant Moon here were just making a little gentleman's bet on how the chinks are gonna come at us. You want a piece of the action?"

His voice distracted, his gaze a thousand miles away, Grossman replied, "Quite frankly, Top, I don't give a shit one way or the other."

Then he climbed into his jeep and drove off.

"What the fuck's his problem?" Sean asked.

"I don't know...but something sure ain't right."

They headed into the CP and found Colonel Miles. Patchett asked, "How big's the bug up Lee Grossman's ass, sir?"

Shaking his head sadly, Jock replied, "A pretty damn big one, Top. He just got a *Dear John*. His wife's filing for divorce."

"Dammit," Patchett said. "She got somebody else?"

"Isn't that always the case, Top?"

"Damn right, sir. Can't change horses if you ain't got another one to hop on. He gonna be okay, you think?"

"I'm not sure yet. We're going to have to keep a real close eye on him. Help him out any way we can, okay?"

Patchett nodded, thinking, *Ain't this hot shit? Here the colonel's worried about soothing Lee Grossman's ruffled feathers while he's got his own pile of shit stirring back home. Ain't no telling how this thing with Miss Jillian's gonna play out.*

But I'm pretty sure it won't be with her serving him papers. Their bond's forged in some pretty tough steel after all they went through together back in the last war.

Please don't let me be wrong about that.

As he and Sean left the CP, Patchett said, "Bubba, let's you and me be grateful we never tied the knot with no female of the species."

"Affirmative, Top," Sean replied, adding, "if the Army wanted you to have a wife…"

Together, they finished the refrain: "They woulda issued you one."

*****

In its initial phase, the Chinese assault didn't seem like one at all. The blue haze persisted, and there was no artillery barrage. Instead of human wave attacks, a seemingly endless stream of "civilian refugees" was flooding to the American lines.

In 26th Regiment, Lee Grossman's 3rd Battalion was the first to encounter the "civilians." His men had corralled over two hundred Korean peasants, largely women, children, and old men, but with a surprising number of military-aged men among them.

"Something smells rotten here," Grossman told Jock over the landline from his battalion CP. "I've got the ROK interpreter checking out all these young guys, and he's telling me that only half of them are Korean, probably KPA. The rest are chinks who can half-assed speak the language. Together, they're using the bona fide civilians as hostages. He's telling me we should just kill them all."

"Have you found any weapons, Lee?" Jock asked.

"Not yet, sir. But there are a ton of carts we haven't been able to check yet. And I don't have any real good place to hold all these men or enough people to do it. We can't keep their headcount straight. I wouldn't be surprised if they're slipping away in twos and threes."

Jock had just heard a similar story from 23rd

Regiment down the road at Chip'yong-ni. They hadn't found any weapons among their refugees, either, but had begun to suffer guerrilla attacks by infiltrators in civvies in their rear area. "Best we can tell," the commander of the 23rd told him, "the prisoners are slipping away from us at night because our holding pens are pretty flimsy and we don't have anything available to make them stronger. We believe these escapees are pilfering weapons from rear area detachments and then raiding our line units from behind. They haven't caused much in the way of casualties yet, but they've destroyed a good bit of equipment. In one raid, though, they managed to wound all of my French interpreters, the ones working liaison with the French battalion assigned to me. We had to evacuate the three of them, and I have no idea when I'm getting replacements for them, if at all. As a result, I'm having a hell of a time coordinating my actions with the French. It's been one fuckup after another the last few days. We nearly dumped artillery on their CP until some sharp fire direction officer called a hold on it while he rechecked the target data."

Jock made the most of the information from the 23rd. A group of escaped prisoners tried to raid a motor park in his regiment's rear area that night, but forewarned, the GIs had been ready. They killed four of the intruders and scattered the rest back into the night, with none of their own killed or wounded.

The next morning, a new order from 8th Army HQ went out to all units: *Turn back all refugees. No exceptions. ROK interpreters will make it clear that anyone attempting to bypass the checkpoints will be shot.*

"Them ROKs are gonna love that, the sick bastards," Sean said to Jock. "Nothing they like better than fucking over their own kind. Too bad it'll be GIs having to do the shooting, though."

Patchett told Jock, "You know there are gonna be mistakes, right, sir? If them chinks are using the civilians for hostages, some of them hostages are gonna get dead, even if it's by accident. I can hear the commie propaganda now, crying about how we're murdering innocent civilians."

"That'd be empty talk coming from the people who make it a practice of harming civilians *intentionally*," Jock replied. "Of course we're going to make mistakes, but General Ridgway doesn't care about that right now, and neither do I. Those mistakes will be on the heads of the Chinese, not ours. We've got to keep our men safe."

"Amen to that, sir," Patchett replied.

*****

Patchett was right: there were mistakes. All along the 8th Army line, Chinese infiltrators continued to use civilians as hostages. Most of those groups were turned away at the checkpoints, not to be seen again. But there were some attempts to skirt checkpoints at night, and the GIs, always jumpy in the dark, never hesitated to open fire if a proper password wasn't promptly given. Civilian refugees and Chinese infiltrators alike died. Even two GIs who'd gotten lost during a wire-laying detail were wounded by fellow soldiers when they couldn't provide the right password, despite their frightened bellowing in unmistakable American dialects.

Within forty-eight hours, the guerrilla attacks on American units stopped, and the groups of refugees arriving at the checkpoints no longer included military-aged males. But they were still turned away because orders were orders; in the face of an impending attack, no commander saw the need to amend them.

*****

On 13 February, the Chinese attacked in force, advancing in daylight out of the blue haze, much like the ghosts Sean Moon had predicted. As he'd prescribed, every weapon in 26th Regiment was ready for them. When a Chinese regiment tried to force its way into the Hajin perimeter, bugles and whistles blaring, they were met with a brutal wall of fire that forced them back up Highway 2. Badly battered, the CCF forces did little but probe unsuccessfully throughout the night. Suffering heavy casualties once again, they found no place to achieve a breakthrough at Hajin.

When the sun rose on 14 February, the Chinese facing 26th Regiment had shifted their efforts east to Chip'yong-ni. As they shared canteen cups of coffee after the long and harrowing night, Sean told a sullen Patchett, "I was right, Top. I win the bet."

"Well, goodie for you, Yankee. Now go fuck yourself, okay?"

"Hey, I told you...I'm a Dodgers fan."

"They can go fuck themselves, too," Patchett replied.

*****

As Matthew Ridgway had assumed, the transportation crossroads at Chip'yong-ni was a prime objective of the CCF. Sitting on the western flank of X

Corps, the town promptly became threatened on all sides when two ROK divisions to the east, units Ridgway had placed under General Almond's command, began to collapse in disarray in the face of an assault by surprisingly resurgent North Korean forces. The collapse opened a veritable causeway for the main body of enemy forces in the area—the Chinese—to get behind 8th Army lines. It was the breakthrough they'd failed to achieve at Hajin.

"I need to withdraw Twenty-Third Regiment from Chip'yong-ni," Almond told Ridgway. "They're about to be surrounded. The Chinese are already moving south of the town in force. The Twenty-Third will be cut off and slaughtered if I don't move them immediately."

Ridgway silently cursed his decision to allow Almond control over those now-crumbling ROK divisions: *The idiot placed two of them adjacent to each other, in mutually supporting positions. But what he should've known—like all my other commanders do—is that you don't expect ROK divisions to support each other. When they get into trouble, they cut and run, plain and simple. That's just what both divisions did...and suddenly, we've got enemy forces pouring through a breach in our line a couple of miles wide east of Chip'yong-ni and sweeping south toward Wonju. And it wasn't the Chinese who opened that breach, either. It was the damn KPA, that depleted North Korean Army that's been trying to make a comeback lately.*

This breakthrough should've never happened in a million years. Thank God I've got a big enough reserve to plug that gap and buck up those two fleeing ROK divisions. That'll stop the collapse near Wonju.

But if I let Almond give up Chip'yong-ni, that just

moves the problem west, creating an even bigger salient. And that expanded salient will be filled with Chinese, not battle-weary KPA troops. My entire Army will have to pull back to avoid being enveloped. We could surrender everything we've gained since the start of the new year.

Somehow, someway, I've got to get rid of Almond. The man is oblivious to reality. But every man I've considered to replace him is in Europe or the States and won't be available for a few months, at the earliest. In the meantime, I've got no choice to keep his corps on the line while limiting the damage he can cause.

He told Almond, "Negative, Ned. You'll hold at Chip'yong-ni."

"But all resupply routes have been cut off. They'll run out of ammunition in less than a day."

"They'll be resupplied via parachute drop, effective immediately," Ridgway said.

There was a hint of privileged smugness in Almond's voice as he replied, "I don't think General MacArthur will go along with that decision, sir."

"He already has, Ned. And by the way, I'm taking the ROK divisions away from you and returning them to their Third Corps' control. MacArthur's gone along with that decision, too."

Ridgway found himself enjoying the crestfallen look on Almond's face as he dismissed him.

*****

The *top kick* of Lee Grossman's 3rd Battalion was a master sergeant named Bud Nye. He'd bitten his tongue under Colonel Beemon, the last C.O., although he'd been quite sure from the outset that the man was tactically incompetent and unfit for a combat command. But he'd rationalized his silence: *I could think it all I wanted, but it wasn't my place to say it out loud.* When Colonel Miles relieved Beemon and named Major Grossman as his successor, Nye considered the new commander's level-headed, no-nonsense demeanor a quantum improvement over the delusional bullshit of the previous one. Not only was his new boss a knowledgeable and experienced combat leader, but as Nye put it, *The guy's got balls to spare...*

But something's wrong with Lee Grossman now. He's never discussed his personal problems with me, and I'm not surprised...we don't have that kind of close relationship, not like the one he and Mel Patchett share from the last war. But you don't have to live in each other's pockets to know he's become a few cards shy of a full deck.

When Patchett paid 3rd Battalion one of his frequent surprise visits, Nye took him aside for a private discussion. "I need your help with Major Grossman, Patch," he said. "The man's going off the rails."

His eyes narrowed skeptically as Patchett replied, "You better be real specific, Bud. I ain't got time for no bullshit gripe session right now."

Nye quickly got down to the heart of the matter: Grossman was vanishing without a word every night, abandoning his CP and leaving the battalion functionally leaderless in his absence, since the XO, Nye claimed, *wasn't exactly a ball of fire.* "Sure," he added, "we can usually get Grossman on the radio if we need him, but he's not *here*...and you know as well as I do, a commander's presence can turn things around real fast when it all starts going to shit. We're just lucky the chinks haven't seriously hit us for the past few nights."

Then Nye added, "Even when he is here during the day, his mind's a thousand miles away."

Patchett asked, "You have any idea what the hell he's doing when he's *vanishing*, like you call it?"

"Not specifically, but he claims he's *patrolling*. To me, that sounds like he's decided to do a sergeant's job instead of his own. And that's putting the whole battalion at risk."

"He doing this alone, Bud?"

"I don't think so. I believe he's been taking a handful of *bad apples* with him, guys with a vicious streak he recruited specially for whatever task he's got in mind. Regardless, I'm getting reports from the companies about a few of their guys going missing at night, only to show up before dawn with some bullshit story about where they'd been."

Patchett furrowed his brow and asked, "What kinda *bad apples* we talking here?"

"The kind that were criminals back in civilian life, Patch. Still are, near as I can tell. A judge probably gave them a choice of jail or the Army. It's a shame they picked the service, because those boys all need to do time, real bad. You know the type."

"How many of these *patrols* you reckon he's run so far, Bud?"

"Five, by my count. They started the night we dug in here at Hajin."

Right about the time Lee found out about his wife leaving him, Patchett thought. *I seen it all before. A woman shits on a man's head from ten thousand miles away, and he can't do a damn thing about it. Fucks him up so bad he figures that if he gets hisself killed, she'll feel so guilty it'll ruin the rest of her natural life. Serve her cheating ass right.*

"But don't tell the major I'm the one ratting him out, okay, Patch?"

"Sure, Bud. I'll keep your name out of it. But where is he now?"

"Over at the mortar section."

"Think I'll pay him a little visit," Patchett said.

*****

He intercepted Grossman's jeep on the trail to the mortar section. *Better we talk out here, away from everyone else*, Patchett thought. *If this conversation goes sideways, it won't be fit for tender ears.*

Grossman instinctively knew his visitor hadn't stopped by just to say *hello*. He opened with, "I don't have much time, Top. What's on your mind?"

"Maybe you let your driver take my jeep back to your CP so you and me can talk real private, sir. As soon as we're done talking, you can drop me off."

Reluctantly, Grossman agreed. "Sure. However you want it."

Patchett wasted no time getting to the heart of the matter: "Where the hell you wandering off to at night, Lee?"

The reply was equal parts surprise and defensiveness. "Who spilled the beans on me, Patch? It was that weaselly XO of mine, wasn't it?"

"Ain't no matter who, Lee. Let's just say your whole damn staff is mightily concerned about you. I am, too. But you still ain't answered my question."

"You want an answer, Top? Well, here it is…I'm going to capture myself a chink general. Drag his rice-eating ass right up to General Ridgway's van. That'll be a pretty big propaganda coup for Eighth Army, don't you think? It should put a crimp in all that lying bullshit they're pumping out to the world about *the inevitable defeat of the imperialist aggressors*. You ever listen to that shit on the short wave?"

"Sure I do, but what you're talking is suicide, Lee. How the hell do you plan on finding yourself a chink general, anyway? For openers, that whole damn army don't wear no insignia of rank. You could end up mistaking some old mess steward for a general."

"Nah, it isn't as hard as you think, Top. Some of the chinks I've run into had documents on them that looked pretty high level. They're still being translated by my ROK interpreter, but it's a good possibility that one of the clowns carrying them might've been a regimental commander. So I'm getting pretty close…"

"What happened to those chinks you ran into, Lee? You kill 'em?"

"Afraid so," Grossman replied. "The GIs I've been taking with me…well, you'd like them. They don't have any qualms about killing a man face to face. I must be making an impression with the chinks, because I'm hearing rumors from some POWs my battalion captured this morning that there's a bounty on my head. They say the CCF brass is calling me *The Criminal Street Gang*." He smiled at the sound of his nickname.

"*Street Gang*, like your battalion call sign?"

"Yep."

"I don't get it, Lee. You want to be so famous that

the chinks hunt you down and kill you real special-like?"

"They're already trying to kill me and all the rest of us every minute of every day, Top. What the hell's the difference?"

"The difference is that you're begging for trouble when there ain't no need, Lee. Listen to yourself a minute. How the hell you gonna find a chink general, anyway? He's bound to be in a crowd of people, don't you think?"

"Even generals have to take a shit sometimes, Top."

Patchett fell silent. He felt sure he was trying to talk sense to a crazy man...

A crazy man with a death wish.

"I know what you're thinking," Grossman said after the long and painful pause. "I'm losing my marbles because Rachel walked out on me."

"That did cross my mind, Lee. You know as well as I do that you wouldn't be the first."

"And you're going to have to report all this to Colonel Miles, right, Top?"

"Of course I have to tell him. We can't have you getting—"

"Getting *killed*? If I was worried about that, I would've shot myself in the foot before I ever let Uncle Sam reactivate me."

"No, Lee, I ain't buying that. You never woulda shirked your duty. But yeah, I gotta tell the colonel. And you know what he's gonna do."

"Yeah, I know what he's going to do...nothing. Not a goddamn thing. Hard as it is to get the dogfaces interested in fighting this fucking war, he's not going to stop one of his commanders who's doing it with a vengeance."

"You're missing the point here, Lee. There's smart tactics...and then there's just plain ol' foolishness. And a battalion commander's job is to—"

"You're not really going to tell me what my damn job is, are you, Top?"

"No, Lee, I reckon that'll be Colonel Miles' job."

With a sly smile, Grossman said, "You want to bet on what the colonel's going to tell me?"

"No, thanks. I already lost a coupla bets lately. Can't afford to lose no more." He paused and then added, "But you know I gotta tell him...and then he can say whatever he damn pleases."

They'd reached the Battalion CP. As Patchett climbed from the jeep, he said, "Watch your ass, sir. I mean it. You're fixing to fall into a world of shit one way or another if you ain't careful."

Chapter Twenty-Seven

Tommy Moon sat in pensive silence as the shuttle truck brought him and his crew out to their aircraft, *Moon's Menace VI*. The gist of the pre-mission briefing was still reverberating in his head: *The fight around Chip'yong-ni is a make or break effort for Eighth Army. Even with some rejuvenated KPA units helping them out, the Chinese can't maintain an offensive for very long, not with their meager supply lines stretched the way they are.*

As long as we can stop them from a sustained breakthrough anywhere along the line, General Ridgway is confident this new offensive of theirs will fail...

And when it does, Eighth Army should be able to push them back all the way to the Thirty-Eighth Parallel. It's only forty miles to the north now.

What happens once Eighth Army gets to the Thirty-Eighth, though...that's another question entirely. Will they hold there? Or does Washington want them to push farther into North Korea...and risk another debacle like the one we had a few months back?

I kind of doubt Truman will risk it, despite MacArthur's saber-rattling.

There was no point discussing his last thought out loud, though. Squadron briefings, such as the one they'd just left, were always chock-full of rampant speculation, usually squelched by the commander finally having to say, "Gentlemen, gentlemen...as I've said so many times before, *Opinions are like assholes—everybody's got one.* Now let's knock off the bullshit and get back to the actual facts of the mission at hand."

There was no point, either, in interrupting his two crewmen—Lieutenant Hank Roth and Captain Bill Wild—as they huddled together on the truck's bench seat, comparing navigation and target data, struggling against the truck's turbulent wake to keep the charts on their lapboards in place. Roth, the navigator, asked Wild, "So, Captain, with those two ground stations moved to higher ground and closer to Eighth Army's line, you think SHORAN will work for us below fourteen thousand feet?"

"Yeah, Hank, but not by much," Wild replied. "This system's still a work in progress, you know? And there are still a whole lot of mountains in the way of those radio beams."

Captain Bill Wild—an amiable officer who told everyone to call him *Wild Bill*—was *Moon Menace VI's* new SHORAN operator. He came as a breath of fresh air to Tommy and Roth after they'd endured the disagreeable technocrat Frank Martin for all of one mission before he was booted off the crew and grounded. *Wild seems to be an entirely different sort of technical officer*, Tommy thought. *Unlike Martin, he understands the priority of the mission over his precious box of electrons. Probably comes from him being a mustang— Wild did the last war as an NCO and only took a commission after it was all over.*

The C.O. was right: I think I'm going to like working with this guy.

As the truck came to a stop at their ship, Wild asked Tommy, "Your brother...he's in Twenty-Fourth Division, you say?"

"Yep. He's a top kick in Twenty-Sixth Regiment."

"That's hot stuff that you got to work with him on that *Twin Tunnel* mission. And who knows? You might be working with him again today."

That prospect made Tommy feel very good. He needed those periodic reassurances that Sean was alive and well.

*****

The four B-26s in Tommy's *Switchblade Flight* were leading a squadron of bombers heading north from K-2 to Chip'yong-ni. Each of the squadron's other flights was led by a SHORAN-equipped ship just like *Moon's Menace VI.* The mid-morning sky of 14 February was crystalline blue, with cirrus clouds scattered high above. Against the backdrop of those wispy clouds, Hank Roth saw them first: silvery dots at a much higher altitude than the bombers, shimmering as they reflected the bright sunlight, moving rapidly from west to east as each dot painted a thin white contrail in its wake.

His voice tense, Roth asked, "Do you think they're MIGs?"

"This far south and east? Not real likely," Tommy replied, trying to sound convinced. "Are you sure they've got swept wings?"

"Can't really tell, sir. Maybe when they get a little more overhead…"

From the aft compartment, Bill Wild asked, "What am I missing?"

"Jets, pretty high," Tommy replied. "No positive ID yet."

"They're not coming downstairs, are they?"

"Not yet, Bill," Tommy said. "Don't worry, we'll let you know. In the meantime, we've got big business to attend to."

Actually, Wild wasn't worried at all: *The MIGs won't be much interested in B-26s. We're down too low. They'll waste too much gas yo-yoing up and down between angels thirty and us down here at angels fourteen. The B-29s flying up high are much easier targets for them. Thank God I'm not crew on one of them anymore.*

He'd been on a few B-29 missions over North Korea as part of SHORAN's debut. They'd been hair-raising; MIGs seemed to be everywhere, attacking the big bombers with impunity day and night. It was no wonder the *Superfortresses'* losses were climbing steadily.

After talking with ASOs on the ground, Roth told the crew, "No changes in target coordinates or IP. Hold airspeed at two-one-zero."

"That makes it pretty easy," Wild replied. "I've got the wind data computed. Turn to heading zero-one-zero at the IP."

The IP—*initial point* for the bomb run—was directly over the *fork in the road*: where Highway 24 split into 24A and 24B at the Han River a few miles northwest of the city of Yoju. They were close enough now to identify the fork visually. The bomb run's release point was still seven miles ahead. Once they reached it, the other three ships in *Switchblade Flight's* formation would release their bombs when their SHORAN-equipped leader did. They'd be at the release point in a little over two minutes.

Flying the plane to an accurate drop would consume

all of Tommy's energy now. He told Roth, "Keep an eye on our friends upstairs. What are they doing now?"

"Turning north. Holding altitude."

"Good. If they're bad guys, they've got no plans to engage. Not yet, anyway."

Roth had an idea. "Maybe they're F-86s. Should I give them a shout on the intercept frequency?"

"Not now," Tommy replied. "We're way too busy. Stay on *freq* with the ASO."

The target was a narrow valley along Highway 24, two miles north of Chip'yong-ni. The major CCF logistical route to that city, the highway was reported to be clogged with vehicles and porters toting supplies on their backs, none of whom the aircrew could see through the smoke of battle collecting in the valley. Without SHORAN's blind-bombing capability, this obscured target couldn't be engaged from the safety of altitude at all.

At the IP, Tommy turned the ship precisely to the heading Wild had supplied. From here to the release point, the ship would be under the guidance of the SHORAN operator.

His eyes glued to the flight instruments, Tommy asked Roth, "Anything interesting going on with our friends upstairs?"

"Nope. They're in a wide orbit now, same height."

With Wild's command—*Pickle them!*—the aircraft lurched upward from the release of her ten 500-pound HE bombs. Within seconds, the other three ships in the flight reported *Bombs away*, as well.

It would be hours before the flight crews would see the bomb damage assessment photos back at K-2. Right now, though, ASOs on the ground indicated the bombs were on target.

"Score a tentative victory for SHORAN," Wild said with a laugh. "Now, where the hell are those jets?"

Tommy and Roth scanned the sky, but the only reminder of the jets was the nearly dissipated contrails they'd left behind. "Looks like they went east," Tommy said. "Probably F-86s on their way back to Japan, with one eye on their fuel gauges. Nice to know they were here...even if it was just for a couple of minutes."

Then he asked Roth, "How are we doing on gas?"

"We've got twenty-two minutes of *playtime* fuel, sir."

"Good," Tommy replied. "Let's see what other trouble we can get into."

He ordered *Switchblade Flight* into a high orbit over Chip'yong-ni.

*****

Tommy could hear the frustration in the ASO's voice as he asked, "*Switchblade Leader*, this is *Artemis*. Any chance of you doing some low-level work?"

"What do you have in mind?"

The ASO needed *eyes in the sky* over the west side of Chip'yong-ni. "The Frenchies got that sector," he explained. "I've got no translator, no spotter ship, and their English isn't so hot. They're getting their brains beat in, but I'm not real sure where they want air support. Can you come on down and have a look-see at what's going on?"

"Maybe I can do you one better, *Artemis*," Tommy replied. "Can the Frenchies come up on this *freq*?"

"Affirmative, *Switchblade*."

"Have them switch over. I speak *frog*. I'll talk with them directly."

Wild's surprised voice came over the interphone: "You're going to *parlez vous* with them?"

"Why not, Bill? They need help, maybe we can provide it."

With that, Tommy rolled the ship over into a steep descent.

*****

"*Allo, Allo, Switchblade. Nous avons besoin de soutien…*"

Moon's Menace VI was at 6,000 feet and still in a rapid descent as Tommy made contact with the French battalion at Chip'yong-ni, their plea for assistance coming in loud and clear in their native language. The rest of *Switchblade Flight* was descending more cautiously, awaiting specific instructions—in English—from their flight leader.

Tommy leveled the ship at 5,000 feet as his spirited conversation with the embattled French battalion continued. The ASO's reluctance to call for fire support made sense now: the Chinese had breached the battalion's perimeter along railroad tracks that entered the town, using the rail embankment for cover. The opposing forces had become mixed, with no clear battle lines, making the targeting of artillery or air support a danger to friend and foe alike. Although the Chinese hadn't yet managed to pump any great number of troops through the French perimeter, there was no stopping those still flowing down the embankment. If that flow was not stemmed, it seemed certain the French would be overrun.

From his airborne perch, Tommy could see something those on the ground couldn't: the assembly area for the Chinese coming down the tracks. It was nestled behind a long, narrow ridgeline that lay less than a mile from the French perimeter. There was even a cut in the ridgeline near the tracks through which CCF troops could reach the embankment with little exposure to direct fire.

"We've got to come out of the south," Tommy told his flight. "Too many mountains any other way. *Two, Three,* and *Four,* you take the assembly area first. Once you're clear, I'll take a run at the rail embankment. Is everybody able to identify the target area?"

When all three ships replied *Affirmative,* Tommy said, "Okay, let's do it."

As they rolled into their attack, *Switchblade Flight* had enough fuel remaining for sixteen minutes on station.

*****

As the strafing attack commenced, Bill Wild was little more than a spectator in a very high-stakes game. It was something entirely new to him; all the airborne work he'd done previously was in high-flying aircraft. But now, with his SHORAN system just along for the ride, there was nothing he could do but experience the rapid maneuvers and violent accelerations of a ground attack run for the first time.

He found it exhilarating...and terrifying. He could see nothing of the target area out the two windows of the aft fuselage compartment—one above him, one below. He'd get a fleeting glimpse of it once the run was complete and the ship was climbing away, but he'd been warned in advance that the only thing he'd likely be able to distinguish were enemy tracers chasing the ship.

He'd been warned about something else, too: he was, for all practical purposes, trapped in that aft compartment. The only way out involved jettisoning his compartment hatch and then getting his seat out of the way by unpinning it from the floor and throwing it overboard out the opening. Only then would he have enough clearance to make his own exit while wearing a parachute, crawling headfirst into the sky on hands and knees. The odds were excellent that the ship would crash or blow up long before he got to bail out.

As Tommy began the strafing run, the ship shuddered from the hammering of her eight .50-caliber machine guns. Wild looked between his legs through the lower window and thought, *My God...we're only a couple inches off the damn ground!*

His panicky estimate wasn't off by much.

Then the infernal racket of the machine guns stopped and the ship was climbing rapidly, seemingly standing on her tail as she clawed for the safety of altitude. Wild couldn't see any tracers rising up to kill them.

"Everybody okay?" Tommy asked the other ships in *Switchblade Flight.*

When they all reported no problems, Wild felt sure that was the end of it: *We'll be going home now.*

But it was not to be. There was more chatter in French on the radio now. When it was done, Tommy told the flight, "Okay, let's deal with their other problem now. We'll hose down the south slope of that mountain that's about a mile north of our last target. Attack in *echelon left*—on me—and concentrate on the lower part of the slope, which is crawling with chinks. Everybody ready?"

They all reported they were. "Okay," Tommy told his pilots, "break on my count: Three...two...one...*Break*."

As they headed down into this new attack run, Tommy told his crew, "Too bad we're not carrying napalm this trip. We could've set that whole damn mountain on fire."

*****

The French were delighted with the results of *Switchblade Flight's* strafing runs. By crippling the continued influx of CCF troops from two different directions, those Chinese who'd managed to get inside their battalion perimeter were now greatly outnumbered. They were quickly dealt with.

The commander of Twenty-Third Regiment was delighted, too. Although the fight to hold Chip'yong-ni was far from over, the very real possibility that the French battalion would collapse had been alleviated. The remaining American battalions of the regiment could now focus on their own perimeters without having to worry about Chinese crashing through the French sector and enveloping them from the rear.

Everyone in 8th Army was well aware that the longer the 23rd Regiment could hold off the CCF, the quicker the Chinese attacking Chip'yong-ni would exhaust their ammunition. They wouldn't be getting much more of it, either, as their supply chain was still being battered from the air. When *Switchblade Flight* returned the next day—15 February—to attack that supply chain, it was obvious the Chinese were pulling back; the highways to the north were clogged with fleeing enemy troopers.

And for this mission, the B-26s were armed with napalm, because as any GI could tell you, *The chinks and gooks are terrified of being firebombed.*

*****

Matthew Ridgway was well satisfied with the outcome at Chip'yong-ni. For the first time in this war, an American command had turned back a major Chinese offensive.

And the Air Force is still punishing those retreating chinks, he told himself.

But now my ground force has got to get moving north again in pursuit. It's time to launch Operation Killer.

*****

"Mr. Pitney," his secretary said, "Mr. Peters, the DA, is on line one."

"Put him through," the lawyer replied, a little surprised by the call.

Peters began with, "Mark, I've got something on my desk that I believe will greatly interest you and your client, Mrs. Miles."

"Do tell, Fred. I'm all ears."

"You remember Mrs. Whitelaw, the general's wife?"

"How could I forget?" Pitney replied.

"Sheriff's deputies arrested her two nights ago for driving under the influence. She became extremely belligerent, so much so that the arresting officers thought she might be going for a gun in the glove box. She's lucky they didn't shoot her right then and there. When they searched that glove box, they didn't find a gun. But they did find some very interesting things."

"Oh, man...this is sounding good. What'd they come up with?"

"Foreign passports," Peters replied. "Five of them. And here's the best part...one of them is a Canadian passport in the name of John Arthur Mills. You remember old John, right?"

Pitney couldn't forget him, either, even if he didn't actually exist. John Arthur Mills was the name used to rent a safe deposit box in a Monterey, California, bank, the very box to which Steven Willis, an AWOL US Army sergeant now busted to private and serving time in a Washington State prison for armed robbery, had produced the key he claimed was given him by Mrs. Whitelaw. From that safe deposit box, he'd taken written instructions how to locate and terrorize Jillian Miles. He'd also taken from the box the keys to a car which he and his accomplice, Paul Riddle, another busted Army sergeant, would use as expendable transportation to and from the Miles home.

All these pieces of evidence—the safe deposit box key, the instructions, the car and its keys—were in DA Peters' possession, as was Riddle, currently in the Monterey County jail awaiting trial for the attempted home invasion at the Miles residence. Riddle had been arrested at the scene, unable to flee after the sharpshooting Jillian Miles wounded him in the leg.

Willis had managed to escape this assault gone wrong but had readily admitted his role to an Army CID investigator once tracked down in a Seattle jail.

"This is amazing," Pitney said. "Now we have evidence linking Mrs. Whitelaw to the attack on my client."

"Yeah, it looks that way," the DA replied, "provided your boy Willis hasn't recanted. Don't forget...Riddle still hasn't revealed one bit of information about what he was doing at the Miles home, who he was doing it for, or who he was doing it with."

"Either way, the Army's going to love this," Pitney said. "I'm going to get General Molloy on the phone as soon as I hang up with you. Just one thing...where's Mrs. Whitelaw now?"

"Under Federal house arrest," Peters replied. "As soon as we released her on bail for drunk driving and resisting arrest, the FBI swooped in and arrested her for passport fraud. Considering her husband's position at Fort Ord, she was released on her own recognizance. But the case against her looks pretty strong. All the passports in her possession are apparently bogus. You know as well as I do that it's not uncommon for people running shady business deals to use false passports as ID. The lady's in a lot of trouble."

As good as this news was, Mark Pitney knew that he and his client couldn't allow themselves to become euphoric. There was an excellent chance that none of this would make the judge in Jillian's immigration hearing see her case in a more sympathetic light.

"Just one thing," Pitney said. "Let me be the one to break the news to Mrs. Miles."

Chapter Twenty-Eight

When he'd arrived for the command and staff briefing at Regiment, Lee Grossman was surprised Colonel Miles hadn't given him more than a cursory nod *hello*. He'd expected a much more enthusiastic greeting. *That's okay*, he told himself. *The colonel's just waiting for the right moment to congratulate me on my little project...maybe even make a big deal out of it in front of the whole regiment. Hold me up as an example of that aggressive spirit the generals are always harping about.*

Never mind that what I'm really doing is making a suicide pact with the devil.

The *right moment* came as the briefing was breaking up. Jock pulled him aside and said, "Don't you ever fucking do any of that *kamikaze commando* bullshit again, Major. Do I make myself clear?"

Grossman was stunned to silence. A number of things to say in his defense raced through his mind, each rapidly considered and rejected. Up to a moment ago, he would've considered any one of those responses brilliant and unassailable.

But suddenly, in the face of the colonel's harsh disapproval, they became the ravings of a man out of his depth. His certainty that Jock would applaud his suicidal quest, even use it to inspire his other commanders, collapsed like the house of cards it had always been.

He began to tremble as the plan to escape his shattered world was itself shattered.

"Sit down, Lee," Jock said, his tone shifting once

again, this time becoming paternal. Placing a hand on Grossman's shoulder, he continued, "What you had in mind...you and I have been through too much together for me to let you throw your life away like that. By rights, I could've had you drummed out on a Section 8 already. Maybe I *should've* done that. But then I'd be helping you commit suicide in a different way. It would take away all your veteran's benefits, get you disbarred...all the penalties that go with a less than honorable discharge. You've proved yourself too fine a soldier to deserve any of that. Now I can appreciate the pain you're going through right now, and—"

Grossman cut him off. "Begging your pardon, sir, but I don't see how you can appreciate it. You've never had a woman destroy your life."

"I'm not so sure about that, Lee. I may be losing my wife—and my kids—as we speak. You, at least, know where you stand. I haven't the faintest idea where I am."

Jock paused, letting those words sink in for a moment. But saying them out loud reopened the wound of uncertainty caused by Jillian's pending deportation and its potential to devastate their marriage. He'd managed to keep that wound from festering for months. But now its dormant toxins were active again, awakening the terror of that impending loss:

She had a life in Australia, a very good one. I convinced her to leave that life behind and build a new life with me in the States.

But if Uncle Sam rips that new life from us and she's sent back, will she still want me—when and if I can join her in Australia?

Or will I just become another bloody stupid American, better forgotten?

Then Jock remembered the last time he'd been stricken with this same terror:

It feels just like that entire year back in the last war when I thought she was dead.

But it was Grossman's problem, not his own, that he needed to deal with right now. So he asked, "What's it going to be, Lee? Are you going to help me keep this regiment fighting smart or not?"

It took him a few moments to reply, an awkward silence that had Jock worried he hadn't gotten through to the man. But, finally, Grossman said, "I work for you, sir. However you want it, that's the way it's going to be."

He sounded like he meant it, too.

Patchett approached with a critical and immediate concern: "We just got the word, sir. Kickoff for Operation Killer is in forty-eight hours. We gotta get our ducks in a row *fast*."

*****

The mission of Operation Killer was exactly as its name suggested: kill as many as possible of the enemy troops retreating north after the failure of their *great offensive* at Chip'yong-ni and Wonju. Doing so would clear 8th Army's path to the 38th Parallel and return Seoul to South Korean control for the second time since last summer.

Jock told his commanders, "Twenty-Fourth Division's job is to anchor the western flank of Eighth Army's advance and prevent any CCF or KPA troops from fleeing to and reinforcing Seoul." He circled an area on the map some five miles northeast of their current position at Hajin. "Central to our regiment's area of operations will be the airfield at Sumi-ri. That's where I'll put the regimental CP, along with our direct support artillery. First Battalion, reinforced with a company of armor, will cover Highway Twenty-Four south through the mountain pass to Chip'yong-ni. Second Battalion will cover Highway Two north to Toryong-ni with a company of armor attached. The third company of armor will be a mobile reserve based at Sumi-ri." Turning to Lee Grossman, he said, "Third Battalion will defend the hills east of Sumi-ri and establish an OP on Hill Five-Two-Seven. From that height, we should have a good view of enemy troops approaching from the east."

Jock made it a point to lock eyes with Grossman as he gave him what everyone knew was the most difficult assignment. In the cruel winter weather, establishing effective fighting positions high in the mountains would be a punishing task requiring extraordinary leadership. He'd given the job to Grossman for two reasons:

I need him to know I haven't lost faith in him, and I need to make sure I'm not misplacing that faith.

Inwardly, he breathed a sigh of relief when Grossman's face—its expression brimming with confidence—didn't look away from his gaze for even a second. He showed no trace of the malaise common to leaders who'd lost their sense of purpose. Jock considered it a sign: *Lee Grossman is back. Emotionally bruised, for sure, but hitting on all cylinders again.*

*****

As if the bitter cold and continuous snow weren't

punishment enough for the GIs, nature decided to offer up an improbable blow: an unseasonal warming settled over central Korea on this final week of February. Temperatures rose ten degrees above freezing; falling snow turned to rain. The snow already descended became deep slush; the rock-hard ground beneath softened to a pasty quagmire. Everything that tried to move across that quagmire, from GI galoshes, to truck tires, to tank tracks, was doomed to bog down in the thick mud, often to a dead stop. When tasked to intercept a column of enemy armor, the tank company assigned to 2nd Battalion—Charlie Company—would be the first to realize just how badly the soggy terrain would impair their mobility.

Lee Grossman's OP on Hill 527 had reported five T-34 tanks moving west on a secondary road through a valley, headed toward 2nd Battalion's sector along Highway 2.

"Any infantry with those tanks?" the battalion C.O. asked the OP.

"Can't tell," came the reply. "The visibility's not so hot right now...lots of mist and fog down in the valleys. But we can make out the tanks. Hell, even if we couldn't see them, we could sure hear them from up here."

Battalion wasted no time dispatching Charlie Company—its attached armor—to engage and destroy the T-34s before they could reach Highway 2. The drive along the highway itself was perilously slick; two tanks of First Platoon—which were leading the Charlie Company column—slid off the paved roadway to become mired on the shoulder while still a mile from their objective. The first had slid sideways with such momentum that it peeled a track. Abandoning that vehicle for the time being, the platoon leader employed his other two Pershings in an attempt to pull out the second stuck but still serviceable tank.

This took precious time, however; the company's other three platoons passed them by, pressing on without them.

Within minutes, Second Platoon lost three of its four tanks. One slid off the highway, her hull bottoming out in a roadside paddy during a frantic attempt to drive back to the pavement. Her tracks, no longer in contact with the mushy ground, spun like useless conveyor belts, moving nothing. She'd require the services of a bulldozer to plow an escape path and the armored wrecker to pull her free. Of the platoon's other two out-of-action tanks, one had suffered a transmission failure, the other an electrical malfunction in a junction box that filled the hull with acrid smoke, forcing her choking crew to flee her confines after expending their fire extinguishers only made it more difficult to breathe.

When the Charlie Company commander—a captain named Marsh—tried to call Battalion to report his growing list of problems and ask for help, his radio—the only one in his company capable of communications on infantry frequencies—went dead. He improvised a new plan on the spot: *I'll use the one serviceable tank from Second Platoon as a runner to take my report back to Battalion. She can bring me back a new radio, too...the extra one I should've brought along in the first place.*

I'll send Third Platoon to the far side of the highway bridge—beyond the spot where the T-34s should show themselves—and leave Fourth Platoon on the near side. As soon as the enemy tanks come into view, we should be able to hit them from both flanks.

What Captain Marsh didn't know was that the OP on Hill 527 had a fairly good view of his misfortunes and had already alerted Regiment. As soon as their report came in, Jock told Sean Moon, "I'm going to commit the reserve tank company right now. What're your thoughts on that, Sergeant?"

"I agree, sir," Sean replied. "They've got the dozer tanks, which we're gonna need. I'll round up the wrecker to go with 'em, too." Then he picked up a field telephone, called the tank park, and read the commander of Able Company the order to commit his reserve force. "I'll be there in a minute to give you guys a hand, Lieutenant," Sean said as he rang off the call.

The reserve company was mounted up and ready to roll when Sean's jeep pulled into the tank park. "How do you think I should handle this?" the company commander asked him.

"Cautiously," Sean replied. "Let the dozer tanks take the lead and plow the highway. It's slicker than we thought. Otherwise, half your vehicles will probably slip off the road and get stuck, too."

The lieutenant replied, "Yeah, good plan, but I've got to tell the dozers they're going to lead. I'll be right *baaaa—*"

He never got to finish the sentence. In his haste to climb down from his tank's slick deck, he'd slipped, striking his helmetless head against the fender on the way to the ground. When Sean got to him, he was stunned and disoriented; blood was beginning to flow from a nasty gash above his ear.

The lieutenant quickly came around, saying, "I'm okay, Sergeant. I'm okay. I'll just…"

Still disoriented, he tried to climb back up onto the

deck. But before Sean could stop him, his foot slipped off the sprocket wheel he'd unwisely used as a step, sending him sprawling to the ground again. This time, he didn't try to get up.

"Get him to the aid station," Sean barked at some mechanics nearby.

A tank platoon sergeant, a five-striper named Pearson who'd been watching from the turret of the adjacent Pershing, climbed down and ran over to Sean, asking, "I guess that means you'll be leading us, right, Sarge?"

"Me?" Sean asked. "Where the hell's your XO?"

"He got evacuated last night," Pearson replied. "The official story is dysentery, but my money says he's got the clap real bad. I think he picked up a little more than supplies down at Yoju, if you get my drift."

"Shit," Sean muttered. He knew there were no other officers in the company; each platoon sergeant, like Pearson, was an *acting platoon leader* in the absence of a lieutenant. None of them had been told any specifics of the mission yet, and there was no time for a formal briefing. The T-34s would reach the junction with Highway 2 in fifteen to twenty minutes, and the unlucky Charlie Company might not be ready for them.

"Mount up," Sean said. "I'll have to brief you guys on the fly."

Before he climbed into Pearson's tank, Sean called the regimental CP on the tank park's landline. Patchett took the call, telling him, "The colonel's tied up with Division. What do you need, Bubba?"

Sean explained the how and why of him leading Able Company to reinforce the armor ambush. He finished with, "Just need to make sure the old man's okay with me taking off for a while."

Patchett replied, "Seeing the calamities been befalling you tankers today, I'd be surprised if he *didn't* want you to go and keep things straight. Just stay in touch, okay? I'll cover for you back here."

*****

When Sean got back to the tank, Pearson had dismounted. His personal weapon and gear were slung over his shoulder. Sean asked him, "Where the hell you think you're going, Gene?"

Surprised by the question, Pearson replied, "You're taking over, right? Ain't no room in that buggy for everybody *and* a big bruiser like you, Sean, so I'm giving you my seat."

Sean snatched the rucksack from Pearson's shoulder, hurled it up to the turret roof, and said, "Negative, numbnuts. I'll be glad to take your seat, but you're gonna be equally glad to displace either your gunner or your loader...who also will be very glad. Delighted, in fact. So who's it gonna be, Sergeant?"

Pearson picked the loader, who wasted no time exiting the vehicle. As he hurried to the motor pool, he seemed every bit as delighted as Sean had predicted. Gene Pearson seemed less so.

The two dozer tanks—Shermans with plow blades in front—were already rumbling down the highway, clearing off the foot-deep slush. With Sean's tank in the lead, the Pershings of Able Company followed close behind the dozers, their rubber-cleated treads providing decent traction on the thin layer of ice still clinging to the pavement. With the top layer of slush cleared, the ice would melt soon…but not soon enough.

"Like I told your guys," Sean said to Pearson, "anybody slips off this roadway and gotta get pulled out, it's his ass."

Pearson asked, "How come if the OP can see those chink tanks, the artillery ain't pasting the shit out of them?"

"Simple, Gene. The only artillery we got available at the moment is our direct support one-oh-fives, and the odds of them doing shit to a T-34 with indirect fire is about zip, right? So there's no point wasting precious rounds."

"But what about Divarty? And Corps? They've got the big guns."

"Yeah, big guns…with only a slightly better chance of hurting a moving tank but no better chance of hitting it," Sean replied. "Don't think we didn't ask, though. They're tied up with higher priority targets, so tough shit for us."

They looked up through the hatch at the gray, overcast sky. "And of course," Sean added, "the flyboys won't be helping us out through this soup."

"I don't know, Sean. It just seems like overkill to commit two whole damn companies for a handful of T-34s. I think the colonel's getting a little gun-shy."

Sean gave Pearson a withering look. "First off, Gene, you got no squawks with Colonel Miles. None of us do. Secondly, when you commit your reserve, you commit the whole fucking thing. Sending them in piecemeal is asking to have them destroyed piecemeal. Didn't you learn nothing fighting the Krauts? And who knows…just because the OP can't see no infantry with them tanks don't mean there ain't a battalion or two of them headed this way."

One of the dozer tanks was on the radio, saying, "We got a vehicle coming toward us...but I'm pretty sure it's a Pershing."

"Affirmative," Sean replied. "Let her through so I can have a little chat."

It was the *runner* from Charlie Company, and the *little chat* was over very quickly. The only thing Sean learned that he didn't already know was that Captain Marsh had sent his Third Platoon *across* a bridge, one that had supported heavy vehicles during 8th Army's advance last fall and again during its winter retreat. But it might have been bombed and weakened since then.

"But they got across okay," the runner tank's TC said. "I heard them report to Captain Marsh over the radio that they were in position."

"That's great," Sean replied. "Let's just hope for their sake that bridge is still standing when it's time to come back. That span goes over a small river, and with all this melting going on, you ain't gonna be fording that river, that's for damn sure. Fall in behind me. We gotta get moving."

Sean's column found First Platoon beyond a bend just a short distance down the highway. Not only was the mired tank still stuck, but one of the Pershings trying to pull her out had become stuck, too. The only one of the platoon's tanks still on the road had just broken a track. Her crew was working feverishly to replace the sheared link pins, sparks flying from the repeated metal-to-metal blows of mallets.

The wrecker sergeant asked, "You want me to help them, Sean?"

"Negative. Second Platoon should be right up the

road, and they got one stuck that needs a plow job. Work on that one first, then go back and do what you can for these guys in First Platoon."

Sean found Captain Marsh with his Fourth Platoon at the near side of the bridge. The four tanks of the platoon had taken up excellent hull-down positions alongside the highway, with only their turrets protruding above the level of the pavement. But the mounds of mud splayed around their tracks betrayed their problem: they were all stuck.

"Well, sir, you've got great firing positions, anyway," Sean said. "Let's just hope this don't turn into a running fight. What about the guys on the far side of the bridge?"

"They're not stuck," Marsh replied. "I've concealed them in the village just beyond the bridge."

Sean could just make out the village, almost a mile in the distance. He asked, "What kind of fields of fire they got from way over there, sir? It looks like they won't even see the T-34s until they spill onto the highway. Then we got a real fight on our hands."

"Do you have a better idea, Sergeant?"

"Actually, I do, Captain. One of the dozers is digging out that buried vehicle of yours, but I got the other one right here. Let's rip up the secondary road the T-34s are on about a hundred yards short of the highway...dig a big ol' tank ditch right across it, but not too deep, so one of them *rice cookers* could actually cross it if she wanted to. As soft as this turf is, the digging will only take the dozer a coupla minutes."

Captain Marsh looked skeptical as he asked, "Then what do we do, Sergeant?"

"I don't figure they're gonna wanna back up or turn

around, sir. That's a guaranteed way to get stuck in the mud. So we let the first one through if that's what she wants to do. Once she's on the highway, your boys on the far side can turn her inside out, no problem. It's a long-range shot, but they better have the distance down good, since they already drove it to get where they're at. And they better hit her first shot, because once a T-34 turns toward them, they're kinda exposed. Those flimsy little shacks ain't much cover."

Captain Marsh looked confused as he studied the firing diagram he'd drawn, silently trying to justify his original plan in the face of Sean's proposed revision.

Sean prodded him. "But if we're gonna dig that ditch, we gotta start right now, sir."

Marsh replied, "I just don't see what we gain by doing that."

"What we gain is that we slow 'em down and add an element of confusion. When the first tank gets cooked, and the rest see this ditch in front of them, they're either gonna stop in their tracks or, if they're hardcore, they're gonna try to plow right through. When they hit the ditch, they can move but not shoot. If they stop, they can shoot but not move. Either way, with all the tubes we got sitting here on this highway, the odds are *waaay* in our favor."

Marsh pondered only a second longer. "Go ahead and dig the ditch, Sergeant."

*****

It took the dozer tank five minutes to complete the job. "It would've taken a hell of a lot longer if this ground was still frozen solid," her TC told Sean over the radio. "I'd better get out of here. I can feel those T-34s breathing down my neck."

The dozer had barely gotten back to the highway when the first T-34 roared through the ditch without bothering to slow down. Watching her violently pitching from a few hundred yards down the highway, Sean said, "I bet that TC just injured his whole damn crew, the dumb bastard. There gotta be broken bones and concussions like crazy from getting thrown around like that."

On the far side of the bridge now, the T-34 pulled onto the highway and began to pivot north. Before she could get halfway through the turn, two HEAT rounds from two different tanks of Marsh's Third Platoon—the one in the village beyond the bridge—slammed into her hull. A round from a third tank screamed over the enemy vehicle's deck, flew down the highway, and plowed into soft ground just yards from one of Sean's tanks. Luckily, the explosion did little more than paint the nose of the buttoned-up Pershing with mud.

It took a few seconds, but the T-34 *brewed up* as expected after taking the two killing shots to her flank. Her hatches had blown open, but nothing exited those hatches except smoke and flames. The GI tankers rejoiced in her demise, but it left one big problem: the burning T-34 was straddling the highway, her ammo cooking off, completely blocking the only viable approach to the bridge.

Sean fumed as he thought, *That ain't the way I figured Third Platoon would get itself trapped on the wrong side of the bridge. I was betting that span would drop into the river at the worst possible time.*

Hell, it still could.

Captain Marsh asked him, "Are they chink tanks or KPA, Sergeant?"

"Does it fucking matter right now, sir?"

The second T-34 approached the ditch more cautiously than her vanquished sister. She stopped at its edge, prompting the gunner in Sean's tank to ask, "I can barely see her through the trees, Sarge. Should I take her now, anyway?"

"No, hold up a minute," Sean replied. "Let's see what she's gonna do."

With agonizing slowness, her turret began to traverse toward them. "Typical," Sean said. "The traverse motor's out. They gotta hand-crank the turret around."

Then the T-34 lurched forward, nosed into the ditch, paused at the bottom momentarily, and then slowly continued forward up the revetment, crawling out with her bow high in the air, her soft underside exposed.

"NOW!" Sean commanded. "SHE'S SHOWING HER BELLY. SCRATCH HER ONE GOOD, DAMMIT!"

The shot peeled open the top of her hull like a flower suddenly blooming. Her turret, blown off in the blast, fell to the ground twenty yards behind her.

The three T-34s behind her were still not in the view of any GI gunner. But one thing was for sure: they could no longer try to move forward without leaving the road and getting hopelessly stuck.

Captain Marsh asked, "What do we do now, Sergeant?"

"I'm supposed to be asking you that, sir," Sean replied.

"Then let me put it this way," Marsh said. "What do

you *suggest* we do now?"

"I suggest the best shot in your Third Platoon pulls up to that ditch and knocks out the next T-34 in the column, Captain."

"But it'll be a head-on shot, Sergeant. Not much percentage in that."

"I think their tanks are gonna try to turn around, sir, because there ain't much percentage trying to flee in reverse, neither, slow as that'll be. We just might get a shot at their flanks or their backsides, because turning around ain't gonna be no piece of cake. Lots of back and forth...they gotta keep on that narrow pavement or they end up in the slop. So what's it gonna be, Captain?"

"Fine. We'll do it your way, Sergeant."

"Outstanding, sir. Oh...and while we're at it, let's start getting that blown-up wreck that's blocking the bridge outta the way. Just hook a coupla cables to her and pull her clear. We may need to cross that bridge real soon."

"But that ammo cooking off..."

"Ah, that's over with already, sir. It don't take long."

*****

When the Pershing from Third Platoon arrived at the ditch, the three T-34s still unscathed were in the middle of their laborious attempt to pivot to the opposite direction. The nearest one to the American tank was easy pickings. Once the smoke and flames signaled her demise, the two T-34s beyond seemed strangely inert. They'd both stopped in mid-pivot with hatches open. Their main guns lay at acute angles to the hull lines as if the crews had given up on the idea of traversing them toward the Pershing's threat. The Pershing at the ditch claimed he didn't have a clear shot at either of them.

Sean and Captain Marsh had driven to the bridge, walked across it, and then commandeered the Third Platoon tank that wasn't busy clearing away the vanquished T-34. Once they'd ridden that Pershing to the ditch, Sean took one look at the enemy tanks in the distance and said, "They're abandoned."

"How can you be sure, Sergeant?" the captain asked.

"Because they'd be shooting at us if they weren't, sir."

"So we're done here?" Marsh asked.

"Negative, sir. Not until we blow up those two perfectly serviceable T-34s."

"But how, Sergeant? We don't have a good line of sight on them."

Sean smiled, amused by Captain Marsh's lack of imagination. "Simple, sir. Why don't you wait here while I drive right over this hulk in the ditch, right up to that next flamer, and shoot right over her hull. Then I'm gonna back out. By the time I'm on the highway, the bridge should be clear and we can all go back where we came from, mission accomplished."

The captain needed no further encouragement. He jumped over to the Pershing that would remain at the ditch.

Then Sean did exactly what he said he'd do, with an added bonus; as his vehicle backed down the road, the four Chinese tank crewmen who'd surrendered to the Pershing were marching before her with hands on their heads.

Jumping over to the deck of Sean's tank, Captain

Marsh asked, "How'd you find them, Sergeant?"

"I didn't, sir. They found me. Look at 'em...they got rags for shoes and they're starving. They practically ripped each other apart to get a bite of that chocolate bar I threw to them. I guess what the brass have been saying about the chink supply lines *being a little thin* ain't no lie."

Chapter Twenty-Nine

Jillian Miles' lawyer, Mark Pitney, delivered the news of Mrs. Whitelaw's arrest in person. As she sipped coffee in her Monterey home's great room, Jillian took it calmly, resisting the urge to *pop a cork* in celebration. She told Pitney, "Of course I'm delighted to see that devious witch in hot water—*boiling* hot water at that. But that judge...is it going to make one iota of difference to him?"

"I understand what you're saying, Mrs. Miles," Pitney replied, "but we won't know that until the hearing. It certainly doesn't hurt your case, though."

"That's a very small consolation, Mark. *Not hurting* is a far cry from *helping*. But no matter...there's something else I need you to be aware of."

She pointed to a legal document on the coffee table. "Read that," she said.

He flipped through the pages quickly. "If I understand this correctly," he said, "the US Government is requesting an emergency extension of its contract with your shipping company?"

"That's correct, Mark. The Yanks need my six tankers very badly, apparently. All of a sudden, the British have their hands full with the Iranians trying to seize their oil interests in that country. The Brits' national revenue will plummet—maybe collapse—without being able to peddle oil on the world market that they're getting out of Iran for practically nothing, so they're pulling their tankers from the Korean supply effort to grab all they can get for themselves...before it's too late."

"Is that the dust-up they're calling the Abadan Crisis?"

"That's the one," Jillian replied.

"I don't practice maritime law, so I'm not sure how this works, Mrs. Miles. It says your company—Forbes-Weipa—has a contract that runs for a term of six months, expiring on the thirtieth of April of this year, 1951. That's nearly a full two months from now. Doesn't that give everybody plenty of time to—"

"Negotiate a new contract, Mark?"

"Yes, that's what I'm saying."

"Perhaps," she replied, "but the US Government prefers to operate like everything is an emergency, and they feel their emergency *must* become your emergency. It's all bureaucratic nonsense."

"Are you suggesting they can't invoke an indefinite emergency extension of the contract, like it says here in paragraph three?"

"That's their fantasy, Mark, not mine. Read the side note...that provision only applies to a declared war, which Korea is not. The only way my tankers will keep floating American gasoline to Korea is if the contract is renewed."

"And you don't plan to renew the contract, Mrs. Miles?"

There was no anger in her voice, just cold, confident steel: "Why should I, Mark? What has the American government done for me lately, except kick me out of the country?"

Her words stunned him. Pitney told himself, *The lady knows how to play rough. She's had a potential game winner up her sleeve the whole time, and she's been waiting for the climactic moment to show it.*

But he couldn't help but wonder if she was underestimating the dangers involved, especially the one that could affect her most directly.

"Isn't this ploy a little risky, though, Mrs. Miles? I mean, with your husband in the fight...restricting critical gasoline supplies..."

"Of course Jock's on my mind, Mark," she replied, "but nobody ever wins without taking risks. My husband's a soldier, a combat commander. If anyone understands that, it'll be him."

*****

A few miles farther north up Highway 2, beyond where Sean's tanks had defeated the Chinese T-34s a week ago, were a number of secondary roads and trails that spilled from the mountains to the east. Spotter aircraft had reported evidence of large numbers of CCF troops moving through those mountains on foot, trying to reach the highway that would take them to the relative safety of the 38th Parallel and beyond.

"Push your patrols farther north up Highway Two," Jock Miles told Phil Harper, his 2nd Battalion commander. "Find the best locations for artillery traps at all the places the Chinese are exiting the mountains. According to intel, the chinks must be in a hurry to get away from the pounding they've been taking from our big guns, so they're now traveling in daylight as well as their usual nighttime movements. Have your people man the outposts along with the artillery FO teams so we can provide security for them round the clock."

"Got it, sir," Harper replied. "This will come as

great news to our Captain Papadakis. He's been chomping at the bit to get out there and kill himself some more chinks, and I'll be glad to oblige him. The guy's unstoppable."

"Yeah, I learned a long time ago that you've just got to point Theo in the direction you need him, and then get out of his way. He doesn't need a whole lot of supervision."

"I've come to appreciate that, sir," Harper said.

*****

It had taken Captain Theo Papadakis less than a day to establish the OPs and LPs in accordance with Jock Miles' wishes. Positioned on either side of a ridgeline several miles long just east of Highway 2, those outposts overlooked the two secondary roads suspected of being the prime routes of the retreating Chinese infantry. The southernmost of the LPs also straddled a mountain trail which, from its trampled-down condition, had apparently seen its fair share of traffic, too. Along with the men of his Able Company, *Captain Pop* had under his control two FO teams from Baker Battery, the Negro artillery outfit attached to 26th Regiment.

The FO teams fired in numerous registration points along the roads and trail, numbering each for simplicity when communicating with their battery's fire direction center. With firing data for each point already computed, rounds could be on target in less than forty seconds after being requested, most of those seconds being the time-of-flight of the rounds.

"Setting up all these registration points is the way to go, Captain Pop," said Lieutenant Thackery, the senior

FO from Baker Battery. "I hear that's what saved
Second Division down at Wonju when they were
outnumbered something like six to one. They fired in a
bunch of registration points along likely avenues of
approach to their positions, many more than you usually
would. Once the bad guys started coming, they just kept
pumping out rounds onto those registration points.
Didn't have to adjust much of anything, so no precious
time was wasted. It saved their asses."

"Let's hope it works here, too," Papadakis replied.
"Tonight should be a pretty good test."

Thackery added, "Just so the temperature and wind
don't change much and the guns keep shooting the same
ammunition lot, that firing data will give us first-round
hits every time. But when those parameters do change,
Captain, we should shoot in those registration points
again, if at all possible."

"Agreed."

Papadakis had his GIs set out as many noisemakers
as they could cobble together along the likely paths the
Chinese would travel. The noisemakers were the same
type of crude devices he'd used with great success in the
jungles of Papua, Dutch New Guinea, and the
Philippines: empty ration cans filled with a few small
stones and strung on wire low to the ground. He'd had to
practically stand on more than a few troopers' heads to
get the cans in place; it was another task that many of his
inexperienced GIs considered useless *busywork* when
piled on top of all the arduous digging to continuously
improve their positions. To make it worse, handling the
sharp-edged metal cans and stiff wire was brutal on the
hands in the cold temperatures; some parts of the task
required gloves to be removed for a few moments, so

unprotected skin was lacerated often. But Papadakis knew the effort was worth these hardships: running for their lives, the poorly fed Chinese troopers were exhausted, and exhausted adversaries stumbling through the dark couldn't help but activate the noisemakers. The rattling sound they made—like *maracas* shaken momentarily—was hard to mistake for anything else and carried over great distances at night. Even if you couldn't see the intruders, you could certainly hear them.

And those doubting-Thomas GIs of mine will find out soon enough it was all worth it, he was sure.

The noisemakers proved their worth that first night on the LPs. They betrayed the approaching Chinese at several locations along the roads; the steel rain was falling on them moments later. When the sun rose, Captain Pop's men counted over two hundred enemy bodies. They'd probably killed more; nobody could figure out how to tally the innumerable body parts strewn among the intact corpses. None of his GIs had been wounded or had even fired a shot.

"That's a good haul," Papadakis told his leaders, "but you know for damn sure we didn't get all of 'em...and the ones still walking might have some mighty strong suspicions we're around here somewhere. They'll be looking for us, watching to see if we give ourselves away. So from now on, when the sun's up, we lie real low, with outstanding noise discipline, no fires, no nothing. You got me?"

His men did as they were told. An enemy lurking nearby would've been hard-pressed to detect the well-dug-in American company.

That's how it remained until late morning, when an American helicopter passed overhead, orbited the hill on which Papadakis had set up his CP, and—to the horror of every man in Able Company—landed in a small, flat clearing on the backslope. Her occupants had seen some of the GI positions, since no effort had been made to conceal them from airborne observation; there was little need to do so when your enemy didn't have planes overhead. Captain Pop raced to the helicopter, intent on telling her occupants to *get lost*.

A brigadier general alighted from the Sikorsky H-19—her blades still whirling, the blatant sound of her engine reverberating through the hills—and walked right up to Papadakis. He was trailed by a major, presumably an aide. As they drew near the small, swarthy man, the general's expression changed from stern to quizzical. He asked, "Are you from some *Allied* country? Turkish, perhaps?"

The aide snapped to parade rest behind the general, his face a sneer behind reflective aviator sunglasses.

"Negative, sir," Pop replied. "We're one hundred percent US Army...Able Company, Second of the Twenty-Sixth. And since you're wondering, I'm Greek-American, born and raised in New York City."

The general was still unconvinced; *offended*, perhaps, by this foreign-looking soldier. He asked, "What's your division?"

"Twenty-Fourth Division, sir."

"And what's your position in this *Able Company*?"

"I'm the company commander, sir, Captain Theo Papadakis." Pulling his parka open to reveal the *railroad tracks* on his shirt collar, he added, "Now, how about doing me a real big favor and get that whirlybird the hell outta here? You're giving away our position."

"I'm not going anywhere, *Captain Paaa...*"

He quickly gave up trying to pronounce the name—
which his memory hadn't properly retained in the first
place—and continued, "You're obviously lost, *Captain*."
He spoke the rank with no respect, as if he didn't believe
it possible. "You're in Tenth Corps territory. I should
know, because I'm Assistant G3 in General Almond's
headquarters. You're perilously close to Second
Division's CP. You're lucky I didn't call in artillery fire
on you."

Papadakis repressed the urge to laugh. This general
was so lost—and so belligerently ignorant about it—that
any artillery he requested would've landed miles from
here, maybe on one of his own X Corps units.

*Tenth Corps, eh? I heard that Almond, the corps
commander, is a walking, talking disaster. Looks like his
staff officers are, too.*

Lieutenant Thackery, the Negro artillery FO,
approached the two men, carrying his map board under
his arm. His presence seemed to repulse the general even
worse than that of Papadakis, who thought, *It's gospel
truth in this man's army that Almond ain't real fond of
the colored race. Looks like his staff officers think the
same way their boss does.*

Pop said, "Good...you got the map. Show the
general where he is, Lieutenant. You might want to point
out where the boundary between Ninth and Tenth Corps
is, too."

"*Lieutenant?*" the general said, his face reddening
and not from the cold. "This *nigra* is an officer?"

Pretending to ignore the slur, the seething Thackery
presented the map to the general, who ripped it from his
hands, saying, "I don't need a map reading lesson from
one of *these people*."

"Then to save us all some time, let me do it, sir," Papadakis replied.

In a few quick jabs at the map with his finger, pointing out terrain features plainly visible from where they stood, Captain Pop made his case: the general and his helicopter were miles from where they thought they were.

As he gave his tutorial, Theo glanced up to the elevated cockpit of the Sikorsky H-19. The pilot had a sheepish look on his face as he made a shrugging, palms-up gesture that Pop took to mean, *Look, I tried to tell him…*

The general's error now irrefutable, Papadakis added, "I'm kinda surprised your chopper didn't get knocked down by friendly artillery fire on the way over here, sir. You musta passed right through the *no-fly zone.*"

The general did an about-face and started back toward the helicopter. He told his aide, "Deal with these people, Major."

But the aide had no idea what *deal with these people* entailed. He remained silently at parade rest as the sun, just liberated from a shroud of low clouds, reflected brilliantly off his sunglasses.

Papadakis told him, "Maybe the general means you're supposed to get my name so he can put me up for a medal." He said it with such a straight face that Lieutenant Thackery couldn't help but snicker.

"*At ease*, both of you jokers," the major snarled, snatching a sense of purpose from Captain Pop's wisecrack. "You'd better believe I'm taking your name, but it's not going to be for a medal, that's for damn sure."

"All right, sir...my name's Papadakis, just like I told the man before."

"What the hell kind of name is that? How do you spell it?"

"Standard spelling, sir."

Then he and Thackery turned and started walking toward the top of the ridge, leaving the major sputtering. The only words they could decipher from his rant were *court-martial*, liberally sprinkled throughout.

Papadakis called over his shoulder, "You've been standing still an awful long time, sir. You make one hell of a target, especially with those *signal mirrors* you got over your eyes. I've gotta tell you, there are chinks all over these hills."

When they looked back again, the major was sprinting to the helicopter. She lifted off the second he'd leapt through the doorway.

Thackery asked, "That damn chopper...are we going to have to move now, sir?" The tone of his voice left no doubt that just the thought was exhausting.

"Nah, we'll guts it out right where we are, Edgar," Papadakis replied. "Ain't no better position than this around here, anyway." He paused and then added, "But the only helicopter I wanna see up on this ridge is one that I request. The next whirlybird that shows up uninvited, I'm gonna shoot her down myself. Nobody'll know the chinks didn't do it."

*****

On the evening of 6 March 1951, Jock Miles assembled his battalion commanders at 26th Regiment's Sumi-ri CP. He'd just returned from a briefing with

General Bryan, the division commander, who'd been candid with his combat leaders. Jock extended that same candidness to the leaders of his regiment.

"General Ridgway has officially declared Operation Killer completed, gentlemen," he began. "I'd like to tell you it was an unqualified success, but you all know better, because you were there. True, our advances met the geographic goals, and we did inflict a heavy toll on the CCF. But did we achieve the massive level of destruction in men and equipment we'd hoped? I'm afraid not. The warmer temperatures and soggy ground slowed our ability to pursue the enemy greatly, allowing far too many of them to escape. But as General Ridgway has already made clear, this is not an ass-chewing, because you have no control over the difficulties Mother Nature throws at you. We know we've got the Chinese on the run. We just haven't been able to overtake them as quickly as we'd like. Hopefully, this next phase of our advance will change that."

He removed the sheet covering the big situation map at the head of the room. In big block letters across the top was the name *OPERATION RIPPER*. Jock let his commanders and staff study it for a few moments.

"Notice the phase lines for *Ripper*," Jock continued. "They take us to—and slightly beyond—the Thirty-Eighth Parallel over a period of three weeks. You'll also notice how the phase lines bulge north some ten miles to the east of Seoul early in the campaign. I'm sure you all know why…"

Every man in the room did, in fact, know why: General Ridgway had no intention of waging yet another knock-down, drag-out battle on the streets of Seoul. The city had been through three of them already—changing hands each time—at great cost in lives and materiel. As envisioned, the initial thrust of Operation Ripper would quickly put 8th Army forces northeast of Seoul, in position to encircle it. The CCF would, hopefully, abandon the city rather than be trapped within, allowing it to be reclaimed with a minimum of fighting.

If and when the Chinese did abandon Seoul, those American and ROK divisions to the northeast—24th Division among them—would be in position to cut them off and finish them. Just like Operation Killer before it, the primary goal of Operation Ripper was to destroy as much of the CCF as possible. And this time, the terrain retaken would result in reestablishing the integrity of South Korea's border with North Korea, the 38th Parallel.

Jock concluded with, "If you thought the artillery barrage that kicked off Operation Killer was something to behold, wait until you see the one General Ridgway has laid on for tonight's kickoff of Operation Ripper. It should be Christmas, New Year's, and Fourth of July all rolled into one."

*****

Just before midnight, Patchett and Sean Moon made their way up Hill 527, driving as far as they could up its slope in a jeep. Then, on foot, they took the arduous climb the last few hundred yards to Lee Grossman's CP on the peak.

"Oh, good," Grossman said. "More spectators. Pull up a chair and grab a cup of coffee. The show's just about to start."

No sooner had they settled onto camp stools, their gloved hands wrapped around the warm canteen cups, than they could see what looked like a summer night's storm boiling to the south: several hundred artillery pieces were suddenly firing all at once, their muzzle flashes portraying the lightning, the continuous rumble of the firing that arrived seconds later playing the thunder.

The artillery preparation for Operation Ripper had begun.

They could hear the shrill *whoosh* of countless rounds streaking high overhead, flying north, hoping for a cataclysmic meeting with enemy forces at the end of their trajectory. Most of the GIs—officers and enlisted alike—cheered each salvo as if they were watching a football game.

The old hands, Patchett and Sean among them, watched in awed silence, however. They'd seen before what massed artillery could do, how human flesh offered no more protection than a sheet of paper to the massive power of their explosives...

And none of the old hands had ever seen a barrage quite so colossal.

It would continue until sunrise.

After it had gone on for five minutes, Patchett broke the silence. "Hey, Bubba, as I live and breathe, I ain't never seen this many rounds crashing down on nobody. Even being in the trenches back in France in '18 don't come close. And in the jungle, we didn't even see the artillery most of the time, just heard it. What about you?"

"That turkey shoot in the Falaise Gap back in '44 was almost like this," Sean replied. "Not this many guns, but they were firing on and off for days. Burned out God knows how many artillery tubes. And when the guns weren't firing, my little brother and his flyboy friends took up the slack with their bombing and strafing. When it was all over and you looked at it from a distance, all you could see was burned-out vehicles and dead horses. Thousands of 'em. You had to get a lot closer to see the bodies. And there sure was a shitload of 'em, too."

He paused, taking a long sip of coffee as he gazed at the pinpoint flashes of rounds impacting miles to the north. "But even though we killed damn near an entire Kraut army in that trap, it wasn't enough. Too many escaped because goddamn Monty fucked it up. He wouldn't let us close the door on that damn gap. If he had, we coulda ended Hitler's war right then and there."

They fell silent for a few moments, until Patchett asked, "You reckon we're gonna kill enough chinks this time out?"

"I kinda doubt it, Top. I get the feeling that they ain't never gonna run outta people."

"Maybe so, Bubba…but I don't think it makes no nevermind no more. We finally figured out how to use our high-class firepower to deal with them *hordes* pretty good. As long as they don't get better firepower than us, I reckon we can hold 'em off damn near forever, any place we feel like."

*****

On this afternoon in the second week of March, *Moon's Menace VI* had just led *Switchblade Flight* on a SHORAN bombing mission of the rail yard at Uijongbu, ten miles north of Seoul. Mission altitude was the typical 14,000 feet of most SHORAN sorties. Even in broad daylight, that cushion of sky kept her crew safe from ground fire during the bomb run. The flak sent their way burst nowhere near the B-26s.

Their primary mission done, the flight headed south, following Highway 3 toward Seoul. They descended to 8,000 feet in preparation for possible strafing missions. An aerial observer flying a T-6—a trainer reinvented as an airborne observation platform—came up on frequency, intent on guiding Tommy Moon's B-26s to enemy concentrations in and around the city. The Air Force had issued Seoul the codename *Big Top*. As one pilot put it, the city looked like a circus ground when viewed from the sky, the numerous hills within and around her limits poking up like so many circus tents.

"*Switchblade Leader,* this is *Slowbird Four-Five,*" the AO transmitted. "I've got something right up your alley. Railroad tracks exiting west side of *Big Top*, going northwest through target box *four-niner*. We got us a *huff n' puff* on the run, further identified by the cloud of smoke she's making."

Huff n' puff: a train pulled by a steam locomotive.

The AO added, "I'm over the river, keeping an eye on her."

"Roger," Tommy replied. "Drawing any ground fire?"

"Negative. No tracers, no muzzle flashes visible."

Once down to 5,000 feet over the south side of Seoul, Tommy and his navigator Hank Roth had the train in sight. They counted fifteen cars behind the locomotive and its coal tender. Most were boxcars, the rest open hoppers. Whether there were soldiers in any of the cars, they couldn't tell.

"How much you want to bet that train's carrying a load of chinks evacuating the city?" Tommy asked.

"Pretty brazen—or pretty damn desperate—that they're doing it in the middle of a blue sky day, when they're obvious as hell. This is going to be like France in '44 all over again."

"What do you mean by that, sir?" Roth asked.

"It means I strafed a whole lot of trains in the last war, Hank, so many that I've lost count."

The ship was entering the last revolution of a spiral that would take them down to 1,000 feet, the altitude from which they'd begin a strafing attack. Tommy asked the AO, "Is that track as flat and as straight as it looks? No tunnels, no nothing?"

"What you see is what you get, *Switchblade*. The only obstacles are the hills rising on the north side of the tracks."

None of my other pilots have much experience going after trains, Tommy told himself, *so I'll take Switchblade Two with me and go after the locomotive. Three and Four can attack the freight cars back to front after I've made my pass.*

Once he'd briefed his flight on the attack plan, he told *Switchblade Two*, "Pull hard left after the run and get back to the river. Stay away from the hills. If there are chinks with weapons up there, you'll be flying too damn close to them."

As they rolled in on the locomotive from her eight o'clock, Tommy reviewed in his mind what he'd told *Two* on how to attack: *Go for that big round boiler...anywhere on it will do. Lead her slightly and aim low. Then use just a little bit of rudder and elevator to walk those rounds right across the ground and up into that boiler.*

Down to 400 feet now, *Moon's Menace VI* was

locked onto her target. Tommy told Roth, "Watch for small arms fire from the train so we can give *Three* and *Four* a heads-up what they'll be in for when they make their run."

Roth asked, "Okay, but is that boiler going to throw pieces everywhere when she blows up? You know, pieces that can knock us down?"

"Probably not, Hank. There's going to be a lot of steam venting, though. It might look like she's exploding..."

Six hundred yards out, Tommy had the sight picture he wanted. He waited another instant before firing the eight .50 calibers in the ship's nose. As the first rounds fell short, they threw up plumes of soggy marsh; with slight back pressure on the elevator, he walked the next rounds toward the briskly moving locomotive.

"This is easier than in the jug," Tommy said. "No wing gun convergence to mess—"

His words were cut short as the locomotive exploded spectacularly, hurling large chunks of the shattered boiler into their path. In a flash, they entered the opaque plume of escaped steam, Tommy holding his breath, bracing for those terrible *thuds* of metal striking metal.

They passed out of that plume as quickly as they'd entered, without hearing that tell-tale sound of impending disaster. But they were racing toward the hills Tommy had sworn to avoid.

Hard left, stupid. Remember?

As he stood the ship on her wingtip, Tommy asked Roth, "Any gunfire from the train?"

"Who could tell in all that? I thought you said she wouldn't blow up..."

Tommy didn't answer. He was much too busy flying the airplane through the tight and fast low-altitude turn.

Switchblade Three and *Four* were making their pass at the train now, which was rapidly slowing due to the powerless locomotive. They had less than a second to decide whether to target the cars themselves or the countless figures they could see jumping off and scurrying toward the hills like so many ants. With no time to adjust to this new development, the two pilots maintained their original objective and, attacking in trail, shot the entire length of rail cars to hell.

"Great job, *Switchblade*," the AO called after his own low pass over the smoldering, shattered train, which had come to a stop. "You blew that son of a bitch sky high."

"Thanks," Tommy replied without enthusiasm, "but it looks like the cargo got away. You see any troop activity in the hills we can go after?"

"Negative," *Slowbird* said. He paused a moment before adding, "I guess those chinks live to fight another day."

Tommy didn't bother transmitting a reply. Instead, he turned to Roth and said, "Shit. I'm afraid we only did half the job."

"But it looks like they were running away from Seoul," Roth replied. "That's a good thing, right?"

*****

Hank Roth was right on both counts: the Chinese were abandoning Seoul, and that was a very good thing for the 8th Army troops entering the city. They met little in the way of organized resistance. What they did encounter came mainly from lost stragglers and shaken deserters.

On 14 March 1951, Seoul was returned to the government of South Korea for the second—and final—time since this conflict began. That day, there was no pomp, no parade, and no MacArthur returning the keys to the city to Syngman Rhee.

Chapter Thirty

As the sun rose on the last day of March, the goals of Operation Ripper had been mostly achieved. Eighth Army had advanced to just twelve miles south of the 38th Parallel; despite the skillful retrograde operation waged by the Chinese forces who had abandoned Seoul, Ridgway's forces had not been appreciably slowed in their push northward. The massive destruction of CCF forces he'd hoped for had still not been achieved, but the Parallel, at least, was finally within his grasp.

Twenty-Sixth Regiment held the town of Kap'yong, nestled in the valley of the Pukhan River, with towering high ground on all sides. One such piece of high ground—Hill 425—lay just a mile north of the town, in the sector of Lee Grossman's 3rd Battalion. Anyone on the ridgeline atop that hill had an excellent view of Kap'yong, the river, and the two major roadways that traveled north from the town.

Jock Miles' instructions to Grossman had been clear about Hill 425: "Sure, there may be chinks up there watching our every move, Lee. But I'm not exhausting your men—or anyone else's—climbing that steep bastard. If you think they're up there, just isolate the hill and let the Air Force take care of them."

But several hours later, Jock was startled when Patchett told him, "Major Grossman's on the command net, sir. You ain't gonna believe this, but he's on top of that damn mountain with two of his companies."

"Shit. Tell him to get the hell off that hill right now, Top."

"Says he can't, sir. He's got the peak, but them chinks are ringing the slopes on all sides."

Together, they studied the situation map, looking for some way—*any* way—to prevent a sudden Chinese surge into the division's rear area through the gaping hole Grossman had created by diverting his forces to Hill 425. "He left only one damn company—Baker—with a coupla tanks to block *both* highways," Patchett said. "Pulling units from any other battalion to cover 'em just moves the hole someplace else."

"You've got that right," Jock replied. "Let's do this—pull the armor from First Battalion and put it into Third Battalion's area. Have Sergeant Moon coordinate the shift...and make damn sure those tankers know they're working for Baker Company of the Third now. I'm going up that hill to see what else I can do to straighten this mess out."

Patchett couldn't believe what he'd just heard. "How the hell you gonna get up there, sir? You can't drive it...you gotta climb the bastard on foot. And you ain't gonna be doing it with that leg of yours, that's for damn sure."

"That's why I'm taking the chopper, Top. It'll drop me right on the peak."

"But the pilot's already had a look up there, sir. Says he can't land...it's too damn windy to set down on that narrow ridgeline."

"He's not going to land, just get close enough so I can hop out," Jock replied.

"*Hop out*? How, sir? Your leg's been outta the *hopping* business for quite a while."

"My leg's not the issue here, Top. If you've got a better idea, I'd love to hear it."

But Patchett didn't have one. All he could think was, *This is just fucking great. I thought we were done with officers of this regiment having death wishes.*

He shook his head sadly and said, "As you wish, sir."

*****

The helicopter pilot offered another reason not to be thrilled with the idea: "It's going to be dark in less than two hours, sir. I won't be able to pick you up then."

Jock replied, "Let's not belabor the obvious, Captain. Are you taking me up that mountain or what?"

"Is it just you going, sir?"

"No. Me and my RTO."

The pilot considered the details for a moment. "I'll have to leave my copilot behind, then. We can't afford the extra weight if we're going to be screwing around near that mountaintop. It'll just be me and my crew chief with you two. I wouldn't take the crew chief, either, but I've got to have someone down in the cabin full-time with a better view of that peak than I'll have once we're right over it."

"Whatever it takes, Captain."

"Well, sir...if that's what you want to do...we'll give it our best shot. There's still no guarantee we're going to be able to pull it off, though. If that wind gets to swirling off the peak..."

"I understand, Captain. This isn't my first chopper ride. Now let's get airborne."

*****

It took less than five minutes for the helicopter to arrive over the peak of Hill 425. Jock could see Grossman and a few of his men crouched against the icy wind and rotor wash. His aircraft bobbing like a cork in a stormy sea, the pilot struggled to keep the chopper just a few feet above the peak. The crew chief told Jock, "If you're going, you'd better go now, sir. We can't hold this forever."

Jock and his RTO jumped when it seemed the gyrating ship was as close to the peak as it would get. The moment they were out the door, the helicopter lifted several feet and then barreled forward, skimming the downhill slope, building speed to gain lift. In her quest to escape the perils of the high-altitude hover, those on the peak were pelted by the stones and chunks of icy dirt propelled by her rotor wash.

Jock landed poorly, his bad leg crumpling beneath him as his feet hit the ground. For a moment, he feared he'd undone all the years of therapy that had enabled him to keep that leg, so grievously wounded in 1944. Pain shot through his thigh like electric shocks. When that pain subsided, he found he could stand and walk, not without difficulty and discomfort, but well enough to deal with Grossman and the problem he'd caused.

"You'd better tell me just what the hell you're doing up here against my explicit orders, Lee," Jock said.

"Better I show you, sir."

He led Jock to a circular cluster of boulders that formed a sort of parapet. Seated within that cluster were two Chinese military men, hands bound behind their backs. They were middle-aged, older than the common soldiers the GIs usually captured or found dead. Their uniforms were clean and in relatively good condition, considering the harsh conditions on the mountaintop.

And they wore high-top leather boots on their feet, not the sneakers or wrapped rags of ordinary CCF soldiers.

"We took some prisoners at the base of the hill," Grossman explained, "and they spilled their guts to the interpreters right away. Said there was the CP of a major command up on the peak, watching over the whole valley, coordinating the CCF efforts to stop us."

Unimpressed, Jock asked, "And you figured the Air Force couldn't kill them just as well as you could, Lee?"

"I figured it was too important to leave to chance, sir."

"Bullshit. You knew I would've told you to leave it alone. So now you've got half your battalion under siege up here...and I'm looking at a massive hole in our regimental line."

"But, sir, these chinks we captured...they've got to be colonels, at least, maybe—"

"*Generals*, Lee? Is that where you're going with this? I thought we agreed you wouldn't pull any more of this *kamikaze commando* bullshit to capture some high-ranking chink."

"No, wait, sir! It's not like that at all. I wasn't trying to get myself killed. I wouldn't have needed all these men with me if that's what I had in mind."

Hmm...he's got a point there. But he's still trying to play hero...and he's made a horrendous mistake doing it.

"Trouble is, Lee, regardless of your intentions, there's a good chance you're going to get us all killed, anyway. We've got to get your men off this mountain before it gets dark."

"I've been trying, sir...but they keep blocking us every time we head down."

"How many casualties?"

"Two dead...maybe ten wounded."

"Dammit, Lee. You're wasting good people for no damn reason. Now let's think this through and come up with a plan to get us all out of here in one piece. Show me the withdrawal routes you've already tried."

As they huddled over the map, Jock's RTO said, "Sir, I've got *Backstop One-Five* for you."

Backstop One-Five: Patchett.

The news he reported was not good. Massed Chinese had pushed almost to Kap'yong along Highway 17, the very route some element of Grossman's battalion was supposed to be blocking. That meant CCF forces were now on three sides of Hill 425—north, east, and south. That left only the west slope, which was extremely steep and very lightly wooded. Just a few enemy machine guns could turn it into a killing field that few Americans would escape.

Grossman's people had already tried that route once and been beaten back. That's where two GIs had died.

Jock asked Patchett, "Do the flyboys have any flame ships in the area?"

Flame ships: he was asking for a napalm mission against the west slope. With any luck at all, it would burn a path down the mountain, incinerating some—maybe all—of the Chinese trying to stop them.

It only took Patchett a moment to confer with the ASO. He relayed the answer to Jock: "Negative. We just missed out—someone else got the last dose for today. By the time they refueled and rearmed, it'd be dark, so there won't be no more until morning."

If we're still up here, we'll probably all be dead by then.

And if Lee had called for that napalm two hours ago, instead of launching into this damn fool exercise...

Jock asked Grossman, "Is there an artillery FO up here with you?"

"Negative, sir."

"Well, we'll have to call our own shots, then." Getting back to the radio and Patchett, Jock called in a fire mission on the west slope.

"Just one hangup," Patchett replied. "The cannon-cockers got radio problems. I've been running them a direct landline so I can relay calls for fire. I reckon it'll be another two-zero minutes or so before it's up and running."

Random rounds from Chinese mortars were beginning to fall around the peak. Grossman said, "They've been doing that on and off for the last hour. Haven't hit anything yet. Probably can't see us to adjust fire...and you know how tough it is to fire a mortar with any accuracy when there's a big vertical interval, anyway."

"Let's hope that holds true a while longer," Jock replied.

It had been cold on the hilltop, but the temperature had stayed just above freezing. A sudden wind shift changed all that in a matter of minutes. Frigid air from Manchuria to the north was now swirling over Hill 425.

The sudden bitter cold did more than chill the GIs; they watched in horror as the moist air down at the level of the river began to condense into a thick fog. It wrapped around the base of the hill and then crept upward, the ascent stopping halfway to the 1,300-foot peak. Viewed from above, the still visible part of Hill 425 looked like an island in a sea of white.

"This is all we need," Jock said, "fighting in the blind, dammit."

It might've been an ethereal experience, this perch above cottony clouds, glowing milky white in the late afternoon sun...

Like a castle in the sky.

But this natural wonder, no matter how breathtaking, was conspiring to make their survival less likely:

We can't see a damn thing below us. The chinks could be massing for one of their human wave attacks right under our noses and we wouldn't have the faintest idea.

When Patchett finally called to announce the artillery was ready to fire the first adjustment round, Jock was almost reluctant to let it fly; he might never see where it hit...or who it killed.

But what choice do I have? I've got to try something.

"Request *splash*," Jock said, asking for that five-seconds-before-impact advisory over the radio.

"Roger on the *splash*," Patchett replied. Ten seconds later, he reported, "*Shot*, over."

The first adjustment round was on the way.

Twenty seconds later came, "*Splash*, over."

The men on Hill 425 could hear the *whoosh* of the round as it flew past, sounding closer than they'd expected it would.

Then, after a few seconds that seemed impossibly too long, the *crump* of impact rolled like a single clap of thunder from the white mist below and promptly began

echoing through the valleys. They'd seen no flash, and
the echoes mocked their attempts to determine the
blast's direction by sound alone.

The only rough indication they had of the impact's
location came from Patchett: "The tankers sitting on
Route Seventeen-Able say they just nearly got beaned
by a round. Probably yours. They saw the flash through
the fog, so it musta been pretty close."

Close to the tankers, perhaps, but nowhere near
where Jock had wanted it.

"I'll bet the vertical interval is screwing up the
artillery firing data, too," Grossman offered.

Jock asked Patchett, "Do the tankers know their
exact location?"

"Negative. They can't see much of anything in that
soup, neither. But we can probably work up a rough
location where that round hit. Let us do a little arithmetic.
Stand by..."

*A rough location's better than nothing. Just so we
have something we can adjust up the slope...and maybe
see the flash of that next round.*

Jock started to say, "There may be some hope
yet..."

But then the chattering sound of gunfire on the *east*
slope shattered the silence. Grossman's radio came alive
with frantic voices: his Charlie Company was being
attacked. CCF troopers were rising toward them from
the fog like ghosts materializing out of thin air. The
Chinese weren't visible until they were less than fifty
feet away. Despite being cut down in droves, more kept
coming.

"I'm telling Charlie to pull back up the hill about
fifty yards," Grossman told Jock. "They need some

cushion so they can at least see the chinks."

"Agreed," Jock replied.

Then Able Company on the west slope reported they were under attack, too. The company commander's assessment of the enemy's strength: "They're everywhere!"

"I'm pulling them back, too," Grossman said.

Jock didn't hear him. The noise of gunfire from both flanks was deafening. When Patchett called with the estimate of where the adjustment round had landed, he could barely hear him, either.

But the data Patchett provided made sense, at least. And with the Chinese surging in from both sides, Jock knew there was no time for further adjustments.

I've got to take the risk. If I'm right, we win.

If I'm wrong...well, we're screwed, anyway.

He called the correction: "Right four hundred, drop one hundred, fire for effect."

Patchett cringed as he wrote down the data. *Cannon-cockers are gonna hate that shit. Everybody knows that corrections that big are a stab in the dark...and probably a waste of precious rounds.*

But they gotta give us what we ask for.

When the rounds finally came—six this time—they seemed to *whoosh* so close overhead that they couldn't help but land on the heads of GIs.

But they didn't. This time, Jock could see the dim flashes of impact through the fog. With any luck at all, they'd landed on the Chinese attacking Able Company.

The Able Company commander confirmed that luck had been with them, his excited voice on the radio saying, "Hey, that was good! Can we have it again?"

Grossman was crouched beside his RTO, a radio

handset pressed to one ear, a field telephone to the other. Jock asked him, "What's the story with Charlie Company, Lee?"

Before Grossman could answer, the men of Charlie came into view as they raced toward the peak, firing wild, unaimed shots down the eastern slope. *I can't shift the artillery to help them*, Jock told himself. *The chinks are too close. Even if the shift of fire was accurate, it'd probably kill us all...because calling in fire on your own position only has a chance of succeeding if your men are well dug in, and there's no time and no place for our guys to do that.*

He told Patchett to repeat the *fire for effect* on the west slope, thinking, *If I can cripple the chinks facing them, maybe Able Company can come over the peak and save us all.*

Some of Charlie Company was on the peak now, only feet away from Grossman's CP, with the Chinese close behind. Some GIs were firing; others were dragging wounded buddies, screaming *Medic!*

This was no longer a tactical military operation; it had become a disorganized street brawl. Bodies swirled in a macabre dance as desperate men clinched their enemies like exhausted boxers, so close to each other that bayonets were more useful now than firearms.

Only one man at the CP—Grossman's RTO—saw the sizzling device some Chinaman had hurled into their midst. He screamed a one-word warning— *GRENADE!*—as he dove behind a boulder.

For the others at the CP, it was already too late. Those fractions of a second it took to process the RTO's warning had doomed any chance of their reaching safety.

Jock's only thought was to hurl the grenade away

before it exploded: *Surely, we've got a second or two...*

The grenade was just a few yards from him. He whirled in its direction, tried to lunge for it...

But his leg, still strained by that leap from the helicopter, crumpled before he could take a step. Flat on his stomach, all he could do now was turn his face away from the imminent blast.

Lee Grossman wanted to hurl the grenade away, too, but he was much farther from it, with Jock's prone body halfway between. He knew he'd never cover the distance in time.

But there was still something left of the *kamikaze commando* in Lee Grossman, no longer suicidal, perhaps, but selfless and unafraid.

He flung his body across Jock's.

There wasn't even time to draw a last breath.

*****

Concussed by the blast and still flat on the ground, Jock was only vaguely aware of the next few minutes. He felt as if he was under sedation, the drug altering the sights and sounds of the world around him. The fighting was still going on; it seemed to be happening right above him, a cone of chaos around which spun the shapes of men in mortal combat, whirling to the staccato beat of automatic weapons, with their shouts and curses— distorted to unintelligible yet frightening wails— providing a dissonant counterpoint. He couldn't move, as if fate was a wrestler who'd pinned him to the ground and wouldn't let him up.

Then it fell strangely quiet, the only sound the soft rustling of men moving about. He tried to turn his head, but a white-hot pain that blinded him and screamed like sirens in his ears put a stop to that effort.

He heard a voice—he swore it was Jillian's, *But how could that be?*—telling him, "Can you hear me, sir? Don't move. You're gonna be okay...I've almost got it out."

It was slowly coming back to him now—the fight, the artillery, the grenade. But the details were a muddle. There was a man beside him. Jock's first thought was that the man was giving him a haircut...

But then he felt the wrapping of the bandage completely around his head from chin to crown. The pain had miraculously eased; his eyes were coming back into focus. The first thing he saw was a GI helmet—*my helmet?*—on the ground before him, a thin, jagged piece of steel protruding from it. He reached out to touch it; it seemed just a sliver.

"You're lucky, sir," the man wrapping the bandage said. "That grenade fragment cut right through your steel pot, the liner, and your *bunny hat*, but only a little ways into your scalp. Burned you some, but didn't bleed much."

That didn't explain why the helmet and his parka were smeared with blood.

Then Jock saw two other medics working diligently on a man not three feet away. He asked, "Who's that?"

"Major Grossman, sir. He got it pretty bad."

"Is he going to make it?"

The medic didn't answer, just kept working on the bandage.

Full awareness returned to Jock like a bolt of lightning. "Who's in charge here?" he asked.

"Aren't you, sir?"

"No. I mean who was running the show while I was out?"

"I guess that'd be Captain Williams, sir."

Williams: Bob Williams, the C.O. of Able Company.

*****

Nobody had a pair of pliers handy to pull the grenade fragment from Jock's helmet, so he used a rock to pound over the sharp point that had penetrated inside. Captain Williams suggested he not tamper with the piece of the fragment protruding outside the steel pot: "It can be like a good luck charm, sir," he offered. "You know, like a gladiator's plume or something."

Jock took the suggestion and left it alone. But he knew what—or who—had really been his good luck charm: *Lee Grossman. That crazy son of a bitch better not die. I don't want to be pinning a medal on him posthumously.*

Williams filled him in on how the fight ended. "Whoever put that artillery on the chinks in my sector did a hell of a job. By the time the dust settled, there was only a handful of them left, and they beat it down the hill. I hear our tanks cut them to shreds when they reached the road."

"Let's just say that artillery was a team effort," Jock replied. "A couple of people had to make some outstanding guesses to pull it off. So, what happened after that, Bob?"

"Well, sir, we could tell Charlie Company was in a whole lot of trouble, them not getting the benefit of artillery like we did. I left a squad of mine on the west slope as a rear guard, and then the rest of us turned around and moved up to the peak. It was touch and go for a little bit, but for once, at least, we had numbers on the chinks, and there's no place to hide up here, so..."

"How many casualties, Bob?"

"I don't have an exact number yet, sir, but I've got one killed and five wounded in my company, above and beyond the couple we lost before the big fight. Charlie Company's in rough shape, though. Looks like they took about thirty casualties, including Rick Suarez."

"Suarez...the company commander?"

"That's right, sir," Williams replied.

"Well, add in me, my RTO, and Major Grossman to the wounded list, too. All in all, that makes it a pretty costly little operation." Jock wanted to add, *And one that should've never happened,* but he held his tongue.

"Gather the seriously wounded here on the peak," Jock said. "We've got a little time before the sun sets, so I'm bringing the choppers in to get them out. It'll be tricky, but the winds have died down quite a bit, so we should be able to land and get those boys on board. You've already got the walking wounded moving down the hill, Bob?"

"Affirmative, sir. Litter bearers are carrying the dead down, too."

"Good. I want every man off this damn pile of rocks before dark."

Together, they roamed the battle area one last time, making sure they were leaving no man behind. On the west slope, they came across the bodies of the two Chinese officers Grossman had captured. Williams dispassionately rolled the bodies over to reveal a bullet wound in each forehead, execution style.

"A pistol had to do this, sir," Williams said. "Hard

to tell who pulled the trigger without digging out the slugs. But I'm here to tell you that none of my guys would've had the time or the interest for gangster shit like this. Not in the middle of the fight we were in, that's for damn sure."

*****

General Bryan, the division commander, was waiting at Jock's CP when he returned well after dark, after the Chinese trying to force their way into Kap'yong had finally been driven back. Not a happy man, the general asked, "Just what in the hell happened up on Hill Four-Two-Five, Miles? I thought your plan favored isolation of mountain enclaves rather than costly fights like the one you got yourself into."

Jock replied, "One of my battalion commanders saw a fleeting opportunity to capture a major command post and took the initiative, sir. It wouldn't have been my choice to do it like that, but once it was underway, I took command of the operation."

Bryan eyed the bandage wrapped around Jock's head and said, "It looks more like you took a licking, Miles. What about that battalion commander? It sounds to me like he needs to be relieved immediately for inability to follow orders."

Patchett stepped in and said, "Begging your pardon, sir, but the commander in question, Major Grossman, is being prepped for immediate medical evacuation to Japan. He's hurt bad, sir, real bad. The doc thinks he's got a chance to make it…but it's gonna be a real close-run thing. From what I'm hearing, he did some mighty heroic stuff up on that mountain."

Jock was relieved that Patchett had deflected the issue, at least temporarily. His after-action report, however, would have to be far more candid about what actually transpired on Hill 425.

But for now, he decided that perhaps this wasn't the best time to discuss with General Bryan the Medal of Honor paperwork he planned to submit for Lee Grossman.

Let the dust settle on this fiasco first.

Chapter Thirty-One

They were up to the dessert course, but Judge
Hobart Riggs still wasn't sure why the senator from
California had invited him to dinner at San Francisco's
posh Bohemian Club. The judge was no stranger to
pressure from politicians; just last year, some senators
from the Midwest had pressured him to vacate the
deportation case of a Swedish businessman that was
before his immigration court. They hadn't been very
subtle about it, either, letting Riggs know that he served
at the pleasure of the Secretary of State, who, in turn,
served at the pleasure of the President of the United
States. Neither of these august gentlemen would look on
the judge with any pleasure at all if he didn't let that
Swedish businessman remain in the US as an honored
guest. Some big political donors had too much to lose if
the Swede was forced to take his steel-making
technology—and his money—to a more hospitable
nation.

The dinner invitation from Senator Garrett Wilford
had come as something of a mystery, which had yet to
be unraveled through the course of the meal. The
conversation had been pleasant and general, without a
hint of the senator trying to influence any issue before
Riggs' immigration court.

And what case of mine could it possibly be, anyway?
the judge asked himself. *The convicted Mafioso who'll
be on his way back to Italy very soon? Not likely. The
assortment of people who've overstayed their visas?
None of them would be worth the trouble. And that rich*

*Australian woman—the Army colonel's wife—who tried
to buy up some California real estate? The government's
case against her is ironclad. She'll be sent back to her
native land in just two weeks' time, her spousal visa
annulled. And good riddance, I say.*

*Wait a minute...maybe it's not that I'm being
pressured at all. Perhaps the senator is a messenger
from above bearing good news: somebody in
Washington has finally noticed my no-nonsense, by-the-
book approach to the law and I'm being considered for
elevation to a higher federal court.*

Yes, that must be it!

But that wasn't it, not by a long shot. As the waiter
rolled the lavish dessert cart away, Senator Wilford
looked up from admiring the chocolate cake on his plate
and said, "By the way, Hobart...I can call you Hobart,
right?...it would be a wonderful thing for *all* concerned
if you'd dismiss the case against this Jillian Forbes-
Miles woman. No judgment is necessary, just
administratively dismiss it as *without merit.* You'll
receive the thanks of a grateful military and a grateful
nation, too. I guarantee it. Okay?"

Judge Riggs felt as if the wind had been knocked
out of him. The senator kept casting that cold, insincere
grin his way as he struggled to form an objection to the
fait accompli just handed him. The best he could come
up with was, "But the prosecutors, Senator...what do I
tell them?"

"You don't have to tell them dog squat, Hobart.
They have bosses who want to keep their jobs, too, you
know. Now, would you like more coffee?"

Later that night, as the senator was being driven
across the Golden Gate to his home in Marin County, he

watched a tanker steaming below the bridge on its way west across the Pacific. He smiled as he told himself, *Can you believe it? That lady with all those tankers...we should've been kissing her ass instead of trying to pitch her out on her ass. That's the trouble with this government—sometimes it can't even figure out which side its bread is buttered on.*

*****

Several nights later, General and Mrs. Molloy were Jillian's guests for dinner at her Monterey home. The evening's get-together was both a celebration and a gesture of thanks. The general had suggested the dinner be at Fort Ord's Officers Club—where he would've been happy to pick up the tab—but Jillian had firmly but politely refused, suggesting it be at her home instead. She reaffirmed her reasons as she served the appetizer: "I don't want to seem ungrateful, sir, but I just can't see myself setting foot on that post right now. I'd prefer not to be present when some gossipy Army wives are whispering behind my back, regardless of whether they're on my side or the Whitelaws'. It would be difficult not to say something very rude to them."

"Understandable," Molloy replied. "Did you get a reply from Jock confirming he received my radiogram about your case being dismissed?"

"I certainly did. It came just a little while ago, so thank you again for expediting that message."

Nancy Molloy—the general's wife—raised her wine glass in a toast: "To Jillian: you've won! All this deportation nonsense is over, once and for all. And that miserable witch Priscilla Whitelaw is going to get what's coming to her. She'll be in jail for the rest of her life, I'll bet. Imagine...a general's wife a criminal!"

"Oh, I doubt she'll do very much time, ma'am," Jillian said. She turned to Dick Molloy and asked, "What did they say the maximum penalty for passport fraud was?"

"Ten years," he replied. "But I'm inclined to agree with Jillian, *Nance*. I doubt our Mrs. Whitelaw will get the full boat. She's an *aristocrat*, remember?"

"But the fraudulent passport...that's just *one* charge," Mrs. Molloy protested. "What about her indictment for being the mastermind behind the assault on this lovely home? Surely, she'll do time in California for that, too, once she's out of Federal prison."

"Maybe, maybe not," Jillian replied. "I spoke with the DA earlier today. He has no choice but to charge her separately from those two mongrels who actually tried to pull off the assault. As a result, he's not very confident he can get the full weight of the conspiracy charge against her to stick for any real prison time. True, there's that one piece of damning evidence against her—that bogus passport—but he feels that proving an ironclad connection between that and the actual assault will be a tough one. And, of course, if she somehow beats the rap for the passport..."

"That'll never happen," the general said. "They caught her red-handed with the goods. I wouldn't be surprised if she just pleads guilty and throws herself on the mercy of the court. What else is she going to do...blame her husband for that fake passport being in her car?"

Jillian asked, "Speaking of General Whitelaw, what's going to happen to him once his wife goes to the slammer?"

"The minute her trial is over, he'll be forced to retire...with a reduction in grade to colonel," Molloy replied. "He's lucky that's as far as the regs allow the board to reduce him in retirement. They take a very dim view of a general officer's wife having a felony indictment, let alone a conviction."

The grandfather clock struck six. Nancy Molloy said, "Oh, it's time to turn on the radio. The president's giving an important speech."

"You bet it's important," the general said as Jillian switched on the receiver. "Rumor has it he's firing MacArthur."

The two women looked at him, dumbfounded.

"What the hell did you expect was going to happen, ladies? MacArthur's been trying to run his own foreign policy for months, contradicting the administration's position right and left. He wants to attack Red China, for cryin' out loud, and he keeps announcing it to the whole world. Making foreign policy isn't a soldier's job, not even one wearing five stars. Can't blame Truman for clipping his wings. I'm surprised it's taken this long, considering how many times Washington's told him to shut his self-righteous mouth."

"But so many people think MacArthur's a god, Dick," his wife said.

"Well, they'd better get used to the fact that he's not, *Nance*...and damn quick, too."

Once Truman began to speak, there was no doubt Dick Molloy had been right: MacArthur was being relieved.

As the speech went on, Jillian said softly, "I never thought I'd see the day." She seemed delighted to be able to say those words.

Nancy Molloy was worried, though. She asked, "But who'll take his place?"

"Matt Ridgway," her husband replied. "He's more than earned it."

*****

Ned Almond was annoyed; he'd been ready to depart for Tokyo when the airplane was pulled out from under him for an unspecified *higher priority* mission. Threatening to end the career of every officer in the Kimpo Airfield operations office, he demanded they call 8th Army Headquarters to get that ruling reversed. "We can call if you'd like, sir," the operations officer told him, "but the order's come directly from General Ridgway. Oh, and by the way, I just got a message that says he wants to see you within the hour."

When Almond stormed into Ridgway's office ready to air his grievance, he was told, "*At ease*, General. You're not going back to Tokyo because you don't have a job there anymore."

Almond recoiled, as if he'd been slapped in the face. "But, sir, be realistic," he said. "You're going to need a chief of staff who knows his way around FECOM. I've been doing that job for two years now, and—"

Ridgway cut him off. "And now that job's finished, Ned. MacArthur's gone, and my people are already moving in. You will remain here in Korea as Tenth Corps commander for the next few months, until you're due for rotation. That's all, General. You're dismissed."

"But, sir...I choose not to be rotated. I want to stay in command. General MacArthur guaranteed me a—"

"That's not his call anymore, Ned, or yours," Ridgway interrupted as he pointed toward the door.

Still grasping for some semblance of his crumbling status, Almond asked, "Can I ask one question, sir?"

"Sure."

"What *higher priority* claimed *my* aircraft?"

"The new commander of Far East Command, General. *I'm* the higher priority, and I'm taking that ship to Tokyo...just as soon as they load her up with litter cases who need a lift."

*****

In the Dai-ichi Building—which housed FECOM Headquarters in Tokyo—Ridgway's hand-picked staff were deep into the task of assuming control of that command. MacArthur's high-level people had been sent packing along with him. Lower-level staff were kept in their jobs to maintain—for the time being, at least—administrative continuity. General Ridgway would be arriving from Korea that evening. They planned to present him with an orderly transition in progress.

The colonel assuming the job of G1—the admin and personnel officer—asked the hold-over staffers in his *shop* for a tour of their record-keeping facilities. When it was done, the colonel noticed an unmarked file cabinet that hadn't been mentioned. He asked the captain who'd been leading the tour, "What are we storing in there?"

"Oh, that's just the *dead letter office*, sir. Paperwork where no further action is required, that sort of thing." Then, perhaps foolishly, he added, "We call it *limbo*."

"Limbo, eh?" the colonel said. "Sounds biblical. Let's see what's inside."

"You don't need to trouble yourself with anything in there, sir, it's all—"

"Unlock the fucking cabinet, Captain."

As the colonel rifled through the files, he was horrified to find just how much of it was promotion endorsements and decoration requests for enlisted men.

Scanning the decoration requests, the colonel said, "Hmm...it seems this headquarters is only interested in hanging *fruit salad* on officers. I can assure you that's going to change immediately." He pushed the tall pile of decorations paperwork across the table to the flustered captain.

Then the colonel began to thumb through the promotion endorsements. One jumped out at him right away, if for no other reason than it was signed by Matt Ridgway himself. Enraged, the colonel asked, "Was it a policy of this headquarters to sideline anything with General Ridgway's signature?"

"Absolutely not, sir."

"Then how can you explain why this promotion request—of a colonel to a one-star, no less—is rotting in this damn drawer with no action taken one way or the other?"

The captain had no reply.

"I want everything in this cabinet with General Ridgway's signature on my desk in thirty minutes' time. Is that clear?"

Thirty minutes later, the colonel had not only Jock's promotion paperwork to brigadier general but also the confidential letter Ridgway had written to Washington, advocating for the dismissal of the deportation proceedings against Jock's wife, Jillian Forbes-Miles. He told the captain, "Quite the coincidence, isn't it? I've seen some petty bullshit in my day, but this takes the cake. Now hear me good…you'll have this sorry situation rectified by 1800 hours today, or you'll be kissing this cushy, *non-combat* position of yours goodbye."

*****

Patchett had a feeling of *déjà vu*. It was making him sick.

Twenty-Sixth Regiment was twelve miles north of the 38th Parallel, digging in on a ridgeline that overlooked the critical intersection of Highway 3 and Route 124. But they were doing much more than just *digging in*:

Division's ordered a complex of trenches…not just fighting holes, but goddamn trenches, lined up one behind the other like soldiers on a parade field. We got engineers here carving up this ridge with bulldozers, scoop buckets, explosives…

And that ain't all. My men are busting their asses stringing barbed wire all over the place. Laying mines, too—all to make a permanent hidey-hole for whatever outfit relieves us next week. I guess we stopped fighting a war of movement once we took back that made-up boundary they call the Thirty-Eighth Parallel. This army's gonna hunker down right here…for Lord knows how long.

I seen this before, dammit. This is France in 1918 all over again…goddamn trench warfare, plain and simple. You don't move nowhere. You just die in place.

Ain't no general decided this. It's the work of politicians…and it stinks to high heaven.

But if they were going to dig trenches, Patchett knew the engineers were doing it all wrong. He pulled their officer-in-charge aside and said, "I'm here to tell you, sir, that these trenches you're plowing ain't worth shit."

"Why, Sergeant? What's wrong with them? Not deep enough?"

"Negative, Lieutenant. They're plenty deep…but they're straight as a damn arrow. You're making parallel lines that are just as useless as the ones them politicians drew on the map."

"Useless? Why's that?"

Patchett expelled one of those weary sighs the deeply experienced reserve for novices showing their ignorance. "If a trench ain't got sharp angles in it, sir, the blast of one shell or one grenade dropping in there can get channeled a long way down that trench and kill a whole lotta people. But if the trench got angles in it, that blast don't go too far."

"That's going to take a lot of extra work, Sergeant."

"Your machines are doing most of the work, anyway, sir. And unlike your troopers, they don't give a rat's ass about *doing extra* as long as you keep feeding 'em gasoline. So how about it? You gonna save some GI lives today, or are you gonna help get them killed?"

*****

April 1951 was a time of change not only for Far East Command, but 8th Army, 24th Division, and 26th Regiment, as well. Ridgway replaced MacArthur, General James Van Fleet replaced Ridgway as 8th Army commander, and 24th Division was about to be pulled off the line for a much-needed rest and rebuilding.

Many of the 8th Army's front-line commanders and troops had earned enough points to rotate home, if they so chose. Among them were Jock Miles, Melvin Patchett, and Sean Moon.

As they prepared the regimental CP to be turned over to their relieving unit, Patchett asked, "Anybody know this Van Fleet fella?"

"I do," Sean replied. "He was a corps commander in Patton's Third Army. Good general, real straight-up guy."

"Is he as good as Matt Ridgway?" Patchett asked.

"Maybe so. And he ain't Airborne like General Matt, so at least he's got the good sense not to jump outta perfectly good airplanes."

Jock smiled as he listened to his two sergeants but said nothing. He'd been waiting for the right moment to ask them both a very important question. But he had to lay some groundwork first. He asked, "You both know that my wife's deportation problem has vanished into thin air, right?"

"Of course we do," Patchett said. "Ain't no other reason for you to be as damn happy as you been the last coupla days. But I gotta ask you, sir…how's that gonna figure in to you getting that star?"

"Let's just say that it shrinks my biggest obstacle a whole lot, Top."

"So you gonna take it?"

"I'm meeting Jillian and the kids in Tokyo next week. If she's on board, then yes, I'm going to accept the promotion."

Both sergeants rushed forward to shake his hand.

But Patchett had one more question: "You and me known each other a long, long time, sir. And I know why you stayed in after the last war...although it didn't make a damn bit of sense for you to do it after marrying the richest lady in Australia."

"Come on, Top. She's not the richest lady *down under*."

"If not, she's damn close, I reckon. I know I asked you this before, sir, but I gotta ask you again: Ain't there a point where you gotta know that your account's been paid in full?"

"Maybe I just don't know where that point is, Top. An awful lot of fine men fought and died under my command. That's just too big a debt to simply walk away from. I don't know any other way to honor their sacrifice except to keep being a soldier."

After a long pause, Patchett said, "Well...amen to that, sir."

"Now, there's something I need to talk to both of you about," Jock said. "After a couple of weeks' leave with the family—and with Jillian's concurrence—I'm coming back to Korea. Before he left, General Ridgway discussed forming a mobile combat team—not as big as a division but more than a regiment—to act as a *fire brigade* anywhere Eighth Army needs it. Since it looks like most units will be pretty much fixed in place from now on while diplomats try to crank up negotiations to end this damn thing, he wants a large mobile reserve to put a cork in any breeches that might occur before they can develop into catastrophes."

Sounding enthusiastic, Sean asked, "And this *brigade's* gonna have lots of armor, right, sir?"

"Affirmative, Sergeant. Now, unless something

changes drastically in the very near future, Ridgway's going to offer me command of that outfit."

"Hot damn, sir," Patchett said. "It'll be another *Task Force Miles*."

"Something like that, Top, but a hell of a lot bigger and much more potent than the last one."

Sean asked, "Begging your pardon, but what the hell's *Task Force Miles*?"

"A little before your time, Bubba," Patchett replied. "It's when we were in Australia…and you were doing the bidding of *Ol' Blood and Guts* in Europe."

Jock continued, "So what I'm asking you two is this: Will you join me in my new command? I'll understand completely if you want to pack up and go home, but—"

"To hell with that *going home* stuff, sir," Patchett said, rolling out his strident Southern preacher's voice. "You keep me outta those goddamn trenches they're building and I'll follow you to hell and back. I done my time in them linear graveyards."

"But I thought you'd want to take a break, Top. You've been at it a long, long time, and—"

"And what, sir? So I can go back to *Bumfuck, Alabama*, and maybe find me a job carrying the mail if I'm lucky? Or maybe try to grow crops like my dirt-poor daddy did?"

Sean added, "You can count me in, too, sir. I'm only halfway to my twenty years, so I might as well hang around here. You know what they say: *I've had better assignments, but I've never been with better people*."

Patchett reached into one of his field cases and extracted a bottle of whiskey. "Been saving this for just such an occasion," he said. "Let's have us a toast to the new *Task Force Miles*."

As they savored the spirits in their canteen cups, it was clear there was something else on Patchett's mind. With a little gentle prodding from Jock, he opened up: "Seeing them trenches, sir...it just seems like such a giant step backward. I can't help but worry that the longer we keep the heat off the gooks and chinks, the more big guns and tanks the Russians are gonna send their way. Our Air Force may be damn good, but we all know they ain't gonna blow up all them heavy weapons before they start hurting us ground-pounders. Ever since the Pusan, we've had better firepower than them...*way* better. We need something that's gonna make sure it stays that way."

Jock replied, "You're not talking atomic weapons, are you, Top? Washington's made it pretty clear that we're not going that route. The only person in the whole world who said out loud that we should drop the A-bomb on Red China was MacArthur...and he got himself fired for it."

Patchett shook his head sadly. "Maybe so, sir...but we still need *something*. And it better be a *big* something."

Chapter Thirty-Two

Watching his two young children run to him from the airliner that had brought them to Tokyo, Jock couldn't believe how much they'd grown in the past ten months. He scooped up one in each arm and held them close as Jillian—smiling, unflappable, a beautiful force of nature—strolled across the ramp and joined the collective embrace. As the family clung to each other, she said, "Nice to see you again, *General Miles.*"

Jock couldn't have been more stunned. "Wait a minute," he said. "My surprise...it's been ruined. Who told you?"

"General Molloy got word to me right before we took off from San Francisco."

Wearily, she added, "And then, we began thirty-something hours of stomach-wrenching hell. I feel like we've been on an airplane for a bloody year."

"We landed five times, Daddy," his six-year-old son Jif added, the words brimming with a child's enthusiasm. "One of them, we bounced *bloody hard.*"

"Uh oh," Jock said, gently touching his forehead to his son's. "Somebody's just put another penny into the *barracks mouth* jar."

Jillian said, "That jar's been overflowing for quite a while, Jock. I think it paid for the plane tickets."

"Well, we'll talk about that later," Jock replied. "Let's get you tired travelers to the hotel on the double."

*****

As the staff car took the Miles family into Tokyo, Jock said, "You know, Jill, I haven't officially accepted the promotion yet. I was waiting to talk to you before—"

She silenced him with a finger to his lips. Then she said, "Did you really think I'd say *no*, silly boy?"

Then he told her about returning to Korea to assume a new command. With a curious smile, she asked, "Do you need my approval for that, too?"

"Of course I do, Jill."

She was silent for a few moments, long enough to convince Jock she just might withhold that approval.

But then she said, "I married a soldier, so I've learned to take these things in stride. Of course you have my blessing."

Later that night, as the children slept, they talked quietly in the hotel suite over after-dinner drinks. He sat and listened, sometimes amazed, sometimes horrified, as she filled him in on every detail of what she'd done and what others had tried—and failed—to do to her. When she was finished, he was speechless.

It took a minute to find his voice again. Once it returned, he described his fear that the deportation would cause her to reject all things American, including him.

When he was finished, it was her turn to be speechless.

Not sure how to interpret her silence, he added, "Patchett said I was crazy, insisting you'd never leave me. Not after everything we've been through."

She smiled, laid her head on his shoulder, and replied, "Patchett was right, you bloody mug, you."

*****

Over breakfast the next morning, Jillian asked, "Your leg, Jock...is it going to carry you through?"

"Generals don't have to walk very much, Jill. I think I can manage."

"And Patchett's really going to stay with you?"

"Yeah, he is, the crazy old coot," Jock replied.

"Good. I'll feel better knowing he's there. What about the other lads from our time together in the jungle? Is Theo still *The Mad Greek*?"

"I'm afraid so. Five years as a civilian didn't mellow the warrior in him one bit."

"And Lee Grossman...you say he's expected to recover?"

"That's what we're hearing. The war's over for him...his arm's going to need a lot of work, and he'll carry the scars for the rest of his life. He's in a military hospital here in Tokyo, you know. I thought maybe we'd visit him together."

"I'd very much like to do that, Jock. I need to thank the man who saved my husband's life in person." She took a sip of coffee and asked, "Is he really getting the Medal of Honor?"

"Probably not. I'm sure it'll get kicked down. The conventional wisdom lately seems to be that you've got to be dead to win it. I just hope it doesn't get reduced any further than a Silver Star."

Their five-year-old daughter Jane, still in her pajamas, ambled to the table. Propping her arm against its polished teak as if holding a rifle in the firing position, she said, "Daddy, did you know that Mommy's famous? Everyone in California calls her *Annie Oakley*."

"Yes, I've heard, sweetheart," Jock replied. "Would you like some breakfast?"

"No, thank you," the child said. "I've got postcards to write." Then she ran back to the bedroom.

He asked Jillian, "Postcards? To who?"

"Our little Janey is the belle of her nursery school, Jock. Several young lads have already asked for her hand in marriage."

"Oh, dear," Jock said. "It's starting already? Whoa...hang on. I think I get it. It's her Australian accent...that's the allure, right? You know how that works on American boys."

"It certainly worked on you, Jock Miles."

*****

Later, as they strolled the busy streets of Tokyo, Jillian surveyed the hundreds of American servicemen wandering about. She asked, "Jock, are the Yanks going to win this bloody war?"

"I think the point now is just not to lose it, Jill."

"How does an Army go about doing that?" she asked. "And how long will it take?"

"I'm afraid those are questions only the politicians can answer," he replied.

"In other words, what they're saying about *die for a tie* is true, then?"

His pained silence was all the answer she needed.

*****

Sean Moon's final destination for his two-week leave was Tokyo, but his first stop would be K-2

Airfield at Taegu. It didn't take long to find his brother
Tommy, who wasn't flying that day; the rain and
accompanying overcast in central Korea had kept most
of the Air Force's attack ships on the ground.

When they first made phone contact, Sean told him,
"I ain't setting foot in no officers club, *Half.*"

"Okay," Tommy replied, "then how about I meet
you at the NCO club? You know where that is, right?"

"Where the hell do you think I'm calling from? Get
your scrawny ass over here, *sir.*"

Thirty minutes later, as they sat around a big wire
spool pressed into service as a barroom table, Tommy
said, "It's funny, but nobody's called me *Half* since I
saw you at Sunchon back in November, Sean."

"Nobody in your squadron ever calls you that
anymore?"

"Nope."

With a devilish grin, Sean said, "Will you look at
that? My little brother's all grown up now."

Eager to change the subject, Tommy asked, "Did
you hear about Mary Alice having another baby?"

"Yeah, I did. What is it with our sisters, anyway?
None of 'em are even thirty yet, but between the four
of 'em they got like thirteen kids already, right?"

"All boys, too," Tommy added. "Pretty soon, they'll
have their own platoon."

Sean laughed out loud. "That's pretty good,
Half...*The Moon Platoon.* I like that."

"Except none of those kids are named Moon, Sean.
Our sisters are all married, remember?"

"Don't be a wiseass, *Major.* You know what I
mean." He took a big gulp of his beer and asked, "So
how long until you rotate home?"

"I'm still twenty-eight missions shy of my hundred, Sean, so it'll be a while."

"Then what?"

"Not sure. But you'll be the first to know."

Sean eyed his brother skeptically. "Don't bullshit a bullshitter, Half. You wanna pull jet duty back in Germany so you can be near *Madame Bergerac* again."

"Something wrong with that, Sean? I haven't seen Sylvie in months."

"Nah...I just thought you might wanna stick around Korea and help us lowly ground-pounders grind those commie chinks to dust, that's all. It's gonna be a long, drawn-out fight now that them politicians have decided we're just gonna hold the line at the Parallel and not pursue them bastards no more. Can you believe that shit? You got your enemy on the ropes but you're not gonna pursue? Fuck me! Patton's rolling over in his grave right now, I'll bet."

"It may not take as long as you think, Sean. As long as we can keep the MIGs off us, the Air Force will keep bombing the hell out of every CCF supply line in North Korea. The chinks will be begging for peace before you know it."

"I ain't so sure about that, Tommy. We keep hearing stories that every mile of track you blow up, every bridge you knock down...it's all back in service within forty-eight hours. They must have about a million *coolies* on their repair crews."

"That's why a fair percentage of the stuff we drop is time-delay bombs, Sean. They don't explode until hours later, when the repair crews are on the scene."

"Sounds real clever, Half, but something tells me it's not working out that way. You may nail 'em the first coupla times, but the chinks ain't completely stupid. They're gonna get wise and work around them time-delay bomb craters."

"So what're you saying, Sean?"

"I'm saying that if this war's gonna be fought at a conference table, we're gonna need a bargaining chip *on the ground* that scares the crap outta the chinks."

*****

Spring had come early to Germany in 1951, and the summer promised to be a very warm one. Sylvie Bergerac—*Madame Bergerac*, as Sean Moon had called her—stepped off the Frankfurt tram, cursing herself for still having only her winter clothes. When she'd gone undercover two months ago near Grafenwöhr, Bavaria—close to the border with Czechoslovakia—it had still been the dead of winter. Now, the woolen skirt, sweater, and heavy socks she wore were hot and uncomfortable, but they were one of her few outfits that had survived that mission intact.

I was lucky to get out of there alive. There's a chance the Soviet agents I duped figured out my identity. I've been on their kill list since that mission in East Berlin back in 1945. Despite my many aliases, I only have one face.

By rights, the CIA should send me out of the country. But they won't. The fact that I'm still alive undermines my story of possibly being identified...

And they need somebody for another mission. That somebody is me, apparently.

She was on her way to a meeting that would lay out that mission. It wouldn't be at CIA headquarters in the

IG Farben Building, however; it was probable that Soviet agents surveilled and recorded the comings and goings there twenty-four hours a day. It would be a dangerous place for an undercover operative to show her face:

Especially one who suspects she's been compromised.

But I want to remain in Germany. There's an excellent chance Tommy will be stationed here soon, too, once his tour in Korea is over.

It's worth the risk...and I've been in worse trouble so many times before.

A popular restaurant had been chosen as the meeting place, with an open air beer garden teeming with lunchtime diners now that the weather had warmed. Tracking and identification by Soviet spies would be difficult there; eavesdropping on conversations would be practically impossible.

As Sylvie entered the restaurant, she spotted her handler immediately. The tall, blond American in well-cut civvies looked authentically German and spoke the language flawlessly. He was a major in the US Army named Joe Bachmann and, like her, could blend into any Frankfurt crowd.

Seated beside him, though, was a man whose looks and mannerisms positively screamed *American* with unrelenting clarity. The inelegant cut of his Sears and Roebuck clothes, his cheap haircut, and military low quarter shoes conspired to leave no doubt.

Sylvie slid into the booth as Bachmann filled a stein from a pitcher for her. They wasted no time getting down to business.

The American's name was McCarthy, a civilian

employee of the Army's White Sands Proving Ground in New Mexico. He explained he was a nuclear weapons engineer, engaged in a top secret project to produce tactical nuclear projectiles for American artillery. These projectiles would be of a much smaller yield than was possible with air-dropped bombs but could engage close-in targets and troop concentrations, day or night, in any weather condition, with pinpoint accuracy.

"That's something you can never be sure of with an airplane," McCarthy said. "You know that the bomb dropped on Nagasaki actually missed its aiming point by several miles, don't you? If it'd been off much more, it would've landed behind a mountain range and done almost no blast damage to the city at all."

When Sylvie and Bachmann shrugged in ignorance, McCarthy continued, "The issue with nuclear artillery ammo is size. We've determined that the smallest we can make the shell is two hundred eighty millimeters—that's about eleven inches. Currently, we don't have a land-based cannon in the inventory that can fire a shell of that caliber, so we're building one."

Sylvie asked, "How long will that take?"

"About two more years."

"Two years?" Bachmann said, his impatience bristling. "So why the hell are we even talking about this now?"

"Because *your* bosses, Major, believe that just the threat of nuclear artillery will drive the Chinese and North Koreans to the bargaining table very quickly. The only way they've been able to succeed in Korea is by massing their forces to astounding levels. But those massed forces could be wiped out by the tens of thousands by just one nuclear shell. If they're smart, they'll take a negotiated settlement while they can. Otherwise…"

Sylvie finished the sentence: "…we can turn them to dust."

"You catch on quickly, Miss Bergerac," McCarthy replied.

"That's *Missus* Bergerac. *Madame, s'il vous plaît.*"

"Oh, pardon me. I didn't realize you were married."

"I'm not. I'm a widow…a war widow."

"Okay," Bachmann said, "this is all well and good. But how can my people help you with this bluff?"

"Oh, it's not a bluff, Major Bachmann."

"I beg to differ, Mr. McCarthy. If you're trying to scare people with a weapon that's nowhere near ready yet, *that's* a bluff. And what if the Russians are developing nuclear artillery of their own? I mean, they finally did get the bomb."

McCarthy's body language was dismissing Bachmann's point before he'd even finished speaking. "The Russians are years behind in this technology. Decades, maybe. It's not a factor right now."

Bachmann was the dismissive one now, but he said, "Well, give us the details anyway, and we'll see what we can do. Sylvie's pulled more than one rabbit from the hat in her illustrious career. She can probably do it again."

McCarthy laid out the details of moving the faux *atomic cannon* to Germany. When he was done, he had one question of the operatives: "What I don't understand is why we're sending this little circus here instead of Korea. If your bosses are just interested in putting on a show, wouldn't it be better doing it closer to the action?"

Bachmann glanced at Sylvie and asked, "You want to take this one?"

"I'd be glad to," she replied. "Even though this is the first we're hearing about the technical details, I can tell why it's coming to Germany. Washington may be interested in driving the Chinese to the conference table, but they want to drive fear into the hearts of the Russians while they're at it, who you claim are *decades behind*. Based on the sophistication levels of the various Soviet intelligence networks, there's a far better chance they'll pick up on your mock-up *atomic cannon* here in Germany rather than in Korea. There are no Russian agents in Korea—they'd be too easy to spot—so they're using Korean surrogates, who aren't very skilled and are poorly compensated for their efforts, if at all. We've killed or captured most of them already. You put that fake gun into Korea and word might never get to Moscow or Beijing. Put it here in Germany, though, and Moscow will know about it the very next day, Beijing the day after. And they'll both be *very* worried about it, at least for a while."

Bachmann was nodding his agreement the whole time she spoke. Then he added, "But if you want to hang a real threat over their heads, you'd better hurry up and get the real thing working—and demonstrate it—or they're going to catch on that it's all been a big fraud."

Chapter Thirty-Three

On a sunny afternoon five days later, Sylvie laid her bicycle against an old stone wall in Baumholder outside the sprawling US Army base. She watched as the massive—but fake—cannon maneuvered slowly down the narrow streets of the town. To heighten its mystery, tarps covered the long carriage and gun tube, concealing their details from view. The tractors on both ends of the carriage skillfully performed the coordinated dance to maneuver the sham weapon's eighty-four-foot length through curves and around corners. Inevitably, though, there was damage to civilian property, and a few streetlamps were knocked over as well, snapped like twigs by tons of unforgiving steel in motion. Army engineers stood by to make immediate repairs or file paperwork to compensate in cash, the usual practices as American mechanized might couldn't help but harm German towns and countryside even when ensuring peace.

The movement of this massive charade from the railroad yard to the base had been a spectacle that was impossible to miss. To make sure the townspeople would be forewarned along with the Soviet agents in the area positioned to keep an eye on US Army activities at Baumholder, Sylvie had begun a whispering campaign about the new *super weapon*, suggesting the massive cannon was nicknamed *Atomic Annie*. The campaign had worked; among the many bystanders lining the road, she'd seen a man and a woman she was fairly sure were spies for the Soviets taking photos.

So far, so good, she told herself. *But if they only knew that beneath all that canvas is a long length of oilfield pipe dressed up to look like a cannon from a distance. Up close, the tinny sound of knuckles rapping against the barrel or the lack of rifling on the interior would give its secret away.*

But this was only prologue. The main act was yet to come.

*****

The day after the fake cannon arrived came its phony nuclear ammunition. Sylvie had made sure the whispering campaign was still going strong among the civilians in Baumholder. At a printing shop she trusted, she created sham handbills on *atomic awareness*, each copy displaying and identifying the symbol for nuclear material—a black-rimmed circle containing six concentric, pie-shaped wedges: three black, three yellow. The handbills' crudeness gave the impression they'd been produced by some underground cabal protesting the American military presence and suggested the likelihood the Americans were stocking nuclear weapons at their Baumholder base.

But merely driving a deuce-and-a-half carrying the dummy ammunition through the town of Baumholder— even with the requisite nuclear symbols hanging on all sides as a warning—might not make a strong enough impression. American trucks rumbled through the town every day, drawing little attention beyond a scowl or grumbled complaint. This transit—theater that it was— would have to be unequivocally memorable.

That's where her pool of ex-Wehrmacht soldiers

came into play.

She'd worked with these German veterans before. As civilians, they'd struggled to make ends meet in a nation all too slowly recovering from the ravages of war. US dollars had convinced these men, still skilled in the military arts, to set aside their hatred of Americans and wage the occasional act of insurgency against the Soviets, who they hated far more and offered them no compensation.

They were good men—*tough* men—and they knew how to keep secrets.

As long as the US was paying in hard cash, the former German soldiers had no problem taking orders from a French woman—now a naturalized American citizen barely thirty years old—who was once a fighter in *La Résistance*. They had no doubt she was a seasoned guerrilla who had, in all likelihood, taken the lives of fellow German soldiers. Despite her quiet but forceful charm, they had the distinct impression she wouldn't hesitate to take their lives, too, if she suspected them of double-dealing.

But she was the paymaster, so she was obeyed.

Sylvie had selected two of the Germans—both of them *fallschirmjäger*, or paratroopers—to man the deuce carrying the fake nuclear ammunition. When she offered them the job, she'd posed it this way: "You both know how to fall, don't you?"

When they answered, "*Ja,*" she continued, "Good, because you're going to jump out of a moving truck. Is that something you can handle?"

The price was right. They could handle it.

She needed eight men total: three in the lead jeep, three in the trail jeep, and the two in the deuce. They'd all be posing as American servicemen in vehicles borrowed from the US Army. They'd carry American small arms but have no ammunition, just empty pouches. Only she would have a loaded pistol, the same Beretta she always carried.

"We'll involve two GIs in this operation," she told the eight Germans, "because, unfortunately, we need them. I'd prefer not to use Americans at all—most of them can never keep their mouths shut about anything—but none of you can expertly drive a Pershing tank, and we're going to need experts."

The acknowledged leader of the Germans was an ex-*hauptmann* named Franz Ulrich. He'd been skeptical of Sylvie's plan before he'd even heard it. Knowing a little about it now, he asked, "If you don't trust the GIs, why are you using them at all? Is the tank so crucial?"

"Absolutely crucial," she replied. "And to ensure those GI tankers don't spill the beans about what went on here, the Army's shipping them back to the States the moment this operation is over. They don't know about that, so let's not tell them."

Then she explained the plan in detail, using a chalkboard in the meeting room of a church basement to depict it visually. She made a point of saying that the deuce-and-a-half they'd use was headed to the scrapyard, anyway. "It's old, burns oil badly, and the transmission leaks. The Americans have declared it *uneconomical to repair*, so they couldn't care less how we bang it up. The jeeps, on the other hand…let's try to keep them undamaged, please." She pointed to boxes full of US Army fatigues. "Now let's get you *ersatz soldaten* outfitted. We only have a few hours."

*****

To Sylvie's surprise, the crowd watching the phony nuclear ammo truck parade through Baumholder was even bigger than the one that had viewed the arrival of *Atomic Annie*. Even when perched atop the same stone wall from which she'd witnessed the fake cannon's arrival, the throngs made it more difficult to pick out the suspected Soviet agents. But she had little doubt they were there, somewhere:

We scattered those pamphlets all over town. They were bound to see one...and once they did, they'd want a bird's-eye view of the proceedings.

Then, almost too quickly, the game was on. The lead jeep came into view a few streets away, with Franz Ulrich in the front passenger's seat wearing the uniform of a US Army lieutenant, playing the *officer-in-charge* of this three-vehicle convoy. Sylvie mounted her bicycle and rode as fast as she could to the base gate, doffing her bright red flat cap as she passed the guard shack. That was the signal for the Pershing, which had been hidden behind a building near the boundary of the post, to start moving. Then she crossed the street, parked her bicycle, and stood in the doorway of a butcher's shop. Her plan would play out directly in front of her.

It was all going flawlessly. Ulrich's jeep reached the gate, drove a hundred feet past, and stopped, blocking any traffic that might be coming from the opposite direction. The deuce with its nuclear markings and fake ammunition crates was thirty yards behind. As it drew near to the gate, the Pershing lurched onto the road, her turret facing backward so the overhanging gun tube would not strike anything in the imminent crash. The tank played its roll perfectly, turning onto the road but at too great a speed; the resulting attempt was much too wide, as planned. A head-on collision with the ammo deuce was just a split-second away. The two German *fallschirmjäger* leapt from the cab, their bodies rolling once across the cobblestones before they were on their feet and sprinting to safety.

The tank driver, relishing the chance to play *demolition derby* in earnest, steered his massive vehicle so it met the front of the much lighter deuce at a slight angle, creating the collision that seemed a careless accident. It was anything but.

The Pershing's overwhelming inertia knocked the truck onto its side, a result Sylvie hadn't planned on. The four heavy ammo crates in the truck bed—each containing nothing but multiple industrial-sized tin cans filled with cement—spilled onto the cobblestone street with startling violence. Sylvie breathed a sigh of relief they hadn't broken open; she'd insisted they be banded with steel straps, and those straps had kept the crates intact. Lying in the street, the nuclear warnings and bogus technical data stenciled on the boxes were plain to see.

This is a little more spectacular than I had in mind, she thought. *I would've been happy just to have an upright truck stopped in the middle of the street until the wrecker could get here, with those nuclear symbols on its side making their ominous point...and maybe have some civilians try to get a look inside the truck.*

And among those civilians would be Soviet operatives, no doubt.

But with the crates in the street, they'll have an even better look...

Just so those fucking things stay closed.

A civilian mob was forming around the toppled deuce and spilled crates, preventing her Germans—her fake GIs—from forming a security cordon as was the plan. Now Sylvie was worried: *I can't let the Russian spies find out what's really inside. This mission would go from success to farce in seconds. It would be an embarrassing failure...*

And I don't fail.

She started toward the mob but strong hands seized her from behind in an unbreakable grasp, covering her mouth and dragging her backward into the butcher's shop. Trying to free just her hand so it could reach the pistol in her musette bag, she saw the mute, cowed faces of the old butcher and his wife standing behind the counter as her captor dragged her to the rear of the store. Her fingertips brushed the pistol's grip but could do no more.

Another man rushed in from the street, moved quickly toward her, and brandished a knife, which he waved in her face. Then he took that same knife and cut the strap on her bag, allowing him to seize it from her shoulder. Finding the semi-automatic pistol inside, he held it on her.

Sylvie recognized the man holding her gun: *Steigmeier...that MGB mole from East Berlin. We heard he'd been killed by some Russian officer over a woman. But I guess that was planted misinformation, because that scar running down his cheek is unmistakable.*

The man with the vise-like grip on her—whose face she still couldn't see—asked Steigmeier, "You've got the photos?" Though he was speaking German, the accent was decidedly Russian.

"Of course," he replied, sounding insulted to have been asked.

"Put the camera in my pocket."

Steigmeier did what he was told, slipping the miniature device into his comrade's jacket. When he was done, he stepped back in front of her and began running the pistol's barrel through her hair like some crazed hairdresser.

He won't shoot, not as long as his partner is still holding me.

I'm far more worried about that knife.

An exultant leer on his face, Steigmeier said, "So...Sylvie Bergerac. Or is it Isabelle Truffaut? Or Sylvie Kohler?" He rattled off the rest of her aliases before asking, "Which name will the Americans put on your grave? Oh, you can't answer with that hand clamped over your mouth, can you?"

She tried to kick him but he stomped on her foot.

"Hold her still," he told his partner as he stepped to her side, raising the knife to her throat.

A shot rang out. Steigmeier's head exploded in a cloud of pink mist.

Franz Ulrich was crouched behind the counter, wielding a US Army .45 pistol he held with both hands. The man restraining her had pivoted so she shielded him. Tightening his grip on her, he began to back toward the shop's rear exit, dragging her with him. Ulrich jumped over the counter and followed, the .45 at the ready.

When he considered himself close enough to the door, the Russian shoved Sylvie toward the man in the GI uniform and sprinted outside. Ulrich dropped to one knee and took careful aim. Sylvie grabbed his arm, jerking the barrel upward.

"Let him go," she said. "We need him to report what he saw or this is all for nothing."

They ran to the front door of the shop, Sylvie offering hurried apologies for the mayhem to the butcher and his wife as she wiped Steigmeier's blood and brains from her face. Back on the street, she was relieved to see the other Germans in GI uniforms had finally established the cordon around the phony ammo boxes. None of them had been opened.

When she tried to thank Ulrich, he told her, "I couldn't let them kill you. You haven't paid us yet."

"But who gave you the bullets? That was strictly forbidden."

He looked at her like she was crazy and asked, "You're not really complaining, are you, *Frau Bergerac?*"

*****

At the debrief, Joe Bachmann was a very satisfied boss. "It sounds like another jackpot, Sylvie," he told her. "Very fine work. Washington thinks the phony intel you planted is already in Moscow's hands. They're now watching very carefully for signals that the Chinese and the North Koreans are showing some interest in coming to the conference table."

But she didn't seem pleased. Bachmann asked, "Something wrong?"

"The Russians know I'm here…it's a certainty now. They know my face, they know my name…or should I say *names*, all of them. I'm compromised."

"Yeah, I know," Bachmann replied. "You'll be on the next plane out of Frankfurt. You're being reassigned to Washington."

That wasn't what she wanted.

Something Tommy once told her kept echoing in her head, something he'd referred to as Brooklyn wisdom:

No good deed goes unpunished, Syl.

Chapter Thirty-Four

The imperatives of warfare have a way of mocking even the best laid plans. The new unit Brigadier General Jock Miles would form and command—the 247th Regimental Combat Team—was supposed to be assembled and intensively trained in-country over a period of two months. Only after that training period was complete would it be deployed to the 38th Parallel, ready for immediate commitment to battle as needed.

A renewed Chinese offensive in mid-May 1951 changed all that. Northeast of Seoul, 8th Army units were withdrawing south of the Parallel as much as twenty miles, yielding ground to dissipate the blow. For the most part, it was never a rout but a series of skillful retrograde operations to deny the CCF the ability to employ its daunting numbers against obligingly stationary objectives. Once the Chinese assaults faltered, as they now did with regularity, 8th Army would be poised to regain the ground they'd ceded.

MacArthur had criticized Ridgway for this strategy, but few could deny it was achieving the political goal that Washington—and the rest of the United Nations—had set as a means to end this war: bleed the Chinese dry so they'd be forced to negotiate an end to hostilities.

When General Van Fleet, the new 8th Army commander, ordered Jock to immediately bring his nascent unit north to Hoengsong, the RCT had been in existence barely two weeks. The unit wasn't fully formed yet, either, as it was still short two of the infantry battalions he'd been promised, leaving Jock with only four.

Sean Moon took an optimistic view. "Might not be such a bad thing, sir," he told Jock. "With what we got at the moment—the four infantry battalions plus the two artillery battalions and the two armor battalions—we're more like one of them armored cavalry regiments we formed in Germany than an RCT. The only difference is our infantry will be riding in deuces instead of armored carriers. Still, we're light enough to move pretty damn fast but still pack a hell of a lot of firepower."

Before he put Sergeant Moon's contention to his five staff officers—three of whom hadn't even arrived until that morning—Jock turned to Patchett and asked, "What are your thoughts, Top?"

"I gotta agree with Bubba, sir," Patchett replied. "If we're gonna be this mobile *fire brigade* like General Ridgway figured, I think the way we're set up right now—even though we're a little low on dogfaces—might just be the way to go. Besides, we're lucky that the units we got ain't green. All we gotta do is lay down the law how they're gonna work together. And the way I see it, *rule number one* gotta be this unit don't never get split up and farmed-out piecemeal. Otherwise, we're gonna end up just being road guards or a manpower pool for the rest of Eighth Army."

"Damn right, Top," Sean added.

"I'm glad you both agree," Jock said with a smile, "because I'm with you one hundred percent on all counts."

"I got something else you'll wanna hear, sir," Patchett said. "Our boys have come up with a crackerjack nickname for this outfit, because the *Two-Forty-Seventh RCT* is kind of a mouthful. They're taking to calling themselves *Brigade Miles*. They sound pretty proud of it, and I believe I like the name a whole lot myself. Beats being called *Trench Rats* any damn day."

Sean Moon said, "Sounds pretty good to me, too, sir."

"Outstanding," Jock replied. "You've got to love a morale booster the men invented all by themselves. Makes our job so much easier."

Patchett replied, "Amen to that, sir."

*****

Leaving their training camp at Wonju, *Brigade Miles* covered the ten miles to Hoengsong in a little over an hour. Sean Moon griped, "If it hadn't been for all that fucking traffic moving away from the battle, we coulda been here in half the time."

But they'd only stay at Hoengsong long enough to get a new set of orders from 8th Army's forward CP. General Van Fleet told Jock, "Elements of two CCF divisions are forcing a gap near the village of Soksa-ri, about thirty-five miles east of here. Air power's been a huge help slowing them down, but airplanes can't be everywhere at once and can't hold terrain." Pointing out the village on the map, he continued, "I imagine you'll want to take Highway Twenty to get there. Can you make it within three hours?"

Jock replied, "If there are no traffic jams, we could do it in three, sir. But the odds of no traffic are about zero. To make the move as fast as possible, can the MPs give my boys priority on the highway?"

A pained look came over Van Fleet's face. "Jock, right now I can't guarantee the highway's going to be open all the way to Soksa-ri. It sits right on the boundary between our Tenth Corps and the ROK Third Corps."

Jock clenched his teeth: *Tenth Corps—that means General Almond. This isn't the first time he's had a problem keeping a boundary secure. This sounds like Twin Tunnels all over again.*

He asked Van Fleet, "So I'll be reporting to General Almond, sir?"

With what sounded like an air of apology, the 8th Army commander replied, "Yeah, I'm afraid that's the way it works, General Miles."

*****

The traffic had been heavy and chaotic, just as Jock surmised. It took three hours just to reach the village of Changp'yong-ni, which was five miles west of Soksa-ri along Highway 20. There, Jock conferred with the C.O. of 3rd Infantry Division, a two-star named Bob Soule.

"Good to meet you, Jock," Soule said. "I've heard a lot of good things about you. How'd your armor hold up on that motor march from Hoengsong?"

"Lost two to breakdowns."

"Out of how many?"

"Seventy-one."

"Man, that's fantastic," Soule replied, "because I'm down to about a company of tanks."

"You've got a better excuse than I do, sir—you're in contact with the enemy. All I've been doing is driving. So what are we up against here?"

"A couple of ROK divisions are caving again, Jock. I had to put most of my men into a blocking position at Habae-jae. Otherwise, I would've had the fleeing ROK

Seventh Division and Lord knows how many CCF divisions streaming into my sector. We've stopped them there, but on our right flank, the 3rd Corps ROKs have been giving up whole stretches of Highway Twelve like it's going out of style. Almond wants me to split my force and set up another blocking position at Soksa-ri, but I just don't have the people. You do, though."

"Yeah, I could do that," Jock replied, "but listen to this…I got a message from Almond's headquarters about thirty minutes ago. He wants me to push east through some damn mountain trails, passing well south of Soksa-ri, and buck up the ROKs at Hajinbu-ri, of all places. As far as Eighth Army is concerned, that's the one area the ROKs aren't under serious pressure and haven't had to pull back much at all. I could do what Almond's ordering, but by the time I get there, most of my armor will have broken down on those mountain grades. I won't be much help to anybody then."

Soule added, "And if the chinks pull a breakthrough at Soksa-ri, you'll be fighting them in those mountains with both hands tied behind your back. All those artillery pieces and tanks of yours will be next to useless." He paused, knowing full well that both of them were considering ways to *interpret* Almond's orders into actions that would make more sense…and maybe do some good.

Jock studied the map for a few moments more. Then he said, "You know, I can go straight up Highway Twenty to Soksa-ri as if I'm actually headed to Hajinbu-ri, staying out of those damn mountains, and be in position to block the chinks at either village. Nobody can really say I'm not following Almond's orders. I'm just choosing a faster route."

"Sounds like a plan, Jock...but speaking of fast, you'd better do it *now*."

*****

Brigade Miles found Soksa-ri practically deserted. Sean Moon had led the lead element of tanks into the town, jokingly declaring it an *open city* over the radio.

But everyone knew that was no joke: the ROKs' desertion of the village and its crucial highway junction had nearly created a gap through which the CCF could've poured, allowing them to envelop the 8th Army line in any number of places.

Sean had convinced the tank battalion commanders to leave platoon-sized detachments—all mutually supporting—at the likely exits of the mountain trails the Chinese might use to bypass Highway 12 and encircle Jock's forces at Soksa-ri. The bulk of the armor, though, formed a steel barrier at the junction of Highways 12 and 20. As they established a defensive position within the village, Jock's infantrymen were able to make use of the bunkers and fighting holes the ROKs had prepared and then abandoned. His artillery battalions emplaced themselves west of the village, able to deliver massed fires in any direction. Hastily occupied as it was, it wasn't a perfect position. But it was more than good enough to absorb the onslaught of infantry the CCF unleashed against it.

All along its line, *Brigade Miles* repulsed that onslaught without giving up a foot of ground while sustaining a mercifully low casualty rate. Despite the superior numbers of Chinese, the GIs were never in danger of being encircled: the outlying armored outposts

Sean had championed stopped all such attempts cold, at tremendous cost to CCF forces.

From the vantage point of a ridgeline behind the village, Jock and Patchett watched the battle rage. "Them chinks are getting butchered," Patchett said, his eyes glued to binoculars. "But they keep coming, the stupid bastards. They gotta have about five thousand dead lying out there already."

"They'd be a hell of a lot more formidable if they could adjust their tactics when things aren't working out for them," Jock added. "But without much in the way of radios, those bugles and whistles just can't communicate well enough to change plans on the fly. So they keep getting cut to ribbons...until they finally run out of steam."

"I hear you, sir," Patchett said. "Funny thing is, we probably got gaps in our line all over the place, rushed as we were to set up out here. But the chinks ain't found 'em, so too damn bad for 'em."

The Chinese attack *ran out of steam* as the sun grew low in the afternoon sky, about to drop behind the towering mountains to the west. Their survivors melted away to the north, into the hills flanking Highway 12.

Patchett said, "It's a cryin' shame we ain't got enough daylight to pursue with anything but artillery. We coulda kept putting the hurt on 'em real good."

A communications sergeant approached with a message. "We just picked this off the command net, sir," the sergeant said. "Figured you'd be real interested in it."

The message was from General Almond, addressed to General Van Fleet at 8th Army. In its text, Almond was taking full credit for *the brilliant victory at Soksa-ri* by troops under his command.

Patchett roared with laughter as Jock read it out loud. "I reckon if we done it his ass-backwards way, the disaster woulda been all your fault, sir."

"No doubt about that, Top."

Looking up from the clipboard on which he'd been jotting notes, Patchett said, "Been doing a little figuring, sir. I reckon that when you add up all the tank rounds, artillery shells, and small arms fire we just expended this past two hours, we let loose with about half a million projectiles."

"Okay...what's your point, Top?"

"Well, sir, since the chinks never seem to stop coming by the tens of thousands, I was just wondering how long we can keep something like that up."

"You know the answer to that as well as I do, Top. We'll keep it up as long as we have to."

"Sure we will, sir...but don't think me crazy if I'm still hoping for that one *magic bullet* that'll end this little adventure here once and for all."

* * * * *

* * * * *

About the Author

William Peter Grasso's novels explore the concept: *change one thing...and watch what happens.* Focusing on the WW2 era and beyond, they weave actual people and historical events into a seamless and entertaining narrative with the imagined. His books have spent several years in the Amazon Top 100 for Alternative History and War.

A lifelong student of history, Grasso served in the US Army and is retired from the aircraft maintenance industry. These days, he confines his aviation activities to building and flying radio-controlled aircraft.

Sign Up For New Release Announcements at:
wpgrasso@cox.net, with Mailing List as the Subject

Connect with the Author on Facebook:
https://www.facebook.com/AuthorWilliamPeterGrasso

Follow the Author on Amazon:
https://amazon.com/author/williampetergrasso

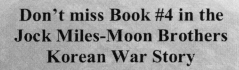

Don't miss Book #4 in the
Jock Miles-Moon Brothers
Korean War Story

Available Fall 2020

*Sign up to be added to the mailing list
for New Release Announcements at*
wpgrasso@cox.net,
with Mailing List as the subject

More Novels by William Peter Grasso

Jock Miles-Moon Brothers
Korean War Story

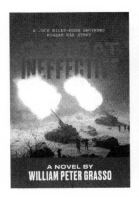

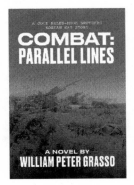

Moon Brothers WWII Adventure Series

4-Book Series

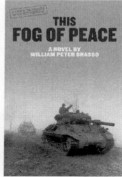

Jock Miles WW2 Adventure Series

5-Book Series

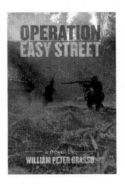

Standalone WW2 Novels

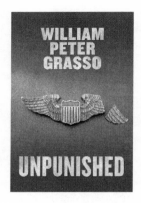

Made in the USA
Middletown, DE
11 May 2020